ROUSING A... ...
TEXAS LEGENDS SERIES:

"Mr. Shelton skillfully blends historical figures
and actual events with made-up characters
and imaginary situations."
—*The Dallas Morning News*

• • • • •

"Engaging . . . filled with
the details and flavor of the West."
—*Publishers Weekly*

• • • • •

"A fast-moving story brightened by
cowboy humor . . . Shelton's familiarity with
ranching and cowboys lends authority to his story."
—*Amarillo News-Globe* (TX)

• • • • •

"A classic Western tale . . . bring[s]
the 1860s of Texas alive."
—*Tyler Morning News* (TX)

Gene Shelton Books
from The Berkley Publishing Group

MANHUNTER

THE LIFE AND TIMES OF
FRANK HAMER

GENE SHELTON

BERKLEY BOOKS, NEW YORK

MANHUNTER: THE LIFE AND TIMES OF FRANK HAMER

A Berkley Book / published by arrangement with
the author

PRINTING HISTORY
Berkley edition / October 1997

The Putnam Berkley World Wide Web site address is
http://www.berkley.com

ISBN: 0-425-15973-6

BERKLEY®
Berkley Books are published by The Berkley Publishing Group,
a member of Penguin Putnam Inc.,
200 Madison Avenue, New York, New York 10016.
BERKLEY and the "B" design
are trademarks belonging to Berkley Publishing Corporation.

PRINTED IN THE UNITED STATES OF AMERICA

10 9 8 7 6 5 4 3 2 1

To Mary Kate Tripp—

Who took a green kid under her wing and patiently taught me about writing in the newsroom of the *Amarillo Daily News* and *Globe-Times,* and in the process became my counselor, confidante, good friend, banker when cash ran low and college tuition was due—and even stand-in mom—this work is dedicated with love, respect, and gratitude.

FOREWORD

This is a work of fiction based on the life and times of Texas Ranger Frank Hamer, one of the most famed and fearless lawmen ever to pin on a badge.

While Frank Hamer is most often remembered as the man who tracked down Clyde Barrow and Bonnie Parker, that case represented only a small portion of his long and illustrious career, which began in the days of Winchester and horseback law enforcement and continued into the days of the telephone, radio, and automobile. Although this work is intended to reflect Hamer's entire career, many interesting cases, episodes, and anecdotes have been omitted due to the length restraints of a single volume.

Many of the individuals portrayed in this novel actually existed. Some of the names herein have been changed to avoid any potential embarrassment to descendants of certain parties; in a few instances, the true names are unknown to the author.

Every effort has been made, within the framework of the fiction novel, to portray as accurately as possible the actual dates, locations, and sequence of events that shaped the life of Captain Franklin Augustus Hamer. Any historical inaccuracies or erroneous conclusions reflected in these pages are the responsibility of the author, but with no malice toward or disrespect for any person, living or dead, intended.

ACKNOWLEDGMENTS

The author wishes to express his gratitude to many people who made this work possible through their help, guidance, and encouragement. To name all those to whom I am in debt in this project would be the equivalent of a book-length work unto itself.

I am especially grateful to Dr. Jim Conrad, head of the archives section of the Gee Memorial Library at East Texas State University in Commerce, and the library staff, for invaluable assistance and enthusiastic detective work in researching this project.

Special thanks also to Tom Burks, former curator of the Moody Texas Ranger Museum in Waco, Texas; my agent, David H. Smith of Dallas, for his faith and hard work on behalf of this book; my editor, Gary Goldstein of Putnam Berkley Publishing Group, New York, for his patience and guidance; and to my personal cheerleading section, who took it upon themselves to keep my spirits up and dole out enormous amounts of encouragement when the project seemed almost overwhelming.

My deepest appreciation also to the following authors and their works: *"I'm Frank Hamer"*, *The Life of a Texas Peace Officer*, John H. Jenkins and H. Gordon Frost, State House Press, Austin, Texas, the most extensive biography to date of Captain Hamer; *Ambush: The Real Story of Bonnie and Clyde*, Ted Hinton as told to Larry Grove, Shoal Creek Publishers, Austin, Texas; *The Bienville Democrat*, Arcadia, Louisiana, May 24, 1934, edition; *The Texas Rangers*, Walter Prescott Webb, 2nd edition, 7th printing, University of Texas Press edition; *Trails and Trials of a Texas Ranger*, William Warren Sterling, University of Oklahoma Press; *The Killing of a Black Man: The Case of George Hughes,* Mary Elizabeth Crabb, Master's Thesis, East Texas State University, August 1987; the *Texas Almanac,* published by *The Dallas Morning News; Lone Star,* T. R. Fehrenbach, American Legacy Press, 1983 edition; Bartee Haile, Texas historian; and the many scholars' and authors' books, monographs, and historical works pertaining to the Texas of Frank Hamer's days.

And finally, a heartfelt thanks to my colleagues in the Western Writers of America, Inc., the DFW Writers Workshop, and the Northeast Texas Writers Workshop, for their individual and collective help, encouragement, and friendship.

PROLOGUE: TRAIL'S END

Ringgold Highway,
Bienville Parish, Louisiana
May 23, 1934, 9:20 A.M.

THE BIG MAN in black ground his half-smoked cigarette beneath a heel, ignored the mosquitoes and deerflies that buzzed about his ears and fed on his flesh, and peered through the tangle of pine boughs and brush at the side of the asphalt road.

Waiting was the hardest part of any manhunt.

Boredom worked on a man's nerves more than the chiggers that burrowed beneath his skin, more than the knowledge that there likely would be gunplay, more than the possibility of death.

Franklin Augustus Hamer, special investigator for the Texas State Department of Corrections, played the waiting game well. It was a game learned from his lifelong fascination with Indians.

Indians had patience.

Patience was the hallmark of the hunter, whether the game walked on four legs or two. For most of his half century of life, Frank Hamer strived to be like an Indian. Once again—for the last time as a hunter, he hoped—he felt more Comanche than white. Seven hours behind a blind, senses tuned to each noise, scent, and flicker of movement in the Louisiana forest, calmed his nerves rather than stretched them.

Frank glanced along the line of man-made hunting blinds where other members of the party waited. None of them seemed overly tense or jumpy, he noted with satisfaction. They were professionals. This was no game for amateurs, no place for nervous men. Especially when the two most wanted killers in the country were on the loose. And headed this way. This morning. Frank knew they were. He didn't know how he knew. He just felt them.

He still clung to the faint hope that it wouldn't come to shooting, but he accepted the fact that the odds were against it.

Clyde Barrow and Bonnie Parker had vowed never to be taken alive. Frank knew they would keep that vow. He had come to know them well in 102 days on their trail.

He hated the idea that he probably would have to kill a woman. But his dislike for the prospect was tempered by the fact that Bonnie Parker, all four feet, ten inches and ninety-four pounds of her, was as dangerous as the slightly built man she rode with. In his mind's eye, he pictured the red-haired woman standing above a wounded, possibly already dead, state trooper. Pumping two rounds from a shotgun into the lawman's body. Laughing at how the body had bounced when the heavy shot charges struck home.

What worried Frank the most was the steadily climbing sun. Time was running out. If Bonnie and Clyde didn't show in twenty minutes, the waiting lawmen would call off the stakeout for the day.

He was satisfied with the posse's tactical situation. They waited on the east side of the narrow road that ran north and south at the crest of the low hill. The sun, already high enough and hot enough to wring sweat from a man, would be at their backs. Sunlight filtered through the tops of pines and dappled the tree stump that marked Clyde Barrow's "mailbox" on the other side of the road.

The isolated spot held another significant advantage. The road was little traveled, the area sparsely populated. There would be almost no chance of an innocent person being hit when the shooting started.

Despite the muggy heat, Frank's oversized hands were dry against the metal of his Remington Model 8, .35-caliber autoloading rifle with its special twenty-round magazine. The other hunters were armed with shotguns, Browning Automatic Rifles, or other powerful long guns, and each carried at least a pair of handguns. Hamer figured they had at least as much firepower as the two killers they sought.

The irony of the situation wasn't lost on Hamer. But for a couple of quirks of fate or the deliberate hand of God, he could have been in the two outlaws' shoes, riding toward a near-certain death. Or preparing a sermon to be delivered over their bodies. He had come within a few minutes of turning into a bank robber, and within a buckshot cloud of becoming a preacher.

The Creator, he mused, sometimes played tricks on a man. . . .

Frank's heartbeat remained steady at the distant sound, the distinctive hum of a Ford V-8 engine revved to high speed. He figured the car to be three miles away. He knew he had been the first in the waiting group to hear the car motor; the keenness of his senses had always been downright spooky, as his Texas Ranger friends often said.

He slipped the safety of the Remington rifle to the ''fire'' position and waited, almost idly wondering if he was about to collect a few more wounds to go with the two dozen he'd accumulated in his years of law enforcement. He still packed a few chunks of lead in his six-foot-three, 230-pound frame. The wounds bothered him at times.

Not now.

Moments later the urgent whisper came down the line of waiting lawmen: ''Here they come.''

The tan Ford sedan topped a distant ridge, still moving fast, towing a dust-cloud rooster tail, and dropped from sight, but not from sound. The pitch of the engine changed as the car slowed, began the climb up the north side of the hill.

Frank shouldered his rifle. It ends today, he thought. It ends here. . . .

BOOK ONE

Buckshot and Bridle Reins

CHAPTER ONE

Llano County, Texas
June 1896

THE KILLER WAS nearby.

The youth who sat silent and unmoving beneath the post-oak grove along the banks of the shallow creek sensed its presence. He felt the wary gaze on his skin, a sensation stronger than the sharp sting of the heel-fly bite on his bare forearm. He made no move to brush away the insect. The hunt was near its end.

In a day of tracking and three more days and nights of watching and waiting, the young man had come to know the animal as well as the killer knew itself. The fox had sealed its fate when it found the family-farm chicken coop easy pickings. Until then, the youth was willing to live and let live.

The fox would be circling now, pausing to sniff the light breeze, keen senses tuned to the slightest movement that would mean danger.

The youth sat patiently. He was in no hurry. School was out, his father could spare him from the blacksmith shop for a few days, and he could think of nothing better to do than enjoy the hunt, the warm late-spring days, the outdoors, and all that nature supplied for his personal entertainment. He felt no particular need for playmates or boys' games. He knew that some folks thought he was a bit peculiar; some even said it was a bit "spooky," the way he disappeared for days at a time carrying his old rifle, a pocketknife, a couple of fish-hooks, and a single blanket, living off the land. He didn't especially care what other folks thought. At least not those outside his immediate family, and they understood.

God's creations provided all the diversion a boy needed. He held the thought a moment. That might make a good sermon topic when he stepped into the pulpit one day.

He also knew all the admonitions he had heard from the
preacher. God loved all creatures. Thou shalt not kill. The
youth saw no conflict in those words while waiting to dispatch
a chicken-killing fox. God didn't seem to get overly upset
when Mother killed a plump pullet or two for Sunday dinner,
or when he shot a rabbit, squirrel, wild turkey, feral hog, or
deer for the table. The more he thought on it, the more the
boy felt the Creator was a pretty reasonable fellow.

Besides, the fox had already violated the Word.

The fox had killed. Not just for food, but in blood frenzy.
Three or four prime laying hens at a time, just for the pleasure
of killing and maiming. Now the fox would pay for its raids.

For the last two mornings there had been no clear shot that
would mean a quick, certain kill when the fox returned to its
den after a night's hunt. A clean kill was an absolute necessity. Ammunition was expensive. There was no money for
target practice, but that didn't matter. He didn't need it. He
knew he could put the slug where he wanted to put it. It had
to be a head shot. The fox pelt would bring a dime, maybe
fifteen cents, in town.

He could wait.

By now, the fox would have become accustomed to the
human scent. It was part of the predator's environment, as
much a part of its life as was its home.

Twenty yards away, a hole in the reddish bank of eroding
soil across the dry creek marked the opening of the killer's
den. The end of the stalk was only minutes away now, the
youth sensed. He was in perfect position. The early-morning
sun was at his back. The fox would be reluctant to stare directly into the sun. Even if it did, the animal probably would
never see the boy. The trunks of the post-oak trees broke up
the outline of the hunter's body.

The youth felt no particular sense of elation or thrill that
the end was near. He didn't kill for fun, only from necessity.

The long days and nights of the stalk would have driven
most twelve-year-olds well past the point of crushing boredom.

Franklin Augustus Hamer wasn't an ordinary twelve-year-
old, and he knew it. In his mind, he wasn't even Frank Hamer
at the moment. He was Indian. Each rustle in the tall grass

and whisper of breeze through the trees spoke to him, each
flicker of movement noted in the steady gaze from blue eyes
in the round face, each birdcall a clear statement to his keen
ears, every slight scent on the gentle breeze told its own tale.

He was Comanche now. Not the son of a cavalry trooper
and regimental blacksmith in Colonel Ranald Slidell Mackenzie's 4th Cavalry. He was Indian. It was a feeling he had
worked to develop ever since he had read the big book on
Indians a year ago at school. . . .

The sense of being watched grew stronger. Frank's
breathing rhythm didn't change; his heartbeat remained
steady against his ribs. The slender lines of the old Remington
rolling-block single-shot .22 rifle nestled comfortably in his
hands.

Hamer was well aware that he was big for his age, tall and
heavy-boned. His arms and shoulders already showed ripples
of muscle toughened by hours over his father's blacksmith
forge, wielding a heavy hammer and bending metal straps.
Being big had its advantages. The older boys at school never
tormented him. At least not more than once.

He also knew that despite his size, he would seem no threat
to the fox. Unless he moved.

He had no intention of moving. Not yet.

The flutter of wings and irritated, raspy buzz off to his right
told the boy the fox was within a few yards. Frank had already learned the habits of wildlife in the rolling hills of
Llano County. One of his most valued allies on the hunt was
the mockingbird. The gray-and-white-feathered sentinel could
always be counted on to raise a fuss when a predator was
near.

Without moving his head, Frank cut his gaze toward the
raucous, buzzing hiss of the mockingbird. A sprig of underbrush flickered on the west side of the creek, a movement
that didn't fit the motion of bush in the breeze. Two alert,
small eyes turned toward him; the fox lifted its muzzle, tested
the breeze. Frank could easily make out the shape of the fox's
head in the early-morning shadows. Still, he waited. The time
wasn't right.

The fox's head drew back and vanished into the brush.
Frank ignored the mosquito lancing its way into the side of

his neck. He eased the hammer of the .22 to full cock, his movements so deliberate that the action took almost a full half minute. He never shifted his gaze from the berry thicket a yard from the opening of the den.

Another five minutes passed, by his estimation, before the fox slipped, silent and cautious, from the thicket. The animal was in full view now. A less attentive hunter might have missed seeing the fox. Its reddish-gray coat blended well into the clay soil along the creek bank.

Still, Frank made no move. He knew the fox's routine. Just before entering its den, the animal would momentarily drop its guard to sniff at the opening, to make sure no danger waited inside.

The fox stopped a foot from the den, its nose extended toward the hole in the creek bank. Frank lined the sights and stroked the trigger.

The pop of the .22 short rimfire cartridge barely disturbed the early-morning air. The fox's head jerked and the killer collapsed, all four feet beneath its body.

Frank sighed in satisfaction. The hunt had ended as he had hoped, with a clean head shot that dealt instant death. The fox had not suffered. The pelt was undamaged. And the family chickens were now safe.

In a way, Frank mused, the fox had gotten better than it deserved with the whack of the .22 slug beneath its left ear. The fox had showed no such consideration for the Hamer chickens.

He broke the action, extracted the spent cartridge, and chambered another. Not for the fox; he could tell by the way the predator fell that it had died instantly. But there were rattlesnakes about. He didn't want to waste a cartridge on a snake, but sometimes they didn't give a fellow an option. The man who stayed alert and prepared didn't have to worry so much about snakebite.

Frank removed his shoes and socks, waded the ankle-deep waters of the spring-fed creek, and strode to the reddish-gray carcass. He stood for a moment staring down at the dead animal, aware that a real Indian would have something kind to say to the spirit of the fox.

He could think of nothing to say. The fox had done wrong.

That meant, to Frank's thinking, that it had lost whatever soul it might have had. In a way, the concept disturbed Frank. It meant that he wasn't fully Indian. Indians could see the spirit, the soul, in most anything. Even rocks and trees.

He let his gaze drift about, his nostrils flared to the breeze, testing the air for scent much as the fox had done, head tilted as he listened to the lazy drone of insects, the scuttle of small forager feet in the brush, the cries and calls of birds. Moments after the single shot, nothing seemed out of place.

He glanced at the sun. He could pelt out the fox and cover the four miles back home well before noon. He propped the Remington within easy reach against a tangle of exposed roots alongside the den, pulled his pocketknife, tested the keen edge of the blade with his thumb, and went to work.

The weathered wood-frame house that stood beside Oxford's single dirt road looked a bit rough on the outside, Frank knew, but it was as good a home as a boy could hope to have.

The home's weathered clapboard siding and slightly crooked, hand-hewn oak porch supports gave the Hamer house the outward appearance of poverty. It wasn't much different in appearance from most homes in Oxford. But the Hamers had never been truly poor. At least Frank had never thought so. The house was warm enough in winter, reasonably cool in summer, the furnishings simple but sturdy and functional.

Frank Hamer had no complaints.

The scent of yeast bread set his mouth watering as he strode toward the front porch, his shoes barely disturbing the dust. The Hamer family didn't have much cash, but they were in better shape than a lot of folks in Llano County. They ate regularly, and usually well. His father's blacksmith shop, which stood silent and empty at the moment a few steps from the house, brought in a few dollars every now and then.

Frank's rifle and the family chickens, pigs, and garden plot, along with some barter with merchants and other farmers in the area, supplied the raw materials for Mrs. Hamer's considerable kitchen talents.

Frank didn't remember ever going to bed hungry. For that,

and for his family, he thanked the Good Lord in his prayers each morning and again at night.

Harrison Hamer, Frank's younger brother, boiled out of the house to greet him with an almost frantic burst of energy. Frank grinned at the sight. Harrison usually was more reserved; in many ways, he seemed older than eight. And, Frank freely admitted—at least to himself—Harrison was his favorite in his growing brother-and-sister herd.

"Did you get him, Frank?"

"Sure did, Harrison." Frank rumpled the boy's tousled hair in fondness, then handed over the pelt for his wide-eyed inspection. "You watch the place while I was gone?"

"Real good, Frank. Can I go with you next time?"

"Sure, partner, if the folks will let you." Frank paused at the door. "Do me a favor, Harrison? Show Mother the pelt."

"You bet, Frank." The boy's eyes glittered in excitement. "Dad was hoping you'd come home today." He darted inside before Frank could ask why.

Mrs. Hamer, a petite, attractive woman with a pleasant smile and the soft drawl of a native Texan, greeted Frank with a motherly embrace. He could be gone for an hour or for days at a time, and her greeting never changed.

She finally turned him loose. "Dinner will be ready in an hour, Frank," she said. "I'm afraid it's just stew again."

"The best stew in the world," Frank said. "If you made it, it has to be. Where's Dad?"

Lou Emma Hamer swirled a wooden spoon in the stew pot and said over her shoulder, "Gone to put some new straps and hinges on Mr. Baker's barn door. We'll get some nice new pullets in trade."

Frank nodded. Barter was the way of life in cash-strapped Llano County. It held things together, whether those things were barn doors or families. Trading might not be easier than paying cash, but it made a man feel good, somehow. Indians traded all the time.

Mrs. Hamer wiped her hands on her apron and studied the fox skin Harrison held. "It's a nice skin, Frank."

"Harrison and I will pelt it out."

Mrs. Hamer nodded. "Harrison, you and Frank take it out to the barn to work on it—and be sure to wash your hands good when you're finished. Foxes carry all sorts of vermin, you know."

"Yes, ma'am." Frank steered Harrison toward the back door with a hand on the boy's shoulder.

The two had almost finished the initial scraping of flesh and fat from the pelt when the elder Frank Hamer strode into the barn. Frank nodded a greeting to his father, who squatted beside the boys as they fleshed the fox skin. The elder Hamer was, like his namesake son, a big man—not tall, particularly, but powerful of build, with the sloping shoulders and thick forearms that were the hallmark of a longtime blacksmith.

"Head shot?" Mr. Hamer said after a time.

"Yes, sir."

"One round?"

"Yes, sir."

Frank's father nodded in approval. "Good job, son. If I was still with Mackenzie, I'd want you by my side in any Indian fight."

Frank tried to accept the comment lightly, but his chest swelled a bit anyway. His father, the veteran Indian fighter, didn't pass out such compliments like buttered corn. He was also slow to criticize, yet tolerated no insolence from his children. It was one of the main reasons Frank's father stood tall in his eyes. The man was honest.

He was also intelligent. If not in formal education, in common sense. Frank had heard the story of how his father, caught alone and in the open by a band of prowling Comanches, had pretended to be insane. The Indians watched the white man run in circles, howling and barking like a dog, then rode away shaking their heads. To kill a crazy person was bad medicine.

"You have plans for tomorrow, son?"

Young Frank shook his head. "No, sir."

"Good. I could use a hand. Mel Bulleau is bringing his wagon in for some work." Mr. Hamer's voice still held a trace of his native Virginia. "Between the two of us, we can get it done in a day, I think." He stood. "Dinner will be ready in a few minutes, boys. When we're finished eating, Frank, I need your help on some ciphering."

"Sure," young Frank said. "We'll be right there. We're

almost done scraping this pelt. Harrison and I'll have it
stretched and hooped before bedtime."

Frank and Harrison strode to the house, scrubbed up at the
basin, and took their seats. Young Frank offered grace; he
was better at it than anyone else in the family, but that seemed
natural for a young man who planned to become a preacher.

After the noon meal, sister Estill and Harrison turned their
attention to helping their mother wash the dishes and utensils.
Frank's father pulled a battered ledger book from a drawer
and handed it to Frank.

Frank scanned the numbers on both sides of the ledger,
looked up, and said, "We made nine dollars and twenty-six
cents profit last month."

The elder Hamer shook his head. "I can't figure out how
you do that, son. Just look at a string of numbers and come
up with the answer without ciphering it out with a pencil."

"He's never needed a pencil," Mrs. Hamer said over her
shoulder. "It fuddled his teachers some, too."

Frank shrugged. "I've never had any problem with arith-
metic unless they ask me how I got the answer. I can solve
it, but I can't explain the different steps."

His father closed the ledger. "Nine dollars and change isn't
bad, I guess, considering business has been slow for everybody. It'll buy flour, coffee, and sugar enough to last us
awhile." He leaned back in his chair. "Did you check the
crops on the way back, son?"

Frank's brow furrowed. "Yes, sir. There's a few weeds in
the cornfield that have to be chopped before they spread too
much. Harrison and I can take care of it this afternoon. We
could use a good rain, though. All the crops are showing some
wilt. I'll do a little praying on it. Maybe an Indian rain dance,
too."

Frank's father chuckled. "Sure couldn't hurt to do both.
Man's going to talk to the Creator, he might as well cover
God and the Indian spirits at the same time. You never know
until that one fateful day who's really in charge."

Frank motioned to his younger brother. "Let's go, Harrison. We've got some weeds to chop."

Harrison winced, but didn't protest. The youngster was a
hard worker for an eight-year-old, and he already knew that

jobs that needed to be done had to be done. Even when it might be a better day for fishing.

The boys' parents waited until the door closed behind the two brothers.

"We did well, Lou Emma. They're good boys."

"The best, dear," Mrs. Hamer said.

"You really think Frank has the makings of a preacher?"

"Whatever he does, he'll be good at it." She sighed. "Sometimes I worry about him. He's only twelve, but at times I get the feeling he's already a man grown."

"In many ways, he is," the former trooper said. He finished the last of his coffee and smiled at his wife. "Might be nice to have an ordained preacher in the family, at that. We'd save a lot of money on marriages and funerals."

Llano, Texas
August 1898

The power of the Holy Spirit throbbed through the crowded Llano Methodist Church and surged through young Frank's veins as he waited to shake the Reverend Lucius Miller's hand. Frank stood last in line on purpose. He wanted a private moment with the preacher.

The traveling evangelist was, Frank admitted, an imposing figure—tall, hawk lean, dark eyes glittering beneath a thick shock of silver-laced brown hair, and even more impressive in the long black swallow-tailed coat.

"That was quite a sermon, Reverend," Frank said. "It was sure worth the ride up from Oxford."

"Glad you got the message, young man." The preacher's voice was a deep, booming baritone, and seemed to show no strain from the hour's worth of fire and brimstone he'd just spewed from the scarred pulpit. "It's always a delight to see a fellow such as yourself come rededicate his life to the Lord's work. I trust you have been baptized?"

Frank nodded and half smiled. "Enough that I wrinkled up like a prune, sir."

The preacher chuckled. "I daresay it took, then."

"Sir, do you have a minute to talk?"

Miller glanced around; most of the crowd had already begun to disperse. Saddle leather creaked and buggies groaned as folks from two counties around prepared to go home. "Of course, son. Something troubling your soul?"

"No, sir, not at all. I just wanted to talk some about preaching. I plan to be a minister myself."

The Reverend Miller clapped a big fist against Frank's shoulder. "Wonderful, son, wonderful. There are never enough messengers to carry the Lord's word. Tell me, what brings you to the calling?"

"It's just something I've always wanted, Reverend. I've felt it ever since I can remember."

"A good sign. Yes, a very good sign." The preacher's brows narrowed. "Have we met? You seem familiar."

"The name's Hamer, sir. Frank Hamer. My family and I heard you preach at a revival down in Oxford last fall. I sat on the front row all three days."

"Yes, yes, I remember now. Your father has the same name. I recall being confused as to how to refer to you." Crow's-feet lines crinkled the corners of the preacher's eyes at his smile. "Little Frank and Big Frank fit somewhat at the time, but as much as you've grown since then I don't know what to call you."

"It has been a problem," Frank said, "but most folks around Oxford just call me 'Pancho.' That's the Spanish name for Frank. Helps keeps things straight when my father and I are in the same room."

"I see. You speak well, son. Have you had much schooling?"

"All I could get, Reverend Miller. I finished the sixth grade. That's all we have in Oxford. We don't have the money for private schooling past that. Is that important to a preacher?"

Miller stroked his chin. "Seminary-school training helps one prepare for the calling, no question. On the other hand, there are many very good ministers who have little formal education. I would advise continuing your education if possible. The more one knows about the world, the more effective his ministry."

Frank's heart sank. More education, especially at seminary

schools, was out of the question. The money simply wasn't there. "But," Miller continued, "while helpful, it isn't necessarily a requirement—as long as you can read."

"That wasn't my best class in school, Reverend, but I can read. Not as well as I can cipher, but I can read pretty well. And write some, too, but I'm not real good at it."

A slight frown touched Miller's lips. "If you're not good at writing, how do you plan to prepare your sermons?"

"I thought I'd just kind of talk to the congregation. Sort of like friends. Tell them what the Good Book says and how we should follow its teachings."

"Hmm. Not a bad approach, at that. Fire-and-brimstone rantings get folks excited, but they often forget the message when the enthusiasm fades in a day or two." Miller put a hand on Frank's upper arm. The grip was a lot more powerful than Frank expected. "Tell me, son. Do you plan to carry the story of Jesus to the pagans—the red savage Indians?"

Frank's lips lifted in a slight smile. "It seems to me, Reverend, that the Indians do quite well with their own religion. I had sort of planned on trying to teach some Christianity to these Christians."

Miller chuckled and shook his head. "Son, I do believe there's a place for you in the ministry. The Good Lord knows there's a need for missionary work among our own." Miller paused for a moment, then said, "Frank Hamer. I remember now when I last heard of you. Wasn't it last July Fourth when you won that shooting contest in San Saba?"

"Yes, sir. My father entered me."

"I understand you won hands down—rifle, pistol, and shotgun. A clean sweep. Quite impressive for someone so young. What are you, Frank? Sixteen?"

"Fourteen, sir. I've always been big for my age."

The reverend shook his head in disbelief. "I'd never have guessed that. Especially someone so young being good enough to beat the best marksmen in two counties."

Frank shrugged, a bit uncomfortable with the turn of the conversation. "Shooting has always come easy to me, Reverend Miller. My father says I'm just a natural shot. Is it wrong for a preacher to know how to use guns?"

"Not at all, son, not at all. Any man should utilize his God-given talents.'' He lifted the lapel of his black swallowtail coat. A walnut-handled six-gun nestled in a shoulder holster beneath the preacher's left armpit. ''As men of the cloth, we sometimes have to ride into or through rather harrowing country. If the Good Lord hadn't intended man to protect himself, Colonel Colt would never have been born.''

Frank nodded, relieved. ''Yes, sir. I suppose you have a point there.''

The preacher's lips pursed pensively for a moment. ''God doesn't give a man a talent—any talent—without a reason, young Frank. Bear that in mind always.''

''I'll do that, sir.''

''And if your plans to take up the ministry should not work out, for one reason or another, perhaps that talent will serve you well in whatever calling you choose.'' Miller glanced at a gathering of expectant faces nearby. ''I must go visit with the rest of the flock, son. May the Lord bless and keep you and yours.''

''You, too, sir. And thank you.''

Frank watched the tall preacher walk away, back straight, head held high, his strides long and confident. Frank's chest swelled in admiration.

Maybe, he thought as he made his way to the picket line where his horse waited, there was a way to get the education he would need to be a good preacher. A man who wasn't afraid to work hard could find something. If he couldn't land a steady job on a ranch, there was always farming. The Hamer family didn't own enough land for a big farm operation, but there were others who did. Others who were always looking for someone to do all the work for part of the profits.

Sharecropping was half a loaf, but it was more than an empty breadbox.

CHAPTER TWO

———————◆———————

Spring Creek, San Saba County
June 1900

FRANK HAMER CALLED a soft command to the team of mules at the end of the row.

The mules, ears flopped and apparently half-asleep, made the turn and started back on the next row. The two weren't the world's most handsome mules, but they were the best team he'd ever worked. They knew what to do. He figured they could probably work the field themselves, if they were able to set the depth of cut. He shoved the control lever and felt the tines bite into the earth.

Satisfied that the cultivator was running straight and true, Frank draped the reins around his left forearm, lifted the bandanna around his neck, and wiped the sweat from his forehead with the gritty cloth. His heavy work shoes sank into the freshly turned earth as the cultivator tines ripped the weeds from between the rows of young, calf-high cotton plants.

Farming was not Frank's favorite form of work. He would have preferred to have been back on the Welch Ranch, working cattle from horseback. But a man did what a man had to do. There were no horseback jobs to be had this spring, and the sharecropping arrangement should bring in some much-needed cash.

Plodding along behind half-asleep mules wasn't that bad a way to spend the day, he admitted. Nature had a way of paying a man for working outdoors. She didn't pay in cash, but in other ways. The smell of fresh-turned earth, the scent of man and mule sweat, the songs of birds, the flicker of movement from rabbits and field mice along the rows, eased the boredom. And a man had plenty of time to think when he was out in the fields.

"Frank?"

Harrison's call from a couple of rows over brought Frank back to the moment. He called the mules to a halt and turned toward his younger brother.

Harrison was twelve now, going on thirteen, but worked as hard as a lot of boys older than he. He was more wiry and slighter built than Frank had been at that age, but he was strong. Frank himself was in another of his periodic growth spurts. At sixteen, he stood an inch over six feet and packed a hundred eighty pounds of muscle on his big-boned frame.

"Yeah, partner?" Frank said.

"Ready to swap places for a spell?" Harrison, the hoe handle propped against his shoulder, studied his palm. "I've cracked a callus. It's starting to sting some."

Frank wrapped the lines around the depth lever of the cultivator. "Sure, Harrison," he said with more enthusiasm than he felt. It was his turn on the hoe handle anyway. That was the hard part of farming. New plows and improved implements came on the market almost daily, but even if they could afford the latest equipment, it still took a man with a hoe in his hands to keep the weeds whipped out of a field.

A slight half smile touched Harrison's lips. "If hard work builds character like Dad claims," he said, "we're going to be sure-enough characters before this season's over."

"Some around here say we already are, Harrison. Just think about the money we're going to make."

Harrison's grin faded. Frown lines creased the layer of dirt between his dark brows. "Doesn't really seem fair. We do the work and old man McSwain takes half the cash."

Frank shrugged. "It's his land. Without it, we'd just be working for day wages. Grab the lines, partner. We can get this field finished by sundown if we put our backs to it."

He waited until Harrison picked up the reins and clucked the team into motion. Frank stepped over the young cotton plants, careful not to crush any of them, and picked up the hoe Harrison had left behind. He noticed the pinkish smear of Harrison's blood on the hickory handle. Harrison might be just a kid, Frank thought, but he was tough as a black walnut. Harrison didn't whimper or back off from work.

He and Harrison were like the mules, Frank thought as he flicked the hoe blade at the weeds between the cotton plants;

they came as a team, all but inseparable. Where one went, the other went. Frank liked the arrangement. He had always been fond of Harrison. They didn't squabble constantly the way some brothers did. On the rare occasions when they did argue, they listened to each other and rarely got mad over a disagreement. They were friends as much as blood kin.

And they were just different enough to keep things interesting.

Harrison attended church services and revivals, but it was pretty obvious he didn't get as caught up in the Word as deeply as Frank did. In their schooling, Harrison struggled with math, but handling and understanding numbers came naturally to Frank. On the other hand, Frank had never been a top hand at reading; Harrison was. Frank had finally talked Harrison into reading Wilbarger's book, *Indian Depredations in Texas,* but they each got different messages from the accounts of Indian raids on white settlers. It was that book that left Frank wanting to be more like an Indian; Harrison wasn't impressed with the red man, but identified more with the Texas Rangers and Indian fighters in its pages. It had made for some interesting conversations, but not to the point of argument. Frank granted any man had a right to his opinions, as long as those opinions didn't hurt anyone.

A shadow flicked across the cotton rows and drew Frank's gaze to the sky. A sharp-shinned hawk circled overhead, its silhouette dark against the cloudless spring sky. Frank could see the bird's head turn this way, then that, as the hawk rode the air currents and hunted its dinner.

On impulse, Frank crouched, placed the hoe on the ground, and cupped a hand against one side of his mouth. The sound that came was the high-pitched squeal of a rabbit in agony.

Frank waited a few heartbeats as the hawk narrowed its circles, then repeated the cry. The bird dropped closer to the ground, its head cocked toward Frank. Moments later he had called the hawk to within thirty feet. The bird looked puzzled, Frank thought; the hunter heard its dinner, but its keen eyesight picked up no sign of an injured rabbit.

Frank made no move for his father's old top-break Smith & Wesson .32-caliber handgun he carried tucked into his belt. He had no intention of shooting the hawk. He simply enjoyed watching wild creatures up close. It was a game, to see how near he could call them by mimicking their prey or their own mating cries. The hawk was only a few feet overhead when it loosed a shrill cry, wheeled on strong wings, and darted away.

Frank stood and glanced around, curious as to what had spooked the hawk. His gaze settled on an approaching wagon pulled by a big but gaunt bay. Frank frowned at the condition of the horse. Dan McSwain wasn't one to waste money on feed for his working livestock. Frank picked up the hoe and dispatched a few more weeds, pausing at the end of the row as McSwain reined in.

"Afternoon, Frank," said the owner of the land Frank and Harrison sharecropped.

Frank nodded a greeting; he wasn't sure how to take McSwain, a tall, spare man with perpetually hunched shoulders and frown lines that crinkled narrow lips. The landowner was cordial enough to the Hamer brothers, but Frank had heard tales. That McSwain was, beneath the surface, a bitter, vindictive man who would do anything to get what he wanted. Or settle a score. Around San Saba County, the gossip was that a man best stay on McSwain's good side—or else watch his back. He had managed to get involved in feuds with several farmers and ranchers in the country. And, it was said, he could carry a grudge for years.

"Looks like you boys have been busy today." McSwain leaned forward and rested his forearms over the knees of worn overalls. His close-set eyes swept the field.

"Yes, sir," Frank said. "We should be through with this field by sundown."

"How's it shaping up? Good crop?"

Frank thought it was an unnecessary question. McSwain was a farmer. He could tell by looking what the prospects were. "If the rains come at the right time and the weevils don't, we'll do all right."

McSwain nodded. Frank could tell from the expression in his eyes that something besides the condition of the crops was on the farmer's mind.

Frank waited. He wasn't much for small talk, at least where McSwain was concerned. He had discovered early in life that with certain people, the best thing to say was nothing. The man would get around to saying his piece eventually. Or just leave. Frank hoped it would be the latter.

Frank glanced toward the cultivator. It stood at the turn row a few feet away; Harrison had finished a pass while Frank played with the hawk, then stopped the team and strode behind a stand of cottonwood trees across the rutted field access road, apparently to relieve his bladder.

"Been watching you ever since we made the sharecrop deal, Frank," McSwain said. "Couldn't help but notice you're one of the best shots I've ever seen."

Frank shrugged. "Guess I'm better than some folks."

"How'd you like to earn some extra cash? Say a hundred and fifty dollars?"

"That's a lot of money. Who do I have to kill?" Frank joked.

"Jack Clifford." McSwain's gaze didn't vary from Frank's face. The smile died on Frank's lips as he realized this was no joke. The man was serious. The cold set of his eyes said so.

The whole county knew of the bad blood between McSwain and Clifford. It dated back several years, to the murderous San Saba feud, when opposing secret organizations—one backed by Clifford, the other by McSwain—took turns bushwhacking and lynching each other. McSwain's faction, Frank had heard, was the worse. At least Clifford's group gave a man the chance to leave the country first. They didn't just bushwhack him.

Whatever their problem, it wasn't enough to justify killing.

Frank lifted a hand. "Now, wait a minute, Mr. McSwain," he said, his words tainted with the disbelief that swirled in his brain, "I was just kidding. I didn't mean I was going to kill anybody. As a matter of fact, I intend to be a preacher, and I just don't think a preacher could go about killing people."

McSwain's close-set eyes narrowed and glittered even more. The slight movement of his face muscles gave Frank the impression of a bird of prey pondering its unsuspecting dinner.

"Well," McSwain said after a moment, "if you're on that kind of bent, I'll up my offer to two hundred."

"McSwain, I said no." Frank's disbelief gave way to a glowing ember of anger in his gut.

McSwain ignored the declaration. "Here's what I want you to do. I'll ask Clifford for a meeting to settle our differences. I'll hide you in a covered wagon, and I'll work it so that Clifford and I'll stand right beside the wagon. While we're talking, you take out your pistol and shoot him through a slit in the canvas. Nobody will ever know what happened, and you'll be two hundred dollars richer."

The spark of heat in Frank's belly flared into a burst of anger and disgust. He leveled a hard stare on McSwain.

"Hell, no!" Frank snapped. "I'm not going to kill that man for you! As a matter of fact, I'm going to tell him what you've asked me to do."

McSwain's face reddened. Hamer turned on his heel to stride away. "If you let one word of this out, I'll kill you!" McSwain all but shouted at Frank's back.

Frank didn't look around. He picked up his hoe and attacked more weeds. Dirt clods flew from his violent slashes; almost blinded by disgust and anger, he accidentally hacked down a perfectly healthy cotton plant. At the moment he didn't care.

His brain was still seething when he felt a hand on his shoulder. He hadn't heard Harrison's approach. Harrison's brow was furrowed in worry. Frank thought he saw a touch of his own anger reflected in his brother's eyes.

"You heard?" Frank asked.

Harrison nodded solemnly. "I heard. I can't believe it, but I heard it. Frank, Mr. McSwain was serious. And he was mighty mad when he left."

"He's not the only one mad. Harrison, I'm not going to let this slide."

"What are we going to do?"

"Just what I told McSwain I'd do," Frank said. A muscle at his temple pulsed. "I'm going to tell Clifford."

Harrison squatted and toyed with a dirt clod for a moment, thinking, before he glanced up.

"That could be dangerous." Harrison's words were soft, laced with worry. "McSwain threatened to kill you."

Frank dropped the hoe, a cold expression in his blue eyes.

"McSwain's a coward. Nobody but a coward would hire somebody to do his dirty work for him. I'm not afraid of him."

"But—"

"Harrison," Frank interrupted, "if we don't tell Clifford what McSwain's up to, Clifford will wind up dead. There's plenty of folks in this county who wouldn't hesitate to bush-whack a man for ten dollars, let alone two hundred. Clifford *has* to be told. If I don't warn him, I'll be just as guilty of murder as the man who pulls the trigger on him."

Harrison was silent for a moment, then nodded again. "You're right, Frank. We have to warn him."

Some of the anger drained from Frank. The disgust re-mained, but now a calm determination settled in behind his belt buckle. "Not 'we,' little brother. There's no need for you to get involved. I'll tell Clifford myself. If McSwain has the guts to come after me—which I doubt—at least you'll be in the clear."

Harrison's young jaw set in a firm line. "We're in this together, Frank. Besides, McSwain may know that I heard what he said. He's sure to figure that you told me." The younger Hamer squared his shoulders. "Even if he didn't know, it doesn't matter. I'm going with you. When do we leave?"

Frank glanced at the sun. "Soon as we get finished with the day's work here. Then we'll head home like always. There's no need to let McSwain know our intentions by leav-ing right now. Maybe he's just a hothead and popped off. Maybe he'd been drinking and will forget about what he said. We'll wait until after supper, then saddle up and ride."

Jack Clifford rose from his chair on the front porch and flipped his cigarette butt over the rail in an arc of sparks as the two young men reined in before the ranch headquarters.

The sun had set more than an hour ago, but Clifford had no trouble recognizing the two men through the soft shine of the high quarter moon and the circle of light cast by the twin-globe lantern on a table at his side.

"Frank, Harrison," Clifford said by way of greeting,

"good to see you boys. Climb down and come in. There's coffee left."

"Much obliged for the offer, Mr. Clifford," Frank said, "but this isn't a social visit. Something happened today you need to know about."

Clifford could tell from the tone of Frank's voice that whatever it was, it was serious. "What is it?"

"McSwain. This afternoon, he offered me two hundred dollars to kill you."

"You take him up on it?"

"No, sir. I told him not only no, but hell no."

"That's true, Mr. Clifford," Harrison said. "I heard the whole thing. McSwain wanted Frank to bushwhack you from a covered wagon."

Clifford's eyes narrowed. "So it's come to that, eh? I wondered if the damn fool might get himself a crazy notion of some kind. He'd like nothing more than to see me dead, but hasn't got the guts to do it himself."

"That's what I figured, Mr. Clifford," Frank said. "I also told McSwain that I intended to tell you what he tried to do, because there might be somebody out there who'd take the offer."

Clifford nodded. "There's men in this country who'd kill their own grandmother for less." Frank didn't think Clifford seemed overly worried about McSwain. The rancher looked mad, if anything. "What did he say to that? That you were going to tell me?"

"That he'd kill me if I did."

"You don't seem too worried about it."

Frank shrugged. "No more than you are. I don't think McSwain would brace a man in a face-to-face fight. He could have been just making noise. He could have been drunk."

"Regardless, you took a chance coming to me," Clifford said. "Thanks for the warning. I'll keep my guard up and my mouth shut. If McSwain finds out you've come here, he won't hear it from me. What are you going to do?"

"Go back to work, just like nothing happened." Frank paused for a moment. "We don't have any choice. We're counting on our half of the crop money. And the way I see it, if I don't go back to the fields, McSwain will know for sure I've been to see you."

"And maybe kill you."

"He may try. Even if he does find out, I've never backed down from anybody. Especially a coward who hires his dirty work done. I don't intend to start now."

Clifford sighed. "Can't find fault with your logic there, Frank. But while I'm watching my back, you'd better watch your own. Drunk or sober, McSwain can be a dangerous man."

"Harrison and I'll stay on our toes, Mr. Clifford. Don't worry about us."

Clifford reached for his wallet. "If my life's worth that much money, information like this ought to be worth something."

Frank shook his head. "I don't want your money. I just don't want to see you hurt or dead."

Clifford paused for a moment, his gaze on Frank's face. "I suspected you'd say that, Frank. It's a comfort to know there's one man in this county with a sense of right and wrong." He extended a hand. "Sure you won't stay a spell? You're welcome to overnight here."

Frank took the offered hand. "No, thanks, Mr. Clifford. We've got to get back home. We have to put in a day and a half's worth of work between sunup and sundown tomorrow." He picked up the slack in the reins, turned his horse, and said over his shoulder, "Watch yourself."

"You do the same, boys."

Clifford watched as the two Hamer youths reined their horses about and moved off at a slow trot. "There," he muttered to himself, "go two good young men. The country could use more like them."

Harrison called the team to a halt at the end of the row beside a chinaberry tree. Something hadn't been right for the last twenty feet or so. The breaking plow felt loose in his hands.

Harrison wrestled the plow onto its side and kicked a few clods free of the blade. Solving the problem didn't take long. Two rivets had loosened on the left sweep. The long blade wobbled at his touch.

The sight left Harrison a bit disgusted. The plow belonged to McSwain, and the landowner obviously didn't believe in spending money on good equipment. This particular breaking plow was a pile of cheap junk. It seemed to Harrison that he and Frank had spent more time fixing the plow than working the land over the last two days.

At least it wouldn't be too hard to fix. A couple of whacks with the blacksmith hammer against a steel punch or hand anvil from the Hamer wagon would reset the rivets. For a time, anyway.

He wasn't surprised at the amount of trouble they'd had, and the cheap plow wasn't the sole cause. This piece of land was more rocks and tree roots than it was soil. Snapping a rivet or plow tip was nothing new.

He swiped a sleeve across his face and glanced toward Frank, who squatted in the scant shade of the brothers' wagon, rasping a file across the blade end of a grubbing hoe.

Breaking new ground was one of the hardest jobs in farming, an occupation that never had ranked real high on a lazy man's list of preferred jobs, Harrison thought. Frank had sharpened the grubbing hoe twice already today, and the sun wasn't even straight overhead yet.

Harrison idly wondered why McSwain picked this particular ground for breaking. The soil was not good. Harrison doubted it would support much of a late-season vegetable crop even if they did manage to get the bigger rocks cleared and thickest roots grubbed away. The new field was downwind from McSwain's house, barely fifty yards away. If it didn't rain soon and the wind kicked up, McSwain would have most of the soil inside his home.

Harrison strode toward the wagon, stumbled and almost fell over an exposed loop of tree root, caught himself, and stopped as McSwain's buckboard, pulled by the gaunt bay, came into view beyond the chinaberry grove. Harrison had kept a wary and frightened eye on McSwain in the two days since he'd tried to hire Frank to kill the rancher.

McSwain acted as if the incident had never happened. He had even seemed more hospitable than ever; at times, he even appeared chipper. That wasn't like him. Harrison studied the man on the wagon seat. McSwain didn't appear to be armed, though he usually carried a shotgun or rifle with him anytime he left the house. The only thing out of the ordinary today was the tarp in the back of the buckboard. Canvas sheets were for keeping the rain out. There wasn't a cloud in the sky.

"McSwain's coming," Harrison said as he reached the wagon.

"I know," Frank said, still scraping the file across the angled edge of the grubbing hoe.

Harrison reached into the wagon, tucked the hand anvil—a steel chunk shaped like a railroad spike—into his pocket, and thrust the smithing hammer under his belt, the way Frank carried the .32 revolver. "Wonder what he wants?"

"Guess we'll find out soon enough." Frank tested the cutting edge of the tool, put the file back in the wagon alongside his New Testament, and waited as McSwain's buckboard pulled alongside.

"How's it going, boys?" McSwain said. His tone was cordial enough.

Maybe, Harrison thought, McSwain *had* been drinking the other day. Or maybe he didn't know they had warned Clifford. At any rate, he'd been all sweetness and light the last couple of days. That wasn't something a man could take comfort in.

"Going pretty slow," Frank said casually. "This piece of ground's a bear to work. Full of rocks and tree roots. We're not much more than halfway through and we've just about worn out the turning plow."

McSwain nodded. "Expected it would be. But it'll be a good spot for fall greens." The landowner set the buckboard brake, climbed down, and glanced at the sun. "Getting on toward dinnertime. You boys got anything to eat out here?"

"Few biscuits and some bacon left over from breakfast," Frank said. "I'm afraid we didn't bring enough for three, though."

McSwain waved a hand. "I hadn't planned on sponging grub off you. As a matter of fact, I think you two've earned a decent feed. Frank, why don't you go down to the house. There's a hank of ham and a loaf of fresh bread on the sideboard, a cupboard full of tinned peaches and tomatoes, and a crock of buttermilk in the cooling house. Fetch 'em, and we'll have us a big dinner right here.''

Frank nodded and started for the house.

McSwain waited until Frank was out of earshot, then turned to the younger Hamer. "Harrison, how about bringing a new trace chain and a couple of U-bolts from the barn? Noticed that plow chain's showing some wear.''

"Yes, sir. I'll water the mules, too.'' Harrison unhitched the mule team and led the animals to the water trough at the barn. He saw Frank go into the back door of the farmhouse as he swung the corral gate closed. He left the mules to drink and rest, found the chain and U-bolts, and started back for the wagon. While he was at it, Harrison thought, it wouldn't take but a minute to stop by the plow and fix the loose rivets.

He pulled the hand anvil from his pocket and reached for the hammer in his waistband. He glanced toward the McSwain wagon. It was out of his line of sight, behind the chinaberry trees.

Harrison placed the anvil against the end of a loose rivet and drew back the hammer.

He never delivered the blow.

He heard a clatter behind him, glanced around, and saw Frank squat down to pick up a couple of cans he had dropped—and a flicker of movement at the edge of his field of vision caught his attention.

Harrison's heart leaped into his throat.

McSwain crouched no more than fifty feet from Frank. He held a double-barrel shotgun in his hands. The weapon swung toward Frank.

Chapter Three

McSwain Farm

"LOOK OUT, FRANK!" Frank glanced up at Harrison's sharp yell; his heart skipped a beat as the twin bores of the shotgun in McSwain's hands lined on his chest.

Frank threw himself to the side. The tin of peaches he had dropped disappeared in a cloud of dirt and dust as the heavy shot charge ripped into the earth where he had crouched to pick up the fallen cans a split second before. Frank rolled to his feet and sprinted for the nearest cover, an uprooted tree stump a few strides away at the end of the turn row.

He didn't make it.

A sledgehammer blow against his upper back and alongside his head sent him down. The muzzle blast of the shotgun slammed against his ears. He lay stunned for a moment, heart hammering, brain struggling to comprehend what had happened. He felt no pain, just a heavy weight against his left side pinning him to the freshly plowed earth. The soil felt damp and cool against his right cheek. The swirl of sensations subsided under the realization that he had been shot.

The sticky heat of his own blood against his skin triggered a quick curse and a sudden burst of rage.

He forced shocked muscles and nerves into action, twisted his body, and pulled the .32 revolver from beneath his waistband. He cocked the weapon and swung the muzzle toward McSwain, still partially obscured by the gray-white powder smoke of the shotgun blasts. Frank squeezed the trigger and heard the distinct thump of lead against flesh.

McSwain grunted and half spun. The shotgun dropped from his hands. Frank thumbed the hammer and fired again as McSwain went down between two furrows. The slug went over McSwain's body and clipped a limb on the chinaberry tree above Harrison's head.

Frank tried to line the sights for a third shot, but had no target; from where he lay, he couldn't see McSwain. The farmer lay between rows of earth turned up by the breaking plow. Frank lowered the handgun as Harrison sprinted past the spot where McSwain had gone down. Frank thought he heard McSwain groan over the thud of Harrison's footfalls.

Frank's head spun. A wave of nausea rippled through his gut as the first stab of pain lanced from the torn muscles of his back and shoulder. He tried and failed to push himself to his feet as Harrison skidded to a stop alongside.

"Frank! Are you hurt bad?"

"He hit me—pretty hard," Frank said through clenched teeth. "Help me up—gotta kill that—son-of-a-bitch!"

Harrison slipped an arm under Frank's right shoulder and hauled him erect. At the edge of his vision, Frank saw McSwain struggle to his feet and run, stumbling, toward the house. Frank couldn't bring his revolver into play; Harrison's helping arm restricted his movements. He tried to shift the revolver to the other hand, but his numb fingers didn't respond to his will. By the time he had worked his gun hand free, McSwain was out of effective range of the short-barreled .32, lurching toward the back door of the farmhouse.

"We've got to get out of here, Frank!" Harrison's voice quavered in fear. "McSwain'll kill us both! Come on!"

The earth tilted under Frank's feet. The pain in his back started a quick climb toward white-hot agony. He leaned against Harrison and forced heavy legs to move as the two brothers ran.

"The hill," Harrison said, gasping from the effort of running through fresh-turned soil and the strain of carrying a portion of Frank's weight. "We can hide in the gully on the other side."

The hill, little more than a slight rise in the farmland, was a hundred yards past the field. It seemed to Frank that they had half run, half staggered, for a mile before Harrison all but dragged him to the rocky crest. Searing pain from the shotgun wound spread through his body. The black rage in his mind tempered the agony a bit as they topped the low hill.

Harrison glanced back and cursed. "He's got that old buffalo gun, Frank—and he's on horseback. We have to hide!" He practically dragged Frank down the hill and into a tangle of berry vines and fallen timber in the bottom of the draw choked with brush, driftwood, trees, and rocks.

Frank lay on his belly beneath the brush cover, teeth gritted, and fought an inner battle to control his breathing. His lungs screamed for air, drained from the demands of the run, but each deep breath sent a knife thrust through his chest. He became aware that his shirt was warm and sticky from the blood that plastered the cloth to the skin of his back. He felt a trickle along a cheekbone and swiped at the track. His hand came away smeared with blood. He didn't know how many times he had been hit, but he sensed he had caught almost the full load of shot in his back and shoulder. A few pellets had slammed into the left side of his head.

Harrison's breathing soon settled into a steady rhythm, unlike Frank's shallow, labored gasps. The younger Hamer cocked his head, listening. His face seemed to pale even more.

"He's coming, Frank," Harrison whispered. "Don't move. Be as quiet as you can."

After a few minutes Frank heard the click of a shod hoof on stone. He realized he still held the .32 revolver in his right hand. And that he still had three of five rounds left. If McSwain rode past within pistol range, Frank promised himself, one farmer was going to be a dead man.

The scratch of brush against cloth only a few yards from their hiding spot reached Frank's ears. If McSwain kept his course, he would pass within thirty yards of their hiding place. And Frank would have a clear shot when McSwain rode into the open space between timber stands to cross the creek. He cocked the revolver and pointed the muzzle toward the bottom of the draw.

Harrison's hand fell on Frank's forearm.

"No, Frank," he whispered, "don't try it. He's got that big rifle. That buffalo gun will shoot a lot farther and hit a lot harder than your pistol. Let him go. We've got to get away from here alive and get you to a doctor."

Frank started to argue. The protest never came, quashed by a sudden surge of weakness and a shuddering chill. He had to admit Harrison was right. If he didn't kill McSwain with the first shot, the landowner would probably kill him—and Harrison, too. Frank wasn't even sure he could put the handgun slug in the right place. His vision wavered. The front sight of the little revolver flickered in and out of focus. If Harrison hadn't been beside him, Frank would have tried it anyway. But he knew he couldn't let his own pain and fury cost Harrison's life.

"All—right," Frank whispered back, his voice raspy, "but if he—finds us—I'll have—to try and take him down."

The brothers lay silent, unmoving, as the cautious hoofbeats drew nearer. McSwain came into view through the break in the covering brush a few yards away, his head swiveling back and forth as he studied the surrounding terrain. Frank fought back the urge to line the sights and pull the trigger; in his condition, he couldn't be sure of a killing head shot. The gamble wasn't worth it, not with Harrison's life at stake.

McSwain rode past, crossed the shallow creek, and urged his horse up the far creek bank. Harrison waited until the sounds faded, then crept to the edge of the thicket. He crabbed his way back to Frank's side.

"He's gone," he said. "We've got to get out of here before he comes back. Can you walk, Frank?"

Frank's shoulders quivered under a fresh blast of agony. "I'll—manage." His voice sounded weak and shaky in his own ears.

"Okay, let's get you back to the wagon. The best place to go now is home. He won't come after us there. Then I'll get the doctor." Harrison took the revolver from Frank and tucked it into his own waistband, then helped his brother wriggle from beneath the cover and onto his feet.

The wagon seemed an impossible distance away, Frank thought.

The trip home in the jolting wagon was a vague, blurred memory in Frank's mind.

He lay facedown on his cot, his brain fogged from the foul-tasting liquid the doctor had given him. It helped ease the pain a bit as the doctor probed for the shotshell pellets. Still, Frank's breath came in short, wincing gasps as the physician worked. At the edge of his vision he could see his mother's face, narrow furrows of worry between her eyebrows. His father sat nearby, a rifle across his knees as he stared out the window.

Frank heard the faint tink of lead against porcelain bowl. A moment later he flinched as something cold and wet built the fire in his back to a taller blaze.

"That's about all I can do for him, Mrs. Hamer," the doctor said. "He took more than a dozen pellets. Fortunately, they weren't big buckshot, or they could have penetrated even deeper and caused more damage. A few of them are so deep in his back and shoulder it would be more risky to take them out than to leave them in."

"Are you sure, Doctor? I've heard of people getting lead poisoning. . . ." Mrs. Hamer's voice trailed away.

"He may carry them the rest of his life, but the human body's a remarkable piece of work, ma'am. I doubt they'll cause him all that much discomfort later. The head wounds don't seem to be bad. Lucky the pellets hit at an angle and didn't penetrate the skull, or he'd be dead now."

"Then you're saying he'll be all right?" Mrs. Hamer asked.

"You never know with gunshot wounds, Mrs. Hamer," the doctor said solemnly. "If there's no infection, he should recover." Frank winced again as a weight pressed against his damaged shoulder and back. "I'll drop in every couple of days for a week or so and check on his progress."

Frank felt a hand on his upper arm. "Can you sit up, son?" the doctor said. "We've got to tie off this bandage."

Strong hands and arms helped Frank to a sitting position and quickly tied the wrappings. The doctor grunted in satisfaction. "Don't move around any more than you have to for a few days, Frank. We don't want you losing any more blood."

Frank had to try twice before he got the words out. "How long—until I—can work again?"

The physician scowled. "I won't coat it with sugar, son.

You've been hit hard. Some of the wounds were pretty deep. It's going to take time, even for someone as young and strong as you. You have to be patient. In a few days the wounds will stop weeping and start to scab over. With luck, the only lasting effects you'll have will be a few scars. How are you feeling?''

Cold sweat beaded on Frank's forehead and upper lip as the doctor wiped the blood from his probe and other instruments, doused them with alcohol, and stored them in his bag. The room tilted. Frank didn't know if it was from the laudanum or a delayed reaction to being shot. The bitter, acid taste of bile was sharp against the back of his throat.

"Not so good," Frank said.

"Better lie down again. On your belly. For what it's worth, Dan McSwain isn't feeling real perky, either, but he's going to be down for a while himself. Your slug hit him in the upper chest. Just missed a lung and two big blood vessels.''

"I'll do better next time." Frank's voice was weak, but the tone was still tight and hard.

"I didn't hear you say that, son," the physician said. "Now, let's get you stretched out. You'll be more comfortable.''

Frank ground his teeth, but couldn't help moaning aloud as the doctor, Harrison, and Mrs. Hamer eased him back facedown on the cot. The physician's voice seemed faint and far away.

"As soon as he's able, ma'am, try to get some food into him. Broth or thin soup at first. When he's able to keep that down, solid food, and as much of it as he can hold. Make sure he drinks plenty of water." Frank heard a slight slosh of liquid. "Give him a couple of teaspoons of this if the pain gets too bad, but don't overdo it. I've seen patients get addicted to the stuff. Laudanum's a hard habit to break. It's just opium extract and watered-down alcohol.''

"Where's—Harrison?" Frank hardly recognized his own voice.

"Tending the barn chores," Mrs. Hamer said. "Don't worry about a thing, Frank. Just try to rest.''

"What if—McSwain comes—to finish the job?''

"I seriously doubt that Mr. McSwain will be going anywhere soon," the doctor said.

"If he does come," Frank's father said, his words tight,
"he won't leave except facedown across his saddle." It was
the first time Frank remembered his father having said a word
since the initial flurry of questions and frets when Harrison
had reined the wagon team up to the front door. "Harrison,
your mother, and I'll take turns keeping watch. All of us are
fair rifle shots. Don't worry about him."

"My chores—"

"We'll handle them, son. You concentrate on getting
well."

"Young man," the doctor said, "I'm no lawyer, but it
seems to me you would have a strong case against McSwain
if you want to press charges."

Frank shook his head. "No. I'll handle—McSwain myself.
As soon as I'm able. It's between him and—me now...."
Frank's voice trailed away. He let himself slide into the com-
fort of darkness.

"Something bothering you, Pancho? Besides the back, I
mean?"

Frank pushed himself away from the porch post he had
been leaning against and nodded to Harrison. "Cabin fever,
I guess," he said.

"I can imagine. You've been cooped up in the house almost a month. Still hurting?"

"At times." Frank sighed. "I might as well be honest. I
hurt most of the time. I never thought it would take this long
to get back on my feet."

Harrison frowned. "The doc said it would take a while.
That you'd have to be patient."

Frank tried to flex his upper back and left shoulder. The
movement pulled at the tender red skin beginning to grow
over the wounds and sent a twinge of discomfort through his
body.

"Want to come inside and lie down?"

"No. I've had enough of that bed to last me a lifetime."
Frank heard the strained disgust in his own words. After all
this time he was still unable to do any but the simplest, less

demanding chores around the farm. He even had to all but fight his mother to let him do what little he could. She thought he should do nothing but sit or lie around the house and grow skin while she waited on him hand and foot and Harrison or his father stood guard. One or the other was always nearby, a rifle at hand. It was disrupting the normal routine of his family's daily living.

Frank felt responsible for that. It made him even more itchy and restless. And helpless. The helpless feeling hurt worse than the shotgun pellets still in his body. Frank knew the itch that consumed him was more than the slow healing process. It came from deep within. He was bored. Plain and simple bored.

Harrison sat down on the porch steps, his father's rifle across his knees. Frank studied his younger brother for a moment. Harrison had always seemed older than his years, and he had aged more since the McSwain affair. His eyes were bloodshot. His gaze constantly scanned the roads and land around the Hamer house, watching for any sign of McSwain. Frank doubted the landowner had the nerve to come after him, but the man's existence was enough to set everyone's teeth on nervous edge.

Damn McSwain, anyway, Frank thought; what he did to me was bad enough. What he's doing to my family is even worse. There would come a day, he promised himself, that McSwain would pay.

The buzz of cicadas and fat blowflies seemed almost deafening in the July heat. There was little wind today, only an occasional rustle of leaves in the trees among the cluster of buildings that was Oxford. The air was heavy, the humidity oppressive to the point a man had to work to draw in a lungful.

Frank reached in his pocket for the makings and rolled a cigarette. He hadn't smoked all that much before, but when a man was stove up and couldn't do much else, tobacco was a way to pass the time. He rolled the quirly, scratched a match against the porch post, lit the cigarette, and drew the smoke deep into his lungs. "I'm leaving, Harrison," he said.

"What?"

"I said I'm leaving home for a while." Frank shook out

the match and tossed it aside. "I'm just in the way here. I know I haven't been easy to live with—"

"Frank, that's not true!"

"Yes, it is, partner, and we both know it. Even if you don't want to admit it. Besides, I think I can heal faster somewhere else."

Harrison fell silent for a moment. He knew Frank well enough to know his brother's mind was made up and nobody was likely to change it by arguing.

"Where?"

Frank dragged at the cigarette and let the smoke trickle from his nostrils. "West."

"How far west?"

"As far as it takes to find a place that suits me. A place where I'll not be underfoot all the time, where I can think on things and finish healing up. The doc says there's nothing more he can do to speed things along. I'll be leaving tomorrow."

Harrison started to rise. "I'll go with you."

Frank put a hand on his brother's shoulder. "No, Harrison. Mother and Dad need you here now, more than ever. And where I'm going, you'd be as bored as I am now."

Harrison didn't argue. After a moment he cleared his throat. "Mom won't like that."

"She'll get used to the idea. And I don't think she'll worry all that much. She's used to me being gone camping and hunting for days at a time anyway." Frank took a final drag at his smoke and ground the butt under his heel.

"When will you be coming back home?"

"When I'm back on my feet and able to do a day's work like everyone else, little brother." Frank's tone hardened. "And when I'm ready to settle up with McSwain."

Rio Grande
September 1900

Frank stood in the cool semidarkness of the cliff cave near the confluence of the Pecos River and Rio Grande and studied the Indian pictograph high above his head.

The drawing, almost startling in its attention to detail, portrayed a young Indian woman walking down a trail toward a water hole. At the side of the trail was a large, coiled diamondback rattler, poised to strike.

Frank wondered what story the painting told. Did it depict a tragedy, the end of a pretty young woman's life before it had really begun? Or was it the basis of yet another Indian legend? Did the girl escape the rattler's fangs, befriend the snake, and somehow be granted special spirit powers?

At first he had wondered who painted the picture, what tribe it represented. He suspected it was of Apache origin, but these caves might have been used long before the Apache came. The more he studied the drawing, the less important the origins of the artwork seemed in relation to the story it told.

He promised himself that someday he would try to find the answer. Maybe he would cross paths with an old Indian who had heard the legend of what happened at this particular campsite in some long-ago time.

Frank strode to the mouth of the cave, his steps longer and more fluid than they had been since McSwain's shotgun blast ripped into his back. He was mending, gaining strength by the day. His back and shoulder were still a bit stiff, and some mornings it seemed he could feel the lead-pellet lumps deep in his flesh. But he was satisfied that he had made the right decision.

The dry climate and the heat of the desert sun was a better physician than the doctor from Oxford ever could be. The sun and the solitude, the time to think things through, to plan the payback with McSwain, and being no one's burden had lifted his spirits even as his flesh began to mend.

The rugged, canyon-laced country where the Pecos and Rio Grande met was outwardly an inhospitable land. But to those who grew to know it, as Frank had, it was a land of plenty—deer and other wild game, fish, and edible plants abounded. Those who didn't know how to live off the land, he thought, would starve in the midst of plenty.

On the way west, he had reached one inescapable, if expensive, conclusion. The little .32 rimfire wouldn't cut the cheese as a handgun. The next time he hit McSwain, he'd stay hit. So Frank stopped at a store and spent a hefty chunk of his seminary-school savings on weapons. He rode away from the store with a new Colt Single-Action Army .45, a used but serviceable holster, and a .44-40 Winchester lever-action carbine that had seen use but still had a smooth action and a clean bore. He had gone through a box of revolver cartridges and half a box of rifle rounds in practice and on the hunt. Both weapons shot where he pointed.

Frank had gained weight along with strength. He wasn't the only one. The first couple of weeks, his bay saddle horse started to take on the shape of a hair barrel on the rich green grass that grew on the riverbanks.

Frank now was near full recovery. It was time to go.

There was unfinished business back home. Frank had reconciled himself to the fact that he would never realize his dream of being a preacher. Preachers didn't kill. And he was going to kill Dan McSwain.

CHAPTER FOUR

———◆———

San Saba County
October 1900

FRANK HAMER REINED his bay to a stop at the edge of a peach orchard, stepped from the saddle, and studied the McSwain house thirty yards away.

A wisp of smoke rose from the chimney and drifted away on the mild northeasterly breeze. Through an open window beside the back door, Frank caught a glimpse of a familiar figure and nodded to himself, satisfied. McSwain was home.

The anger that had sustained him during the long weeks of recuperation was no longer a cold knot in his gut. His heartbeat was steady, his palms dry. Frank knew he was about to go up against a man who would shoot back, but he wasn't overly concerned for his own safety. And, he admitted to himself, this wasn't a matter of simple revenge.

McSwain was a killer. Maybe he didn't always pull the trigger himself, but that didn't wash the blood from his hands. If anything, it made the stain worse, as far as Frank was concerned. A man stomped his own snakes. A bushwhacker and coward hired somebody else to do the job. This time, McSwain was on his own. He'd face the man he tried to kill.

Frank knew the layout of the place well, but he still took the time to study it with care once more. He had planned his approach for weeks. Charging blindly into a shoot-out wasn't part of the plan.

The most important thing was to determine that McSwain was alone. The last thing Frank wanted was to endanger an innocent person. That would be murder, not justice.

Frank took his time, rolled a cigarette, and peered past the smoke until he was sure no one was in the house but McSwain. He had no intention of just riding up to the front door and calling McSwain out. If McSwain spotted him coming, it likely would mean a rifle slug in the chest before he could face the man. He also knew he could wait at the orchard until McSwain came out the back door and plunk a slug into him. He had no intention of doing that. Blasting a man from ambush was the McSwain way. Not the Hamer way. Frank wanted to look into McSwain's eyes before he pulled the trigger. He wanted McSwain to know who was killing him. And why.

Frank finished his smoke, looped the bay's reins around a low limb, and absently patted the horse on the neck. He slipped the .45 Colt from his holster and thumbed a cartridge into the sixth chamber, which he normally left empty under the hammer. He eased the revolver back into the leather.

It was time to collect on a debt.

Frank moved cautiously, circling through the cover of buildings and fences, to the side of the main house. He listened for a moment, marked McSwain's movements in his mind, then chanced a glance through a side window.

McSwain stood beside the cast-iron stove, a coffee cup in hand. He had a revolver tucked into his waistband.

Frank stepped around the corner to the front of the house, stopped a few feet from the front door, and dropped his hand

to the butt of his holstered Colt. He rapped on the wall with
his free hand.

"McSwain," he called, "come out here!"

After a moment the door swung open. McSwain stepped
through. His eyes widened in surprise.

"Hamer! I thought I'd finished you!"

"Not by a damned sight, McSwain. I'm here to settle accounts!"

McSwain yanked at the revolver in his waistband. Frank
swept his Colt from the holster, cocked the hammer as he
drew, and fired. McSwain grunted aloud and staggered back
a step as the heavy .45 slug tore into his chest; his revolver
blasted harmlessly into the dirt. Frank thumbed the hammer,
ready to fire again. McSwain's gun hand opened. The weapon
dropped from numbed fingers. McSwain stumbled again and
went down.

Frank stepped to McSwain's side, the Colt trained on the
downed man's head. He knew at a glance he wouldn't need
a second shot. McSwain had only moments to live.

"Damn—you—Hamer." McSwain's words were weak,
barely audible. Bloody spittle frothed at the edge of his lips.
"Thought you'd—crawled off somewhere—died."

"Looks like you beat me to it, McSwain," Hamer said.
"A man shouldn't start what he doesn't finish."

McSwain coughed once and died. Frank stared at the dead
man for a moment. He felt no remorse. McSwain had made
his own bed. He'd died in it.

If Frank had any regrets, it was that he had violated the
biblical admonition "Thou shalt not kill." He could never
take the pulpit now. Minutes later he was in the saddle,
headed home.

Ketchum Ranch
Pecos County, Texas
Spring 1901

Frank hazed the half-dozen shorthorn cows up the rocky trail
out of Fourmile Draw toward the spring gather on the prickly-
pear flats a half mile away.

He reined the Ketchum Ranch palomino aside to head off a wide-eyed yearling before the heifer had a chance to bolt back into the draw.

Spring roundup was the best part of a working cowboy's year, Frank mused. Especially on days like today, with the fresh scent of last night's rain heightening the smell of greening grass and the pleasant odor of horse beneath a warm, friendly sun, topped off by a cool breeze.

The lowing of cattle milling in the distance fell easy on Frank's ears. A blue quail sounded its distinctive *chiing* cry from a nearby yucca patch, warning its covey mates that strange, large creatures were moving past. A green Mexican jay raised a nattering fuss from its perch on a mesquite limb, little more than arm's length away, threatening Frank with dire consequences if he dared approach the hidden nest.

Frank nattered back at the Mexican jay; the bird fell silent. Frank chuckled to himself at the mental picture of a totally confused green bird standing guard against something that spoke its language, yet obviously was not one of its own kind. It was a game he enjoyed, the banter with different birds and animals. He had even learned the calls that summoned the curious roadrunner, paisano, almost to his side. Paisano was a bit of a clown, once you got to know him well.

Frank waved a hand at his brother as Harrison appeared, trailing behind another small band of Ketchum cattle a couple of hundred yards away. At fifteen, Harrison was almost a man grown, a good hand around a herd despite his youth.

Frank hadn't argued much with Harrison when he said he wanted to come along. The Ketchum outfit needed another hand, anyway. Frank liked his younger brother's company, there was little to do around the family homestead these days, and Harrison had finished what little schooling was available in Oxford. As cowboys, they could at least earn a semblance of a living. And it was a lot more enjoyable than plodding along behind a mule team or swinging a hoe.

The two groups of cattle drifted together a couple hundred yards short of the main herd on the flats ahead.

"Looks like a good gather," Harrison said. "How many you think?"

Frank stood in the stirrups to study the bunches of cattle

being thrown toward the main herd, then shrugged. "Three or four hundred, probably a hundred and fifty or so branding-size calves. We're in for some work this afternoon, it appears."

Harrison half smiled. "Oh, I don't know. Branding's work, all right, but sort of enjoyable. Given the right company."

Frank nodded. The Ketchum outfit ran a crew of thirteen men, not counting the chuck-wagon cook and wrangler, during roundup and branding seasons in spring and fall. Most of the crew were decent enough sorts, especially after the day's work was done. Frank enjoyed the constant joshing and frequent practical jokes. Maybe the old saying he had heard was true, that the only thing dumber than a cow was a cowboy, but it didn't make them any less fun to be around. Especially a couple of them who had ridden on the shady side of the law.

Barry Ketchum, the owner and range boss of the outfit, was the brother of Black Jack Ketchum, recently decapitated in a botched hanging at Clayton, New Mexico. As far as Frank knew, Barry hadn't run with Black Jack's bunch of outlaws, which had preyed on stores, trains, banks, and stages over three or four states until most of them were shot to pieces or captured in Folsom, Arizona, in July of 1899. Black Jack escaped and decided to go it alone. That turned out to be a mistake. A solo train holdup that went sour left him with an arm shattered by a shotgun blast and led him to the gallows, to get his head yanked off by a noose.

A couple of the Ketchum hands had ridden with Black Jack at one time or another. Frank found himself drawn into their campfire tales of holdups, shoot-outs, and wild times on the outlaw trail. Harrison seemed equally fascinated with the stories. At times, listening to those yarns, Frank wondered if he might have been born twenty years too late. He figured he'd missed out on the best of the wild times.

Hearing about them from those who had been there was something that stirred a man's blood, anyway. He knew he'd never forget those yarns spun on the Ketchum outfit. The way the outlaw mind work fascinated him. Even discounting the probable exaggerations, those yarns made fine entertainment.

It sure sounded like outlaws had more excitement in their lives than farmers and preachers did. . . .

San Angelo, Texas
Spring 1903

Frank squatted beside the rangy McKenzie Ranch bay, the reins draped over his forearm and waited for the boss to return from contacting the buyer in town.

Two McKenzie wranglers lazed in the saddle in the near distance, keeping an eye on the remuda that grazed at the outskirts of San Angelo. The horses, trail-wise and gentle, needed little attention. The horse buyer would be getting quite a few decent cow ponies to offset the handful of spoiled mounts and just plain jugheads in the McKenzie cavvy.

The McKenzie Ranch wasn't the best outfit he'd worked for since he and Harrison had left the Ketchum spread, but it wasn't the worst, either. Frank wished Harrison were here. He missed the company of his brother, but Harrison wasn't among those picked for the horse drive.

Frank rolled and lit a smoke and let his gaze drift around the half circle of McKenzie riders who had trailed the horses from ranch headquarters at Marathon to San Angelo and now waited the foreman's return.

Of the five other hands, four were young, near Frank's age or even younger. A sixth, who had just reined up by the waiting group after a quick horseback ride through town, went by the name of Mort Cafferty. He was in his thirties and looked older.

If half what Cafferty said was true, Frank could understand why the man looked older. He had packed a lot of living into his years. Cafferty claimed to have ridden with Butch and Sundance's Wild Bunch, then with Black Jack Ketchum's gang a few years back. He spun some interesting and exciting stories about those years. The gimp in his right leg, he said, was courtesy of a posse that had chased him, Cassidy, and Sundance from a Colorado train holdup almost to Hole-in-the-Wall.

The younger McKenzie hands had spent many an evening

around the bunkhouse table soaking up Cafferty's tales of wild times on the outlaw trail, with its easy money and easy women. The lean, dark man was quick with a whiskey bottle and six-gun. He wielded almost as much influence with the younger hands as the man who handed out their pay every month.

"How'd you boys like to earn some easy money?" Cafferty asked.

"How much, Mort?" one of the men asked.

Cafferty's dark eyes sparkled. "How does a couple thousand or so apiece sound?"

"That's a heap of money. Where do we get that much?"

"At the place where they keep a heap of money." Cafferty dragged at the smoke and nodded over his shoulder. "The San Angelo bank."

The young cowpunchers sat in surprised silence for a moment. Finally, Curly Broadnax broke the quiet. "You mean—"

"I mean, rob the place," Cafferty said. "If ever a bank was ripe for the pickin', that one is. No guards, just one old teller on duty, and the law's out of town. We could just waltz in, help ourselves to the cash, and ride out. Easy as pluckin' persimmons off a short tree."

Frank's gaze shifted to Broadnax. The stocky young man with the pocked face grinned and nodded. "Sounds good to me. You got a plan, Mort?"

Cafferty shrugged. "Doesn't take much planning to hit a bank like that one. We'd be in, out, and gone quicker'n a rattler's strike. Take the money, cross the Rio, and set us up a big ranch down in Mexico. Wouldn't have to ever work for wages again, and we'd be up to our butts in tequila and señoritas the rest of our natural days."

"Count me in," Broadnax said, his reedy voice rising in pitch as his excitement grew. "Always wanted to take a crack at something like that."

One of the other punchers, eyes wide, nodded. "I'm in."

Cafferty stared at Frank. "Well, Pancho?"

Frank paused for a moment, trying to reason his way past the surge of excitement in his veins. Finally, he nodded. "Might as well."

"Good," Cafferty said. "Pancho, you and I will go in the front door. Curly, you watch the back. Dan, Jake, you two sidle up alongside the front door. I doubt there'll be any shootin', but be ready just in case you need to cover us."

"What about me?" The red-haired youth at Frank's side sounded worried, as if he was afraid he'd miss out on the fun.

"You hold the horses, Toby—mine and Pancho's. We'll be wantin' to light a shuck from San Angelo pretty quick. I know places where we can lose any posse easy. We'll be in Mexico in a couple days." Cafferty glanced around the group. "Let's go, boys. There's big money waitin'."

Frank swung into the saddle and rode alongside Cafferty toward town. "You others let Pancho and me ride in first, boys," Cafferty said. "When we step down outside the bank, move in. Look casual about it, like you was just goin' to get a beer. Ready?"

Frank surprised himself; despite his inner excitement and anticipation at his first venture into the life of outlawry, his heartbeat remained steady and his palms dry as he and Cafferty moved onto San Angelo's main street at a slow trot. He even caught himself calculating the best and least risky escape routes along the way. A few more minutes and he'd be riding Cafferty's outlaw trail, living all the stories he'd heard—

"Hey, boys!"

The call from the front porch of a hotel at the side of the street brought Cafferty and Frank up short.

"Yeah, boss?" Cafferty said as they reined in.

The McKenzie Ranch foreman stepped into the street, a smile twitching the ends of his droopy handlebar mustache. "Sorry, gents, but there's no time for a drink now." He untied the reins of a leggy roan and swung into the saddle. "The buyer finally showed up. I just closed the deal on the horses. We're moving them to the holding grounds a mile north of town until his crew gets here about sundown."

Frank glanced at Cafferty. The former outlaw merely nodded at the foreman. "Sure thing."

Frank and Cafferty reined their horses around and fell in behind the segundo's roan. Cafferty glanced at Frank, caught the question in his raised eyebrow, and shrugged as if to say, Well, maybe another time.

The sun had set before Frank fully realized how close he had been to becoming a hunted man. His initial disappointment at missing the bank job gave way to relief. He lay on his blankets and studied the sky overhead, now coming alive with a wash of stars.

He had come within minutes of playing the fool.

He could now admit to himself that it was the prospect of adventure, not the lure of easy money, that had almost turned him into an outlaw. He made a silent vow to the stars above that he'd never be that impulsive again.

The life of a cowboy might be long on work and short on pay, but it beat being on the run. And maybe facing a lynch rope.

A wry smile tugged at his lips as he wondered what Harrison and his folks would have thought, with son and brother a wanted man, a bank robber, on the run from the law. Or dead in a dusty street somewhere.

The slight smile faded as Frank realized that something even worse could have happened. What if innocent people had been hurt? He had already killed one man, but that was different. The thought of his bullet knocking the life from an innocent bystander—maybe a woman or child—chilled his blood.

He remembered what the Reverend Miller had said about his natural talent with a gun. That God didn't bless everyone with the same abilities, but the special gift a man received from the Almighty was not granted without purpose.

Frank idly wondered what that purpose might be. . . .

Carr Ranch, Pecos County
August 1905

"Easy, boy. Nobody's going to hurt you," Frank said softly as he eased the saddle blanket onto the young chestnut's back.

The skittish three-year-old colt walled its eyes, fluttered its nostrils, and tried to spin away from the strange thing on its back. Frank stayed with the horse, talking softly, his hand keeping its firm grasp on the hackamore headstall. The skin on the chestnut's shoulders and flanks quivered.

Frank patiently held his grip on the hackamore. He didn't blame the horse for being spooked. The animal was what the hands called a "long three," almost four years old, and this was only the second time he'd been exposed to human touch. The first time had been as a yearling, when he'd been roped, branded, and castrated. Frank figured he'd be a bit yippy himself if he'd had the same experience that the horse had at men's hands.

"Steady, now," Frank said to the horse, his tone steady, voice soft and soothing. The chestnut's skin quivered, but he slowly accepted the saddle pad. Frank took his time. Good horses weren't "broke," their spirit destroyed by fear. That didn't make the horse a partner, and a good cowhorse had to be part of a team. A horse that worked in fear of its rider and a possible beating was too busy being scared to learn how to do his job. Slow and easy was Frank's way. Abusing a horse was the mark of a sorry man, not a sorry horse, as far as Frank was concerned.

Frank patted the horse on the neck and ran his hand across the chestnut's muscled shoulder. "That's enough for now, partner," he said. "Tomorrow, I reckon you'll be ready for the saddle."

"Got him coming along good, Pancho."

Frank glanced up at the voice from outside the corral. Hap Carr leaned against the peeled log fence, wiry forearms resting between two rails. Carr had a real first name, Frank supposed, but to most people in the country he was just "Hap."

"He's a smart one, boss," Frank said. "He'll be a top pony." He stepped back and studied the horse with a practiced eye. "Built for quick speed, stout, and smart. Got the makings of a fine rope horse."

Carr grunted his agreement. "Been watching you with these broncs, Frank. I never had a rough string twister who could gentle a horse as quick. And without 'em pitching."

Frank shrugged. "Never saw the need for a bronc ride when there's better ways to do it. A horse isn't hard to talk to." He let the hackamore reins drop and strode to the fence.

He reached into his pocket, shook out a ready-roll smoke, and offered one to Carr. The boss shook his head.

"Thanks, I've got my own—"

Something in Frank's expression caught Carr's attention. He turned. A rider was coming in at a lope.

"Looks like Dugan's got a burr under his blanket," Carr said. "Never knew him to run a horse toward the barn unless something was up."

The man called Dugan reined in a few feet from the two men, his weathered face drawn into a scowl. "Trouble, Hap," he said, anger tight in his words. "Somebody stole two horses from the Escondido camp sometime last night. Took the bridles and saddles, too."

Carr's face darkened. "Any idea who?"

"No. Tracks looked like two men done it." Dugan leaned in the saddle and spat. "Lost the sign about three miles northeast of the camp. One thing's for sure, and that's I ain't no lawman. Thought you'd best call Sheriff Barker on that newfangled talkin' machine."

Carr muttered a curse. "I'll call him. But by the time he can get out here, they'll be long gone on a cold trail. At least he can get the word out in case they try to sell 'em."

Frank wasn't sure exactly how the new gadget called a telephone worked. It didn't seem possible a man could talk to somebody that far away just like he was sitting at the same table. But the thing did seem handy to have around. The Carr outfit had had a phone for a couple of weeks now.

"When you talk to the sheriff," Frank said, "tell him to swear out a warrant. I'll go get those jaspers. There's nothing in this world I hate worse than a horse thief."

Carr turned to stare at Hamer. "Go after them alone, with the start they've got on you?" He shook his head. "You'd never find them, Frank. If you did, you could get shot for your trouble. As much as I hate losing two good horses, I'd hate even worse to lose a top hand."

"You won't. Don't expect me back right away. This may take a while."

Frank reined the rangy buckskin to a halt and sniffed the breeze. He hadn't been mistaken. The scent of wood smoke was faint but distinct in his nostrils.

He'd found his horse thieves.

After two full days of scouting, he'd finally cut sign on the stolen stock. Two more days of tracking, and now the hunt was over. Dugan was right. The tracks said two men. Frank was comfortable with those odds.

He eased the buckskin forward at a slow walk. The wood-smoke smell was stronger now, overlaid by the scent of bacon frying. Frank grunted in satisfaction. With their minds on their bellies, the two outlaws wouldn't be paying attention to much else.

Frank checked the buckskin a hundred yards upwind of the camp and on the far side of a low ridge. A dry creek off to his left led toward the draw. He dismounted, hobbled his horse, pulled his Winchester from the saddle boot, and set out on foot for the cover of the dry creekbed.

A quarter hour later he crouched behind a greasewood clump at a sharp bend in the creek and studied the men a dozen yards away. They sat beside the fire, backs to Frank, leaning over the tin plates on their laps. Four horses were tied to a makeshift picket line on the east side of the camp, including a piebald bay and a stocking-legged sorrel wearing the Carr brands.

Frank eased the Winchester hammer back to full cock and stepped into the open.

"Nobody move, gents," Frank said. "You're under arrest."

The shock of his words snapped the two men's spines upright. After a moment one of the horse thieves twisted his head, eyes wide. His face paled as he stared into the muzzle of Frank's rifle. The outlaw glanced at his own rifle, leaning against a saddle within arm's reach.

"Try it and you're dead." Frank's tone was calm, almost as if he were discussing the weather. "It would save the state the cost of a trial."

The man abandoned the idea of going for the rifle as quickly as the thought had come. "Horse thieves?" He swallowed hard. "What are you talkin' about?"

"You have two Carr Ranch horses on the picket line. I'm taking them back. And you. You can go back sitting up in the saddle or facedown across it. Doesn't matter much to me.''

The man who was looking over his shoulder shook his head. ''You'd drop a hammer on a man for stealing a horse?''

''I would. Figure yourselves lucky. A few years ago you'd be hanging from a tall tree on a short rope instead of facing a stretch in the state pen. Well, gents? What's it going to be?''

A half hour later Frank stepped back into his saddle. The two horse thieves weren't going anywhere. Frank had their hands tied behind their backs and the pair necked together with one of their lariats. The end of the hemp rope was tied hard and fast to Frank's saddle horn. The stolen Carr horses trailed behind the thieves on loose lead.

''Let's go, fellows,'' Frank said. ''We'll have you tucked away in jail by sundown.''

The older man's eyes narrowed. ''It's a long ways from here back to Fort Stockton. You think you're hoss enough to get us back there by your lonesome?''

Frank fired a cigarette and stared at the horse thief. ''I'm hoss enough. But we're going to Crockett County. It's closer. The sheriff there'll hold you until Dud Barker picks you up.'' He reined the buckskin toward the southwest.

''Mister,'' one of the thieves called after a half mile's ride, ''you got a name?''

''I'm Frank Hamer.''

''Lawman?''

Frank shrugged. ''Cowboy. And a man who can't abide a horse thief. Might keep that in mind—and your mouth shut— until we get to the Crockett lockup.''

The sun had set by the time Frank turned the prisoners over to the Crockett County sheriff. He nodded toward the phone on the wall. ''Mind if I use that thing? I need to let Mr. Carr know we've got the horses back.''

''Sure. Help yourself.''

Frank hesitated. ''Show me how to use it?''

CHAPTER FIVE

Carr Ranch
October 1905

FRANK LOUNGED AT the table in the big house, nursed a cup of coffee, and listened to the breeze rustle the golden leaves of the cottonwood tree outside the dining-room window. He idly wondered if they were in for a tough winter this year.

The coarse rasp of the telephone caught his attention. Two longs and a short—the ring for Charlie Witcher's place. Frank strode to the phone and lifted the earpiece from its hook. Several ranchers shared the same line, and none of them seemed to mind if somebody listened in on a conversation. If they did, they'd just tell whoever was listening to butt out. Besides, it helped pass the time when there wasn't much else to do.

"Charlie, I need to ask a favor." Former Texas Ranger turned rancher and sheriff Dud Barker's voice sounded a bit tinny over the line, but except for the occasional static, it was clear enough. "Fellow stole a horse over this way. Joy's black. He's headed your way. Man we're looking for is about five-nine, little on the skinny side. Got a scar from his right ear down to the jawbone. Reckon you could run him down for me?"

"Sorry, Dud," Witcher said, "but I've got so much to do I haven't got the time. Why don't you go after him yourself?" Witcher, a former deputy of Barker's, now owned a ranch midway between Fort Stockton and the Carr spread a few miles outside of Sheffield. That meant the thief would be coming through Carr Ranch country, Frank thought.

"Can't, Charlie," Barker said. "I got a jail full here at Fort Stockton, my deputy's out of town, and Saturday night's coming up. I can't hardly find time to eat as it is. Besides, this coyote's got such a jump on me it'd take a spell just to catch up with him.''

Frank cut in. ''I'll go get him, Sheriff.''

''Who's this?'' Barker asked.

''Frank Hamer.''

''Oh. Howdy, Frank. You've already caught a couple horse thieves for me, but if you can gather this fellow I'd be mighty happy. I'll tell you what he looks like—''

''No need,'' Frank interrupted. ''I heard you describe him to Charlie. I think I've got a good idea where he'll be.''

''Well, Frank, if you can catch him, I'd sure appreciate it. I'll ride out tomorrow and lend a hand.''

''I'll have him for you by the time you get here, Sheriff.''

Barker hesitated for a moment, then said, ''Okay, but watch out. This fellow's likely to start shooting if somebody tries to stop him. You're not drawing cowboy wages to get killed.''

''Don't plan to,'' Frank said. ''See you tomorrow.''

Frank hung up, sipped at his coffee, and grimaced. It had gotten lukewarm during the conversation. Frank hated cold coffee almost as much as he disliked folks who'd rather steal other people's property than work to earn it. He tossed out the stale brew, refilled his cup, and studied the problem.

It wasn't that hard to work out. The Carr Ranch had the only good water between Fort Stockton and Sheffield. A man with a gaunt horse would likely stop at the windmill in the north pasture. It was isolated, well away from any main roads or ranch houses, and the water was cool and pure. By the time Frank finished his coffee, he'd decided the best way to lay the trap. He rinsed the cup, refilled the pot so that all he had to do early in the morning was light the fire, and turned in for a short sleep.

At daybreak, Frank crouched behind the brush-covered earth dam that formed a stock tank fed by overflow from the three-foot-tall round metal tub at the north pasture mill.

The windmill blades spun lazily in the wakening breeze. The soft gurgle of a thumb-sized stream of water from the windmill pipe lay restful on the ear. Frank noted the scratchy squeak as the sucker rod worked, and made a mental note to tell Carr the well leathers needed grease.

Frank checked his rifle to reassure himself that a round was chambered. If he had figured right, the horse thief would get here soon. The sun would be at Frank's back, in the fugitive's eyes. If it came to shooting, that gave Frank the advantage.

The sun was barely above the eastern horizon when Frank spotted the horseman approaching, still a good half mile away. He was pretty sure it was his man. The horse looked to be a black, the rider medium height and tending toward the wiry side.

Frank sat patiently and watched the rider draw closer. The slender man either wasn't much of an outlaw, figured there was nothing to worry about, or else was too tired to care. He wasn't even paying attention to where he was going. Frank eased back the hammer of his rifle.

The rider made no effort to rein in and look around as the black neared the metal tank. The horse was gaunt in the flanks and sweaty, but seemed to be in good shape.

The rider tilted his head back and yawned. The white mark on his face all but gleamed in the rays of the morning sun. Frank nodded to himself, satisfied. The scar branded the man.

Frank studied the rider, noted the rifle butt protruding from the saddle scabbard and the handgun holstered at the man's left side, butt forward, cross-draw style. He didn't look like a shooter, and the fast-draw yarns Frank had heard were just that. Yarns. He'd met one man who had set out to be a fast-draw artist. That man was now called Gimp. He'd shot his right kneecap off practicing his quick draw.

Frank didn't worry about the horse thief's weapons. A gun in the hand was worth more than a dozen still in the leathers. Nobody could pull a rifle or sidearm before Frank could stroke the trigger on an already cocked Winchester.

Frank waited as the rider dismounted and stretched. The gaunt black already had its nose crammed into the tank up to the nostrils. The rider took off his hat, crouched over the stream of water from the mill pipe, cupped his hands, and drank. Frank stood and leveled the Winchester on the man's shirtfront.

"Hands up!" Frank called.

The scar-faced man started at the unexpected challenge. He glanced up, water dribbling from his chin and cupped hands.

For a moment Frank thought the thief was going to try for the gun. He didn't. Staring down the barrel of a rifle tended to make a man cautious. The thief's shoulders slumped. He lifted his still-dripping hands to shoulder height.

"You picked the wrong man to rob, feller," the scarred man said. "I'm flatter'n last year's cowpatties."

"Wasn't what I had in mind. You're under arrest."

"What for?"

"Stealing that black. Now, slow and easy, unbuckle that gun belt and lay it across the mill pipe."

The scarred man did as he was told.

"Step back."

Frank plucked the gun belt from the pipe, draped it over his shoulder, and slid the thief's rifle from the scabbard.

"What now?" the prisoner asked.

"Soon's the black drinks his fill, we go for a ride. Back the way you came. Sheriff Barker's on the way. Why'd you steal that horse?"

The scar-faced man shrugged. "Seemed like a good idea at the time. Stealin's cheaper than buyin', especially when a man's flat broke. Who the hell are you?"

"I'm Frank Hamer."

"You the law?"

"Just a cowboy with a Winchester. The black's had his fill. Mount up and we'll move out. You in front. Might be a good idea to keep in mind that a horse can't outrun a rifle bullet."

The two rode in silence at a steady walk, the thief in front and Frank trailing behind, rifle in hand. The gentle slopes of the low, rolling countryside slipped past as the sun rose.

After a couple hours the scar-faced man said over his shoulder, "You don't have to be so damn chipper about it."

"What?"

"Quit that hummin'. It's gettin' on my nerves."

Frank didn't realize he had been humming. He had to admit he was kind of pleased with himself, though. This felt like the most natural thing he'd ever done, trailing an outlaw toward justice. But he stopped humming.

They had covered sixteen miles before Frank called out to the captive to rein in. A buggy topped a hill a couple of miles off, the team stepping out at a fast trot.

"Here comes your ride the rest of the way," Frank said. "That's Sheriff Barker's rig."

"How the hell can you tell that from this far off? You got eyes like an eagle or something?"

"So it's been said." Frank fished out a cigarette. He had finished the smoke when Barker reined the team to a halt and peered at the prisoner.

"See you got our man, Frank."

"Nothing to it, Sheriff. He's all yours."

Frank kept his rifle at the ready until Barker had the man handcuffed, then stowed the Winchester. The sheriff boosted the thief onto the buggy seat and turned to Frank.

"This is the second time you've done my work for me this year, Frank. You did a mighty fine job of catchin' this man. Looks to me like you've got the gift to be a top lawman." Barker removed his hat and ran his handkerchief around the sweatband. "How'd you like to be a Texas Ranger?"

The question caught Frank off guard. After a moment he said, "Never gave it much thought before, but it sounds pretty good. What do I have to do to get in?"

"You let me take care of that." Barker climbed onto the buggy seat and picked up the lines. "Keep in touch. It may take a spell. The Rangers don't sign on just anybody, but you'll be hearing from 'em. Much obliged for catching this polecat." The sheriff reined the two-horse hitch back toward Fort Stockton.

Frank stood and watched as the buggy rolled away, the team stepping out at a trot, rooster tails of dust kicking from the wheel rims, the recovered black hitched to the tailboard.

Texas Ranger Frank Hamer sure had a nice ring to it, he thought. When people talked about lawmen in Texas, they mostly talked about the Rangers. That was the outfit folks called when they had big troubles. Frank admitted that he'd honestly had the most fun of his life tracking down those three horse thieves.

It wasn't the danger that appealed to him. It was the chase, the hunt, the challenge. And knowing that the outlaws he'd run down wouldn't be bothering decent folks for a long time. Frank knew his chest had swelled up like a strutting tom turkey's. He didn't care at the moment. He had outthought the horse thief, outmaneuvered him, caught him, and nobody had been hurt. He had a right to feel a bit smug. It would, he thought, take a heap of money to get one Frank Hamer to sell out right now.

Maybe Dud Barker was right. Maybe he did have a talent for law enforcement. And that meant that the Reverend Miller must have been right, too, in that long-ago conversation after the revival.

"The Lord doesn't give a man a gift for nothing," Frank muttered aloud. "He expects him to use it, one way or another." Frank knew those weren't the preacher's exact words, but they were close enough.

A wry smile touched Hamer's lips. The Creator must have a sense of humor. Who else would take a man who wanted to be a preacher, have him kill a man, then lead him within a whisker of turning into an outlaw and bank robber, and just might make a Ranger out of him? On the other side of the coin, maybe the good Lord wasn't playing a joke. Maybe he'd sized Frank Hamer up as a spreader of the gospel, found him wanting, then put a hand on his shoulder and turned him away from the outlaw trail. Maybe that all-seeing, all-feeling hand had pointed Frank down the road he was born to ride.

As a lawman.

Frank mounted and reined his horse toward Carr Ranch headquarters. He'd been up since midnight, it was well past noon now, he'd covered forty miles or so on horseback, and he wasn't the least bit tired.

He hummed to himself as he rode.

Sheffield, Texas
April 21, 1906

Sergeant Jim Moore, Company C, Texas Rangers, leaned against the counter of Sheffield's general store and sized up the young man standing before him.

Moore liked what he saw.

The man recommended by the adjutant general's office to take the oath as the newest member of Company C stood six-foot-three, weighed in at 193 pounds, and had the sloping shoulders that marked him as a powerful man and natural athlete. He was twenty-two years old and still growing muscle, with strong forearms and oversized hands. He didn't look twenty-two, Moore thought; more like eighteen, with that round, moon-shaped face. Some would say Frank Hamer was baby-faced. Moore figured someone would say it, eventually, but it wasn't going to be him.

It wasn't Hamer's physical stature that impressed Moore as much as it was his eyes. Moore saw determination and a quiet confidence in those blue eyes that somehow seemed wise beyond their years. And, Moore thought, a solid dose of common sense behind them. That combination was what he looked for in a Texas Ranger.

"Well, Hamer," Moore said, "the adjutant general was pretty impressed with Dub Barker's account of how you caught three horse thieves in the span of a few months. The sheriff said he was especially taken with your ability to size up a situation in a hurry and come up with a plan, instead of just tearing off after some bandit. That's pretty high praise for a man your age."

Hamer nodded. "Thanks, Sergeant."

"No need to thank me. You've heard of Captain John H. Rogers?"

"Yes, sir. I've heard stories about Captain Rogers most of my life. He's quite a man."

"That he is, Hamer. He's checked you out and thinks you've got the makings of a fine Ranger. Word is that you're a crack shot with handgun or rifle, a fine horseman, and long on common sense. Still want to give it a try?"

"Yes, sir," Frank said, trying to hide the excitement that had his heart thumping an Irish jig in his chest.

"Why?"

Frank didn't hesitate. "Because I think I can do some good."

The expression in Moore's eyes softened. "That's exactly what I wanted to hear. Now, you'll be expected to supply your own mounts and weapons. The state pays for ammunition and certain personal equipment lost in the line of duty. We also reimburse some, but not all, of your service-related expenses—provided we can pry the nickel from those tightfisted bean counters in Austin. Safest thing to do is get a receipt for everything you buy and sort out later what you get paid back for.''

"Yes, sir.''

"You won't get rich on the Ranger payroll, Hamer, but I don't think you'll be bored. If you don't mind being shot at from time to time.''

"I don't mind so much, as long as whoever's doing the shooting happens to miss,'' Frank said.

Moore's smile widened into a grin. He offered a hand. "Welcome to Company C, Frank. Captain Rogers is waiting at Alpine. In a few days you'll be chasing bandits instead of cattle.''

"Sounds fine, Sergeant.''

"Call me Jim. Most of us go by first names or nicknames, at least among ourselves. Captain Rogers is just 'Cap' when we don't have to be formal.''

By noon the next day, Franklin Augustus Hamer was a duly sworn private in Texas Ranger Company C.

Frank didn't remember ever being quite so proud as when Rogers handed him the distinctive star-in-circle badge. Frank pinned it to his shirt.

"Looks good on you, Hamer,'' Moore said.

"Feels mighty good.''

"I have to warn you,'' Captain Rogers said solemnly, "that badge can get heavy at times.''

Frank nodded. "I expect so, sir. If it ever gets too heavy for me to carry or you think I'm not toting it right, I'll hand it back to you.''

"Fair enough,'' Rogers said. "By the way, we don't, as a matter of course, wear the badge openly in public. Most people can recognize a Ranger from the way he sits his horse and looks them in the eye. We usually just carry the star in a leather wallet or folder.''

Rogers's grip was firm, the hands callused. "Glad to have you with us.'' The shake reinforced Frank's opinion that the captain didn't shy away from hard work or long hours. If Rogers was half the man his reputation indicated, he was a good man to ride with, Frank thought. "Need a couple of days to get your personal affairs in order?''

"No, sir. I've got my stuff on a packhorse outside. I'm ready to go to work right now."

Rogers turned to the sergeant. "Jim, get Hamer fixed up with any supplies and ammunition he needs. I'll be hanging around the office shuffling papers if you need me. Otherwise, I'll see you men tomorrow."

Moore led Hamer from the spartan Company C headquarters office into the bright late-afternoon sunshine that bathed the streets of Alpine. The sun seemed hotter than usual in the thin air high up in the Davis Mountains. Frank liked the high country. Sounds carried better up here, and the air seemed to clean out a man's nostrils and sharpen his thinking.

Rogers introduced Frank around. The members of Company C didn't look like hard men, but he noted the confidence in their bearing, the set of their jaws. If he had turned outlaw, he decided, he wouldn't want these men on his trail. He liked what he saw.

There were a couple of other Franks in the company, so by nightfall, Frank Hamer was answering to Pancho—the Spanish version of the handle. Moore said it wouldn't do to have three men holler "huh?" when he yelled for Frank.

After the introductions, Rogers handed him two thin booklets. "Get yourself settled in and study these. The tan one is the Ranger code of conduct, organization structure, chain of command, procedures to follow so that arrests you make will stand up in court. It's dull reading, but important.

"The black book is commonly called the Ranger Bible. It's a listing of wanted men, with their descriptions, habits, last known places of residence or sightings, what crimes they're charged with. Memorize as much of it as you can. You never know when a man walking down the other side of the street might be one we want. It works out a lot better if you see that man before he sees you."

Frank palmed the books and nodded.

"How much ammunition do you have?" Moore asked.

"A hundred cartridges for the handgun, fifty or so for the Winchester."

"Good. Man doesn't want to get caught a few rounds short if a shoot-out develops, and in this business, you never know when that might happen." Moore sighed. "I have an idea we may be seeing some of that before long. There's bandit trouble down on the Mexican border, and the Army's not doing a real good job of handling it. Company C doesn't have any really pressing business in Alpine, and I suspect we may get handed that little chore.''

Del Rio, Texas
December, 1906

Texas Ranger Private Frank Hamer reined the big chestnut gelding back to an easy walk and studied the veteran campaigner who led the four-man Company C patrol back into the sunbaked, dun-colored adobe settlement called Del Rio.

Frank was still a bit in awe of Captain John H. Rogers.

Most everyone who knew the man felt the same way.

Rogers was of the old Frontier Battalion mold, but nothing about him was coarse or crude. He rode with erect dignity despite the effects of a half-dozen wounds accumulated over years of breaking up feuds, running down outlaws, and taming wild towns.

Frank already had learned a lot about the rangering business from following Cap Rogers. He knew he couldn't have found a better teacher.

Rogers even looked the part of a veteran Ranger. He stood nearly six feet tall, thick in chest and shoulders, and wore a thick gray mustache. He had lost a bit of bone to an outlaw bullet some years back; one arm was noticeably shorter than the other, but it didn't affect his ability to handle a rifle or six-gun. His somewhat squinty hazel-brown eyes could, it seemed to Frank, look straight through a man's face into his soul. He was soft-spoken, but when he did speak, wise men listened.

What intrigued Frank most about the captain wasn't the way he rode, his ability with weapons, or his long experience afield.

Despite his often violent occupation, John H. Rogers was a deeply religious man, a Presbyterian who never missed an opportunity to attend worship services and who taught Sunday-school classes whenever his duties permitted. He never

cursed, even when facing down a would-be lynch mob or
going up against an armed and deadly suspect. He had never
been known to drink anything stronger than camp coffee.

Rogers was, Frank now knew, a good man to follow when
riding into a hornet's nest. And that's what Del Rio was—a
no-man's-land that drew ruffians, bandits, and killers from
both sides of the Rio Grande. Company C's assignment was
simple enough on the surface. Put an end to the lawlessness.

Already, Frank thought, they had made a sizable dent in
the outlaw population. The local lawless element had little
respect for the army, but they wanted no part of the Rangers.
While the military chased its tail, Cap Rogers's company
chased bad men. Sometimes they caught them. Sometimes
they didn't. Like this time out.

They had intercepted the stolen cattle a mile and a half
north of the Rio Grande. The Mexican bandits spotted the
rinches coming and high-tailed it across the river before the
men of Company C could get into rifle range. The Rangers
recovered the stock and returned the herd to its rightful
owner, so the hunt hadn't been a waste of time.

Frank could tell it galled Captain Rogers when an outlaw
got away, but Cap never let it show.

Del Rio was quieter now. The number of gunfights, killings, and robberies had dropped dramatically in a few weeks
since Company C had arrived. Several bad hombres took one
look at the Ranger column as it rode in and immediately left
for greener pastures. Others who hadn't been so cautious accounted for Del Rio's major growth business at the moment,
the care and feeding of prisoners in the town lockup. They
had converted a vacant adobe into a makeshift jail to hold the
overflow.

The problem with having so many prisoners was that a
number of Rangers always had to stay behind on guard duty
while the rest went afield. Nobody in the company wanted
the dreary boredom of guard duty when there were outlaws
to chase.

The army was no help. Miffed that the Rangers seemed to
be quickly solving the problem they had been unable to handle, the military commander declared the outlawry to be a
civilian problem. There was no glory and little chance for

advancement in rank in guarding prisoners. Company C was on its own in an arid, rugged land of scrub brush, mesquite, and cactus, where deep, twisting arroyos and canyons meant possible ambush at every turn.

Despite the dust raised by the criminal element on its way out of town, Del Rio still had a plentiful supply of bad men, Mexican and Anglo alike.

As they rode down the main east-west street Rogers seemed to stare straight ahead, but Frank knew the captain's gaze took in everything that was happening along the way.

"Reckon today's payday."

The comment from the rider alongside brought Frank back to reality. He lifted an eyebrow at Duke Hudson. The square-jawed, dark-haired young man had become his closest friend among the riders in Company C.

"Payday?"

"December first. The eagle screams this afternoon." Hudson flashed that infectious grin that drew the attention of young ladies wherever they went. When they went places where there were young women.

"Couldn't be payday, Duke," Frank joshed. "You've still got a few dollars left."

"No thanks to you, partner. You want to just take my pay outright from Cap, or do you plan to cheat me out of it with the pasteboards?"

"I tried to tell you I'd rather not gamble for money, but you wouldn't listen. It's not my fault you can't play poker worth a flip."

Hudson snorted. "I was the top poker hand in the outfit before you signed up."

The banter ended abruptly as Rogers waved the patrol to a halt and kneed his horse into a trot. A man on a lathered sorrel reined in beside him. The man's hands seemed to be motioning in six directions at once as the two talked.

After a couple of minutes Rogers returned to his men. "All right, gentlemen, gather around. We've got a killer, name of Ed Putnam, holed up in a house north of the railroad tracks. He's holding hostages. We've got to get him without innocent people being hurt."

Rogers wasted few words in summing up the rider's message. Putnam had murdered a man named Rolston at a ranch near Box Springs, stolen the victim's sheep, and trailed them to a spot near Del Rio. Putnam convinced a local sheepman, B. M. Cauthorn, to inspect the sheep on the idea of going halves on their purchase. A few miles out of town he shot Cauthorn in the back and took the would-be sheep buyer's money.

The man on the sorrel had seen the killing and chased Putnam, but the killer made it to the Glass Sharp home before the witness could close to shooting range.

"Putnam's a dangerous man," Rogers said in conclusion. "He's suspected in a number of holdups and murders. I'm going to try to talk him out of the house, or at least see if I can convince him to let the hostages go. Watch yourselves and be ready for anything. Any questions? All right, let's go get him."

CHAPTER SIX

Del Rio
December 1, 1906

FRANK PULLED HIS horse to a stop and watched as Cap Rogers rode almost up to the front door of the Glass Sharp home, a well-tended two-story frame north of the railroad tracks.

Frank glanced at Hudson and saw his own worry reflected in Duke's face. Rogers was in plain sight, within easy pistol shot of the house. Putnam could drop the Ranger captain with a single round if he wanted. Almost as one, the five Rangers pulled Winchesters from rifle boots and thumbed back the hammers.

"Hello, the house!" Rogers called. "Georgia, you in there?"

The door opened and a young woman stepped out. Frank had seen Georgia Glass around town, knew that she was the older sister of the family, but little else about her.

Rogers and the girl talked quietly for a moment; at one point Georgia lifted her hand to her mouth as though surprised or startled. Finally, she turned and went back into the house. Rogers reined his horse around and trotted the few yards back to the waiting Rangers.

"I don't think Georgia knew what Putnam has done," Rogers said. "She's going to try to convince him to give up, or at least to get the others out."

A few minutes later the door swung open. Glass Sharp, his wife, and three younger children hurried outside to the waiting Rangers.

"Where's Georgia?" Rogers asked.

"Still inside," Mrs. Sharp said, her face pale, eyes wide in fear. "She's trying to talk him into giving up. Oh, God—my little girl—"

"Don't worry, Mrs. Sharp," Rogers said, his tone calm and reassuring. "We won't put Georgia in danger. We want Putnam, but not so badly we'll get your daughter hurt. Mr. Sharp, would you please take your family to safety until this is settled?"

Glass Sharp looked for a moment as if he might object, then swallowed hard and led the woman and children away. When Cap Rogers made a request, it was an order.

"What do we do now, Cap?" Hudson asked.

"Wait. As long as Putnam's got Georgia in there with him, he's holding the winning hand." Rogers glanced around the group. "You boys spread out. Pancho, take the left side of the house so you can keep an eye on the back door. Duke, you drop off about halfway between Pancho and me—" The front door banged open, cutting off Rogers's orders. Georgia Glass ran toward the men, tears streaming down her face.

"He won't come out, Captain Rogers! He's got a—funny look in—his eyes—says he won't—give up!"

"Okay, Georgia," Rogers said soothingly, "you just go on back there with your family—"

Smoke billowed from a front window. Frank was on the move at the report of the pistol shot. One of the Rangers wheeled his horse, scooped Georgia up behind him, and spurred away as two Rangers opened up with Winchesters. Glass shattered from a front window. At the corner of his vision, Frank saw a slug kick sand near Hudson's boots. Hudson levered three quick rounds in reply and dove behind a low earth mound.

For a few seconds the crack of Ranger rifles and the flatter bark of Putnam's six-gun rattled the afternoon air. The firing stopped; Frank glanced around. The Ranger who had carried Georgia Glass to safety spurred back toward the house, dismounted, and took cover.

"Give it up, Putnam!" Rogers yelled. "You're surrounded! There's no place to go!"

Putnam answered with a pistol shot.

The air filled with the crackle of gunfire as the Rangers opened up again. Frank fired twice as a shadowy figure flickered past a shattered window. Clean misses. He worked his way behind a hackberry tree thirty yards from the house, held his fire until he was sure he had a target, and at the same time wondered how anyone could survive the hail of lead that raked the home.

The gun battle raged for almost an hour as Frank studied the situation patiently, finger on the trigger. The curtains at a window on his side of the house fluttered, pulled aside by a six-gun barrel. A slug whacked into the trunk of the tree two feet above Frank's head.

Frank ignored the near miss. He had Putnam's pattern now. The man darted from window to window, blazing away with a handgun at each post. Frank was sure that so far, no Ranger had been hit—and if Putnam had been, you'd never know it from the volume of lead he threw from inside the house.

The curtains fluttered and gun smoke again boiled from the window. The slug splatted into the dirt a foot short of the hackberry trunk. Frank settled in to wait, his gaze fixed on the window, ignoring the constant thunder of rifle fire.

He was ready when the window curtains moved again. He lined the sights and squeezed the trigger. A split second after the muzzle blast from his Winchester, he heard the distinct thump of lead against flesh. Putnam slumped over the windowsill. His six-gun tumbled to the ground beneath the window.

"He's done, Duke!" Frank yelled to Hudson a few yards away. "Pass the word to Cap!"

The gunfire slowed, then stopped.

Rogers approached cautiously, his rifle still at the ready. Frank nodded toward the figure slumped over the windowsill. "He made one too many mistakes, Cap," Frank said. "I think I nailed him pretty hard. He hasn't moved."

Ed Putnam would never move again.

Rogers grunted in satisfaction as he examined the body. Frank's slug had taken the crouching outlaw in the left cheekbone, tore through his lower jaw, drove into his left shoulder, and buried itself in the outlaw's heart. Putnam's pockets held more than a hundred handgun cartridges.

"Good thing you got him, Pancho," Rogers said. "He had enough ammunition to hold us off until dark. If he'd made it that long, he could have slipped away. Let's go see what's left of Glass Sharp's house."

There wasn't much.

Every piece of furniture had been riddled by lead; even the cast-iron legs of the cookstove had been shot away. The Rangers counted more than three hundred bullet holes in the walls of the home.

Four of the five Rangers were down to less than ten rifle cartridges each.

Frank Hamer had fired three times.

Frank hadn't expected to be the center of attention in Del Rio after the shoot-out. He couldn't understand why everyone was in such an all-fired hurry to make a hero out of him just for doing his job.

He couldn't seem to go anywhere without wading through a mess of backslappers or turning down drink offers. Some folks seemed to get downright insulted when he told them he didn't drink.

Worse yet were the wide-eyed expressions of disbelief on the faces of newcomers, who couldn't comprehend that a baby-faced twenty-two-year-old could be a man killer and a crack shot. Every edition of the *Del Rio Times* seemed to have a rehash of the fight or a fawning editorial each time the presses rolled for weeks afterward. Frank had even been photographed, kneeling with his Winchester in hand.

Frank wanted to let the whole affair slide, but Captain Rogers wouldn't let him. "It's good for the Rangers, Pancho," Cap said. "The politicians in Austin read the papers, too. Stories like this will help your own career, and maybe get us more appropriation money, too."

Finally, Frank sighed. "Okay, Cap. I don't like seeing my name in the papers so much. The way they write the stories, nobody else gets any credit, like I was the only one there. But if it will help the service, I'll put up with it for a while. I'd appreciate it, though, if you'd find me something to do out of town as often as possible."

"No problem there," Cap said. "We've got plenty of territory to cover."

Frank turned to go, then paused. "Cap?"

"Yes?"

"Why do you suppose Putnam let the girl go? If he'd kept her as a hostage, we'd never have gotten a chance at him."

Rogers shrugged. "I don't know why. I don't suppose we ever will. There was no boy-girl stuff between them as near as I can tell. Maybe he didn't want her hurt, maybe he just wasn't thinking." The veteran Ranger sighed. "There's a lesson here, Pancho. When you're dealing with men, always expect the unexpected."

"Yes, sir," Frank said. "I learned that a long time ago."

Del Rio
September 1908

Cap Rogers had been a man of his word. He'd gotten Frank out of town. All the way to Terlingua for a three-month stint of standing guard over a silver mine.

It had been a boring time, but not wasted. After the Rangers started posting two-man guards on a rotating basis, the mine and its ore burro trains hadn't been hit by bandits. And it had given Frank a chance to polish his Spanish in off-duty conversations with the mostly Mexican mine labor force. He had also been able to establish a number of contacts and informants on the south side of the Rio Grande.

Still, it had been good to get back to Del Rio at the end of his guard shift. At least there was some action going on. Del

Rio was some quieter now—not quite a buggy mare gentled to the harness, but not as wild as a raw mustang, either. Even the chili at the Rio Cafe seemed to have improved in his absence. It had a solid jalapeño bite to it now.

Frank finished his meal, decided there was no sense in putting off talking to Rogers, and strode to Cap's office.

Cap looked up from the stack of forms on his desk as Frank walked in. "Something on your mind, Pancho?"

"Well, sir, I've been offered a job. As town marshal in Navasota."

Rogers lifted an eyebrow. "That's one of the toughest towns in Texas. It goes through law officers faster than a duck through cornbread. They average at least two killings a month over there. The last town marshal they had lasted one week, I understand."

"Yes, sir. I'm aware of the situation."

"And the political atmosphere there? You know that there are several distinct power groups. The old-money crowd, the new arrivals, Klan members, Negroes. Each of the factions with its own notions about justice regardless of what the law says. It's a town where a badge is a target, not a symbol of authority."

"I'm aware of that, too, Cap."

Rogers leaned back in the chair. "Frank, Dud Barker had you pegged right when he recommended you for this job. You're one of the best Rangers I've ever worked with. But before I say anything one way or another, let me ask you one question."

"Yes, sir?"

"Why would you want that job? The extra pay?"

"It's more than the money, sir. Somebody has to bring that town into line. I believe I'm the man who can."

A slight frown creased Rogers's forehead. "It's the challenge of the job, isn't it?"

"Yes, sir. I suppose I have to admit that. I don't like outlaws and bullies. Of any stripe."

Rogers steepled his fingers and studied Frank for a moment over his fingertips, then nodded. "Take the job, Pancho. Even if I could, I wouldn't stop you. And while you're there, you'll be in my prayers."

Frank rose and extended a hand. "Thanks, Cap. That means more to me than you realize—the prayers, I mean." He rose and reached for his hat.

"Pancho," Rogers said as Frank turned to go, "anytime you decide to come back to the Ranger force, we'll have a badge waiting for you."

Navasota
December 1908

One thing about Texas, Frank thought as he stood and stared out the smudged window of the city marshal's office and surveyed his new town—a man could move from one country to another and never leave the state.

Navasota was about as far removed from Del Rio as any two towns could be, and not just in miles.

Del Rio was frontier west with a strong Spanish influence reflected in its language and customs, adobe homes, and businesses shimmering in desert heat waves. Navasota was Deep South, more like the lingering plantation culture of Louisiana or Mississippi than it was Texas. Most businesses lining the downtown streets were three-story constructions of stone or timber hewn from nearby forests.

Rain was a cause for celebration in parched Del Rio; here, it was almost a daily event. Even now, puddles of brownish water stood in the muddy street. Fat, heavy gray clouds above promised more rain. Del Rio was a horseback-and-wagon town; Navasota's streets often carried as many as two or three noisy, sputtering automobiles a day. The sticky mud kept most of the automobiles from the roads today. At intervals along the main street, boards had been placed as crosswalks so the locals didn't have to muddy their boots or shoes getting from one side to the other.

Even the populations were different. Del Rio was home to a sizable Mexican population, with only a sprinkling of Negroes. Navasota had few Spanish-speaking people, and almost a third of Grimes County's census was black. The Negroes and poor whites eked out a living as sharecroppers, farmhands, and day laborers.

Navasota did top Del Rio in one area, Frank had found. It was a darn sight tougher. There had been more than a hundred killings in the past three years. Fistfights, shootings, knifings, and arson were almost a nightly affair. Lynchings were less common, but not unknown, and many a black man had felt the bite of the night riders' bullwhips and clubs.

Navasota had the reputation of a wide-open town where anything went as long as a man had the power to get away with it. The city's dice and poker games were legendary in southeast Texas. The crap shooters, cardsharps, and professional gamblers made no attempt to conceal their ventures.

It was Frank's first day on the job, but he had already picked up on the rumors. The town council had been split on hiring him to begin with, until some of the "old guard" argued that it would be no problem to control the young marshal. It should be easy, they thought, to hire a wet-behind-the-ears kid and train him the way they wanted him. And if he wouldn't train, just buffalo him.

Frank also had heard that the old guard planned to test his mettle that same day. He didn't waste time fretting about it. He had already told the council he would tolerate no lawlessness from any individual or group, regardless of political power or financial stature. Break the law, he told them, and you're going to jail.

He did admit to a degree of curiosity about how the first showdown of his new career would be staged.

He didn't have long to wait.

Across the muddy street, an old man with a long, gray beard strode into view, followed by a dozen or so men and a sprinkling of women, some of them with young kids in tow. Frank recognized the bearded man, a patriarch of one of the prominent old-time families, a political force in the community, one of the leaders of the old guard. And, Frank suspected, a Klansman of high rank.

The old man stopped, stared for a moment toward the marshal's office, then threw back his head and let fly a piercing rebel yell. And another.

Frank stepped out of the marshal's office and studied the crowd behind the yelling man. There was a definite air of expectancy in the group. Several had knowing smirks on their faces. With the old man's yells hammering his eardrums, Frank strode across the loose boards to the other side of the street. He stopped within arm's length of the bearded man.

"Mister, I'm Frank Hamer, the new city marshal," he said, his tone calm and composed. "You know there's an ordinance against disturbing the peace. If you yell like that again, I'm going to put you in jail."

The bearded man looked Frank defiantly in the eye, then let loose another window-rattling yell.

Frank knew he was facing his first test. What he did in the next few seconds would determine whether or not he would gain the upper hand or be laughed out of Navasota.

He reached out, grabbed a handful of wiry gray beard, pivoted, and yanked. The old man's yell ended in a squawk; Frank's powerful pull on the beard sent the man flying. He landed facedown in the muddy street. Droplets of rainwater and thin mud flew.

Frank turned to the crowd as the old man struggled in the squishy mud. "You folks saw and heard what happened," he said. "I told this man if he hollered again, I was going to take him to jail. And that's exactly what I'm going to do."

A surprised murmur rippled through the crowd. Frank stepped from the boardwalk, hauled the old man to his feet, and led him across the street to the jail.

"What you think you're doin', you whelp?" the old man croaked, rubbing a muddy hand across his stinging chin.

"Charging you with disturbing the peace," Frank said casually. "It's a misdemeanor offense. Spend a few hours in the lockup, pay your fine, and you're free to go. Hopefully to get a bath. You look like you've been wallowing in a pigsty."

The bearded one grunted in disgust, but grudging respect glinted in the dark eyes. "Gotta hand it to you, son," he grumbled as the cell door clanged shut behind him, "you got plenty of guts for a wet-eared young whippersnapper."

Frank turned the key. "Just doing my job, mister."

"You ain't heard the last of this."

"Maybe not." Frank smiled at the mud-soaked old man. "But I'd better have heard the last from you, because if you pull a stunt like that again, you'll be back in that cell." He left the yeller sitting sullen and silent on a hard jail cot, strode to the window and looked across the street.

The crowd was breaking up. They were a lot quieter now. From time to time, one of them glanced at the jail, as if wondering what Navasota had gotten itself into.

January 1908

For the last few days, Frank mused, Navasota had been unusually quiet.

He had jailed a couple of drunks, escorted a known cardsharp to the train station with a quiet but sincere request never to return to Navasota, arrested a drifter wanted on a Houston assault warrant, and broken up a rooster fight, confiscating the gamblers' money.

He did notice that when he walked into a saloon or business owned by one of the old guard, it suddenly got quiet. He hadn't missed the sullen glances in his direction as he patrolled the streets. There had been no knifings or shootings, just routine stuff.

He made a final notation, bringing his marshal's logbook up to date, and glanced up as a man clad in a suit, vest, and cravat with a pearl stud strode into his office. Frank glanced up. "Help you with something, Mr. Stillman?"

Stillman, owner and operator of a plantation a mile outside the city limits, sat down without an invitation, removed his spectacles, and peered down his long nose at Frank.

"I just wanted to clear up something," he said, a threatening note in his voice despite the outwardly friendly smile. "Hamer, you need to know how the cow eats the cabbage in Navasota. There are a number of us who take care of our own, in our own way, when problems come up. We don't allow our kind to be arrested."

Frank leaned back in his chair. "Law enforcement is my concern now, Mr. Stillman. If your kind don't want to be arrested, there's a simple solution. Don't break the law."

"I'm serious here, Hamer," Stillman said. "Even if our people have a little too much to drink and raise a bit of hell in town, you're not to interfere. We expect you to confine your efforts to the outsiders and the darkies. That comes straight from the town council. We hired you. We can fire you.''

Frank lifted an eyebrow. ''True, but that's beside the point. I was hired to enforce the law in Navasota. I intend to do just that, regardless of who the lawbreakers might be.''

Stillman stiffened. ''Just watch your step, Hamer, and remember what I told you. Our kind won't be messed with.''

''You've said your piece, Mr. Stillman,'' Frank said. ''Now, if you'll excuse me, I have work to do.''

''Are you throwing me out of the office, Marshal?''

''No, sir. Anytime any citizen in this town has a problem, my door's open. And anytime a citizen in this town breaks the law, I'm coming after him.''

Stillman flushed. ''We'll see about that.'' He stood and stalked out of the office.

Frank watched him go. The new marshal had already developed some reliable sources. He had it on good authority that Stillman and most of his old-guard cronies were Klansmen. The KKK's idea of justice was to lynch, burn out, or just generally terrorize anyone who disagreed with them.

It will be interesting, Frank thought, to see what happens the first time one of them steps out of line.

That time came less than six hours later.

Frank had just pushed back his dinner plate at the Corner Café and nodded for a refill on his coffee when the first gunshots sounded.

Frank dropped a quarter on the table, pushed his chair back, and strode outside. The gunfire came from a saloon three doors down. He hurried to the crowd that milled outside the building.

''Marshal,'' one of the men said, ''George Conner's in there, roaring drunk, shooting up the place. Stillman and some others of Conner's clan are in there, egging him on.''

Frank nodded. ''I'll take care of it.'' He shouldered his way through the crowd and pushed open the saloon door as a six-gun slug shattered a bottle on the back bar. Through the powder smoke Frank saw the spidery bullet holes in the back-bar mirror, the cracked plaster on the walls—and the burly George Conner, bottle in one hand and short-barreled revolver in the other, drawing a bead on a quart of Old Taylor. Stillman sat at Conner's table. It was obvious that he was packing a fair load of whiskey himself.

"Quarter says you can't take the neck off it, George," one of the men said.

Conner closed one eye. "Call the bet."

"That's enough, Conner!" Frank called. He made no effort to draw his own weapon. He didn't see the need.

The gunman turned a watery gaze toward Frank. "Says who?"

"The law," Frank said. He ignored Conner for a moment as his steady gaze raked the Stillman group. "I understand you men don't allow 'your kind' to be arrested."

Stillman's mouth opened as if to speak, but the comment died when he stared into Frank's eyes.

Frank strode up to Conner and held out his hand. The drunken gunman tried to focus his unsteady gaze, finally figured out what the young marshal had in mind—and meekly handed over the six-gun. Frank tucked the weapon into his waistband, took Conner by the elbow, and started for the door.

"What do you think you're doing, Hamer?" one of the Stillman group demanded.

"Arresting this man."

"You can't. He's one of ours."

"He's mine now," Frank said. "I warned Mr. Stillman that anyone who broke the law went to jail. And that includes his brother-in-law here. Any more trouble tonight, and I'll come back for the rest of you and let you have a nice, long family visit in the lockup. Let's go, Mr. Conner." He deliberately turned his back on the scowling group and led the intoxicated man to jail.

With the prisoner secured, Frank checked his Winchester and waited to see what happened next.

The rest of the night was as peaceful as a Methodist camp meeting. Frank turned in about three in the morning, sleeping on the cot in the marshal's office, his rifle close at hand.

As he made his usual rounds six hours later, several men stopped him to shake his hand.

"Word's getting around that Navasota's got a marshal now

that can't be hoorawed,'' one of the men said. ''Couple of the crap tables and poker games folded up after you arrested Conner. Saturday's rooster fights have been called off. And it looks like quite a few folks already are heading out of town.''

''That's nice,'' Frank said. ''It'll save me the trouble of asking them to leave.''

The man hesitated. ''Marshal, you know you're making enemies here. Now, I appreciate what you've done, and so do most of the good people in Navasota. But be careful. They're still going to see how far you'll push, you know.''

''I know that. And I hope by now they know I push back.''

CHAPTER SEVEN

Navasota
June 1909

FRANK PUT DOWN his pen, closed the ledger where he kept track of arrests and fines, and leaned back in the creaky chair. He stared at the open window, trying to will a passing breeze inside to stir the sultry heat that had come to Navasota.

Dust eddied in the wake of a passing car. Almost two weeks without rain—normal in Del Rio, but a drought in Navasota that wilted people and plants alike. Even the magnolia and cypress trees drooped beneath the heat.

He turned from staring out the window as one of the city's prominent merchants strode into his office. The store owner was a weathered, stooped man with a perpetual scowl who never had forgiven Lee for the surrender at Appomattox, or Lincoln for freeing the slaves. The story was that the man's father had lost a big Georgia plantation and a fortune in the Civil War.

Frank remained seated. ''Something I can do for you, Mr. Scranton?''

"Marshal," Scranton said, "what are you going to do about those damned darkies?"

"What about them?"

"Juneteenth is coming up." The way he said "Juneteenth" made it sound like a cussword. "There's always trouble then, what with those uppity coons parading up the street like they owned it, making lewd remarks to our women, getting drunk, and acting like they were just as good as us white folks. Last year they broke one of my plate-glass windows. Threw an empty quart jar through it. We near had a riot on account of them."

"So I've heard." Frank lifted a reassuring smile at the merchant. "Don't worry about it. There won't be any trouble this year."

"You gonna tell 'em they can't strut around our town?"

"No, sir. The last time I read the Constitution of the United States, it said they have the right to a peaceful celebration just like anyone else."

The merchant snorted in disgust. "Always suspected you was one of them darkie lovers. There's folks around here won't stand for no more Negro troubles."

Frank's smile faded. His eyes narrowed. "I just now told you there wouldn't be any trouble from the black folks. And I'm also telling you there won't be any trouble from the white folks, either. I'll arrest anybody who causes a commotion, and I don't care what color he is. I won't have it in my town."

"Since when did this get to be your town, Hamer?"

"Since I pinned this badge on." Frank stood. "Now, I've got to go see a man. Go on about your business and leave this to me, Mr. Scranton."

The merchant sniffed in disgust and turned toward the door.

"By the way," Frank said, "do me a favor and save us all some grief. Tell your fellow Klansmen that the first man who tries to start trouble is going to regret it."

The old man shuffled from the office. Frank reached for his hat. It was time to pay another visit to the section of town where few white folks ever went.

Twenty minutes later Frank strode down the narrow street in the inner belly of the black section of Navasota, a small package wrapped in brown butcher paper tucked beneath his left arm.

The air felt heavy from the weight of poverty and need as much as the heat and humidity. The acrid scent of outhouses mingled with the pervading smell of fatback, greens, and cabbage boiling within weathered homes that looked more like hovels than places of residence.

Navasota was two different towns within the same city limits. Few whites entered the section called Darktown, or by less complimentary names, and the blacks crossed the boundary into the Anglo side only if they were fortunate enough to have jobs in white homes, gardens, or businesses.

The two towns were further divided into other communities. Among the whites, one faction of dedicated Negro haters wanted the blacks run out of town or eliminated. A second faction tolerated the dark-skinned people as a source of cheap labor, or even urged cooperation and coexistence. In the black community, the white outsiders who ventured in were hated and mistrusted by many, greeted warmly by others.

Both towns and all their factions had their own leaders, beliefs, and standards—and their own ready supply of fine, upstanding citizens, devout Christians, thieves, drunks, wife beaters, lawbreakers.

Yet, Frank noted anew, the overall feel of the place called Darktown was not the desperation, underlying fear, and hate he had sensed on his first visit here after he had pinned on the badge.

He instinctively slowed his stride as he passed a vacant lot where a dozen boys played a game of rotation baseball. The first baseman across the diamond waved a greeting. Frank waved back. Seconds later a high pop foul fluttered toward him, a flap of torn leather sending the ball in erratic flight. Frank took a couple of steps to his right, speared the foul tip with his left hand, and examined the ball. It had seen better days. It was almost black from dirt and overuse, held together only by a few frayed stitches.

The third baseman held up his worn leather glove and waited for Frank to toss the ball back. Frank reached into his pocket and pulled out a new baseball he'd paid eighteen cents for at the general store.

"Try this one, Freddie," he called as he casually tossed the new ball to the infielder.

The action brought a chorus of shouted thanks, waved arms, and wide grins from the players. Frank pitched the dirty, frayed ball back also, casually waved a "you're welcome," and went on his way. Eighteen cents for a baseball might turn out to be a major investment in keeping some black kid out of trouble, Frank figured. Frank liked kids, regardless of skin color. He enjoyed their innocence, their innate curiosity.

From time to time as he walked Frank nodded a greeting to an acquaintance. He ignored the occasional dark stares of suspicion or open dislike cast his way by some who didn't know him—or had felt the toe of his boot and bearlike slap of his open hand, powerful enough to down a big man, when they stepped out of line.

Frank felt neither animosity toward, nor any special sympathy for, the black people of Navasota. Poverty and hard times were a fact of life in many cultures, black, white, or red. Frank had brought the same message to them that he had to the whites—if a man broke the law, he would pay the price, no matter the color of his skin. He did not expect to be welcomed into their culture with open arms. He had earned their respect. That was enough.

He paused before a house slightly larger than the others. It needed paint and repairs, but otherwise it was well kept and clean. The yard had been swept, the porch steps still damp from the morning mop. A small girl with a bright red ribbon tied into wiry hair sat in a child-size rocking chair by the door, scolding a rag doll for some imagined infraction of play rules.

"Morning, Jolena," Frank said. "Is your father home?"

The child stopped fussing at the doll, looked up at the big white man, then nodded and went into the house without speaking. Moments later a black man stepped outside.

He had to duck his head to make it through the doorway.

Frank seldom had to look up to meet a man's gaze, but if this took too long, he might get a crick in his neck. The man's mostly gray hair was nearly seven feet up from the soles of his shoes. From side to side, he would have made two Frank

Hamers if melted down in a rendering pot and recast.

"Mornin', Marshal." The big man's smile flashed white, even teeth. His speech was pure Deep South plantation black, the words slurred into one another. "Come in and set. My woman's got some fine herb tea brewin'. Picked the leaves herself."

Frank shook his head. "Thanks, Sam, but I just finished off a pot of coffee. I slosh when I walk."

"Drink too much of that brew, Marshal, and your skin'll turn black as mine." Sam chuckled at his own joke, then sobered. "What brings you down here on such a hot day?"

"I have something for you, Sam." Frank handed over the brown paper package and waited until the big man untied the string, which he pocketed with care, and unwrapped the bundle.

A wide satin cloth burned crimson in the bright sunlight.

"Mighty nice, Marshal, mighty nice." Work-hardened hands the size of small hams stroked the smooth satin. "What's it for?"

Frank smiled. "It's sort of your badge of honor, if you'll agree to wear it. Juneteenth is coming up. I'm appointing you parade marshal of your people, Sam. That red sash is so they can tell who's boss."

Sam's impressive chest swelled a bit more. "Parade marshal? We ain't had one of them before. How come you picked me?"

"Because, Sam," Frank said solemnly, "your people respect you, and with good cause. You've earned the right to lead them in the parade. Now, we both know there's been some trouble in the past with these Juneteenth celebrations. If we work together, you and me, your people can have their Juneteenth holiday, and others, without any problems."

Sam's brow wrinkled for a moment, then the grin returned. "I reckon we could, at that. What you want me to do?"

"Just keep the rowdier boys in line. Pick three or four helpers and make sure everyone behaves. I'll make sure the white folks don't cause trouble for you. That way, you can have your parade, enjoy your holiday, and I won't have to arrest anyone."

The huge black man ran his hand over the sash again, the

corners of his thick lips upturned in a grin. "You can sure enough count on me," he said. "And I got me a silk top hat I put on just for special occasions like marryin's and buryin's. And parade marshalin'."

Frank nodded. "That would be a nice touch, Sam. Sort of a uniform. Any parade marshal worth his salt has some kind of uniform."

"They'll be able to see ol' Sam comin' from a mile off, Marshal. Why, ever' cute young gal down here'll set up and take notice when I steps out in front of that parade—"

"They better not, you old coot!" The bark from inside the house widened the grin on Sam's face; the big man winked at Frank. "I'll whup any woman does that, and then I'll whup you, you big ox, your eyes gets to wanderin' where they ought not!"

Frank grinned. "Sounds like Sarah's got you pegged, Sam."

"Just baitin' the old gal some, seein' can I get a rise outten her like a bluegill takin' to a cricket. She knows there ain't but one woman for this ol' darky. Won't stop me from lookin', though." Sam's smile faded. "Don't you worry none about no parade, Marshal. There won't be no trouble."

Frank turned and strode back toward downtown, satisfied. Sam and his handpicked helpers would keep any rowdies in line. The best way to stop trouble was not to let it start. Make friends with the biggest dog in the pack, and the rest would give a man no grief.

He made a mental note that this was another favor he owed the huge black man. Sam knew everything that went on among the black folks from the cotton fields in the Bottoms beyond the town to the deadline between the races. Once Sam had decided he could trust the young town marshal, he had helped Frank develop a spy system among the darkies almost as good as the network of informants Frank had built among the whites.

The old axiom of the good lawman kept paying its way. Information was more valuable than any weapon when it came to keeping the peace. Frank found himself humming "The Girl I Left Behind Me" as he strode back to his office. He was off key and knew it, but he didn't care.

June 19, 1909

Frank Hamer stood on the boardwalk outside Navasota's main bank and watched the long line of blacks marching three abreast approach.

At head of the Emancipation Day Parade, big Sam strutted, resplendent in tall silk black top hat, scarlet sash across his thick chest, a hickory walking stick clutched in his oversized right hand. Sam touched the stick to his hat brim in salute as he strode past Frank's post. Frank acknowledged the greeting with a nod.

Many of the Negroes laughed and sang as the procession moved along. The able-bodied men were mostly afoot, the women and children in horse or mule-drawn buckboards and buggies. Every last one of the blacks, from the deepest ebony-skinned to those the color of creamed coffee, were dressed in their Sunday finest. Their clothes ranged from somber black to flashy yellows, reds, and greens, suits and dresses freshly laundered and ironed. Even the poorest of the poor strode or rode with heads held high; those who owned a pair of shoes had polished the worn leather to a gleaming black or brown.

The wheeled vehicles also carried old men and weathered women who rode with stooped, hunched shoulders that likely had felt the white slave owners' lash as young people.

Frank's gaze drifted from the passing parade to the boardwalks lining the main street.

Few whites had turned out to view the parade. Most of Navasota's white population simply ignored the celebration. Scattered clumps of Anglos bunched here and there along the route cast bleak stares of distrust and outright hatred toward the passing Negroes.

Frank didn't like the looks of one such cluster a few strides away. The set of jaws and shoulders and dark mutterings told him that these were potential troublemakers. He strode to the back of the group.

"Damn them uppity coons," the apparent leader of the group, a stocky, swarthy man muttered. He balanced a fist-sized stone in one hand and a bottle in the other. "They got no business prancin' down *our* street like they was as good as us white folks."

"That's for sure 'nuff the gospel, Howie," another, younger man said. "Just a minute ago back down the street, I seen that smart-ass young nigger walkin' beside that red wagon stare right straight at a white woman."

"That a fact?" Howie's face darkened even more. "Reckon I'll just bounce this here rock off his kinky noggin and change that coon's mind—" He drew the stone back.

Frank grabbed the man's fist in his own big hand and squeezed. Howie glanced around, dark eyes blazing. "Let go my hand, damn you."

"Mister, nobody's starting any trouble in this town today. Black or white." Frank tightened his grip on Howie's hand. "Now, you have two options," he said casually. "Either behave yourself or get this hand broken around that rock in your fist."

Howie's face paled in pain as Frank's fist threatened to crush his fingers against the stone. "Damn you—Hamer," he croaked through clenched teeth. "You got no call—treatin' a white man like this—"

"I keep the peace. If you want to keep that hand, it's your call." He squeezed harder. Howie's knees started to buckle.

"All—right. My hand—"

"I'll turn you loose if you agree to give me the rock, and then get away from here. And take your friends with you."

"We can take him, Howie, you give the word," the man at Howie's side said.

"Give that word, Howie," Frank said, "and I'll deck him first, then break every bone in your hand. Well?"

"Let it—go, George." Howie's voice went up an octave. "It ain't—worth—the trouble—"

Frank released his grip and pried the stone from Howie's bruised and numbed hand. "Glad you saw the light, Howie." He turned to the other men. "Now get. And if I hear of any of you causing trouble, I'll lock up the lot of you and toss the key in the horse trough."

The surly expressions faded, replaced by a touch of wariness. "You ain't heard the last of this, Hamer—you and your pet niggers," one of the men said.

Frank glared at the speaker. "I'm not hard to find, mister. I'd as soon not have to whip the lot of you, though. I just

bought this shirt. Be a shame to get blood all over it. But if
you insist—''

The challenge died as the men turned away and left down
an alley. Frank turned his attention back to the parade.

Four husky black men, handpicked by Sam, strode beside
the parade, a couple of paces away from the main body. Their
gazes constantly swept the parade column to intercept and
stop any potential trouble.

A quarter hour after the last of the parade had passed, the
streets started filling again with white faces.

Before sundown, at least a dozen people had told Frank it
had been Navasota's quietest Juneteenth celebration in years.

July 1910

Frank leaned against the porch post of the corner café, worried a bit of bacon from behind his left eyetooth, and gazed
along the street.

It hadn't been an easy thirteen months since he'd pinned
on the city marshal's badge, but he was satisfied with the job
he'd done. Navasota was at least mostly civilized.

Women could walk the streets and shop without fear of
being accosted now. They could even let their husbands out
alone at night and be reasonably sure the mister wouldn't lose
the grocery money in a poker or crap game, and not bring
any unwanted souvenirs home from the sporting houses.

Professional gamblers and prostitutes were in short supply
in Navasota these days. That didn't mean there was a serious
shortage of amateurs or semipros in either profession. Or
thieves, wife beaters, drunks, and other assorted riffraff on
both sides of town.

At least now it was quiet enough that he was able to catch
a few hours' rest from time to time. He had a deputy marshal.
Av Averetts wasn't a town tamer, but he was a solid, dependable man, tough enough to tote his own water bucket.

Frank strolled toward the marshal's office, aware of the
occasional hostile glances or outright glare cast his way.
Bringing the law to Navasota meant making enemies. It
hadn't been often that a day had passed without some kind

of challenge to his authority. Add the drifters on the run from other towns or states to the mix, and it was anything but dull in Navasota—

Frank stopped in his tracks.

At the intersection three blocks away, a black buggy with red painted hubs, a hat-sized chunk of wood missing from above the right rear wheel, rolled across the main street. The driver, the larger of two men on the buggy seat, glanced toward Frank. He seemed to start, then popped the reins against the rump of the horse pulling the buggy. The bay broke into a quick trot. The buggy disappeared from view, but not before Frank noted the bay's distinctive piebald face and the hock-high white stocking on the left hind leg.

It was the horse and rig the Bryan city marshal had called about yesterday. The marshal said the two men were headed in the direction of Navasota. Both men, he added, were dangerous types, quick on the trigger, and wanted on several charges of robbery and horse theft.

Frank broke into a run for the marshal's office and yelled for Averetts.

Ten minutes later the two Navasota officers were saddled up and moving out of town at a fast trot in pursuit of the stolen buggy. Averetts kneed his sorrel into a lope, but reined in at Frank's call.

"No need to run our horses into the ground, Av," Frank said. He pointed toward the crown of a low ridge a good mile away. The buggy was a black dot in the distance, a plume of dust in its wake. "They've got a big start on us. Save our horses, keep the pressure on, and we'll catch up. The bay can't last forever at that pace."

After a couple of hours of hard riding, Frank was beginning to wonder if he'd underestimated the bay buggy horse's endurance. The animal still stepped along at a brisk trot, but the tracks the bay left told Frank the horse was tiring. The toe marks dragged, the horse stumbled frequently, and flecks of lather splotched the roadside vegetation and dotted the earth between the buggy tracks. The lawmen had gained ground. The buggy was less than a half mile ahead.

Averetts cast a quick, questioning glance at Frank.

"Not yet, Av. We'll wait until they hit Froneberger's fence

line a mile up the road, then make our move.''

The two rode in silence, gaining steadily on the buggy.

Frank drew his handgun as the buggy pulled to a stop and the passenger jumped from the seat to open the barbed-wire gate.

"Now," Frank said.

The two lawmen spurred their horses into a lope. "Take the left side, Av. I've got the right. Stay on your toes in case they decide to fight."

The passenger, a lean, hawk-faced man, had just dropped the wire gate and turned toward the buggy when Frank and Averetts pulled their mounts to a sliding stop, bracketing the fugitives.

"What's this?" the man on the ground said.

"We're taking you in for stealing this horse and buggy," Frank said. "Raise your hands and nobody will get hurt."

The hawk-faced one lifted his hands. The stocky man on the buggy seat yanked out a revolver. Frank and Averetts fired, the two shots almost as one. The impact of the slugs slammed the stocky man back against the buggy seat. The gun fell from his fingers. He coughed once and slumped across the footboard.

"Don't shoot!" the man on the ground yelped. "I give up!"

"Smart decision, mister," Frank said. "Av, search that buggy and make sure they don't have any other guns in there."

Fifteen minutes later, with the hawk-faced man handcuffed and dejected on the seat beside Frank, the dead man tossed into the back, and Frank's horse tied to the tailboard, Frank reined the tired bay harness horse back toward Navasota.

The chase had lasted thirteen miles.

Their arrival created a considerable stir. The irony of the commotion brought a faint, wry smile to Frank's lips. Navasota had come a long way from the days when a dead man was little more than a nuisance to traffic, he thought as he reined the stumbling bay in before the marshal's office.

"Av, call the Brazos County sheriff and tell him we've got the horse and buggy back, along with one live outlaw and one dead one, while I lock this man up," Frank said. He turned to the sizable crowd that had gathered around the buggy. "You folks go on about your business. There's nothing to see here but a thief and a dead man, and you've seen both before."

Chapter Eight

Navasota
August 1, 1910

FRANK FINISHED THE last of the paperwork on his cluttered desk, leaned back, lit a cigarette, and glanced at the mantel clock on the shelf beside the gun rack. It read 10:30 P.M.

So far, so good, Frank thought, a relatively quiet night in Navasota. The jail held only one inmate, a traveling patent-medicine salesman who had downed a bit too much of his own mostly alcohol nostrum and turned quarrelsome. The ragged snores from the troublemaker's cell and the ticking of the clock were the main intrusions on the quiet of the still, windless evening.

The quiet ended with an urgent rap on the door.

"It's open," Frank called.

E. N. Simmons, foreman of the Central Railroad, burst into the office, out of breath, his face flushed.

"Marshal, I—we've—been robbed!" Simmons gasped. "Took my wife's rings—my money—"

"Anyone hurt?"

"No—but my wife—it almost scared her to death—"

Frank put a hand on the trainman's shoulder. "Calm down, Mr. Simmons, and tell me what happened."

The story was similar to those Frank had heard before from the rail yards, the one place in Navasota where whites and blacks, good and bad, workers and bums, congregated to work or loaf.

Simmons's wife had just delivered his supper when the couple was accosted by a big black man armed with a large pocketknife. The Negro threatened to carve up Mrs. Simmons if the couple didn't hand over all their cash and jewelry.

"He'd've done it, too, Marshal," Simmons said. "He took my wife's rings, a necklace, thirty dollars in cash, and my pocket watch."

Frank reached for his hat as Simmons finished his story. "I'll take care of it, Mr. Simmons," he said. "You go make sure your wife's all right." He didn't wait for a reply.

The Navasota rail yards were reasonably well lighted in the depot area. Frank checked for footprints outside the foreman's office where the robbery had occurred, but found little to go on. There had been too much foot traffic in the area.

He loosened his Colt in its holster and went to prowl among the clutter of boxcars and jumbles of freight. Away from the main loading docks and depot, patches of pitch-black shadows alternated with the weak light from scattered lanterns in the crowded yard. The scent of oil, grease, and locomotive lay heavy in the still air.

Frank's search turned up one bearded hobo who reeked of whiskey and unwashed body and a local youth out for a late-night prowl, but nobody who fit the description of the robber. The smattering of night-shift workers he questioned, black and white, had seen and heard nothing. There were no obvious suspects among the laborers.

A slight movement in the shadow of a boxcar caught Frank's attention. He strode to the car and looked down at the figure crouched beside the rear wheels.

The man was black, and he was big—maybe an inch taller than Frank—and a cross tie wide through the shoulders. The whites of his eyes showed wide as his gaze nervously shifted about. Frank sensed he had his man, even if he had no proof except the man's skin color and enormous bulk.

"Evening," Frank said. "Nice night. Not as hot as usual."

"Yes, sir. Reckon it is right nice, at that." The words seemed to quaver a bit. Simmons had said the robber's voice was deep, husky, and distinct, without the slurred speech common to the majority of blacks raised in the Deep South. The voice fit.

Frank said, "How about coming out here in the light so we can talk better."

The big man stood and stepped into the rectangle of light between two boxcars. Frank noted the steady shuffle of over-sized work shoes. Sweat droplets streamed down the ebony face. This, Frank decided, was one nervous man. It was time to make him even more nervous.

"Don't remember seeing you around Navasota before," he said, a note of accusation in his tone. "Move here recently?"

The black man shook his head. "No, sir. Just passin' through."

Frank narrowed his eyes when the black man finally looked him in the face. "Where you headed?"

"New Orleans. Got a job waitin' for me on the levee crew."

"I see." Frank paused for a moment to let the tension build, his eyes narrowed in suspicion. "Where you from?"

"Hempstead, sir."

Frank paused again, this time for several minutes, his frown deepening. Let the man stew a bit longer.

"Hempstead, eh?" He let the tone of disbelief deepen in his words. He leveled a steady gaze on the man's face. Sweat flowed down the ebony cheeks. The scuffle of shoe leather grew more intent, the whites of the black man's eyes flashing as his gaze darted about. Frank knew what was going through the man's mind—that he'd been caught in a lie. It was exactly what Frank wanted him to think, even though he had no ob-vious reason to believe otherwise.

After a moment the man cleared his throat and swallowed a couple of times. "No, sir," he said. "I mean Waller. I come from Waller."

Frank knew then he had his man. It was time to twist the knife a bit.

"You know, we had some trouble here in the yard an hour or so back. Somebody robbed the foreman and his wife. Pulled a knife on them. Scared the poor woman half to death. Know anything about that?"

The black shook his head vigorously. "No, sir. I don't know nothin' about no robber."

"Then," Frank said pointedly, "I don't suppose you'd mind turning your pockets inside out for me."

Panic flashed across the ebony features. "What you—you think I—"

Frank's scowl deepened. "There's one way to find out. Turn around and put your hands up against that boxcar."

The man did as he was told; Frank felt the tension in heavy muscles as he patted the big man down. He found a big stockman's style pocketknife in one pocket. And in another, two woman's rings, a wad of bills, and a railroadman's watch with the initials *ENS* engraved on the silver case.

Frank stepped back. "All right, mister, you're under arrest—"

The big man spun away. Frank drew his revolver as the man broke into a stumbling run.

"Stop or I'll shoot!"

The fugitive ran faster. Frank fired two warning shots into the air. "Stop!" he yelled again.

The black man ignored the order. Frank leveled his revolver and fired twice. The man staggered and went down. Frank knew from the way he fell that he was hit hard. The shadowy hulk twitched a couple of times, then lay still.

A couple of laborers working nearby ran up as Frank knelt by the big man. He put a hand against the downed man's neck, then looked up. "He's still alive. You, there"—he pointed at one of the laborers—"fetch a doctor. You," he said to the other, "go find Mr. Simmons. Tell him I've got the man who robbed him, but I'll need a positive identification."

The wounded man died the next afternoon. One of Frank's slugs had taken him in the kidney, another in the lower ribs. Simmons identified the man as the robber. It was largely a formality, since Frank had recovered the stolen items.

The body was barely cold when replies to Frank's telegrams seeking an identification of the dead man began pouring in. Deputy Marshal Averetts's lips formed in a silent whistle as he thumbed through the wires.

"That," he said, "was one bad hombre. Manny Jackson, alias Kid Jackson. Prison escapee. Wanted in five states. Quite a record. Robbery. Escape. Assault. Rape. Murder. You name a felony, that man's done it."

Frank nodded. "He won't do any more of them."

"How'd you know he was the man robbed Simmons?"

"I didn't, at first. He just had the look about him of a man who had something to hide. I gave him a chance to convince me he was guilty, and he took it."

Averetts was silent for a moment, then cleared his throat. "Frank, does it bother you—like it does me—to kill a man?"

Frank looked up, then shrugged. "In a way. Take a man's life and you can't put it back. I'd a lot rather settle for an arrest instead of pulling a trigger. That's a last resort. But I don't beat myself with a harness strap when the man deserves it." He sighed. "People like Jackson are human wolves, Av. When they decide to pull down innocent people, they've made themselves fair game."

April 1911

Frank Hamer stowed the last of his personal belongings and paused for a final look around the town he had patrolled for two and a half years.

Navasota was still busy and occasionally boisterous, but it was more like a gentle saddle horse than the wild and untamed bronc it had been when he had arrived. People could walk the streets unarmed and without fear now.

It wasn't a bad legacy to leave behind.

He doubted that Navasota would forget him, and had to admit to a bit of pride in that doubt. A sizable chunk of the city's population wore scars from his boots; more than a few were a touch hard of hearing from the wallops of his open hand, which occasionally punctured an eardrum. But the rougher elements had gotten the message. Navasota was as law-abiding these days as any town in Texas.

It hadn't been easy, but it was time to move on. His job here was done, and a new challenge waited in Houston. Baldwin Rice, mayor of the bayou city, had been after Frank for months to join the police force as special investigator. The job offer was more than a compliment. It paid better. And there were more interesting cases in Houston. The city had a more sophisticated class of criminals.

Frank instinctively picked up a pen before he realized he

no longer had to sign the Navasota marshal's duty log. In the near distance, the wail of a train whistle sounded.

He picked up the travel case that held his more treasured personal possessions, shouldered his Winchester, and strode from the Navasota city marshal's office for the last time.

Houston
April 21, 1911

Frank slipped the special investigator's shield into his pocket, shook hands with Mayor Baldwin Rice, and immediately went to work on his first case for the Houston Police Department.

He had changed from his denim pants, work shirt, and boots into a simple black business suit, white shirt, tie, and comfortable walking shoes. Boots were for horseback work, not walking. This case was going to take a good bit of shoe leather.

After the introductions, he settled into the straight-backed wood chair behind his desk in the open squad room, sharing space with three other special investigators and a uniformed sergeant in the cramped police headquarters.

He flipped open the first case folder and began to read.

Four Houston police officers had been gunned down from ambush in the last few months. The details confirmed that the killings were planned executions. In each case, the dead officer had been alone. Each had answered a suspicious-person or domestic-disturbance call at an address that proved to be either a vacant home or a deserted warehouse building. And each had been shot by at least two gunmen, the bodies riddled by buckshot and pistol bullets.

The question was why.

There was nothing in the dead officers' files to indicate they had lived higher on the hog than was possible on a Houston policeman's pay. If they were on the take, accepting bribes, or anything but honest policemen, they were mighty good at covering up the fact. Still, it was a possibility Frank didn't discount out of hand. Crooked officers were as much a fact of life as houseflies and mosquitoes. But if they weren't on the take, that could be significant, too.

All four men had worked the waterfront and warehouse district. That wasn't unusual. Most every foot patrolman in Houston drew that beat at one time or another.

It kept coming back to the missing link—the "why" they were killed. Once he had the why, it was just a matter of legwork and following a paper trail to come up with a who.

"Officer Hamer?"

Frank stubbed out his cigarette in the overflowing ashtray and glanced up at the ruddy-faced uniformed sergeant. "Yes?"

"It's seven o'clock. You've had your nose buried in those reports for more than eight hours. Why don't you call it a day? The case'll still be there in the morning."

Frank glanced at the clock, surprised that the time had slipped away so fast. He closed the fourth and final folder. "Guess you're right, Sergeant." He sat back for a moment, flexed his shoulders, then shook his head. "I'm missing something. A link between the four dead men. Did you know them?"

The broad shoulders lifted and fell. "Not well. Just to say hello, how's the wife and kids, that sort of thing."

"They ever run around together, maybe play poker or something, when they were off duty?"

"Not that we've been able to find out, and there were four of us digging into the cases before the mayor dumped them in your lap." The sergeant rubbed a hand across his stubbled jaw. "We couldn't come up with anything to tie the killings together. Figured it was just a case of four cops who happened to be in the wrong place at the wrong time."

Frank stood, the case folders in his hand. "Any problem with my taking these home with me and studying on them some?"

The sergeant shrugged. "Mayor says you've got the run of the place and to give you whatever you need. Any ideas yet?"

"Not yet." Frank didn't add that even if he had, he was under direct orders not to share the information with anybody but Mayor Rice. He reached for his hat, listened to the rumble of thunder in the distance, and became aware of a slight head-

ache as he headed for the door. Eyes that were accustomed
to looking at far-off horizons and down busy streets every
few minutes got tired studying papers all day. He was going
to have to change his habits some, being a city cop.   ·

Two fourteen-hour days later Frank found his link.

He muttered under his breath, scolding himself. He had
read the narrow page of the dead officer's notebook four times
and hadn't, until just now, realized the significance of the last
entry: *CW, Muskrat, two A.M., Jenny's.*

CW were the initials of the fourth policeman shot. The
officer who had written the note was the third.

At least now he had a couple of names. Muskrat and Jenny.
He leaned back in his chair and stared at the big floor fan in
the corner. It wasn't doing much good except to turn the stale,
humid, still air of the squadroom into stale, humid, moving
air. His shirt was plastered to his back, as wet with sweat as
the driving rain that hammered against the squadroom windows.

Muskrat. Nickname, obviously. For an officer or informant.
He scanned back through the notebooks of the other slain
officers. There was no mention of a Muskrat. But the name
"Jenny's" showed up twice.

Frank unbuckled the big .45 Colt revolver and cartridge
belt from around his waist and stowed it in his desk. He
retrieved his snub-nosed .38, tucked the hideout gun in his
waistband, and dropped a dozen extra cartridges into his
pocket.

He shrugged into his oilskin raincoat, caught the quizzical
gaze of the duty sergeant, and strode from the building into
the heavy, slashing rain. He hadn't walked twenty feet before
water poured in a steady stream from the brim of his hat.

Frank walked six blocks before he ducked into a gloomy,
almost deserted bar, a hole in the wall that smelled of stale
smoke, spilled beer, and urine. He shook the water from his
hat and coat, ordered a beer from the bored man behind the
bar, and fired up a smoke. He sipped at the beer and winced.
He had never cared much for beer or hard liquor.

"Nasty night out there," Frank said. "Rain this much here
all the time?"

The barkeep snorted. "Sometimes it really rains. Not this mouse-pee drizzle. Must be new in town."

"Yeah." Frank forced himself to take another sip of the rye. "Buddy of mine over in 'Paso said if I ever got to Houston, I had to drop into Jenny's. Know where it is?"

The bartender snorted again. "Jenny's. Cheat you out of your skin there. You want a woman, I can fix you up better. Cheaper, too."

Frank flashed a grin. "No, thanks. Gotta be Jenny's. Buddy told me to look up a pal of his, some guy named Muskrat."

The barkeep's eyebrows bunched. "Muskrat? Don't know anybody by that moniker. But I don't hang out with that Jenny's crowd. Think too much of my hide."

"Tough joint?"

"Tough neighborhood."

Frank tossed a quarter onto the stained bar. "How do I get there?"

"Three blocks south, two east." The barkeep pocketed the coin. "Between two warehouses, end of Dock Four. If you ain't packin' a pistol, better ask for the loan of one at the door."

"Thanks. I'll keep that in mind." Frank left the beer unfinished, flipped his cigarette butt through the door, and followed it outside.

One thing Jenny's wasn't, Frank saw at a glance, was pretentious. The two-story, unpainted clapboard was a whiskey parlor and brothel. A place where a man could get separated from a month's pay or his spine—or both—in a hurry. The raucous clientele marked Jenny's as mostly a gathering place for seamen, longshoremen, and teamsters, along with a handful of men in business suits. A sense of tension lay beneath the laughter and joshing. The place was about one spark away from a full-fledged riot.

A tall woman, thin to the point of gauntness and wearing a gown so low-cut the neckline could pass for a belt, sidled up to Frank. Her smile was forced and strained; her gray-green eyes held the vacant, hopeless look of the aging prostitute trying to earn what little she could before time, wrinkles, and gravity ended her career.

"Hi, sugar." Her raspy voice held the legacy of too many

cigarettes and too much bad whiskey. "My, but you're a big 'un. Huntin' a little action, honey?"

Frank forced a grin. "Another time, maybe. You Jenny?"

She looked disappointed. "Nah. I just work here. Buy me a drink?"

"Sure," Frank said. "But there is something you could do for me that would pay better than the drink-hustling kick-back." He reached in his pocket and pulled two dollar bills from his wallet. "I'm looking for Muskrat. Know where I can find him?"

The gaunt woman shook her head, but the bills disappeared beneath a wide red garter on a spider-veined leg. "Hasn't been in here lately. Sorry."

Frank pulled a slip of paper from his pocket and handed it to her. "If he shows up, here's my phone numbers, home and office. Tell Muskrat I'm a friend of C.W.'s. My name's Hamer. I've got some easy money for him."

The paper went under the garter along with the dollar bills. "I'll tell him. If he shows up. Sure I can't do something else for you, big boy?"

"Maybe later, when I have more time," Frank said with a gentle smile. Even whores deserved some measure of dignity and respect. He went back out into the pelting, windblown rain. The downpour hadn't managed to wash the scent of fuel oil, wet cotton bales, mildewed canvas, fish, and human offal from the night air.

It smelled a lot better than the air inside Jenny's.

"Hamer speaking," Frank said into the squadroom phone.

"Muskrat. Effie says you've got some easy money for me."

Frank sighed in relief. After two days he had all but given up on the man named Muskrat. "I'm buying information, if you've got it to sell."

"How much?" Muskrat's voice was thin, a bit reedy.

"Depends on how good the information is."

There was a moment's silence on the other end before Muskrat spoke. "I checked you out, Hamer. Word around Navasota is you don't turn on your informants."

"I don't. Unless they feed me a line instead of the truth."

"What if they do?"

"I take care of that personally. Or put the word out on the street that somebody's talking out of turn and to the wrong people. Same result, usually, but a man's better off taking his chances with me."

"Fair enough. I've got good stuff, Hamer. Just keep my name out of it."

"You have my word on that."

"Meet me in Sam's Billiard Palace. Know where it is?"

"I'll find it."

"Nine o'clock tonight. It'll be crowded enough we won't be noticed. Bring cash."

CHAPTER NINE

Houston
April 25, 1911

FRANK LINED UP a two-cushion shot, kissed the eight ball into the corner pocket, grounded his cue, and retrieved his cigarette from the edge of the billiard table.

"Thought you hadn't played the game much, Hamer," Muskrat said. "Didn't know a man lived could take me two straight."

Frank dragged at his cigarette and peered through the smoke at the short, stocky man leaning against the table. The nickname fit. Muskrat's front teeth protruded past a thin lip that sported a narrow, wiry mustache. Close-set black eyes topped a stubby nose that looked like it might have been bobbed in a bar fight. His worn brown suit seemed a bit mothy, like he was in the molting season. Frank didn't know Muskrat's real name. And didn't want to.

"Played some in Navasota," Frank said with a shrug. "Fairly simple game. All that's needed is being able to figure angles."

"You got the angles, all right," Muskrat said. "So have I.

Names, dates, places. If the money's right . . .'' His voice trailed away in an unspoken question.

"I pay what the information's worth. And I'm ready to do some serious talking," Frank said.

Muskrat talked. For more than hour. At times his voice dropped so low that Frank had to lean forward and all but read his lips against the background click of pool balls and voices.

"These boys I've named are bad fellows, Hamer," Muskrat said as he pocketed the bills Frank slipped him unobtrusively. "If it gets out that I've been talking to you, I'm a dead man."

"It won't get out. These men you named—local?"

Muskrat frowned. "Most of 'em. But they get their orders from the big boys up in Chicago and St. Looie." His voice dropped again. "Ever hear of the Black Hand?"

Frank nodded. Everybody in law enforcement had heard of the Black Hand. An extension of the Sicilian group, maybe even more vicious than the Mafia families in New York. Narcotics, prostitution, arson, gambling, extortion, murder, theft. The little snub-nosed .38 in his jacket pocket felt a lot more reassuring all of a sudden.

"C.W. and the other boys weren't on the take, Hamer," Muskrat said. "They were honest cops. It got them killed. Likely, they talked to somebody on the force about it. I'd say they talked to the wrong man."

"I won't make the same mistake."

"Try to take them down, Hamer, and you'll be a marked man," Muskrat said. "They'll come after you. They'll kill you. Just like they killed C.W. and the others."

Frank shrugged. "They may try."

Muskrat stared at the big, moon-faced officer for a moment. "You don't look nervous, Hamer. Does anything scare you?"

"Yep," Frank said with a half smile. "Dentists. Much obliged, Muskrat. Those boys won't be around much longer."

"For what it might be worth in the future," Muskrat said, "I've got contacts all along the coast. Even up to Dallas."

"Then we just might have a long and mutually rewarding friendship, Muskrat. As long as the information's good."

May 1911

Frank strode casually up to the front door of the stone office building in the downtown Houston business district, flicked his cigarette into the gutter, and checked his watch.

It had been a long ride on this trail, but the payoff was only minutes away now. Every name, every lead Muskrat had given him panned out. He had the paper trail. Witnesses who would testify. And four men who, until a few hours ago, had been Houston police officers, already in custody and yelping like coyotes in wolf traps. It was impressive, the way the hint of a reduced sentence loosened a man's tongue.

Frank loosened "Old Lucky," his .45 Colt single-action revolver, in the holster at his belt. He hoped he wouldn't need it, but it was a comfort to know it was there.

He checked his watch a final time. Half a minute and the same scene would be played out at homes and businesses across the city—officers handpicked by Frank and the mayor, ready for the climactic raid. He nodded to the ruddy-faced duty sergeant at his side. "Let's take them."

The thick door swung open easily on oiled hinges. A beefy man behind a desk looked up, the bulge of a shoulder holster obvious under the left armpit of his neatly pressed suit.

"Can I help you, gentlemen?"

"Yes, sir, as a matter of fact you can," Frank said. "Mr. Angleton in?"

"Do you have an appointment?"

"One especially issued by the Harris County District Attorney's Office," Frank said. "You and your boss are under arrest. Sergeant, if he makes a move toward that shoulder holster, kill him."

The big man blanched, then raised his hands. Frank strode to a mahogany door off to the left. He didn't bother to knock.

The man behind the massive desk was tall, trim, and lean, his expensive gray linen suit immaculate, every hair in place. Eyebrows so neat they seemed to have been plucked lifted in surprise.

"What—"

Frank flipped his leather wallet shield open. "I'm Frank

Hamer, special investigator with the Houston Police Department, Mr. Angleton. You're under arrest.''

"What!'' The pale face went almost beet red. "You're out of your mind, mister! Get out of my office, before my associate—''

"Your associate is occupied at the moment. Being cuffed. As are your other associates around the city. Turn around and face the wall, please.''

"This is—absurd, simply absurd,'' Angleton sputtered. "You have no right—''

"Against the wall. Now.''

Angleton turned and put his hands against the mahogany paneling. "I'll have your badge for this, Hamer!''

"You don't want it, Mr. Angleton. It doesn't pay in a year what you've made in a week. Up until now.'' Frank patted the man down. Angleton wasn't carrying a weapon. "Hands behind your back, please.''

"I suppose''—Angleton's voice turned cold and hard—"you have a specific charge in mind, or is this just general harassment of an honest businessman for political purposes?''

Frank snapped the handcuffs into place. "I'm not into politics, Mr. Angleton. In brief, you're charged with accessory to murder for ordering the deaths of four Houston policemen. Along with arson, extortion, interstate transportation of stolen goods, loan-sharking—shall I go on?''

"I demand the right to call my attorney,'' Angleton snapped.

"No need,'' Frank said. "You'll see him in a few minutes. He's busy right now. Being arrested.'' He put a hand under Angleton's elbow and led him toward the door. "If I were you, I'd think about getting another lawyer. Several of them, in fact.''

February 1913

Frank leaned back his chair, steepled his fingers, and contemplated how fast the world was changing.

The rumble of motorized traffic was a near-constant sound on the streets outside the Houston police station. Horse-drawn hacks, wagons, and buggies were rapidly becoming the curiosity that horseless carriages had been not so many years back.

Frank even had his own telephone now, an odd-looking black square-base box with the transmitter and receiver in one piece. You talked into one end and listened from the other. It freed up one hand for taking notes.

The pistol at his hip was one of the new semiautomatics in .45 caliber, developed for the army. He still carried Old Lucky if he knew he was going into a situation where shooting was likely. But the automatic had its advantages. It carried more cartridges in its spring-fed clip than Old Lucky's six-round cylinder and reloaded more quickly. Drop out one magazine, slap in another, and you were ready to go again. The automatic was easier to wear concealed when he was working undercover or didn't want to advertise the fact that he was carrying a weapon. The auto's advantages over the revolver, however, did not extend to superior accuracy. Old Lucky would still shoot rings around it.

"Problem, Pancho?" one of his fellow investigators asked. "You look like a man with a lot on his mind."

Frank glanced up and smiled. "Just thinking, Jonah. About how much and how fast things have changed in the last few years."

"Can't argue that. Sometimes I think all these new gadgets help the crooks more than they help us." He sighed. "Going to the practice range today? I could use some pointers. Can't hit anything with the Thompson submachinegun."

Frank shook his head. "Sorry. Got a date with a man downtown."

Jonah nodded at Frank's code word for meeting an underworld informant. He started to say something, glanced over his shoulder, and muttered a disgusted curse. "Here comes the chief's number-one spy."

Frank didn't curse, but he felt like it. The uniformed lieutenant who had just walked into the room was one of the main troublemakers in the growing political feud between the chief of police and the mayor's office. Frank had no patience with politics and politicians. Both got in the way of getting the job done. Neither had any business getting involved in police work. That it happened was a fact of life. It was also a fact that Frank didn't have to accept it with any particular grace.

The lieutenant stopped at Hamer's desk as Jonah deliberately turned his back and strode away. The officer frowned at the retreating figure, then turned to Frank.

"Any new leads yet on that burglary and theft ring?"

"Some," Frank said, noncommittal.

"The chief says tell you he expects to be kept posted on your progress." The way he said "chief," it came out in capital letters.

Frank leaned back, fired a cigarette, and let the smoke out in the lieutenant's direction. "Tell the chief you delivered the message."

"And?"

"And what?"

"You'll keep us informed, as he said?"

"I'll let you know when it's wrapped up."

The lieutenant's face reddened. "Listen, Hamer—you know how the chief feels about the mayor's special-agent cowboys not cooperating with the rest of us—"

"Lieutenant," Frank interrupted, his tone even and calm, "I don't really give a rat's rear what the chief likes or doesn't like as long as the job gets done. Anything else you want to say?"

The uniformed officer spun on a heel and stomped away. Frank watched him go with a mixture of relief and disgust. The mayor said the chief was merely jealous because the special agents, and Frank in particular, had gotten results where the uniformed force had failed. And had gotten more newspaper space in the process. Frank conceded that point. But it went deeper than just jealousy between departments. It had grown into a personal feud between the mayor and the chief.

Special investigators like Frank didn't ask to get their names in the newspapers. It cut into their anonymity, which made their jobs that much harder. Several of his compatriots had already lost the services of valuable informers because of the press exposure. Frank still had his snitches, anchored by the reliable Muskrat. They knew they could talk to Frank and their names would never be known.

Frank's personal notoriety had started with the breakup of the cop-killer ring and continued when he helped crack a few other high-profile cases.

The trackdown and capture in Louisiana of Matthew Young, alias Mississippi Red, a black man who had killed a Houston constable, fueled the press fires. Mississippi Red now was in his grave, courtesy of the Huntsville electric chair.

The ink had flowed again with the capture of fugitive Charles Smith, who had evaded detection by the uniformed branch while living under their noses. Smith had publicly sworn he would never be taken alive, but gave up without a whimper when Hamer showed up at his door in Houston's First Ward.

And when this case broke in a few hours, he was going to be knee-deep in reporters.

The phone buzzed.

"Hamer," Frank said. He listened intently for a moment, then grunted his thanks and hung up. He found Jonah in the break room, waiting for the coffee to brew.

"The trucks are moving," Frank said, his voice low. "Get the squad together. On the quiet. We can get this thing wrapped up before midnight." He opened a fresh pack of cigarettes. "I'll get on the phone to some people I trust in the other towns."

Jonah nodded and strode away. Frank fired his smoke, shook out the match, and glanced at his watch. In a few hours—if everything went according to plan—one of the biggest burglary, theft, and hijacking rings in the country would be out of business. The Mafia and Black Hand boys weren't going to be happy people come midnight.

Shortly after 12:15 A.M., Frank replaced the telephone in its cradle on the Houston warehouse desk and studied the six men in handcuffs seated alongside the wall. Jonah stood beside them, arms folded across his chest.

"That's the last of them, gents," Frank told the prisoners. "I'm afraid you're out of business. As are your partners in Austin, San Antonio, Dallas, Fort Worth, and other places. I have to admit you had a nice operation going here." He rose and glanced at his watch. "Let's go. I'm afraid you've missed supper, but the jail does serve breakfast."

It was almost noon the following day before Frank finished presenting his evidence to the mayor and district attorney.

"So you knew who the thieves were all along, Mr. Hamer?" the DA asked.

"Yes, sir. But they were little fish. We let them alone until they brought the stolen stuff to Houston." He lit his last cigarette, crumpled the empty pack, and tossed it into the mayor's wastebasket. "Now we've got the big ones hooked, too. We've put a multistate theft ring out of business."

The district attorney grinned. "Excellent work, Mr. Hamer, excellent. All I need now is the names of your sources—"

"Can't let you have them," Frank interrupted. "I made a deal with them. I'll stand by that agreement. You have more than enough evidence for convictions without them."

The DA sighed. "I figured you'd say that, Hamer. And you're right. You *have* provided plenty of evidence. My staff can fill in any holes, if we find any. My compliments again, sir. Now, if you'll excuse me, I think I'd better get to work. I'm going to be covered up with lawyers in a few minutes, I fear. Mayor Rice, do you wish to make the announcement to the press? Reporters are already wearing our phones out and banging our doors down."

Rice glanced at Frank. "By all rights, Agent Hamer should make the announcement. He uncovered the ring, planned the operation, and brought it off without a drop of blood spilled. He's earned the right."

Frank frowned. "I'd as soon not get involved in that part of it, Mayor Rice. There were seven other agents involved here and another twenty top lawmen across three states. It wasn't just me." He dragged at his cigarette. "I don't care for newspapers, don't want the publicity, and was just doing the job I was hired to do. I'd rather someone else take care of it."

Rice nodded, steepled his fingers, and waited until the district attorney left. "The chief of police isn't going to be happy about our leaving him out of the operation and all. He'll squeal like a pig under a gate."

"I couldn't possibly care less how he feels," Frank said

as he stubbed out his smoke. "Deal me out of this political poker game, Mayor." He stood. "Now, if you don't mind, I have a lot of paperwork to do, and I'd like to catch a couple hours' sleep."

"I'd say you've definitely earned a day or two off, Frank. You're getting quite a reputation, and a well-deserved one at that, as a man who gets things done."

Frank's lips twitched in a wry smile. "In this business, a reputation can work two ways, Mayor Rice. It can help get the job done. Or it can get a man killed."

April 1913

Frank Hamer had had enough of the political infighting at city hall. He walked into Rice's office, handed over his resignation and shield, and walked out into a muggy spring day where the air felt heavy as a wool blanket and the gray skies threatened to open up at any moment.

Saying good-bye to Houston wasn't going to be all that tough.

BOOK TWO

BOOTLEGGERS AND BADMEN

Chapter Ten

Del Rio
March 29, 1915

FRANK HAMER FELT he'd come home.

The badge identifying him as a Texas Ranger of Company C was in the leather wallet, and the .45 revolver holstered at his hip and the easy, powerful motion of the horse between his knees were comfortable and familiar sensations.

Capt. E. H. Smith had wasted little time putting his newest Ranger to work. Frank had taken the oath of office less than four hours ago, and he already was in the saddle.

There was no shortage of work. With World War I raging in Europe, the Germans were trying to organize an invasion of the United States by Mexico. An intercepted message from German foreign minister Dr. Alfred Zimmermann detailed the Plan de San Diego, a call for Mexico to declare the independence of Texas, New Mexico, Arizona, Colorado, and California; every North American man over age sixteen was to be put to death. The Indian tribes, notably the Apaches, were to be enlisted in the overthrow attempt.

The plan might have been carried out if not for the constant political turmoil in Mexico. Even so, it was bad enough.

Mexican bandits, the most prominent gangs led by Luis de la Rosa and Aniceto Pizaña, seized the opportunity to raid into Texas, hitting ranches between Del Rio and Brownsville. There were some U.S. Army and Cavalry units along the border, but the primary defense against the raiders fell to ranch hands and Texas Rangers. The border war would be a lot more interesting than the special investigator job Frank had just left, chasing fence cutters and small-time rustlers.

The dry desert air of the rough, rocky border country held the promise of a scorching summer as Frank kneed his bay horse past a clump of huisache. Even the scent of dust was

welcome in his nostrils, a cleansing counterpoint to the humid
air and heavy smell of civilization in Houston. Out here, at
least, a man could breathe.

Frank reined in as Captain Smith dismounted to study a
patch of ground between a mesquite thicket and a prickly-
pear clump. After a moment the captain straightened and
stared toward the southwest.

"Headed for the Rio," he said. "Six men, twenty horses.
Two mules."

"Pizaña?" one of the Rangers asked.

Smith shook his head. "Bunch of little peppers, not the big
chili." He swung into the saddle. "Let's get a move on, boys.
If we're lucky, we can get to the river before they do."

The sun had dropped to within a hand span of the western
horizon before Frank and the other Rangers had settled in on
either side of the rugged pass, little more than an oversized
arroyo, leading to the ford of the Rio Grande.

Frank's winded bay stood hip-shot and lathered, the reins
tied to a scrub brush a few yards down the arroyo slope. The
metallic click of Winchester actions mingled with the jangle
of curb chains and blowing horses, the only sounds along the
ambush site. None of the Rangers spoke.

Frank saw the bandits a few seconds before Smith waved
a hand. They were a half mile away, the stolen horses
bunched as the trail into the arroyo narrowed. A buzzard circled high above the bandit gang. Frank hoped that was a good
sign.

A slight bandit in a silver-studded sombrero and vest entered the pass, checked his mount, and studied the ridges on
either side. If the scout's grulla mustang caught scent of the
Ranger horses, the ambush would be blown. Frank breathed
a sigh of relief as the point rider reined his mustang back
toward the approaching column.

Frank picked his target, a big man with bandoliers crossed
over his chest and an old Springfield trapdoor rifle in the
crook of an arm, as the bandits rode into the pass a few
minutes later. A few more yards, and they'd have the renegades in a cross fire.

One of the bandits glanced toward the far ridge and yelped
a warning; a split second later a dozen Ranger rifles cut loose.

Frank stroked the trigger, saw the puff of dust from the X where the bandoliers crossed on his man's chest, and heard the solid whack of lead against flesh. The slug tumbled the man over the rump of his pony.

Three minutes later the last echoes of rifle shots died away. Four bandits were down, three dead where they fell, the other hit hard, shot through the gut. The other two, riding drag on the stolen remuda, turned tail and ran; the stolen horses raced through the pass into the brush-studded plain below.

The Rangers approached the downed men cautiously, rifles at the ready. The renegades had had almost no chance to return fire. One Ranger had a spot of blood on his cheek, a nick from a shard of rock hit by a bandit's wild shot. There were no other injuries among the patrol.

"We go after those two that got away, Cap?" the man with blood on his cheek asked.

Smith shook his head. "Our horses are done in. We'll get them another time." He toed the body of the bandoliered man. "Anybody know who nailed this one?"

"I had him in my sights, Cap," Frank said.

"Only one of the bunch I recognize. Goes by the name of Ligarto, the Lizard. Guess he's stolen his last horse and killed his last gringo." Smith turned to Frank. "Pancho, you and a couple of boys gather those ponies while the rest of us clean up here."

Frank and the two other riders had covered less than a hundred yards when a single pistol shot sounded.

"Guess Cap solved the prisoner problem," the Ranger at Frank's side said. "Too bad. That *bastardo* would have been a long time dyin', and that wouldn't have hurt my feelin's."

The venom in the man's voice didn't surprise Frank. This bunch had killed two Anglo cowboys, wounded the ranch foreman, and raped the foreman's wife and daughter before stealing the horses. They wouldn't be doing that again. It was small satisfaction. But it beat nothing.

August 1915

Frank reined the borrowed King Ranch mount to a halt at the railroad tracks that passed a few yards from the headquarters of the Sauz Division of the sprawling Kleberg spread and stared at the carnage.

He knew now why he and the special force of Rangers, local law officers, and King Ranch cowboys hadn't found the Mexican raiding party on their scout to the south.

The bandits had circled around and hit the ranch.

They found more than they had bargained for.

Seventeen bodies lay scattered along and near the railroad tracks where the ranch hands and a squad of army troopers had met the Mexican charge with rifle and shotgun blasts. The defenders had one minor casualty, a trooper shot in the heel and calf.

Frank could barely keep up with the excited babble of voices, each describing the fight, but the position of the bodies, carcasses of dead horses, and spent rifle and shotgun shells told the story eloquently enough.

He ignored the arguments over who shot how many and reined his horse toward a small cluster of Rangers nearly fifty yards away. He heard the moans of the gut-shot bandit and Captain Smith's barked questions before he reached the group. The Mexican talked like a magpie in between retchings and groans. Smith scribbled name after name in his field notebook.

Finally, the captain stood. "A couple of you watch this fellow for a spell. He won't be with us long." He glanced at Frank. "Pancho, you and Tolliver give me a hand. Between the three of us and these King Ranch boys, we should be able to sort out which bodies we've got here. And that," he said pointedly, "will give us the names of those we don't have."

The better part of an hour and a half passed before Smith crossed the last dead bandit's name from his list, went to the ranch house, and made a couple of telephone calls. The sun stood just below noontime.

A muscle in the captain's jaw twitched as he returned to the special force. "Quite a few from this raid were Texas Mexicans, most from around Brownsville. I've asked customs and immigration services to put as many men along the border as they can before the ones who lived through this can get back into Mexico." He dismissed the local lawmen and cowboys, then gathered his Rangers around him. "Let's hit the saddle, men. We've got some bandits to find.''

Two days later Smith and Frank stood beside the body of a slender Mexican. Or what was left of him. A .45 slug through a man's temple tended to mess up his features a bit. The captain nodded, scratched another name from the considerably shortened list from the raid on the Sauz Ranch, and stood.

''Another suicide for the record,'' Smith said as he tucked the notebook back into his pocket. He ejected the spent hull from his .45 and thumbed a fresh cartridge into the loading port. His lips twitched in a grim smile. ''Amazing how much remorse these bandits feel when they realize they've caused so much grief with their outlaw ways.''

Frank asked, ''Think we'll have any trouble over these 'suicides,' Cap?''

Smith shrugged. ''Suicide, killed attempting to escape, what's the difference? The message will get around. Some politicians may raise a little sand, but the people on the border will sleep better now. That's the last of the bunch we're likely to find, Pancho. Let's go see if the other boys have had as much luck on the hunt.''

The captain had been right, Frank mused as he loosened the girth and stripped his saddle from the rangy sorrel.

Some politicians—mostly those whose pockets were lined by Mexican silver—had put up a token squawk about the Rangers bringing back so few prisoners from the southern border campaign. The fuss hadn't amounted to much. And the organized attacks around Brownsville had come to a sudden halt after word got around about the Sauz fight and its aftermath.

The big raids shifted to the northern border region. Frank and ten other Company C Rangers had been sent to put a stop to those, as well.

Frank paused to stare across the river toward Candelia, the Mexican-side stronghold of the sixty or so bandits who had hit the Brite Ranch in the Sierra Viega Mountains, killed nine ranch employees and three innocent travelers, raped the available women, then cleaned out the ranch pastures of livestock. It was payback time.

Frank hadn't asked to lead this force. Captain Smith, busy with other details, just called him in, said, "Pick ten men and take care of it. Do whatever you have to do. I'll worry about any repercussions."

The captain's unspoken message was clear: go into Mexico if necessary, put this bandit gang out of business, and don't worry about bringing back prisoners.

"Harsh orders," Frank said.

"These are harsh times, Pancho. The war's getting nastier on both sides of the Rio," Smith said. "Don't let them sucker you into the white-flag trap."

"I know better than that," Frank said. The Mexican bandits had added a deadly wrinkle to the international symbol of surrender. Several Anglos, a few Rangers included, had been lured to their deaths. A Mexican waving a white flag would call out, "Don't shoot! We give up!" When the pursuers moved in to make the arrest, other bandits cut them down from the ambush.

Nowadays, the first casualty of the "white flag" ploy was the man who carried the banner toward Ranger guns.

The villages and ranches on Mexican soil had suffered as much as those on the Texas side. Maybe more. The raiders sacked, raped, and burned their own just as they did Anglos. They played no favorites. Plunder was plunder.

Frank slipped the bit from the sorrel's mouth, put the morral in its place, and listened for a moment as the animal lowered its head to eat the oats and cracked corn in the feed bag. He lit a cigarette and stared through the evening shadows toward Candelia.

The celebration had already started. He could hear the Mexican bandits whooping and yelling, occasionally firing a shot into the air. A few hours past midnight, the whole outlaw camp would be either skunk drunk or sleeping off a gutful of tequila.

"Pancho?"

"Yes, Kelly?"

"You still plan to cross the river?"

Frank shrugged. "Those killers over there do. It's time we let them know a strip of muddy water won't save them from paying the price.'' He dragged at his cigarette and let the smoke trickle from his nostrils. ''Worried about the consequences?''

The Ranger called Kelly, new to Company C and barely out of his teens, flashed a grin. He shifted the big ten-gauge double shotgun to his other shoulder. ''Not a bit. In fact, I was hoping you hadn't changed your mind.''

''Never intended to,'' Frank said. ''No coffee tonight. We don't want to risk a drunk Mexican seeing a campfire. We'll ride out about midnight.''

Four hours later Frank and his Ranger force crouched in the brush and catclaw at the edge of the outlaw camp. The big bonfire had started to die down, but it still gave the Rangers more than enough good shooting light. Some of the Mexicans were still on their feet, unsteadily handing bottles back and forth.

Frank picked his target, lined the sights, and squeezed. The man spun and went down as the other Rangers opened up; the night seemed to turn reddish white with muzzle flashes from rifles, handguns, and shotguns.

It was over in ten minutes, except for the occasional handgun blast that dispatched a wounded bandit.

The renegades never had a chance. What few shots they did manage to get off went wild. Tequila-soaked brains couldn't draw a decent bead, even if they had obvious targets.

Frank strode through the camp, counting bodies, and came up with fifty-four. Two other dead men were found in the brush, where they had crawled after being hit by slugs or buckshot.

Kelly stopped alongside Frank and nodded toward the south. ''Signs say a couple of 'em got away. Want to go after 'em?''

Frank shook his head. ''No, let them go. They'll do us more good alive and talking than they would dead. Let them spread the word to their bandit amigos that they aren't safe anywhere. Even across the river.'' He reached for a cigarette. ''See what you can rustle up for supper, Kelly. Might as well camp here until daylight, then we'll gather what cattle and horses we can find and trail them back to Brite Ranch land.''

Del Rio
November 1915

Captain Smith slammed the receiver down hard enough to make the black phone bounce and jingle on his desk.

Frank, sitting across from him, glanced up in surprise. Temper explosions like that were out of character for the staid, all-business Ranger officer.

"Problem, Cap?"

Smith glared at the telephone as if it had just called him a dirty name. "Worse than that." His normally calm voice was more like a growl. "That was headquarters. We're supposed to start ignoring the law."

Frank stiffened. "The arms embargo?"

"Yes." Smith snorted in disgust. "We're supposed to go through the motions, but step back and let guns and ammunition flow into Mexico. In *direct defiance* of the orders of the president of the United States!"

Frank sat for a moment, stunned. Woodrow Wilson had less than a month before declared the arms embargo, as the conflict in Europe deepened and the Germans continued to court Mexico as an ally—and a potential army to invade the western United States. The Rangers had already intercepted half a dozen shipments worth thousands of dollars along the border. In the process they put a score of *contrabandistas* out of business.

"On whose orders?" Frank finally asked.

"All they would say is someone high up." Smith's sun-browned face had gone deep red; a muscle throbbed along his temple.

"What are we going to do about it, Cap?"

"I'm not going to do anything," Smith said. "I've been transferred to a damn desk job—at least long enough to report to headquarters and hand in my resignation. By God, if they won't let me do my job, they can have the job back!" He drew in a deep breath, obviously trying to curb his rage. "It's your problem now, Pancho. I've recommended you to take command of Company C."

It was Frank's second surprise in only a few moments. "Cap, I don't know what to say...."

"Just answer one question for me, Frank. What are *you* going to do about these orders?"

"They aren't in writing, are they?"

"No. Strictly verbal. Whoever made the decision obviously doesn't want to be linked with it."

Frank straightened in his chair. "Then the law is still the law. I'll enforce it."

The anger in Smith's face eased a bit. "I figured you'd say that, Pancho." He reached for his pipe. "If the powers that be are serious about this, they can make things rough for you."

"I've had it rough before. I expect I will again. But, Cap, I won't ignore the duties that come with this badge." Frank lit a cigarette and handed the match to Smith. "What I'm wondering is, why?"

Smith puffed his pipe to life. "What's your gut feeling on the why part?"

"That somebody upstairs, either in our agency or other state offices, has been paid off. Or is in the gunrunning business himself."

"I think you're right," Smith said through the cloud of pipe smoke. "Bandits and bad men aren't the real criminals in this business. It's those damned crooked politicians and greedy, conniving businessmen who ought to be lined up against the wall and shot."

Frank said, "I'd supply the ammunition."

Frank squatted in the shade of an adobe in the small Mexican village of Jiménez and waited.

Cap Smith had been right.

The powers that be were making things rough for one Franklin Augustus Hamer, Texas Ranger. One by one, the men in Company C had been transferred to other units or mustered out of the ranks. Now Company C's roster was down to one man. Frank Hamer. And he had ninety miles of lawless border country to patrol alone.

In theory, it was a good plan. Isolate the one man who didn't follow orders to ignore the laws of the United States of America. Odds were he would be killed in the process.

Frank had a counterplan. There was always a way to slap

a porcupine if a man studied on it long enough and thought the problem through. It all depended on the tall young Mexican and his band of *rurales* approaching the cantina.

The men riding with Captain Carlos Castanada were battle wise, tough, well mounted, and armed to the teeth. And their aims happened to coincide with Frank's.

Frank stood, smiling, as the *rural* captain reined in.

"Ah, my friend Pancho, it is good to see you again," Castanada said as he dismounted and extended a hand.

"It is good to see you, too, Carlos," Frank said in fluent Spanish. "How goes the hunting on your side of the Rio Bravo?"

Castanada's smile faded. "Not well. We chase shadows. The bandits who prey on both our peoples strike, then vanish, leaving but a cold trail. Twice in the last month, the damned Villistas have raided our villages and towns." The Mexican sighed. "A simple thief, perhaps, I can tolerate, even in some cases admire. But not Pancho Villa. He would overthrow my government, yet he uses the title of revolutionary to rob and pillage like a common bandit."

"I understand, my friend. I, myself, have a similar problem. Perhaps we could help each other." Frank briefly recounted his difficulties, knowing all the while that he was not telling Castanada anything the *rural* leader didn't already know.

"So, Captain," Frank concluded, "while I cannot patrol the north side of the river alone, I can help patrol the *south* side. What I propose is that I join your *rurales*. Together, we can fight the gunrunning that brings weapons used against your people as well as mine, and stop the bandits who rob and kill on both sides of the river." He paused for a breath. "I can offer you only one man—myself. But that one man has sources of information on the Texas side that might help you—thus helping us both—in our common struggle."

Castanada fell silent for a moment, brows knit in thought. Then a smile spread over his youthful face. He extended a hand.

"Compadre, there is no other one man I would have at my side. My house is your house, my soldiers are your soldiers. Together, we are more than the sum of our individual numbers, I think. We have worked together in the past at times, but from a distance. Now let us work side by side and clean up this mess along the border we share."

Rio Grande Crossing
December 1915

Frank knelt behind a V-shaped notch in the rocks above the valley that had become locally known as Bandit Ford and listened to the crackle of gunfire from across the Rio Grande.

His information had been good. Carlos Castanada's marksmen were equally good. Ten men herding more than seventy horses stolen from Texas ranchers were finding that out.

The bandido gang had plagued both sides of the river for months, raiding villages in Mexico and isolated ranches in Texas. That, Frank thought in grim satisfaction, was at an end. He leaned against a boulder, lit a cigarette, and waited.

The firing trickled to sporadic pistol shots in the distance.

The shadows hadn't moved far before the stolen horses came into view again, headed back across the ford. The wranglers were different men from than those Frank had watched pass earlier. This time the point rider was Castanada. Frank mounted and kneed his bay down the winding trail to the valley below.

Castanada touched his hat brim in greeting. "Your information was good, amigo," he said. "All the *cabrones* are dead. Here are your horses." He waved a hand toward the cavvy trailing behind.

"Gracias, capitán," Frank said with a smile. "Now there is one less gang to bedevil us."

Castanda nodded solemnly. "Three bandit gangs in as many weeks, but this bunch we wanted more than others, even. They have often raided our villages, stolen our grain and livestock, killed our men, and raped our women. They will do such things no more." The captain sighed. "We have made progress, you and I. But between our two countries, we still have an adequate supply of bad hombres. And my sources tell me that more are on the way. Men perhaps worse than these. *Contrabandistas.*"

Frank's smile faded. "More gunrunners? I thought we had most of them thinned out."

"So I have it in a tip from one of my spies in the Villista ranks. In one week, perhaps ten days, a big shipment of arms and ammunition is to cross the river somewhere north of Brownsville. The details I have are sketchy and imprecise. I do not wish to let these guns fall into Villista hands. Can you help?"

"I'll see what I can find out." Frank offered the *rural* captain a cigarette.

Castanada shook away the offer and reached for a thin black cheroot, then frowned. "It is said—whether it is true or not, I have no way of knowing—that money from someone high in the Texas government is financing this arms shipment."

"All the more reason to stop it, amigo," Frank said amiably. "I'll get word to you as soon as I have the details."

Castanada scratched a match, lit Frank's cigarette, then his own cigar. "It is good. Contact me at Rancho Placido. They have a telephone there now. Sometimes it even works." He shook out the match. "I will send a couple of my men with you to return the stolen horses where they belong, Pancho."

Frank studied the remuda for a moment, then shook his head. "I can handle them, Carlos. They know where their home range is. I'll be in touch." He offered a hand.

Frank pulled the cinch tight on his bay as sparks from the two burning wagons drifted into the early-evening sky. Heavily loaded Conestoga freighters made a big fire.

The ambush of the gunrunners couldn't have gone better. Half the armed escort went down under the first volley of *rural* rifles. All but a few of the remainder lasted less than ten minutes.

The six survivors, four Mexicans and two Anglos, a couple of them bleeding from wounds, sat with wrists and ankles bound, eyes wide in fear.

Frank watched the scene that played out before him. A dozen *rurales* under Castanada's supervision stowed recovered rifles and ammunition in their own wagons, carts, and on pack animals.

The weapons would be distributed to Castanada's growing *rural* force and turned against the Villistas and border gangs. Technically, Frank should have taken the rifles back to Texas as contraband. But this was even more appropriate justice. The men who put up the money for the gunrunning operation would lose both their investment and their goods. It amounted to a sizable sum.

Frank led his mount the few yards to the bound gunrunners and studied each man's face. He didn't recognize any of them. One of the prisoners, a stocky, ashen-faced man in the rough range clothing of a brush-country cowboy, apparently knew him.

"What'll you do with us now, Hamer?" the man said, his gaze nervously flicking from Frank to the fifty-odd *rurales* swarming about the place.

Frank shrugged. "Fellow, this is Mexico. It's out of my jurisdiction. You're not my prisoner."

The man's face blanched even whiter. "My God, man, you can't—I mean—we're *white* men, for Christ's sake!"

"The color of a man's skin doesn't mean squat if he's broken the law, mister." Frank paused for a moment and glared into the captive's face. "Now, I might be able to make a deal with the *rurales*, if you've got something of value to trade. Like the name of the man or men who financed this operation."

Panic flared in the man's greenish-brown eyes. "I swear to God, Hamer, I don't know! I'm just a hired hand! Don't you think I'd tell you if I knew?"

"A man should find out who pays his wages when he takes a job," Frank said casually. "If you can't help me, I can't help you."

The cowboy's tone dropped to a whimper. "Get me out of this, Hamer. I'll plead guilty and do my time. Just take me with you back to Texas. Please. I—I got a wife and kids. . . ."

Frank lit a cigarette and shook his head. "Then I'm sorry for your family. You should have thought of them before you threw in with this bunch." He turned to Castanada, who had walked up beside him. "They're all yours, *capitán*."

Castanada, his grim face streaked with powder smoke, dust, and soot from the burning wagons, motioned to a nearby group of *rurales*. "Take care of the prisoners," he said.

The *rurales* hauled the bound men to their feet and dragged them to the edge of a cactus stand. The metallic clicks of half a dozen rifles brought to full cock seemed loud in Frank's ears.

"For God's sake, Hamer!" Tears streamed down the stocky cowboy's face. "You've got to do something! You can't—"

A volley of rifle shots ended the man's words.

Frank turned away from the bullet-riddled bodies on the ground. He felt no remorse for the executed men. They had chosen their own trail to ride. It was brutal justice, perhaps, by American standards, but they had forfeited their right to trial by jury when they crossed into Mexico with wagons carrying contraband. And it was certain justice; these men wouldn't be breaking the law again. Castanada's methods were simple but effective. Nearly a hundred bandits and smugglers had gone down before *rural* firing squads, not counting today's dead.

A hand fell on Frank's shoulder. "Once again, my *rinche* amigo, I am in your debt. The Villistas will see these rifles, but not as they had hoped. They will see them from the muzzle ends. We make a good team, you and I."

"A good team, but one still with a hard pull ahead, Carlos. There are fewer bandits and gunrunners now than before, but still enough to keep us busy." He shook the *rural* leader's hand and mounted. Castanada placed a hand on Frank's scarred shotgun chaps.

"Something bothers you, my friend. Our handling of the prisoners, perhaps?"

"No, Carlos. That doesn't bother me at all." Frank sighed. "What does get under my skin is that I never could find out who was behind this shipment. I would have all but sold my soul for that information."

Castanada was silent for a moment. "The powerful men in your government. They are not pleased with your work here, are they?"

"No, they most assuredly are not. And that, *capitán*, is the one thing I am most proud of." He started to rein the bay back toward Texas, then paused. "By the way, Carlos, you owe me no favors. I'm the one who owes any debts in this game.''

''As long as both our peoples are made safer, who is keeping count?'' Castanada touched fingertips to his hat brim. ''Go with God, my friend.''

CHAPTER ELEVEN

Del Rio
June 1916

FRANK DIDN'T SLAM the telephone receiver down. He replaced it gently in its forked cradle, a wry smile of satisfaction on his lips.

The powers that be were, as Carlos Castanada had said, not all that pleased with Frank Hamer. In the first place, he hadn't cooperated with them by getting himself killed. In the second place, the bigger gangs of bandits and gunrunners had moved their operations to safer territory. The few small-time thieves who plied their trade in his territory now did so in the manner of coyotes—skulkingly, trying to look over their shoulder for Hamer and ahead for Castanada at the same time.

Frank had long ago noticed that certain classes of people bore a resemblance to certain species of animals. Pompous politicians brought to mind strutting peafowl. And he could almost spot a criminal just by the way the suspect moved— like a coyote, always slinking, always looking over his shoulder.

The peafowls and coyotes had invaded Austin.

Governor James E. Ferguson had all but destroyed the Ranger service with his crony appointments. The force was riddled with incompetents from the statehouse down. The agency that was once the pride of Texas law enforcement had been reduced to the status of buffoonery. Good men—the real Rangers—had resigned the force in droves.

Frank was about to join them.

Even if Ferguson were impeached, as appeared likely, the service was ruined in Frank's eyes. It was no longer a source of pride to be a Ranger. He had had enough.

He unfolded the letter from the Texas and Southwestern Cattle Raisers Association and reread it for the fifth time. The association needed a good, dependable man to put an end to the livestock thefts that plagued several areas of the state. Captain John H. Rogers had recommended Frank Hamer.

The association query quoted parts of Rogers's letter. Frank found it a bit embarrassing, but a source of pride nonetheless. The captain had written that Frank was "absolutely void of fear . . . a splendid detective . . . the harder the criminal and more dangerous and hazardous the work, the better he likes it . . . the lawless element stand in awe of him wherever he has worked. . . ."

The money wasn't bad, either. Better than Ranger pay, but there was more to it than money. Most important, there would be no politics involved. No Ferguson cluttering up the landscape with his lackeys, cousins, and political buddies. A man could go to work, do his job, and not be ashamed of the badge he carried.

Frank picked up a pen to write his letter of resignation from the Ranger service—and a note to a friend, *rural* captain Carlos Castanada.

Snyder, Texas
August 1916

Range Detective Frank Hamer sat in W. A. "Bill" Johnson's ranch-house parlor on the Snyder Ranch, barely conscious of the conversation swirling around him.

Harrison Hamer—who now worked for the Snyder outfit and was the reason for Frank's visit—and Johnson were deep into a discussion of range conditions. Frank was deep into a pair of strikingly attractive and expressive eyes.

The eyes, which reflected both intelligence and a mischievous coltish glint, belonged to Johnson's daughter, Gladys. Frank had occasionally seen prettier women, but never one whose total package hit a man so hard.

He tried not to spend too much time staring at Gladys, afraid she might take offense. His eyes weren't paying attention to his brain. And those dancing eyes staring back seemed to reflect an interest in him. It could be just wishful thinking on his part. He hoped he was wrong.

"Any leads on that case you're working on at the E-Bar, Frank?" Harrison asked.

"What? Oh. Sorry." Frank's neck heated up a bit in embarrassment. "I was sort of woolgathering there for a bit."

As soon as he said it, he wanted the words back; Gladys might not take kindly to the comparison to a sheep. But if she took offense, it didn't show. Her eyes twinkled.

Frank forced his attention back to the two men. "I've got some good leads. I expect to have it cleared up in a few more days. I've got a date with a man this evening in Snyder." He glanced at the clock on the shelf. "Which isn't that long off. I'd better be moving along."

Johnson rose and offered a hand. "Drop in anytime, Frank. The door's always open for you."

"Yes, please do," Gladys said. Her voice was as animated as her eyes, with a soft, musical lilt. "Perhaps you'd have supper with us one night?"

Frank nodded. "Thank you, ma'am. I'd like that very much." He reached for his hat.

"Hold up a second, Pancho, and I'll walk out with you," Harrison said. He spent a moment or two with Johnson about plans to move the heifer stock to the north pasture the next day, then strode outside with Frank.

Harrison, Frank noted, had filled out some since they'd last visited. He was not as tall as Frank, or as big, but he moved with the same easy, fluid stride.

The two paused for a moment outside the ranch house.

Harrison winked at Frank. "Big brother, if I didn't know you better, I'd say you've all of a sudden developed a bad case of it."

"Of what?"

"Woman fever. Couldn't help but notice the way you were looking at Gladys."

Frank sighed, reached for a cigarette, and lifted an eyebrow at his brother. "That obvious?" At Harrison's answering grin,

Frank said, "Little brother, I'm going to marry that girl. If she'll have me. But if you say one word about it to anybody, I'll whip your skinny butt."

Harrison raised his hands, palms outward. "Not a word. I get enough bruises from these Snyder Ranch broncs." He suddenly sobered. "You need any help tonight, Frank? There's some bad hombres hanging around town these days. A man could get hurt."

"Don't worry about it, Harrison. You have work to do here. Nothing will happen that Old Lucky and I can't handle."

Harrison glanced at the single-action .45 Colt revolver at Frank's hip. "I reckon you've proved that already." He glanced over his shoulder and lowered his voice. "Pancho, there's trouble brewing for Bill Johnson. I've been hearing rumors that several men are planning to spring a land grab on part of the Snyder Ranch. I'd appreciate it, and so would Bill, if you'd pass along anything you hear about it."

"Be glad to, Harrison."

"I don't suppose I need to point out that would give you an excuse to drop by here pretty regular? Gladys is a hell of a good cook, by the way. Fine figure, too, for a woman with two kids. Pancho, you'll have yourself a tailor-made family."

Frank grinned. "Harrison, you're about as subtle as a sledgehammer. I'd better get moving. Don't want to miss my date with the man downtown."

Snyder
June 1917

Mrs. Gladys Hamer never ceased to amaze her new husband.

They had been married in New Orleans a month ago, and every day Frank wondered anew how he had been so lucky.

The coltish mischief that had showed in her eyes that first meeting on the Snyder Ranch was no act. She could be as teasingly ornery as a kitten, but if she had a mean or waspish streak in her bones, it never showed. He had seen the gentle mother, wife, and homemaker side of Gladys. Now he was seeing a new side. She was not the least bit frightened of guns.

In a pasture outside Snyder, Frank watched as Gladys racked the slide on the little .32 semiautomatic pistol he had bought as a hideout gun a year back. She touched off three quick shots at a prickly-pear pad thirty feet away. Sunlight showed through three round holes in the pear pad.

"Nice little gun," Gladys said. She tripped the magazine release, reloaded the clip, handed the weapon butt-first to Frank, and nodded toward the prickly pear. "Good enough?"

Frank laughed. "Honey, I'd swear you in as a deputy anytime. How'd you learn to handle a handgun like that?"

"Daddy taught me. He said a girl never knew when she might have to defend herself these days, and a gun was one thing that made weak little women the equal of big strong men if it were used right."

"Smart man, your father," Frank said. He fell silent for a moment, almost pensive. "You know, I've been thinking, Gladys. Maybe I should find another line of work. Something less dangerous. I had only myself to worry about before. But now, if something happened to me, or—God forbid—you or the girls should be around and shooting started—"

Her finger over his lips tasted like gunpowder. "Shush up that talk right now, Frank Hamer. The Lord put you on this earth for one reason, to keep the peace and make the world safe for everyone. You're good at your job, you love the work, and I will not tolerate any talk of your changing occupations just because you're now a married man with a family. Do I make myself clear?"

Frank could only nod; her finger was still across his lips.

"Good," Gladys said. "Since you agree, you won't have to sleep in the stable tonight."

Frank started to speak as her finger dropped away from his mouth, but Gladys's lips took its place. Frank forgot that the reason they'd come out here in the first place was to test his new .25 Remington autoloading rifle. There would be time for target practice later.

Bill Johnson waited on the front porch of the Hamers' Snyder home as Frank braked his black Ford sedan at the gate.

Even before he stepped from the car, Frank knew there was trouble afoot. He could tell from the set of Johnson's stubbled jaw and narrowed eyes.

"Problem, Bill?" Frank asked.

Johnson nodded. "I was afraid this was going to happen. One of my cowboys was killed this morning. Shot in the back."

Frank muttered a curse. He had been halfway expecting such news since a handful of ranchers and businessmen from the Abilene area had tried and failed to take over part of Johnson's ranch through the courts.

"The Abilene bunch?"

"Can't prove it," Johnson said, "but I believe they're behind it. I was at the bank when I got word. Sheriff Merrill has the man who he thinks pulled the trigger in jail. The man isn't talking. I was hoping you'd check into it."

Frank put his hand on Johnson's shoulder. "I'll get right on it, Bill. The shooter have any quarrel with your man?"

"Not that Merrill or I know about. As far as we can tell, the two didn't even know each other. I can't shake the feeling there's even more to it, Frank. That's why I came over to ask your help."

Frank slid back behind the wheel. "I'll go talk to the sheriff and the fellow in jail. That'll be a start. And I'll put the word out. I have contacts who know just about everything going on in Texas." He flipped on the ignition switch and stepped on the starter. The Ford rumbled to life. "Go on inside, Bill. Gladys'll feed you. Then get some rest. You look like hell."

Two hours later Frank emerged from the jail and squinted through the late-morning sunshine. Bill had been right. The prisoner wasn't talking. Frank could see in the man's eyes the reason he wouldn't cooperate. It was pure terror, the knowledge that if he talked he was a dead man. That meant someone with power and a long reach was behind the shooting.

Frank had placed four phone calls from the sheriff's office, cryptic messages that wouldn't mean much to anyone who happened to be listening in—switchboard operators and people on party lines had a habit of eavesdropping—but that had meaning to those who would get them.

He climbed into the sweltering Ford, rolled the window down to catch the wind, and headed for the scene of the murder. Land disputes had triggered some of the biggest feuds in the history of Texas. Frank sensed in this one the makings of a big cigar of a brawl. He could only hope Sheriff Merrill and others hadn't botched up all the signs after they'd found the body. Killers always made mistakes, left something behind that marked the start of the trail. All Frank had to do was find it.

Ten days later Frank had his investigation of the shooting wrapped up. The man in the county jail was a hired gun, and not a very bright one at that. He was one cooked goose. Literally.

Frank had found more than enough evidence—circumstantial and physical—to send the shooter to the electric chair. The gunman would be tried at Baird. Before much longer, he'd be waiting for somebody to throw the switch.

The shooter would have company, too, if Frank could tie up a few loose ends. His informants linked the Abilene bunch to the hapless fool who had pulled the trigger.

He barely had time to kiss Gladys hello and hug the two girls, Beverly and Helen Sims—whom Frank planned to formally adopt at the earliest opportunity—when the phone buzzed.

Frank answered, listened for a few moments, muttered a question or two, and hung up.

He turned to Gladys. "Don't wait supper on me, honey," he said. "I've got a date with a man." Gladys nodded in patient understanding. She recognized Frank's code words for meeting with an informant.

"Know when you'll be back, dear?"

"Before noon tomorrow, I hope." Frank grabbed a quick shave and a fresh change of clothes, hugged his family, then paused at the door on his way out. "Keep the doors locked, a shotgun handy, and that .32 pistol in your pocket. Don't leave the house without calling Harrison or your dad to go with you."

Gladys's brows went up. "It's that bad?"

"It could be, honey. I'll know in a few hours."

Abilene

Frank listened intently to the man who stood deep in the shadows of the alley between the bank building and the general store. A price had been put on Bill Johnson's head.

Four thousand dollars.

An even larger sum—the informant didn't know the exact amount—would be paid the man who killed Frank. More money would change hands when Harrison Hamer lay dead. Sheriff Merrill was also marked for murder.

"You're the expert witness, Pancho," the man in the shadows said. "That makes you the number-one target. When they take you down along with your brother, Johnson, and the sheriff, there'll be nobody left to testify. Get rid of witnesses, the killer walks, and nobody'll ever know who's behind the whole thing."

Frank nodded. Killing witnesses was a common defense tactic. "Got some names for me?"

The informant did. A man named Felix Jones had made the hire; one T. A. Morrison was to handle the payoff and personally eliminate Merrill. Former Texas Ranger and ex-sheriff Gee McMeans and two other men were to take care of the Hamers and Johnson.

"Anything else?" Frank asked as the man finished.

"Just that the hired guns are supposed to get together at the defendant's ranch. Sorry, Pancho. That's all I know."

"It's enough." Frank pulled out his wallet.

The informant waved away the cash. "I owe you, Pancho. You got me off when I was facing some big trouble that wasn't my doing, so let's just call it even. Watch yourself. These hired killers are good at their jobs."

Frank stood for a moment, listening to the footfalls as the informant strode away down the alley. He ran through the names in his mind. He didn't know McMeans, the former lawman gone bad. Their paths had never crossed. The others he knew mostly by description and reputation. They were dangerous men. And if they worked like normal assassins, they would hire others.

Frank knew what to expect. And now he understood why a friend had tipped him that Harrison might be killed.

He had no proof of the conspiracy except the word of an informant. At the moment arrests were out of the question. He lit a smoke and made his decision. For now, he would wait. Men made mistakes. When the trial was over and he had enough hard evidence, the whole Abilene ring would be in jail.

Baird, Texas
October 1, 1917

Frank paused outside the Callahan County Courthouse, smiled at his pregnant wife, and drew in a deep breath of the cool autumn air. It was a welcome relief from the closed-in stuffiness and musty scent of the courtroom.

"What do we do now, dear?" Gladys asked.

"Go home, honey. The job's done here." He reached for a cigarette, his first in a couple of hours. "Continuance or no, my part of the trial's over."

"What will happen now? To the defendant, I mean?"

"He'll probably get a date with the electric chair." Frank paused to light the cigarette. "It's an airtight case. The best of lawyers couldn't break the evidence. That doesn't help the Johnson Ranch man he killed, but at least he'll pay for it."

"Then we can relax? They won't be trying to kill you— and the others?"

"I wouldn't count on it, Gladys," Frank said, frowning. "They didn't stop us from testifying, but that doesn't mean they won't be after us."

Gladys sighed and tightened her grip on Frank's biceps. "I guess I knew that. Just wishful thinking on my part." She glanced up at her husband, concern mirrored in her deep, expressive eyes. "Does anything frighten you, Frank?"

"One thing," he said with a slight smile. "When you call me by my full name. When I hear 'Franklin Augustus Hamer,' I *know* I'm in trouble."

Gladys laughed. It was more of a schoolgirlish giggle, but it widened Frank's grin anyway. He didn't add that one thing did, in fact, frighten the absolute daylights out of him. That Gladys or the girls might someday be caught in the cross fire of an ambush aimed at him. The thought was never far from his mind. Especially now, with the baby due in late spring.

He had almost insisted she stay home, not make this trip for the trial. But he couldn't bring himself to treat Gladys like a dutiful, obedient housewife. She had a will of her own, she wanted to go, and that was that. She was his partner in life, soon to be the mother of his firstborn, and his best friend. Frank couldn't ask for a better package.

Frank led Gladys toward the car where Harrison and Emmett Johnson, of the Snyder Ranch Johnson family, waited, their turns on the witness stand done. Harrison opened the car door for Gladys, then pulled Frank aside. "There's some men want to talk to you, Frank," he said quietly. "Over by the drugstore."

"Any idea what's up?"

"They didn't say. But they look serious."

Frank nodded. "Guess I'd better see what's on their minds, then. I'll be back in a minute." He strode to the cluster of men half a block away. No one offered introductions. Frank didn't recognize the men.

"Mr. Hamer, I'll make this short and to the point," the apparent spokesman for the group said by way of greeting. "Don't go back by way of Sweetwater. Word is that they're laying for you there. Take another way home."

"Who's they?"

"McMeans, for one. He'll have others with him."

Frank inclined his head. "Thanks for the tip. I'll keep a sharp eye out." He strode back to the car, slipped behind the wheel, turned on the ignition, and hit the starter. He didn't mention the threat to the others. Rumors didn't always pan out, and there was no need to have everyone fretty and on edge all the way to Sweetwater. Frank had no intention of changing his route. Once a man started running scared, he couldn't stop.

As he drove through Albany, Frank braked the Ford to let a farmer's wagon pass, and glanced at the second floor of a stone building on the corner of the intersection. A lawyer friend of McMeans stood in the open window of an office, a smug smile on his face.

On the far side of town, Frank stopped the Ford, reached

beneath the seat, and casually strapped a second revolver, a .44 Smith & Wesson, onto his gun belt across from his .45 Colt.

"What's that for?" Harrison said.

"Picked up a rumor there could be trouble ahead," Frank said. "Probably nothing to worry about."

"When you start packing two guns, Pancho, I worry." Harrison pulled his own revolver and checked the loads.

Gladys pulled the .32 automatic from her purse and placed it on the seat beside her without speaking.

Sweetwater, Texas
October 1, 1917

Frank muttered a soft oath at the *thub-thub-thub* from the off rear wheel.

"Another flat?" Gladys asked.

Frank nodded and steered the car toward a service station on the southeast corner of the town square less than a half block away. "At least this one happened close to a garage and not out in the middle of nowhere." He pulled into the station driveway before the open, barnlike service bay. There was no attendant in sight.

"Must be in the office," Frank said. "I'll go see if there's somebody here can fix a flat. Might as well stretch our legs while we're about it." He caught a glimpse of Gladys's worried glance; the atmosphere in the car seemed tense. He tried to reassure her with a smile.

"Nature calls," Harrison said.

"Me, too," Emmett Johnson echoed. The two men crossed the alley to a toilet.

"Gladys?"

She shook her head. "I'm fine. I'll stay in the car."

Frank stepped into the deserted office. His call went unanswered. From outside, he heard a sharp cry, then a series of pops, gunshots from a small-caliber weapon. He hurried out the door—and almost into the muzzle of a .45 automatic pistol in the hand of Gee McMeans.

"I've got you now, damn you!" McMeans fired as he

yelled. A heavy blow slammed into Frank's chest and shoulder; his left arm went numb. He slapped McMeans's gun with his free hand, knocked the weapon off-line and down. Another blow hammered into Frank's leg. Frank grabbed the barrel of McMeans's gun, wrenched the weapon free, tossed it aside, and hammered McMeans on the temple with his open right hand.

Through the ringing in his ears, Frank again heard the pop of a small-caliber pistol and the thunk of lead against metal. The shots came from his own car.

Inside the car, Gladys couldn't even chance a glance in Frank's direction. He wouldn't live if she got distracted now. She had spotted a man creeping toward the office with a shotgun in his hands, grabbed the .32 from the seat beside her, and fired at the shotgunner. She missed. The man loosed a startled squawk and ducked behind an automobile. Each time he tried to rise, Gladys squeezed off another shot, emptying the magazine.

The shotgun muzzle swung her way. She ducked down in the seat, frantically trying to reload the clip. She peeked over the door frame and her heart leaped into her throat. The shotgunner darted from behind the car toward Frank, who pounded his open hand again and again into McMeans's face and head.

From the corner of his vision Frank saw the second man appear only a yard away, the barrel of the semiautomatic shotgun leveled. McMeans yanked free; the shotgun thundered. Something hammered at Frank's head. The concussion of the muzzle blast staggered him. He went to his knees.

The shotgunner's yell seemed distant and furry in Frank's battered eardrums: "I got him! I got him—" The yell of triumph ended in a surprised croak as the shooter realized Frank had not gone down, but was still on his knees.

Frank lurched to his feet. McMeans and the shotgunner broke and ran toward a waiting automobile. Frank sprinted after them, stumbled once, regained his footing. McMeans reached into the car. Frank pulled the Smith & Wesson with his working hand. McMeans yanked a pump shotgun from the automobile and turned. Frank shot him through the heart. The man fell behind the car, out of Frank's view. Frank took two more lunging strides, then stopped. Behind the vehicle, the shotgunner crouched beside McMeans's body, the smoothbore still in his hands.

"Get up!" Frank yelled. "Fight me like a man!"

The shotgunner panicked. He broke and fled down the sidewalk. "Turn around, damn you!" The man ignored Frank's yell. Frank lowered his revolver.

Harrison sprinted to Frank's side, raised his rifle toward the fleeing man. Frank knocked the barrel upward as Harrison squeezed off the shot.

"Don't shoot him in the back! Leave him!" Frank yelled.

Harrison sprinted after the fleeing man, who ducked through an open doorway at the side of a café. Harrison flattened himself outside the doorway and waited. The gunman didn't show. After a few minutes Harrison gave up the hunt and hurried back to where Gladys stood at Frank's side, her arm around his waist, his blood on her dress. Several men sprinted toward the scene.

"Somebody get a doctor!" Gladys yelled. "My husband's been shot!"

CHAPTER TWELVE

Sweetwater
October 1, 1917

FRANK SAT IN the courthouse across from the garage, his undamaged arm around Gladys's waist as the doctor stitched his wounds.

McMeans's first shot had hit Frank's pocket watch, driving the twisted metal deep into the flesh of his shoulder. The physician had managed to stem the flow of blood from the bullet hole in Frank's leg.

"No bones or major blood vessels broken," the doctor said. "You're a lucky man, Hamer."

Frank squeezed Gladys's slightly thickened midsection

gently. "I guess you could say that, Doc. In more ways than one." He spoke through clenched teeth. The pain had built rapidly as the shock of numbness gave way to torn nerve endings. Agony screamed inside his head now, despite the painkiller the doctor had given him.

The county sheriff strode to Frank's side. "My deputy caught the man who took a whack at you with the shotgun. H. E. Phillips is the name. He's in the lockup now. I'm charging him with attempted murder. McMeans is dead. Probably died before he hit the ground."

Frank nodded. "Didn't know Phillips, but I heard he was one of them that was hired to get me, Harrison, and some other men."

"We also found a woman waiting for Phillips and Mc-Means in a car a block away," the sheriff said. "She had a paper bag full of ten-dollar bills. Five thousand dollars altogether."

Frank grimaced as the doctor tugged another stitch tight. "Always wondered how much I was worth. That's a lot of money."

"Money won't do them any good now." The sheriff turned to the physician. "How's it look, Doc?"

The doctor glanced over his half spectacles. "Any ordinary man would be dead, Sheriff." He shook his head in disbelief. "Two forty-five slugs at close range. It's a wonder the shock of the bullet hitting his watch didn't stop his heart. Not to mention a shotgun blast two feet from the face that turned his hat into rags. But he's young, strong, and in good shape. He'll live, but he won't be going to any dances for a while."

Frank snorted in disgust. "That was my favorite hat."

Gladys patted him on the undamaged shoulder. "We can always buy you a new hat and watch, dear."

The sheriff went away for a moment, then returned. "The grand jury's come back in. They were in session upstairs when it started. They saw the whole thing. They reconvened and made a ruling on the spot. You're no-billed for Mc-Means's death. And the jurors asked me to pass along their admiration that you didn't shoot Phillips in the back."

"Never saw the need," Frank said. "It was over by then."

"What'll you do now, Hamer? You won't be chasing any bad men for a spell."

"As soon as he's well enough to travel," Gladys answered, "we're going on a long vacation. Maybe spend the whole winter in California."

"But, Gladys, the baby . . ."

"Will be born whenever and wherever he's good and ready."

"He? How do you know it's a boy?"

"I just know. There's another lawman on the way. With his bloodline, what else would he be?"

Hollywood, California
March 1918

Frank leaned against the hitch rail of a fake cantina on the Universal City lot and watched a crew set up for the day's shoot.

At his side, Tom Mix snorted in disgust.

"Look at that, Frank," Mix said, pointing toward a bit actor trying to climb into the saddle across the lot. "That so-called cowboy don't even know what side of the horse to mount from. That's what we've got to put up with around here. If it'd been up to these Hollywood cowboys, we'd all be talking Comanche now."

Frank had to grin. That sounded like Mix. He called the shots as he saw them without a dusting of sugar. It was one of the reasons he'd taken a quick—and mutual—liking to the cowboy movie star. Mix knew horses and cattle. He and William S. Hart were probably the only two actors in Hollywood who knew how to cinch up a mount.

Mix turned to Frank. "Frank, I'm going to try one more time. You could make a fortune in western movies. You've got the looks—big, strong, solid, the eyes of a man who knows right from wrong, and the muscle and guts to back it up. The way you walk, talk, ride, always respectful to the ladies. And you've got the athletic ability for the stunts."

Frank shook his head, a bit embarrassed. "Tom, you've been watching too many of your own movies."

Gladys walked—or rather, waddled, in the eighth month of pregnancy—to the two men and glanced quizzically from one to the other. "What orneriness are you two planning now?"

Mix quickly swept his hat from his head. "I'm still trying to talk some sense into your husband, Mrs. Hamer," he said. "He could make more money here in three months than he could in three years packing a star. And we don't use real bullets here."

Gladys sniffed. "Nonsense. Tom, what you do keeps people entertained. What Frank does is keep them safe. I don't think Frank would be happy doing anything but what he does best. Besides, we have no intention of staying in California." She patted her bulged belly. "I don't want to raise our son in the middle of a make-believe land."

"Don't argue with her, Tom," Frank warned with a wink. "You'd lose for sure. It wouldn't even be close."

Mix's smile was genuine. "Wouldn't even try, Frank. But if you change your mind, just let me know. I'll call on a couple of people—uh-oh. Somebody opened the gates for the *turistas* again."

Frank winced inwardly. The newsmen were bad enough, with all those ridiculous questions; the only story written about him so far that he enjoyed was a slightly acerbic few paragraphs in which a reporter wrote that he was "a giant of a man, and about as talkative as an oyster."

The tourists and local celebrity hunters were even worse than the newspaper folks. "Gladys," Frank said, "I think it's time we made our escape."

"Don't blame you," Mix said. He offered a hand to Frank. "It's been a pleasure, Frank. I don't remember the last time I've enjoyed having someone on the set so much. Sure you won't stay around and get rich?"

"No thanks, Tom, but much obliged for everything else you've done for us. If you ever get out Texas way, be sure to look us up. We'll have the coffee on."

"I'll do that. Meantime, drop a line"—he glanced at Gladys's prominent belly—"and let me know if Gladys is right and it's a boy."

Snyder
September 1918

Frank Hamer smiled into the small, moon-shaped face cradled in the crook of his arm and tickled the baby under the chin. The boy giggled and squirmed.

Gladys had been right. A boy child.

She said it had been an easy birth. Frank didn't want to be around a difficult one. It seemed to him that the Creator could have come up with a better design for putting babies on the ground. Compared with what she'd gone through, a couple of .45 slugs amounted to a bee sting. Frank figured it was about the same thing as a man passing a baseball-sized kidney stone. Just the thought made him wince.

But she hadn't been in labor long, there had been no complications, and she was up and about within four days. The whole event left Frank somewhat astonished, and with an even deeper respect for the woman he married.

Franklin Augustus Hamer, Jr., was nearly six months old now, a healthy, happy baby who seldom cried and almost never colicked. Frank realized that his life had changed for the better—though he hadn't thought that possible—with Frank Jr.'s birth. He loved Gladys's two daughters nonetheless, but there was something about a man holding his own son that mellowed the blood and soothed the soul.

"You two doing all right?" Gladys asked as she opened the oven door to check on the yeast buns. The scent from the stove flooded the room with even more warmth.

"Getting along great, honey," Frank said. "You sure make fine babies."

"I had some fair-to-middling help." Gladys closed the oven door, strode to Frank, and put a hand on his shoulder. "You're getting cabin fever, aren't you, dear?"

Frank sighed. "I didn't know it was that obvious. But then, I should know by now I can't keep anything hidden from you. I'm ready to get back to work. It's time I started earning an honest living for us again."

Gladys gave him a quick kiss on the cheek. "Are you sure you're completely healed and fit?"

"The bullet wounds are healed," Frank said, "but the way

I've been putting on weight from your cooking, I'm not sure about the 'fit' part.'' He paused for a moment, stroked a finger along Frank Jr.'s chubby cheek. ''I've been asked to rejoin the Rangers. The problem is that the job's in Brownsville. I'd have to leave you and the kids here for a while.''

Gladys squeezed his shoulder. ''Don't worry about us, Frank. The girls are in school, and Frank Jr.'s no problem. We'll be fine.'' Her reassuring smile faded. ''It's going to be dangerous, isn't it? With Prohibition and all, I mean.''

''Yes. It's been a month since the law passed, and already the bootlegging's started. You can't wean people from liquor just by passing a law. They'll get it somehow. There's a ton of money to be made, and the crooks know that.'' The baby squirmed and whimpered in Frank's lap. Gladys reached for the child.

''Just like his father—always hungry,'' Gladys said. ''Frank, do you agree with Prohibition? I've never seen you take a drink.''

Frank sighed and shook his head. ''I think it's going to cause more problems than it solves. The big crime rings are already involved, and that means more than just bootlegging. We'll have narcotics, prostitution, gambling, extortion, corruption, and only the Lord knows what else to contend with. Whether I agree or not doesn't matter. The law's the law. It has to be enforced.''

''Then go enforce it, Frank.''

Brownsville
October 1918

Frank escorted the small-time bootlegger into the Cameron County lockup, uncuffed the surly prisoner, and turned him over to the night jailer.

''Got yourself another booze runner, Pancho?'' the jailer asked, reaching for the cell keys.

''Not a runner. Just a small fish,'' Frank said. ''Had himself a homemade five-gallon still a couple miles outside of town. Del Timberlake and I busted it up. Tim's putting the horses away. He'll be here in a few minutes.''

Frank pulled a chair up to the edge of the desk, lit a cigarette, and started filling out the arrest report as the jailer led the whiskey maker to the cell block. It took as much paperwork for a two-bit still operator as it did for a major smuggler, Frank thought. A steel door clanged, and moments later the jailer limped back into the office.

"He give you any trouble?"

Frank shook his head. "Not a bit, if you don't count the names he called us. That man's got an impressive vocabulary of cusswords. In two languages."

The jailer, a former deputy reduced to nursemaiding prisoners by a bullet-shattered hip, settled into a chair and shook his head.

"Hell of a note, this Prohibition business. I've seen more liquor since the law was passed than I ever did before." The jailer snorted in disgust. "You'd think with all the other problems in the country, those fools in Washington could find something better to do than interfere with a man's habits."

Frank stopped writing for a moment, dragged at his cigarette and squinted at the jailer through the smoke. "About all they've managed to do is create a whole new criminal class."

"Sort of puts us lawmen in a bind, too," the deputy said. He reached in his pocket for the makings. The man still rolled his own. "We arrest the bootleggers and their customers get mad at us."

Frank nodded solemnly. The Rangers weren't the most popular people in Texas to a majority of the population, it seemed.

The manufacture of whiskey had been banned in the United States for only a month or so, but already the bootlegging business was booming. Mexican booze went for as much as twelve dollars a quart. Homemade corn whiskey brought five or six, depending on quality.

"Guess we'll just have to live with it," Frank finally said. "The law's the law." He stubbed out his smoke and finished his report on the five-gallon-still case. He handed the paper and search warrant to the deputy.

"Heard anything more about organized mobs being involved?" the deputy asked.

"Nothing we could take to court. But it's common knowledge they're in it. When this much money's at stake, the Black Hand and Mafia boys will get the lion's share. That makes this line of work just a tad more risky.''

"Yeah. Those boys play rough. Heard they had a contract out on you once.''

Frank stood and flexed his shoulders. "Down in Houston. Maybe they still have.''

"Doesn't it worry you?''

"I can't spare time for worrying. A man can get killed as quick and as dead chasing a two-bit cow thief as he can messing with the big boys.'' Frank glanced at his pocket watch. "Guess I'd better get on the way, now that the county's safe from five gallons of bad whiskey.''

He was halfway to the door when the phone rang. The deputy answered, listened a moment, then called to Frank. "It's for you, Pancho. Cap'n Taylor.''

Frank reached for the phone. Must be something big in the works if Captain W. W. Taylor bothered to telephone. The Ranger captain didn't trust telephone operators and party lines any more than Frank did. Frank identified himself, listened for a moment, then hung up.

"Captain Taylor asked me to tell you you'll have the place to yourself for a while,'' Frank said to the deputy. "Sheriff Vann's got a tip there's going to be a big liquor run from Mexico. Vann and some of his boys are going with us.''

"Good luck, Pancho.''

Frank shouldered his .25 Remington rifle and went in search of Sergeant Delbert Timberlake. He found him still at the livery, trimming the hooves of a leggy sorrel gelding. Timberlake was a generally chipper young man, tall and spare of build, a good Ranger. He and Frank had taken an immediate liking to each other. Within a few days they had become a good team—and the best of friends.

"What's up, Pancho?'' Timberlake, bent over the sorrel's hoof, said over his shoulder. "You've got that look in your eye again.'' He made a final swipe with the rasp and let the sorrel have his foot back.

"Call from Captain Taylor,'' Frank said. "Sheriff Vann's got a hot tip. There's supposed to be a big shipment coming across the Rio in two nights. Word is that it's Incarnacion Delgado's bunch.''

Timberlake frowned. Delgado was one of the most notorious bootleggers and bandits along the border. "The big tamale himself, eh? What's the plan?''

"Cap's getting a squad together. We're part of it. Vann's heading the operation.''

"Vann? Why him? This should be a Ranger operation. I'm not convinced Vann knows how to handle a bandit as savvy as Delgado.'' Thin worry lines formed between Timberlake's brows.

Frank shrugged. "It's his tip and his jurisdiction. Cap says we're to let Vann call the shots.''

"Where they coming across?''

"Tomate Bend.''

"Damn.''

"What's the problem?''

"I don't like the feel of that place, Pancho. I don't like it one bit.''

Timberlake had a point, Frank had to admit. Tomate Bend had seen more than its share of blood spilled. The narrow trail through the blind crossing a few miles from Brownsville was choked with heavy underbrush. One rushed shot or bad decision and the smugglers would scatter like spooked quail. Delgado and his band knew the country like the backs of their hands. And the crossing would be at night, when a man couldn't see twenty feet in any direction.

"I'll pick you up in the morning, Tim,'' Frank said. "Don't lose any sleep over it. We've been in worse spots.''

The sun had barely cracked the east when Frank knocked on Timberlake's door and stepped inside. Timberlake had a fire going in the small woodstove. He fed personal letters and papers into the blaze. On the bed an open bag held the young Ranger's few personal belongings.

"What are you doing, Tim?'' Frank asked, perplexed.

"I've got a feeling I won't be needing this stuff after tonight, Pancho.''

"That's nonsense,'' Frank said. "Nothing's going to happen to you tonight. It's going to happen to Delgado.''

Timberlake fed another letter into the stove. He didn't look up. "I can't shake the notion things are going to end for me down at Tomate."

"Aw, you're making noises like an old woman, Tim. Let's go. The others will be here soon. We've got a bandit to kill."

Tomate Bend
October 4, 1918

Frank turned to the man alongside as the group of Rangers and lawmen threaded their way through heavy brush.

"Sheriff, I think you're making a mistake," Frank said. "You can't arrest a man like Delgado—not if he has a chance to shoot his way out of it. I still say we set up the ambush, let him and his band ride in, and cut loose on them. Try to arrest him and you'll get yourself or somebody else shot for sure."

"Sorry, Frank, but I just can't do that," Vann said. "I've got to give him a chance to surrender, not just gun him down. Suppose it isn't Delgado? I can't take the chance of killing an innocent person."

Frank snorted in barely concealed disgust. "And just what in hell would an innocent man be doing in Tomate Bend at that time of the night? Nobody but bandits and smugglers are going to be in that godforsaken place in the dark."

Vann stared at Frank for a moment, then lowered his gaze. "I won't take the chance, Frank. We've got to do it my way."

Frank almost had to bite his tongue. The dispute on tactics had been going on for four miles. Arguing with Vann was like butting a stump. All it got a man was a headache. Frank wished bitterly that Cap Taylor had come along to take charge. This sheriff was going to get somebody killed.

After a moment Frank sighed. "All right, we'll try it. But the minute you yell out, Delgado will open up on us and his men will scatter. We'll be lucky to catch any of them." He held up his hand before Vann could reply. "I've said my piece."

Frank checked his bay, dropped back a couple of yards, and turned to survey the hunting party. A handful of local lawmen and half a dozen Rangers rode behind the leaders.

The men carried shotguns and handguns. Frank was the only one packing a rifle, the .25 Remington that nested in his saddle scabbard.

Del Timberlake rode next in line. He hadn't spoken since the force had left Brownsville. Frank dropped back alongside the young Ranger. He didn't speak for several moments, then nodded toward the shotgun slung over Timberlake's saddle horn.

"Wish you'd brought a rifle, Tim," Frank said.

Timberlake shrugged. "The way I feel tonight, one gun's going to do me about as much good as another."

Frank let the topic drop. He still didn't buy Timberlake's premonition that he'd be killed, but he had tried and failed to talk his friend out of the dark cloud he seemed to be riding through. Maybe they could laugh about it in the morning. One thing was certain, Frank thought glumly: the way Vann was going about it was going to leave them empty-handed. They'd be lucky to catch a burro leader, let alone Delgado.

By the time the sun had set, the lawmen were in position, spaced out amid the rocks and thick brush along the narrow trail. It was going to be a dark, moonless night, Frank thought. Not the best of conditions to catch a dangerous man like Delgado and his bunch of toughs.

Timberlake chose a spot a few yards away from Frank. In the deepening gloom, Frank could still make out Tim's form, and it gave him more cause for concern. Tim wore a light-weight brush jacket that had been washed so often it was almost white. Even the faint starlight reflected from the pale cloth. Frank tried to shake off the feel of foreboding. He told himself it was just Tim's fatalism rubbing off.

Frank settled in to wait, the Remington in his hand with a round chambered, the magazine fully loaded and the safety off. The hours dragged. Stars came out overhead, grew brighter in the moonless night. Frank had begun to wonder if Sheriff Vann's source had fed him bad information when the call sounded clear in the still night air.

It was the bleat of a goat—Incarnation Delgado's signal to his partners. The faint scrape of leather soles against sand placed the bandit leader only yards away.

Vann leaped to his feet. "*Alto!* Halt!" he yelled.

The reply was almost instantaneous; the bandit opened fire with a handgun. Frank heard the whop of lead against flesh, then the blast of Vann's shotgun. Frank swung the muzzle of the Remington toward the spot the pistol flash had come from and opened fire. He squeezed off shots as fast as he could pull the trigger. The flame from the .25's muzzle blasts seemed to light up the night, like one of the kerosene torches cattlemen used to singe the spines from prickly pear in dry times.

"My God," Frank heard someone say a split second after his final shot cracked, "look at Frank use that pear-burner on him."

In the distance, Frank heard the clatter of burro hooves, the scuffle of sandals, and the rasp of brush against clothing as the remaining bandits dove into the thick brush. None of the other Rangers had even gotten off a shot.

"Where'd he go?" one of the lawmen called anxiously. "Did he get away?"

"No, he didn't," Frank said. "Anybody hit? I heard something—" A soft moan sounded. Frank muttered a quick curse and sprinted to Timberlake's side. His heart sank. A pistol slug had ricocheted from a rock near Tim's side. The deformed lead plowed through the lean Ranger's ribs and into his gut. Tim was barely conscious, scarcely able to speak.

"I was—right, Pancho. He—got one into me," Timberlake gasped, then lapsed into unconsciousness.

Frank lowered his head for a moment, ignoring the stunned, muted conversations of the lawmen. Then he stood, pulled a match from his pocket, and scratched it to life. He followed the bandit's tracks and blood spatters for a few yards, other men following cautiously.

Delgado lay sprawled across a cactus plant, his revolver still in the hand that had been partly mangled by one of Frank's slugs. Two other bullets had taken the bandit squarely in the chest. He died within seconds of firing the shot that hit Timberlake.

Vann, his face pale and eyes wide, stared silently at the bandit's body.

"What now, Sheriff?" one of the men asked. "Do we go after them?"

"Forget it," Frank answered, his tone sharp, his gaze locked onto Vann's face. "They're already back across the river. We'll never catch them now. Let's get Tim back to Brownsville."

Vann didn't protest.

The somber posse trussed Delgado's body across a spare horse and carefully strapped the wounded Del Timberlake onto a makeshift stretcher, an Indian travois-style drag pulled by a horse. Frank paused for a moment over the startlingly white face of his best friend.

"Dammit, Tim," he whispered, "why couldn't you have been wrong just this once?"

Brownsville

"Mr. Hamer?"

Frank stepped away from the wall he had been leaning against in the Brownsville hospital corridor and lifted a questioning eyebrow at the doctor. The surgeon's apron was smeared with blood. The doctor shook his head. "Sergeant Timberlake has asked to see you."

Frank strode into the operating room where Timberlake lay beneath a bloody sheet, only his head and face showing. Tim's eyes fluttered open as Frank stepped to the side of the table.

"Pancho," Timberlake said, his voice thready and weak, "there's no chance for me, is there?"

"No, Tim. There isn't."

"Did he—get away?"

"No."

"Then that—helps a whole lot." Timberlake's eyes closed, his body trembled, and the heaving of his chest stopped. Frank pulled the sheet over his friend's face and strode from the room. Several members of the Tomate Bend force waited by a window.

"He's cashed in," Frank said.

One of Vann's men in the group cleared his throat.

"Hamer, if we'd followed your advice, things might have turned out different. We made a mistake."

"Yes," Frank said with a gesture toward the open hospital door and the sheet-shrouded figure inside the room, "and there's the result of that mistake."

CHAPTER THIRTEEN

Hidalgo County
February 1920

TEXAS RANGER SERGEANT Frank Hamer peered into the bloodstained face of the last bandit, scribbled a name in his pocket field report book, and sighed in satisfaction.

Thirteen bodies lay stacked like cordwood a mile north of the Rio Grande, the latest and largest gang to ride into the teeth of a Texas Ranger trap. Four of the dead men were known former associates of the late and unlamented Incarnacion Delgado. Maybe, Frank thought, Del Timberlake can rest easier now. This tally accounted for all but a couple of the Delgado bunch. It didn't hurt Frank's feelings in the least to square accounts with yet another Delgadido. Del Timberlake deserved that much.

These men hadn't been whiskey runners, at least not all the time. The gang had made its living mostly from stolen livestock, with a number of murders and a few rapes thrown in for fun. This was the last of the big, organized gangs in Frank's territory. Or at least the last one that he knew about.

He tucked the field book into his shirt pocket and stood for a moment, surveying the Ranger company he had commanded since a couple of weeks after Timberlake's death. He had almost turned down the promotion to sergeant until he was satisfied the new rank was his, duly earned, and not because Tim had to die for Frank to inherit the rank.

In the year since he'd been made sergeant, he had put together a company of the most competent, tough, seasoned

Rangers on the southeastern Texas border. His group had cleaned up better than a hundred fifty miles of wild border country from Brownsville north and west. He'd lost count of the number of bandits that had fallen before the company's guns. A score of others, lucky enough to escape on-the-spot Ranger justice, awaited trial. Frank had had one man wounded. Himself. It wasn't much of a wound, and it was healing.

Word had spread on both sides of the border that venturing into the land of "Pancho's *Rinches*" was not a way to quick and easy profits. It was a quick and easy way to meet one's Maker. Especially since not one bandit knew if the man beside him might be one of Pancho Hamer's informants. Many gangs had moved their business elsewhere. Frank figured this latest ambush would convince those few who remained to move on as well.

Not all Frank's targeted bandits were from south of the border. The jails and cemeteries in three counties held more than a score of outlaws, white, brown, and black, who had earned a listing in the Rangers' black book.

The lower Rio Grande Valley had become a reasonably safe place for folks to live. Even before today.

A tall, wiry Ranger strode up to Hamer. "Well, Pancho, what's next?"

Frank accepted the Ranger's offered cigarette with a nod of thanks. "I doubt we've worked our way out of a job around here, Andy," he said. "The Good Lord made sure there would always be more bad men than Texas Rangers. We still have plenty of bootleggers and dope smugglers left to chase."

Andy struck a match, lit Frank's smoke, then his own. "That wasn't what I meant," he said, casually pushing a dead bandit's foot aside with his boot. "I meant the whole service. The Rangers. Looks like the damn politicians are about to do to us what bandits, gunrunners, and bootleggers couldn't."

Frank grunted in disgust. "I know, Andy. We're about the only company left in the state that's worth a dime. I'd hoped when Ferguson was impeached, things would improve. The new governor's not a whit different." He drew on the smoke and exhaled explosively. "I promised a man once that if this badge ever got too heavy, I'd turn it in. It did once, on account of politics. So I resigned. And if I see one more drug-store cowboy wearing a Ranger badge, I'll quit again, ride off, and not look back.''

"I was thinking the same thing, Pancho." The two men finished their cigarettes in silence, watching and listening as other Rangers rounded up the scattered remuda of stolen horses to trail back to their rightful owners.

Finally, Andy sighed and gestured to the pile of bodies. "What do we do with them?"

Frank shrugged. "Leave them. I'll put the word out where they are so their families can retrieve the bodies." He finished his smoke and strode toward his tethered horse. "Let's give the men a hand, Andy. We've got a lot of horses to move."

Del Rio
April 1920

Frank tossed the copy of the Austin newspaper to the floor in disgust.

Governor William Pettus Hobby was nothing more, it seemed, than a Ferguson stooge. Hobby was snuff spit, Ferguson tobacco juice, and they both stained the Rangers. Everybody the governor owed a favor or had blood ties with wound up with some sort of political appointment. Entirely too many of them were Rangers.

The force had once been a source of pride to the men who carried the badge, a small, tight-knit, elite agency whose ranks were open only to competent, dedicated officers. The Rangers had been feared by lawbreakers of all stripes.

Now they had become a joke. The force numbered a thousand or so men, and not one of a hundred was real Ranger material. Frank realized he had become ashamed of the badge in his wallet. The thought soured the taste of his morning coffee.

"Sergeant Hamer?"

Frank glanced up. A short, pasty-faced man with double chins and saggy jowls above a potbelly stood by his table. His wide-brimmed black hat, the band studded with silver conchas, was pulled low on the forehead, almost hiding sunken, bloodshot eyes. The man wore crossed gun belts with cartridges in every loop. Two nickel-plated .45 revolvers were slung low on the thighs and tied down, movie-gunfighter style. A polished Ranger badge gleamed from his new black vest.

"I'm Frank Hamer."

The drugstore cowboy extended a hand. "I'm Casey Wilson, personally assigned to your company by Governor Hobby himself."

Frank ignored the hand. He caught a faint whiff of whiskey on the man's breath and fought back the impulse to toss him in the *juzgado*. How on earth, he wondered, could a man hit the jug before the rooster even quit crowing?

The pale face flushed under Frank's snub of the offered handshake and the hard glare from blue eyes. "When you need a good gunhand," Wilson said, "I'll be over at the hotel."

Frank continued to glare at the man without speaking until the new "Ranger" turned and waddled through the door. Then he pounded a doubled fist against the table hard enough to jitter the china and silverware.

"By God, that does it," he muttered. He tossed a half-dollar on the table and left. He didn't wait for his change.

El Paso
October 1920

Prohibition Service Agent Frank Hamer glanced at fellow agent E. W. Walker, then turned to study the tangled mass of brush and tropical growth before him.

"What do you think, Pancho?" Walker asked. "Want to wait for the cavalry?"

Frank shook his head. "By the time the police and provost marshal's boys get here, our rumrunners might be long gone. This could be a hairy one, E.W."

Walker squinted toward the heavy cover of Cordova Island, a spit of land jutting northward from the Rio Grande toward El Paso. "None of 'em are easy, Pancho." He cut a glance at Frank. "How come you quit the Texas Rangers for a piddly job like this one? Nobody likes a prohibition agent."

"I didn't go into the law-enforcement business to win any popularity contest, E.W.," Frank said. "And I didn't quit the *Texas* Rangers. I quit the *Ferguson* Rangers. There's one hell of a big difference." He sighed. "At least in the prohibition service I can do something worthwhile."

"Nuff said." Walker racked a cartridge into his Winchester and nodded. "Let's go, Pancho."

Three hours later the final shot of the Cordova Island battle sounded. Reinforcements from Fort Bliss and the El Paso police had arrived in time to get in on most of the fight.

They hadn't arrived in time to help E. W. Walker. Frank stood over his friend's body and mouthed a silent curse. A rifle slug had torn through Walker's heart.

"Wonder why they didn't run?" the provost lieutenant, his uniform dusty and sweat-stained, asked at Frank's side.

"My guess is they had a big stash already moved to the Texas side and didn't want to leave it," Frank said.

The lieutenant nodded toward Walker's body. "For what it's worth, I'm sorry about your friend."

Frank swallowed against the tightness in his throat. "He knew it was a dangerous business. He wouldn't have done anything else."

"At least he went quickly."

Frank found little consolation in the comment. In the law-enforcement game, it could happen to anyone, anytime. Concern for his own mortality never entered Frank's mind before or during a fight. Moments like this, and the death of Del Timberlake, brought the reality home. Moments like this also reminded him how long it had been since he had held his wife and children.

Frank pulled the canvas field sheet over Walker's body and stood. "I'll call his family. I'd rather they hear it from me than a stranger. He would have done the same for me."

"The bastards who shot him paid for it," the officer said. "We count fourteen bodies. Two prisoners. Another dozen or so got away across the river. It's likely several of them won't live to see sundown."

"I suppose E.W. would consider it a fair trade," Frank said. "He always was something of an optimist."

Snyder
December 1920

Frank bounced Frank Jr. on his instep and listened in contentment to the squeals of the toddler. Playing horse on his father's crossed legs was the boy's favorite game.

"I swear, you two make more racket than a rusty gate." Gladys's smile belied the complaint as she and the girls cleared away the supper dishes.

"Boy's getting too big for make-believe horsey," Frank said. "It's time to get him in a real saddle."

"Frank Hamer! That boy's not even three yet!"

Frank winked at his wife. "Always thought a man should raise a boy the way he raises his woman. Start them young and train them the way you want them."

Gladys's cheeks colored, not entirely from the work of clearing the table or the warmth from the stove. "And do you consider your wife sufficiently trained?"

"Let you know in a couple of hours," Frank said with a casual glance at the bedroom.

"Frank Hamer! Not in front of the girls!" Gladys's half whisper was a blend of admonition and blushing lust. Beverly and Helen, busy at the sink, pretended not to have heard, but Frank could see their shoulders quiver in suppressed giggles.

"Come to think on it," Frank said, "they're growing up awfully fast. First thing we know, they'll be dragging home some punk to show off to us."

"Why a punk?"

Frank shrugged. "No man's daughters ever bring home a young man worthy of them."

"So what'll you do?"

"Shoot them. The punks, I mean. Not the girls."

The giggles from the sink became more audible.

"Maybe that's not such a bad idea," Gladys said. She brought the coffeepot, refilled Frank's mug, and returned for the boy. "Getting along toward bath time and bed, if you haven't gotten this kid so excited I can't get him down.'' Frank Jr. scowled and frumped up, but didn't cry as Gladys peeled him from her husband's leg.

Frank lit a cigarette, sipped his coffee, and watched as the girls finished with the dishes. They were good kids. Not his own flesh and blood, but that didn't matter. He couldn't have sired two brighter, more likable daughters himself. He almost never thought of them as another man's children. They were his in heart if not biology.

Frank Hamer knew he was a lucky man. Gladys had summed it up, even though she had been talking about his work at the time: "The Lord is always tapping you on the shoulder, Frank," she said. He couldn't argue that point.

A hefty bank balance and a big house would be nice, but they got by. Gladys was as good a money manager as she was a cook and a lover and a friend. He had a family he loved, even though he seldom said so aloud. He had a job that meant something. Few men could have that much in life. If the price was getting shot at often and even hit on occasion, Frank would gladly pay the fee.

The only thing that hurt was that his vacation was almost over. A new job at the federal prohibition service headquarters in Austin waited. The hollow feeling in his gut got worse every time he drove away from the house in Snyder. He actually dreaded tomorrow, when he had to say good-bye again.

Later, with a north wind whistling past the windows of the bedroom and Gladys's head nestled against his chest and shoulder and her finger tracing along his belly, Frank sighed.

"Gladys, I've been thinking about something. With this promotion and a few more dollars a month coming in, we might be able to afford to buy a house in Austin. We could be together all the time, not just a week here or two weeks there—"

Gladys's finger on his lips cut off his words. "Not yet, Frank. As much as I'd love to see you walk in the door every evening and despite the fact that I enjoy Austin, let's wait awhile before buying."

"You're right, I suppose. I may not even be stationed there long enough to unpack."

"You'll be stationed there, Frank, but not as a bootlegger

chaser. Prohibition won't last forever. The noble experiment to ban demon rum from society isn't working. I can see that. When it ends, the Rangers will need good men to rebuild the honor of the force. You, Franklin Augustus Hamer, are a Texas Ranger at heart. You always will be. It's what the Good Lord put you on this earth to do."

Frank didn't reply for a moment. As usual, there was the ring of conviction in Gladys's words. He couldn't share her optimism about the future of the Rangers. It was beginning to look like the voters would never come to their senses and boot the Ferguson–Hobby clique out of office. Until that time the Texas Rangers were still a statewide joke. Frank wasn't even sure the damage could be repaired.

"I don't know, honey," he finally said with a sigh. "It's just that—well, when I leave you and the kids in the mornings, I'd like to come home to you that same night."

"I know. I want the same. But the time isn't right, Frank. When you're made captain over the whole Ranger force, we'll buy our house."

"Captain? Are you a seer, dear, or have you been nipping the vanilla extract?"

Gladys chuckled. "Not a drop of extract has touched these lips, Frank Hamer. However, you may do so. The lips, not the extract. After all, you're leaving in the morning. And we'll be needing the paychecks for the new baby in a few months."

"New baby?" Frank sputtered. "When?"

"Six and a half months."

Warmth flooded Frank's chest. "Woman, you're just full of surprises. Nice ones, though."

Austin
January 1921

Frank hung up the phone, leaned back in the swivel chair behind his desk in the state capital city and sighed, a mixture of satisfaction and longing.

Gladys and the girls were fine, Frank Jr. was still growing like a weed. Frank missed them desperately. At day's end, his return to a sterile rented room a few blocks from the office only made the ache in his chest hurt more. A man couldn't occupy his mind for every twenty-four hours of every day with work. There was always a time when the emptiness slipped back inside.

He tried to shrug the thought away. Idle hands, he chided himself silently. There was nothing he could do about it now. But he could do something about a major liquor shipment he had gotten a tip on. It was due to move out of Mexico in four days. Frank hadn't mentioned it to anyone else yet, for a reason.

Something didn't feel right at prohibition headquarters.

Frank was now convinced that he hadn't been promoted to headquarters duty because of the good job he and his fellow agents had done in El Paso. He had been promoted because he had done *too good* a job. The flow of liquor through El Paso del Norte had been barely a trickle when he left. Now the trickle had grown to a stream; it seemed destined to break into a full-blown flood most any day.

During his first year in the border city, there had been a gunfight every night for 236 straight nights. It was still a hairy place, but he and his fellow "prohis," as they were derisively called by smuggler and thirsty citizen alike, had plucked a few of its wilder whiskers.

Frank forced his musings aside to study the job at hand. It was bigger than any liquor shipment. He hadn't been in Austin long, but he had sniffed the breeze often enough to pick up the distinct odor of something rotten, as a Shakespearean character in Denmark had mentioned. The smell came from right here in the prohibition office in Austin.

A couple of agents were living mighty high on the hog for someone on the federal payroll. New cars, big homes, jewels for wives—and even mistresses on the side—didn't quite jibe with the numbers on government paychecks. Neither of the men had outside income, wealthy wives, or rich families.

The biggest spender happened to be the chief prohibition officer of Texas. Frank's boss.

He tried to put aside his personal dislike of the man. He had a hard time tolerating incompetence, even in small doses. He could not, and would not, tolerate corruption. A man who would sell his badge, his honor, was beneath contempt.

Someone in this office had sold his.

Four times in the last month, major-liquor-shipment interceptions and storehouse raids had come up dry despite the reliability of information. In every case, the shipment didn't materialize, or warehouses that were supposed to have held hundreds of quarts of liquor were empty by the time the strike force arrived. In each instance, the bootlegging involved expensive imported liquor from Europe, not cheap Mexican rotgut whiskey or tequila.

The raids that had been successful yielded only inexpensive booze, Canadian labels, homemade corn liquor, Mexican brands. That was significant. It meant that the prohibition war was aimed at the small operators. In effect, it was squeezing the little men and cheaper liquor out of the market. The overall setup smelled to Frank like legal protection for the importers of the expensive stuff.

It was obvious to Frank that the bootleggers had their own sources within the department. Which took money most "honest" bootleggers couldn't afford. Which meant someone, or some group, with deep pockets was involved.

The deepest pockets Frank knew of were those on the britches of politicians, financiers, and organized-crime families. He put his money on the latter. He had no proof yet. It was a gut feeling. Frank trusted his gut. It almost never failed him.

In any investigation, the smart detective followed the money. The money always came from somewhere. It always led somewhere. Money could be tracked and backtracked. Follow the money was a rule that had served Frank well.

"Pancho?"

Frank winced inwardly at the use of his nickname. It implied a familiarity reserved for friends and men he trusted. Darby Smith wasn't one of them.

Smith was a man of medium build, gone slightly to paunch, wearing an expensive wool suit, high-dollar shoes, and a 10X beaver Stetson hat that would have cost a Texas Ranger private half a year's wages. Frank could come up with only one word that fit Darby "Smitty" Smith. Oily.

"Yes?" Frank couldn't bring himself to add, "sir," the

normal titular response when addressing a superior in rank.

"Heard you were asking around about a house a while back." Smith strode to Frank's desk and propped a hip on the corner, a knowing smile on thin lips and in hazel eyes. He smelled of talcum powder and hair tonic.

Frank shrugged. "I was. Found out I couldn't afford the asking price of a decent house in Austin." Part of the comment was the truth. He couldn't afford one. He knew that, and so did Smith. Frank had put the house-hunting story out on purpose. It was as good a worm as he could bait a hook with. If you didn't bait the hook, you didn't catch the fish.

"I might be able to help you out," Smith said. "I've got some contacts in the real-estate game here."

"If it's got indoor plumbing, I can't afford it."

"Maybe. Maybe not. You have time for a drive around?"

Frank glanced at the schoolhouse-style clock on the wall. "I suppose so. It's about time to go off duty, anyway."

"Grab your hat and coat, Pancho. It's a bit nippy out."

A half hour later Smith's government-issue Chrysler, a big brute of a machine, eased to a stop at the curb of a wide, paved street in a fashionable north Austin neighborhood.

"There she is," Smith said.

Frank studied the home. It was a two-story, solidly built native stone with three chimneys and an attached garage. Huge trees flanked the half-circle drive that arced through manicured lawn from street to front door. Electric coach lanterns flanked the heavy oak door with stained-glass inset panels.

"Four bedrooms," Smith said. "Two full bathrooms, formal dining room, parlor, pool table in the basement recreation room. Everything a man with a family needs." He flashed a knowing wink at Frank. "It even has a full bar, stocked."

Frank shook his head. "Way beyond my price range. I can't even afford a partial down payment on a home like that."

Smith pulled a pack of Luckies from his pocket, shook out a couple of cigarettes. Frank took one and accepted a light from Smith's engraved gold lighter.

"Oh, I don't know about that. Like I said"—Smith paused to light his own smoke—"I've got contacts. A thousand down, and you could move your family in within two weeks."

Frank dragged at his cigarette and flicked the ashes out the rolled-down window. "It's a mighty fine house, but too rich for my blood. I couldn't come up with a thousand cash if I could draw hundred-dollar bills with a pencil."

Smith fell silent for a moment, smoking, then lifted an eyebrow. "There might be a way, Pancho. Now, I know what the government pays its agents, but like I say, I've got a bit of influence. I'll tell you what—I'll ask the agent to put a hold on the house. You think it over. If you're still interested in, say, three days, just let me know."

Frank forced a wistful sigh. He had no interest in that particular house. He did have an interest in Darby Smith. "I just don't see any way...." He let his voice trail off.

Smith tossed his Lucky out the car window and reached for the ignition key. "Give it some thought, Pancho. There's a way to get you in that house. I can tell you'd love to have it." He cranked the Chrysler to life. "Talk it over with your wife. Hell, use the office phone to call her. Then let me know. Don't take too long to make up your mind. I'm not sure how long I can keep it off the open market."

Frank nodded. "I'll do that. Thanks for the offer."

"If us lawmen don't watch out after each other, who will?" Smith turned the Chrysler around. The street was wide enough for the big car to take the U-turn with room to spare. "I'll drop you off at your place on the way back, Pancho. Roll up that pneumonia hole of a window. It's cold out there."

A few minutes later Frank stood outside the rooming house and watched the Chrysler blend in with the other traffic, then strode to his rented room. He picked up the phone before he took off his hat.

CHAPTER FOURTEEN

"YOU'RE ON THE right track, Frank," the voice on the pay phone in the Austin pool hall said. "Smith's dirty as a whorehouse towel bin after a busy Saturday night."

"Whose payroll's he on, Marty?"

"Word is that he's in the big boys' pockets. The Chicago syndicate. Specifically, the Black Hand. Bad boys, Frank. Get crossways with them, you'll never see your allotted threescore years and ten."

"I'll take the chance, Marty. I can't walk away from this one. I need your help. I need to know when the syndicate shipments are moving, and where. And if you can find out, where the money changes hands. With that, I can start building a case."

"That's expensive information, Frank. I'm not talking about money. I'm saying it could cost a man his life. But I'll be in touch. If you wind up in the Brazos River with a pistol slug in the back of your head, don't come bitching to me."

"I think I can safely promise I wouldn't do that, Marty. Thanks for the help."

March 1921

Frank sat in the Chrysler's passenger seat and watched as Smith pulled several fifty-dollar bills from his inside coat pocket, tucked them into a plain white envelope, and handed them over. Frank pocketed the envelope without counting the currency. He wanted Smith's fingerprints all over the money when the time came.

"I haven't seen that much cash in one place since I broke up a high-stakes monte game over in Houston," Frank said.

Smith chuckled. "That's just chicken feed, Pancho. Stick with me and you can make twice that much in a week. For doing nothing."

It wasn't exactly nothing, Frank thought. Letting a liquor shipment worth several thousand dollars go by without lifting a finger to stop it didn't qualify as nothing. It went against the grain. But in the bigger scheme of things, it was another investment. One that would pay dividends soon. He had the paper trail and the money trail, and half a dozen names to boot.

"Changed your mind about that house?" Smith asked. "You could have it paid for, free and clear, before summer's end."

Frank forced a grin. "Been rethinking the future. I hear California's a good place for a man with a nest egg to settle down and raise a family. Especially if he's got a big nest egg." He leaned back on the plush upholstery. "What's next?"

Smith hit the starter. "A big one, Pancho. The biggest yet. Half a ship's cargo, straight from the Emerald Isle. The best Irish whiskey that money can't buy in this country. I'll be in touch."

"Drop me off at the bank, will you, Smitty? Man shouldn't carry a big roll around these days. There's a lot of thieves about, I hear."

Smith grinned, nodded, and gunned the engine.

Minutes later Frank put the unopened envelope inside a lockbox and handed it to the chief teller, a man Frank knew he could trust. The teller put the lockbox in the vault and initialed the entry in Frank's notebook.

The note tacked to the frame of his rented room was in his landlady's cramped handwriting. Scribbled beneath the phone number was the message, *They didn't leave a name, Mr. Hamer.*

Frank tucked the message in his shirt pocket and walked the two blocks to a public phone office. He didn't use the phone in his room to contact his sources, or even the same public phone twice in a row. He read the number to the switchboard operator and paid his nickel. She nodded toward a row of booths along the wall. "Second from the left."

Frank closed the booth door and picked up the receiver. A sleepy voice answered on the fourth ring. Frank cut a quick glance at the operator. She pulled off her headset and picked up a magazine.

"How's the pool hustling, Marty?" Frank asked by way of greeting.

"Winning more than I'm losing. You've got troubles."

"Tell me something new."

"The big boys up in Chicago are squirming some with you around, Frank. Word is, there's a contract on you. A hit."

"Thanks for the tip, Marty. I'll stay alert."

"Do that. The world needs more good lerts." The line went dead. Frank hung up and stared at the phone for a moment. He had a pretty good idea who the syndicate had in mind for the hit. Smitty Smith had been acting a bit strange lately. . . .

Two days later Smith wandered into Frank's office at mid-morning. His face was a bit pale; his gaze flicked everywhere except to Frank's face, and his feet shuffled constantly. The man looked like he'd jump nine feet straight up if somebody said "boo," Frank thought.

"Pancho, I need a hand," Smith said. There was a notice-able quaver in his voice. "Got a line on a corn still a ways outside town."

Frank nodded, slipped his .45 automatic into his shoulder holster, and hitched the gun belt that carried Old Lucky around his hips. "Let's go bust them up," he said.

"We'd better take your car. Too many people know that big Chrysler I drive."

Smith had little to say as Frank steered the Ford along the narrow, dusty road that snaked between scrub-oak groves and around heavy brush. Frank drove casually, his left hand on the wheel, and watched Smith from the corner of his eye, thankful that he had always had excellent peripheral vision.

The man had done one thing right, Frank thought. By having Frank take the wheel, Smith was in the passenger's seat, and he was right-handed. The slight bulge of the shoul-der holster and the snub-nosed .38 revolver it held were in easy reach of Smith's right hand. It would be a simple matter to draw and fire.

Frank conceded Smith the advantage. He also knew it didn't make any difference. Smith could sell out to the syndicate, but Frank was sure he didn't have the guts to shoot a man face-to-face.

Despite the cool, early-spring air that flowed into the Ford through the partly opened driver's-side window, sweat dotted Smith's forehead and upper lip. A nerve in the corner of his left eye twitched. He swallowed frequently and seemed to be constantly running a thumb under the collar of his white shirt.

Smith started—almost came out of his seat, in fact—when Frank deliberately reached under his armpit to scratch a non-existent itch beneath his shoulder holster. Smith's face paled even more.

The road narrowed into a rutted path, made a sharp right turn, and followed the lip of a deep arroyo choked with rock-falls and juniper brush.

"Stop here," Smith said.

Frank braked the Ford. Smith had picked a perfect place to hide a body. One shot, roll the dead man over the edge, and the carcass likely would be nothing but bones before someone stumbled across the remains. Frank killed the engine and turned to face Smith. The nervous tic along Smith's left eye grew more pronounced.

Frank waited silently, his gaze steady on Smith's hazel eyes. The man had trouble looking him directly in the face. The boys in Chicago could have picked a more competent assassin, Frank thought. The minutes dragged on. Frank let Smith stew in silence beneath his steady, cold stare. Neither man made a move toward a sidearm.

The tick of a cooling engine block and the warble of a mockingbird were the only sounds audible inside the Ford.

Finally, Smith seemed to wilt even more. "Let's go back to town." His words were little more than a whisper.

Frank said nothing as he tooled the Ford through downtown Austin, eased the car into the agency parking lot, and killed the engine. Then he pinned Smith with a steady, cold glare.

"Well," he said after a moment, "it's all up now. I've got

enough evidence to put you away, and I guess I'd better do it before you get any more foolish notions.''

Smith's mouth opened and closed several times, like a catfish out of water, before any words came out. When they did they were shaky, barely audible. ''No need, Hamer. I've got no choice but turn myself in. Jail's the safest place for me now.''

Newspapers across the state went nuts when the chief prohibition officer of Texas surrendered and pleaded guilty to charges of conspiring to receive, conceal, transport, and sell liquor illegally brought into the United States.

The headlines were in the biggest type the Austin paper had in its trays. Frank could only imagine the expressions on the faces of mob bosses in Chicago when they read the story in the *Tribune* for the first time.

Smith's sworn statement jibed almost to the last *t* with the stack of evidence Frank turned over to the national prohibition authorities. There were arrests in Chicago, St. Louis, Dallas, Brownsville—mostly minor players, importers, distributors, truckers, rail officials. For the most part, the big boys escaped arrest, probably because they owned too many cops, judges, and politicians.

The carefully constructed distribution network of the Black Hand bootlegging operation in Texas and much of the southwest might not be broken, but it was badly bent. Frank was satisfied with that.

He wasn't so satisfied with the press's and public's fawning over him as a hero, one lone ex-Ranger who had brought an entire mob syndicate to its knees. He responded grudgingly to reporters' questions, and then told them only the facts of the case, which they already knew. He shrugged off questions about his own role in breaking the ring.

''Just doing my job,'' was his standard comment.

His reticence and distrust of the papers and radio reporters didn't stop the flowery, mostly inaccurate accolades, the stream of gushy letters from temperance unions and other prohibition groups, or the pleas from antiliquor politicians to have their photos made with him. A New York newspaper offered him two hundred dollars cash for an exclusive interview, and he lost count of the speaking invitations—some offering him up to fifty dollars just for one speech—that he received almost daily.

He turned them all down flat.

It just made the legend grow.

Like it or not, Frank Hamer was a national hero. The whole thing left him more than a bit disgusted. The only real satisfaction he got from the mess was that the exposés in the public press, along with increased pressure from federal agencies, cut deeply into the Black Hand operations.

Frank idly wondered how much his head on a platter would be worth in Chicago these days.

Austin
August 1921

"Frank, I need you back in the Ranger force, and I won't quit hounding you until you agree," Governor Pat Neff said.

Frank stubbed out his cigarette in the governor's ashtray, a stone formerly used by the Indians to grind corn, and shook his head.

"Sorry, Governor, but you know how I feel about that," he said. "The Ferguson Rangers are an embarrassment to the state, to the honor of the service, and to me personally. I'll have no part of that bunch of drugstore cowboys."

Neff pulled a cigar from the humidor on his desk and twirled the brown tube between his fingers. "That's precisely why I need you, Frank," he said. "I want to see the Texas Rangers a respected and competent force again, not a bunch of political cronies. It's going to take a good man to do that."

"In all honesty, sir, I don't think it can be done. The hogs are too deep in the mud now."

"It *can* be done and, by all that's holy, I'm going to do it. With your help," Neff said. "You'll find that I'm a very persistent and persuasive man. I'll have you back in the Rangers before Thanksgiving." He smiled, glanced at the clock, stood, and offered a firm handshake. "I'll be in touch."

Snyder
September 1921

"Franklin Augustus Hamer, for a smart man you can be a real pain in the backside at times." Gladys's tone had drifted toward the tart side.

"Uh-oh. I'm in trouble again," Frank said.

"You haven't seen trouble yet—nothing like you're going to see if you turn down this chance. Sometimes I wonder how you can be such an aggravation. Can't you see the Lord's tapping you on the shoulder again?"

"The Lord? I thought that was Governor Neff."

Gladys stomped a dainty foot beneath the table where they sat, then drew a deep breath. She reached across and placed her hand on Frank's.

"You have to take the job, Frank. It's your destiny, your fate. It's what the Creator put you here to do, and you know that as well as I do."

"But, honey, you know what a mess the service is in—"

"I also know that you're the man who can save it, Frank," Gladys interrupted. "If anyone can, it's you. Now, admit it. Out loud. You *want* to do it. And if you don't, it's going to be mighty chilly around here for a while."

Frank's lips lifted in a wry grin. "That's the only threat I've heard lately that scared me." He reached for a cigarette with his free hand. "You're as bad as Pat Neff about getting under a man's saddle blanket."

"Somebody's got to keep you on the straight and narrow, Frank." At least, Frank noted, she didn't use his full name this time. "Now, tomorrow morning, you get your butt out of my house and into that Ford. Go take the oath of office, *Captain* Hamer."

Frank's grin broke into a smile. "As a matter of fact, I've already told Neff I'd take the job—if you didn't mind."

Gladys patted the back of his hand, then pinched the skin hard enough to make him yelp. "Like I said, you can be such an aggravation. Shame on you, leading a poor defenseless woman on like that." But she was smiling as she said it.

"Defenseless? I never noticed that before." He sighed. "You know, I'm going to be sorry to leave Austin, but it's going to be nice to throw my leg over a horse again.''

"Frank, I'm proud of you. So proud I could pop.'' Gladys's tone softened; Frank thought he saw the glint of moisture in her eyes. ''Now, finish your smoke and coffee. It's getting late.''

Del Rio
September 1921

Texas Ranger Captain Frank Hamer surveyed his former company and snorted in disgust.

For the most part, the men were dirty, unshaven, pale-skinned, and out of shape. He doubted seriously that more than four of them could even ride a horse.

"Ferguson Rangers,'' he muttered to himself. Out loud, he said, "Wait here. I'll be right back.'' He strode to the telegraph office, scribbled out a message, and waited until the keys clacked. The message to the governor's office read simply, *Things have been running mighty loose around here.*

He went back and fired the entire company.

Within a week Company C was on the road back. Frank's initial telegram shook some trees in Austin.

Adequate supplies of food, ammunition, blankets, and other necessities that had been all but nonexistent under the previous command were on the way. Communications with headquarters and other field companies were being revised and improved at Frank's instructions.

Frank was even slightly surprised himself at the power a captain's rank—and a reputation for getting the job done— gave a man. Maybe he couldn't salvage the whole Ranger force, but he could turn Company C back into a unit to be feared along the border. There was no shortage of things to do; the previous outfit hadn't done squat.

He reenlisted the few men he could trust and had begun recruiting other seasoned, competent men who—like himself—had left the Rangers in disgust under the Ferguson and Hobby administrations. For a while they would be at less than full strength. But as he had informed headquarters, he could do more good with these few men than twice the number of political lackeys that had been here.

He crossed the Rio Grande several times, renewed his working relationship with the commanders of Mexican *rural* units, and within days had a wide ranging group of informants on both sides of the border.

By the end of October, the handful of Company C Rangers had put an end to the careers of a half-dozen individual bandits and recovered a sizable number of rustled livestock. A couple of tips paid off in the ambush and interception of liquor shipments. The flow of whiskey across the river abruptly slowed when word got around that *rinche capitán* Pancho Hamer was back in the area.

When the new year dawned, the border country around Del Rio was nearly as peaceful as it had been when he left back in 1919. Company C was again the crack unit in the Ranger force.

Frank wasn't satisfied.

One band of rustlers, smugglers, robbers, dope runners, and killers remained at large along the border—the most dangerous gang Frank had yet stalked. He wanted their leader, Ralph Lopez, also known as "Red," worse than he'd ever wanted any man.

Lopez's trail of blood was long and deep. It had started with a killing in Bingham, Utah, in 1913. During the next year Lopez and his growing band of recruits left at least thirty people dead in a rampage from the Wasatch Mountains in Utah to the Rio Grande. During one train holdup alone, Lopez and his men had cold-bloodedly killed nineteen Americans that had been on board.

Lopez had earned his spot as number one on the list in Frank's "black book."

Two weeks ago Frank thought he had him. The tip had been solid, from a source that had never steered him wrong. But when Company C closed in on the isolated canyon campsite, the bandits had been gone for a full day. Six days later Frank and his Rangers had staked out a river ford. Lopez never showed. They cut his tracks ten miles to the northwest of the crossing.

The near misses confirmed what Frank had suspected for

weeks. Lopez had his own network of spies in this border chess game. Frank had a gut feeling the game would end soon. Lopez wasn't far away; Frank could feel his presence, all but smell the man.

A scuffle of boot soles outside the office door broke through Frank's ponderings. A tall, consumptive-looking man in rough range clothing peered into the office.

"Captain Hamer?"

Frank stood. "Come in, Silas. Something I can do for you?"

The distinct odor of sheep entered the office with the thin man. Silas Herndon ran a scrub flock on a hardscrabble outfit northwest of town. His place had more rocks per square foot than it had grass on the whole acreage. He shuffled his feet and glanced about nervously, twisting the brim of his stained hat in long, knobby fingers.

"Well, I—you know, Captain, times has been kinda hard here lately." He tried to square his stooped shoulders. "I was wonderin'—what's the reward on Red Lopez?"

"Thirty-five hundred at last count." Frank pulled a pack from his pocket and offered Herndon a cigarette.

The sheep rancher's fingers trembled when he took the smoke. "If I take you to him, will you cut me in for a share of the reward?"

Frank nodded. "You know I will, Silas." He scratched a match on the underside of the desk edge. "I want Lopez a sight more than I want the reward money. You know that."

Herndon's cigarette tip jiggled as he puffed it to life over the match in Frank's hand. "I'm takin' a hell of a chance on this, Captain," he said between puffs. "Lopez's got friends. If I didn't need money so bad . . ."

"I understand, Silas. All I can promise is that if someone finds out who tipped us off, they won't hear it from me or any other Rangers in my command."

The sheep rancher hesitated, as if weighing his choice of slow starvation or a quick assassin's bullet, then sighed. "I know one of Lopez's men. A second cousin on my mother's side. He come to my place the other day. Said most of the trails they rode were gettin' a might warm, what with your boys around." He paused for a drag at the cigarette. "I told him I knew a place folks around here ain't thought about in years, that I could lead 'em through. For a price. They'll be movin' through about sundown today.''

"How far is this place?''

" 'Bout fifteen, twenty miles. Captain Hamer, them boys ain't goin' to pay me no guide fee. I know that in my bones. They'll shoot me in the back sure, soon's they're in the clear.''

Frank nodded. "Probably. And most likely they'd kill you if you didn't help them. You did the right thing in coming to me, Silas.'' He glanced at the sun-washed street outside. "There's plenty of time. I'll round up the men.''

Silas Herndon reined his gaunt, leggy sorrel to a stop on a low ridge overlooking a shallow valley that wound its way through rocky hills and nodded toward a depression in the land below.

"This here's it, Captain,'' Herndon said. "Used to be this was a irrigation ditch 'fore the spring upstream dried up years back. This's where I'll be bringin' them outlaws through.''

Frank sat for a moment in silence, surveying the lay of the land. The depression, about three feet deep and flanked by low mounds of earth and progressively steepening ridges, was relatively smooth, mostly sand and gravel. There was no cover for a man caught on the former streambed to duck behind.

"Figgered this'd be a prime spot for you Rangers,'' Herndon said. "You can catch 'em out in the open.''

Frank shifted his gaze to Herndon. Sweat trickled from beneath the sheepman's hat despite the cool air beneath a lowering sun. Herndon's gaze flicked about constantly, never settled on any one thing for more than a second. And on the way here, he had to dismount every couple of miles to empty his bladder. Frank granted that the man had a right to be twitchy.

"See, you can hide your men behind that little ridge alongside the ditch,'' Herndon said, "and I can lead 'em right up to you.''

Frank nodded amiably. "Sounds good to me, Silas.''

Herndon glanced at the sun. "I gotta get goin'. Lopez and

his bunch's waitin' for me now just a short piece from here."
He turned to Frank. "I'd appreciate it when the shootin' starts
if you boys don't put no hole in me by mistake."

"You can count on that, Silas."

Frank sat the saddle as Herndon reined the ribby sorrel into
the abandoned ditch and kicked the animal into a reluctant
trot. When Herndon had disappeared from sight, Frank turned
to the Ranger sergeant who had ridden up alongside.

"I don't like the feel of this place, Pat," Frank said. "I've
got a feeling we're being led into a trap if we play the game
the way Silas lays it out."

The sergeant's gaze swept the abandoned irrigation ditch
again, eyes narrowed. "I'd say you're right. So what's the
plan, Cap?"

Frank nodded toward the stair-stepped hillside behind the
earth berms flanking the ditch. "Ambush the ambushers."

A few minutes later Frank had his men in position. The
Rangers fanned along the higher ridge overlooking the irrigation ditch, their horses safely out of view. The valley
grayed as the sun dropped to the horizon at Frank's back. He
thumbed off the safety of the .25 Remington and settled in
to wait.

The gray light had deepened to near dusk when Frank spotted the twenty heavily armed men creeping up behind the
earthen berm toward the irrigation ditch, their backs to the
Rangers. Several wore broad-brimmed Mexican-style hats,
bandoliers across their chests. Red Lopez was in the lead, his
rifle at waist level; Frank knew Lopez was one of the few
gunmen who fired from the hip, and he was deadly with a
long gun. The cadaverous Silas Herndon was the third man
from Lopez, a shotgun in his hands.

Frank waited until Lopez reached the top of the berm and
peered into the empty ditch, then stood.

"Halt!" Frank yelled. "We're officers of the law!"

Lopez spun and fired, a split second before the other surprised outlaws could bring their weapons around. Frank felt
a light tap and a burn at his cheekbone as he squeezed the
trigger. The Remington slug hammered Lopez in the chest.
Frank swung his rifle muzzle toward Herndon, saw the man

spin and fall before he could fire, then picked out another target.

The aimed volleys from the Ranger ranks ripped into the exposed outlaws. Half a dozen fell in the first few seconds; others scrambled for cover and were cut down by rifle and pistol slugs.

The battle was over in minutes, its end coming with a final pistol shot as a Ranger dispatched a wounded bandit. Frank strode to the irrigation ditch and the riddled bodies. Not a man had escaped.

"You hit, Cap?"

Frank lifted his hand from the Remington receiver and touched his cheek. His fingers came away bloody. He had forgotten about the tap and burn. The slug had grazed him, barely breaking the skin.

"Not enough to count, Van," he said. "Let's see what we've got here."

Frank squatted beside the body of Red Lopez for a moment, then pulled a watch from the killer's shirt pocket. Frank's slug had bored through the gold timepiece and into Lopez's heart. Frank dropped the watch into his own pocket. It would serve the Rangers well as a display, a mute warning to outlaws on both sides of the border.

Herndon wouldn't be using his share of any reward money. Three slugs from the rifles of angry Rangers who didn't take kindly to being double-crossed had seen to that. Frank stood.

"Guess that's that, boys," he said. "Let's find their horses and pack what's left of them into town. I'd say leave them here for the coyotes, but it won't hurt to let folks know what happens to bad boys when the Rangers are around. By the way—since Mr. Herndon is no longer around, every man in the company will get an equal split of the reward money on Lopez."

Chapter Fifteen

"WELL, BOYS," FRANK said to the gathered Company C Rangers, "you'll be getting a new captain soon."

He lifted a hand to stem the protests. "I've been offered a job I can't turn down, a transfer to headquarters in Austin. As senior captain of the whole Ranger force."

The glum mutters gave way to pleased grins. "About damn time somebody got put in charge who knows how it's supposed to be done," one of the men said. The comment brought nods of agreement all around.

"Now, don't think that just because I'm not around to kick your backsides out of the bedrolls every morning, you'll get to loaf around town," Frank said, "We've cleaned up our section of the border pretty damn well, but there's still plenty to do." He paused for a moment to look each man in the face. "And it won't mean that you fellows aren't in my thoughts and prayers every day. I've worked with many a good group of Rangers in my time, and you men are the best of the lot."

Frank wondered why his throat suddenly felt tight. Or that some of the saddle-tough, hard men in his command seemed to be getting a tad damp in the eye. He hadn't said a word that wasn't true, except the bit about booting them out of bed in the mornings. He wouldn't dare use the word aloud, but he had grown to love these men. Facing tight spots and bad men with big guns had a way of drawing men closer than any other of life's endeavors, he mused inwardly. He cleared his throat.

"I'll be leaving tomorrow morning, spend a bit of time with my family, then be in Austin on the first of the year. In the meantime Pat will be in charge as sergeant. I've recommended you for promotion to captain, Pat. You've earned it.''

The sergeant muttered his thanks.

''I can't guarantee you'll get it, Pat, but if you don't, rest assured there won't be some pharmaceutical cowboy sent out to give you orders. Governor Neff has made it clear that he intends to get politics out of the Rangers and rebuild the service into a force to be reckoned with. He asked me to help him do that. If there's anything you need here, all you have to do is wire or phone my office and you'll get it.'' He flipped a hand toward the door. ''Now, get out from underfoot and go chase some bandidos and smugglers. I've got work to do.''

He didn't get out of it that easy.

Every man in the company shook his hand and made some comment. Mostly, the parting words boiled down to the old frontier Ranger saying, ''Keep your powder dry and your hair on.'' The way the words were said gave them more feeling and meaning than the creaky old farewell phrase it was on the surface. Real Rangers kept it simple, almost gruff. They wasted few motions and fewer words.

When the last man filed out of the small building that was Company C headquarters, Frank eased himself into the creaky chair behind the desk and sighed. God, he thought, but I'm going to miss those boys. . . .

Austin
January 1922

Frank had known when he took the job as senior captain of the Texas Rangers that a lot had to be done. He hadn't realized there would be quite *this* many ants to stomp.

In his first four days on the job, he'd fired more than three dozen incompetents left over from the Ferguson–Hobby regimes, hired a sixth that many good men to take their places, and chewed tails on the phone and in person until he was satisfied the Rangers afield would receive adequate supplies and equipment to do their jobs.

He dispatched trusted men to trouble spots as either peace-keepers to put down potential lynchings or riots, or as undercover officers to compile reports on organized gangs and criminal activities.

He saved the most dangerous assignment for himself.

Oil had come to Mexia.

Following on the heels of the gushers were some of the most lawless elements of the Prohibition era. From a quiet country town of 2,500, the population of Mexia had boomed almost overnight to more than 30,000. A sizable portion of the new arrivals were anything but respected businessmen.

Reports from Frank's informants and undercover officers painted a picture of a wide-open, anything-goes town where any vice could be enjoyed, for a price. If ever a town needed a general cleanup, it was Mexia.

Frank glanced at the clock, strode down the hall to the office of Ranger Adjutant General Thomas G. Barton, and paused at the open door until Barton hung up the phone.

"Ah, Captain, come in," Barton said as he rose from behind the desk that almost dwarfed him. Barton, who stood several inches short of six feet, slender of build, with a boyish face and prominent ears, looked more like a bank teller than a competent law-enforcement officer. He was a classic case of a small dog with a big bite in a fight.

"Have a seat, Frank," Barton said. "That was Governor Neff on the phone. He wanted to know if we're ready to start work on Mexia."

"I'm ready. I have Tom Hickman and seventeen good men standing by," Frank said.

Barton nodded. "I'm going along—I wouldn't miss this for all the graft money in Austin—and I've got two good federal agents lined up. That's a total of twenty-two men. Mexia's going to be a tough nut to crack. You've seen the reports."

"Yes, sir, I've read them. Just talked with an undercover agent I've had there for three days. I drove through Mexia myself on the way down." Frank didn't add that he'd driven out the other side of town with a bitter taste in his mouth.

At least nineteen wide-open gambling dens, some in tents thrown up when all available buildings were occupied, operated in Mexia. Bootleg liquor flowed constantly from gaming halls and open bars, with no pretense at disguising the operations. Vagrants, grifters, prostitutes, thieves, robbers, and more violent criminals crowded the narrow streets.

No town could have reached Mexia's state of lawlessness without political graft. Frank idly wondered if any of the local law officers or magistrates weren't on the take. He had no desire to bet a month's salary they would find an honest deputy or justice of the peace in the lot.

Barton asked, "Any ideas on how to handle the Winter Garden and the Chicken Farm?"

"Yes, sir," Frank said. "The quickest and best way in is going to be with a straight assault. A military-style raid."

Barton nodded solemnly. "That's how I had it figured. Hit them fast and hard, maybe we won't have any of our people or civilians hurt. Break up the tables and booze and burn the buildings."

"General, I had in mind something different," Frank said. "Those buildings are fortresses. They've been protecting the bad guys. We might as well make use of the Winter Garden as a headquarters base to finish the cleanup."

"Good idea, Frank. Let's get it moving." Barton glanced at the calendar. "We'll hit them on the seventh. Simultaneous raids. If it suits you, take half the men to the Winter Garden. Hickman can take the others to raid the Chicken Farm."

Mexia
January 7, 1922

Frank Hamer checked the loads in Old Lucky and glanced at the determined faces of the men gathered around half a dozen vehicles.

He hoped he could still count the same number of good guys after this was over. Hitting the two fortified gaming houses and saloons represented a considerable risk. Yet the enforcers had the element of surprise working for them; the strongholds were probably the last places the bad men expected to be raided.

The two structures, specially built outside Mexia for gambling and liquor sales—with, Frank knew, organized crime money—were more like forts than pleasure halls.

Armed guards watched over the roads, patrons frisked for weapons when they entered. Other guards, armed with shotguns, machine guns, or rifles, watched over the main gaming halls from specially built catwalks or balconies.

Tom Hickman and his group faced the more formidable of the two challenges. The Chicken Farm boasted prisonlike watchtowers on the walls, with elaborate trapdoors and escape tunnels designed to let patrons get away in case of raids.

"Ready, Tom?" Frank asked casually.

"Boots and saddles, Cap," said Hickman, the wiry lawman who favored bow ties and western hats with his business suit. "Let's go get 'em."

Frank checked his watch as the call of the nighthawk reached his ears.

Right on schedule. The signal meant Murphy and Olson had taken the two sentries on the road leading to the Winter Garden. Five other Rangers would be in position by now behind the gambling palace, ready to move when Frank's men stormed the front. He had no way of knowing how Tom Hickman's group fared at the Chicken Farm, but he knew Hickman. Tom would hold up his end of the operation.

Frank loosened Old Lucky in its holster. He would leave the Remington rifle in the car. A long gun likely would just get in the way once they were inside the gaming hall. The .45 revolver was more than adequate for the job at hand, and he carried a semiauto pistol in an opposite side belt holster. He nodded to his men.

"Let's go put some people out of business. Watch the guards on the catwalks. If there's any trouble, it'll come from them. Don't shoot any civilians unless you have to."

Moments later Frank braked the Ford sedan to a stop before the Winter Garden and, still behind the wheel, gestured to the two bulky men standing guard at the front door. The guards exchanged puzzled glances, then walked to the car—and found themselves looking down the bore of the .45 in Frank's hand.

"I'm Frank Hamer and you're under arrest," Frank said.

Disarming and cuffing the two men took only seconds. Frank led the way as the lawmen strode through the front door. The raucous whoops of joy and moans of despair from gamblers and drunks assaulted his ears. There wasn't a seat at a gaming table anywhere that wasn't occupied. The long bar where drinks were openly served was packed, customers standing shoulder to shoulder. Four guards armed with Thompson submachine guns prowled the catwalks that over-looked the crowded floor.

"Texas Rangers!" Frank bellowed over the hubbub. "You're all under arrest!"

A split second of stunned silence followed the call. Then a burly man on a balcony at the far end of the hall swung his machine gun toward the officers. A Ranger's bullet put him down. A second man got off a three-round burst before half a dozen slugs tore into him. The other guards abruptly lost their will to fight; they dropped their weapons to the floor and raised their hands.

The stampede of patrons toward the back door ended abruptly as the rearguard Rangers moved inside. The crowd milled for a moment, then gathered, subdued and confused, in the center of the gaming hall. The raid was over within minutes.

"Thought it might be tougher than this, Captain," a Ranger at Frank's side said. "But now we got a problem. Where are we going to put all these people?"

"We'll find a place, Sergeant," Frank said.

One of the gamblers, a paunchy man in an expensive busi-ness suit, blustered, "You can't arrest us! We weren't doing anything wrong!"

"Gambling and drinking is against the law, friend. You're going to jail with everybody else."

The bluster turned to a whine. "But—my business—my family—I'll be ruined. . . ."

"You should have thought of that first."

Sweat pooled beneath the chins of the fat man in the suit. "Look, mister, I've got money—let me walk out of here and I'll give you a thousand—"

"Add attempted bribery of a peace officer to the charges on this one," Frank said to the sergeant. "All right, folks," he called out, "this party's over. Line up, give your names to the sergeant here—politely, if you please—and we'll leave it up to a judge whether you get jail terms or fines.''

Frank ignored the wails of protest. He made a quick tour of the Winter Garden and grunted in satisfaction. It would make a fine headquarters base for the cleanup of Mexia. He picked up a phone and asked the operator to ring the Chicken Farm.

Tom Hickman answered in person.

"How'd it go over there, Tom?"

"No problem, Frank. Had to shoot our way in, but we've got it secured. Some pretty unhappy folks here, though."

"Casualties?"

"Nobody hurt except the bad guys." Hickman sounded chipper. "Four of them decided to fight. Bad decision. Two dead, two wounded. None of our men hurt, no civilians down. You?"

"Two men killed. They weren't ours. Let's wrap it up."

Frank stood outside the Winter Garden amid a stack of gambling equipment that would have filled a sizable barn, and row after row of liquor bottles, as newspaper photographers from across the state snapped pictures.

He left Adjutant General Barton to handle the reporters and shrugged off questions directed to him personally. It took a lot of shrugging. The Mexia raids would make the front pages and radio newscasts throughout Texas and much of the nation. Frank still didn't want personal publicity, but he didn't mind word getting out that the Rangers were serious when it came to bootleg whiskey and gambling.

Already, roads leading out of Mexia were crowded with prostitutes, gamblers, muggers, bootleggers, and others who wanted no part of Hamer's Rangers.

The raids on the two establishments netted almost seven hundred quarts of whiskey and a stash of narcotics big enough to keep most of Texas in a stupor for days. The stack of confiscated weapons would have outfitted a company of Rangers.

The photographers had all but exhausted their supply of film by the time axes, sledges, and the ever-reliable match disposed of the confiscated gaming equipment and booze.

Frank still wasn't satisfied. He knew it would take more

than the Winter Garden and Chicken Farm raids to douse
Mexia's thirst for gambling and liquor. There was plenty of
work yet to be done. And he was running out of places to
keep people locked up—even those who faced only fines for
possession and consumption, or participating in games of
chance.

The rumor making the rounds, and generally accepted as
fact, was that twenty percent of Mexia's population was in
jail or under bond within seventy-two hours after the Rangers
rode into town. The figure was a bit exaggerated, but Frank
made no effort to correct the rumor. That wasn't his job.

And, he suspected, the job was about to get tougher. . . .

January 25, 1922

Frank and Tom Hickman glared in disgust at the fervent
"prayer meeting" going on in a small rural church chapel
two miles outside of town.

The "minister" was a known gambling boss and bootlegger; his "congregation" fell somewhat short of devoutly rev-
erent. Until an hour ago, the "church" had been a gaming
hall and open bar. Now not a hint existed of any illegal activity.

"Brother Hamer," the smug bootlegger called from the
pulpit, "come join us in singing 'Shall We Gather at the
River?' I'm sure you must know the words."

Frank turned on a heel and strode out into the chill morning
air. The north wind smelled like rain, but that wasn't the only
odor in Frank's nostrils.

"Wonder who tipped them off?" Hickman asked bitterly.

Frank shrugged. "Could have been anybody. Lord knows
there's enough local officials on the take here."

Hickman grunted his agreement. "It's like pouring water
up a rope," he said, disgusted. "When we do actually manage
to get a search warrant, by the time we get there, either the
place is deserted or there's a harmless community gathering
going on. What are we going to do about it, Cap?"

"Find a telephone," Frank said.

An hour later, Frank had Governor Pat Neff on the line.

". . . And that's what we're up against, sir," Frank concluded. "The way things are now, we're butting a stump. And besides not being able to get search warrants, I've got a third of my men tied up guarding prisoners. We could use some help."

The voice on the other end of the line was firm though the static of a bad connection. "I'll take care of it, Frank. Hang on a few days. The cavalry will be on the way soon."

February 3, 1922

Frank Hamer allowed himself a slight smile.

Neff had made good on his promise. The cavalry had arrived in the form of the National Guard a day after the governor declared martial law in Mexia.

Commanding General Jacob F. Wolters wasted no time in turning the Winter Garden into a prison camp. Less than two hours after the Guard's arrival, Major Chester Machen had convened a military court to question the prisoners. Armed patrols were ready to move out on the streets to back up any Rangers who might need reinforcements.

"Well, Cap," Tom Hickman said, "looks like we're back in business. Where do we start being lawmen instead of jailers again?"

Frank ground out his cigarette with a heel and smiled. "How about city hall and the county courthouse?"

"Sounds good to me."

Fifteen minutes later Frank strode into the office of a justice of the peace.

"You're under arrest, judge," Frank said.

The man came halfway out of his chair. "What the hell are you talking about, Hamer?"

"I'm talking about official corruption, participating in organized criminal operations, owning a share of an illicit gambling and bootlegging operation. That's for starters. I'll come up with others."

The judge sat down, his shoulders slumped. "It's over, isn't it?"

"For you, yes," Frank said. "And for other crooked officials in town. Mexia's going to be needing new deputies and magistrates. Come along now. There's a special spot reserved for you in the National Guard prison camp outside town."

March 1922

Frank put his signature to the last of the mound of paperwork on his desk, leaned back, and sighed in contentment.

The howling wolf that had been Mexia was a meek puppy again.

Over six hundred arrests were on the Rangers' logbook. Mexia's population had been reduced by some three thousand souls, male and female, who had accepted the Rangers' sincere invitation to leave town.

There were twenty-seven fewer stills, more than nine thousand quarts of bootleg liquor had been destroyed, fifty-three stolen cars recovered, a Black Hand narcotics operation broken up. The largest amount of gambling equipment in history had gone up in flames or fallen to the ax and sledge.

Not a bad month's work, even by Texas Ranger standards, he thought. A few more days and he'd be on his way back to Austin.

"Cap?" Tom Hickman stood at the door.

"Yes, Tom?"

"Ready to have some fun? The soldiers don't believe you're as good a rifle shot as they've heard, so I put down a little side bet that you can break a hundred butter dishes in the air with that pear-burner of yours. We'll use the dishes from the raids as targets."

The first genuine smile in days lifted Frank's lips. "Sounds good to me. Need to get some practice in, anyway."

Two soldiers took turns tossing three-inch butter dishes into the air. Frank ran over a hundred straight targets without a miss from his .25 Remington autoloader before the bettors called enough and settled up.

Frank stowed the Remington in his car and lifted an eyebrow at Hickman. "Who was the fellow taking moving pictures while I was shooting?"

Hickman shrugged. The expression seemed feigned to

Frank. "Some fellow out of Dallas. Probably got word you'd be shooting and came down to see if you were as good as he'd heard."

Frank let it slide. If somebody wanted to drive that far to watch a man shoot a rifle, that was his business. Besides, he had to pack. He offered a hand to Hickman.

"I'm going back to Austin tomorrow, Tom. Our business here's finished."

"I suppose it is, at that," Hickman said with a quick grin. "A thirsty man couldn't buy a pint within miles of Mexia now. What's next for you?"

Frank said, "Thought I might look for a house."

Austin
June 1922

"Yes, dear," Frank said into the telephone, "anytime you're ready, just let me know."

Lee Shannon glanced up from the chair beside Frank's desk. "Another 'honey-do' Captain? I get a lot of those from my wife, too."

"Oh, that wasn't Gladys. Just another death threat."

Shannon put down the case folder he had been studying. "How many does that make?"

Frank shrugged. "I don't know. I quit counting them weeks ago. It's like Shakespeare said, a tempest in a teapot, full of sound and fury, signifying nothing."

"I don't know about the signifying-nothing part, Frank, but there's potential sound and fury in those calls and that stack of unsigned letters. As the Bible says, 'Thou shalt watch thy back.' "

"What verse is that from?"

"Book of Shannon, verse two. Didn't know you read the Bard."

"Haven't had much reading time, but that was one of the books Gladys bought when we moved into the new house." The thought of the hilltop home on Riverside Drive warmed Frank.

The house was no mansion, but it was big enough for the

Hamers and a menagerie of family pets. The house was solidly built and located in a nice neighborhood with good schools. Most important, they could afford the payments on his salary. He had worried about getting the down-payment money together, only to find out he wasted his time fretting. Gladys had squirreled back enough to cover both the down-payment and the moving costs. She seemed to stay a jump ahead of him in a lot of areas, Frank thought fondly.

His only regret was that his horseback Ranger days were over. The riding boots and coarse brush-country clothes were back in the storage closet, replaced by walking shoes and business suits; his saddle, spurs, chaps, and other horseman's tack were also in storage.

Old Lucky was still on his hip, though, and he did keep his favorite hat, even though Gladys thought he should buy a new Stetson. The hat and the handgun were broken in just right. He couldn't part with either of them. He forced his attention back to the job at hand—or in this case, jobs.

There were plenty of cases still hanging fire to keep the Rangers busy until they all retired. One thing about Texas. It had an adequate supply of criminals, homegrown and imported.

Shannon leaned back in his chair. "What's next, Cap?"

Frank tapped a pile of folders and letters on his desk. "Take your pick, Lee—" The phone buzzed again. Frank picked up, listened for a few minutes, interrupted only for an occasional question, then replaced the receiver.

"There's an answer as to what's next," he said. "The political mess in Corpus has finally reached the murder stage."

"What happened?"

Frank briefed Shannon on the new developments. The sheriff, the honcho of one faction, had pistol-whipped grocer G. E. Warren, the opposition leader, in the man's store. In front of his wife. A neighbor, Fred Roberts, had been gunned down when he tried to put a stop to it. Moments after the killing a deputy and a constable ran up and, with the sheriff's help, shot up Warren's store.

"It's a wonder nobody else has been killed so far, but that could change at any minute, Governor Ross said," Frank concluded. "That was him on the phone."

Shannon lifted an eyebrow. "So that boil's finally come to a head. Arrests?"

"No. Warrants have been issued, but nobody in Corpus Christi has the guts to serve them. Ross wants us to handle it. Get a couple of good men who aren't tied up on something else, Lee. Barnes and Westphall should be available. We'll move out in an hour."

Frank reached for the phone. Gladys would understand that rearranging the furniture would have to wait a day or so.

Chapter Sixteen

Corpus Christi
June 1922

FRANK STOOD ON the street leading to the Nueces County Courthouse and glanced over the crowd gathered a nervously respectful distance from the building.

"Captain Hamer!" An aging constable forced his way through the crowd. A murmur went up from the ranks at the call of Frank's name. The constable, sweaty and disheveled, limped to Frank and the three Rangers with him. "We're mighty glad to see you and your men, Captain. We've got us a standoff here. Nobody knows what to do about it."

Frank's gaze settled on more than twenty men who stood before the courthouse, rifles or shotguns in hand. He recognized a few of the men, either from personal experience or description. They were allies of the sheriff's faction, part of the machine that controlled Corpus Christi's politics and most of the city's shady deals.

"There's a dozen more inside." The constable's prominent Adam's apple bobbed. "In the main courtroom. All of 'em armed to the teeth. There's no way to get in there without a bunch of people getting killed."

Frank stood silently for a moment, stared toward the mob

on the courthouse steps, then turned to the constable. "You have the warrants?"

"Yes, sir."

"Hand them over."

Frank took the warrants from the constable. "What you want me to do, Captain?" the aged officer asked.

"Stay out of the way." Frank turned to his men. "Wait here. I'll go get them."

Shannon asked worriedly, "Sure you don't need some help, Captain?"

"Not with this bunch, Lee." Frank strode forward, his revolver holstered, his gaze straight ahead. The mob of armed men stirred, exchanged worried glances—and meekly stepped aside.

Frank went up the steps into the courthouse, kicked open the double doors to the courtroom, and strode inside. A dozen men stood with rifles, shotguns, and handguns pointed at him. For several heartbeats Frank glared at the three wanted men who stood in the center of the half circle of weapons.

"I'm Frank Hamer, Texas Ranger," he said. "I have warrants for the arrest of the men involved in the murder of Fred Roberts. The rest of you put up those guns and get the hell out of here."

Frank ignored the other men, strode up to the sheriff, deputy, and the constable, and started reading the warrants aloud. At the edge of his vision he saw a shotgun-wielding man swallow nervously, glance about, then lower his weapon and head for the door. Others followed. By the time Frank finished reading the warrants, the courtroom was deserted except for himself and the three suspects.

Five minutes later Frank led the handcuffed prisoners out the front door toward the jail adjacent to the courthouse. Not a single gunman from the mobs outside or inside the courtroom remained in sight.

"All right, folks, it's over," Lee Shannon called over the mutters of the astonished crowd. "Go home."

As he passed a small knot of observers Frank overheard one man say, "My God, I've never seen anything like that, one man bracing a mob and just staring them down. Why didn't they open up on him?"

"One good reason," the witness's companion said. "That's Frank Hamer. He ain't no man to mess with"—he emphasized the comment with a squirt of tobacco juice— "and them boys knowed it."

Frank looked up from behind the desk in the sheriff's office, which he had commandeered because the county's major law-enforcement officer, chief deputy, and one constable wouldn't be using any part of it except the cells for a while, as Lee Shannon came in the door.

"All quiet around town, Lee?"

Shannon nodded. "Like a herd of church mice. Not even a fistfight. See the paper today, Frank?" The Ranger held out a copy of the local newspaper.

Frank shook his head. "Too busy catching up on paper-work. Found a dozen warrants the sheriff never bothered to serve, some of them months old and most of them aimed at his political cronies. Classic example of selective law enforce-ment. We'll set that straight."

"You got good reviews on the courthouse case, Captain," Shannon said. "I'll just hit the high spots. The paper says 'they'—meaning the gents in the courthouse mobs—'came near dying when Captain Frank Hamer of Austin showed up on the scene. Hamer is the man they all dreaded, and when they got here they all got good.'—" He paused for a breath, then continued, " 'This is all that saved the day as well as preventing a wholesale killing, which was so imminent that it did not look inviting. But they took to the tall timber when the Rangers made their appearance.' "

Frank sniffed. "A bit flowery, I'd say. Coffee's hot."

Shannon tossed the paper on a chair and poured himself a cup. "Hell, Cap, I was impressed myself. What if they'd opened up on you?"

"They'd have killed me. But it was no big deal. Their kind can't face a man who isn't afraid of them." Frank plucked a telegram from the desk and handed it to Shannon. "Gover-nor's asked us to stick around for a spell and make sure no-body doctors the ballots or tries to intimidate the voters."

Shannon scanned the telegram and grunted. "Only thing worse than a crooked politician is a rigged election. We'll make sure the honest voters get a fair chance to take apart the sheriff's political machine, then head on back to Austin.''

Austin
October 1922

Frank leaned back in his chair, flexed the stiffness from his shoulders, and studied Lee Shannon, who was hunched over his own stack of paperwork.

The Ranger looked like he hadn't slept in three days, which was most likely the case, Frank thought. He was feeling the miles himself.

''Guess that wraps up all the loose ends up on the Ganders Slough case, Lee.''

''All done.'' The agent rubbed his bloodshot eyes. ''Gets tiresome after a while, taming these oil-boom towns. Luling and Caldwell County are now cleaner than a bride-to-be's nightie. What's next on the list?''

''Next up is that we go home and get some rest, amigo.'' The phone rang. Frank jerked a thumb toward the door. ''You'd better go now, before I answer that.''

He waited until Shannon reached the door, then picked up the phone. ''Frank Hamer.''

''Captain,'' the voice on the line said, ''this is Petmecky's. We have a package here for you.''

Frank frowned. He hadn't ordered anything recently from the sporting-goods-and-hardware store, but maybe Gladys or one of the Rangers had. ''I'm headed down that way, anyhow. I'll pick it up in a few minutes,'' he said.

The namesake owner of Petmecky's wore a broad grin as Frank opened the long box and whistled silently. Inside, carefully packed, nested a .30-caliber Remington Model 8F semiautomatic rifle, heavily engraved and gold-inlaid with scenes from Frank's Ranger career. Frank fondled the rifle for a moment in silence, a pleased half smile on his lips.

''Wonder who's behind this?'' he finally asked.

Petmecky chuckled. ''The Remington Arms folks. That Dallas fellow who watched you break all those plates up in Mexia shot some movie film and sent it to Remington. It got their attention for sure, especially when they read that Dallas newspaper story about how you preferred Remington rifles. So they made up this presentation model for you.'' The store owner leaned over to study the fine engraving and rich figured wood of the stock. ''Too pretty a piece of work to shoot, Frank.''

Frank shouldered the weapon a couple of times, getting the feel of it, then lowered the rifle. ''Too nice to carry through the mud and brush hunting bad men. But this one's not just going up on the wall. Feels like it's got many a deer inside it.''

''It'll make a nice match for that silver-plated and engraved .45 Colt the folks in Corpus gave you last July,'' Petmecky said.

Frank shook his head. ''As long as I've got Old Lucky, I'm not lugging that fancy piece of hardware. Whoever heard of a lawman packing a silver pistol, anyway?''

''Tom Mix does. Heard from him lately?''

''We keep up with each other.''

''He still trying to make a movie star out of you?''

''I think he's about given up on that.'' Frank handed the rifle to the store owner. ''Hold on to this for me for a bit. I have to go see a couple of men over at the hotel. I'll pick this up on the way home. Set me aside a couple of boxes of cartridges for it, and I'll see what that baby will do first chance I get.'' He turned toward the door, then paused. ''By the way, did those brass door hinges come in?''

''Got them right here. Still working on the house?''

''And the sooner I can get those doors hung the way Gladys wants them, the sooner I can go shoot.'' He left the store and strode to the nearby hotel.

''Allbright and Simpson still here?'' Frank asked the bored clerk.

The man waved a hand. ''Upstairs. Second room on the left.'' His eyes widened a bit. ''Gonna be any shooting?''

''Hadn't planned on it,'' Frank said. ''Guess it depends on them.''

The door was unlocked. Frank nudged it open a crack with his toe and stood outside, listening. The voices inside were clearly audible.

". . . Couple cans of gas around the stove and back door'll do the trick. That ought to get the message out to those damn Bible-thumpin' prohibitionists."

So, Frank thought, torching the San Saba Baptist Church wasn't enough in itself to teach the preachers that sermons supporting the liquor ban weren't healthy topics. These two planned to take their own brand of sermon to another congregation.

He pushed the door open. Two men, in shirtsleeves and suspenders, sat at a small table in a corner of the room. A .45 automatic nested in a shoulder holster beneath the nearest man's armpit.

"All right, gentlemen, you're under arrest," Frank said.

The men glanced up, startled; the one with the shoulder holster edged his hand toward the weapon. Frank pinned the would-be shooter with a hard glare and silently shook his head. The man's hand fell away.

"What's the charge?"

"Arson. Specifically, burning the San Saba Baptist Church." Frank stepped forward and plucked the weapon from the shoulder holster. "You boys aren't as smart as you think. I've got enough evidence to put you away for a long time. Let's go."

Christmas Eve, 1922

"I think the red one should go here, son," Frank said with a smile at Frank Jr. "What do you think?"

Young Frank, now going on age five, pondered the lower limb of the mostly decorated Christmas tree studiously, then shook his head.

"Better here," he said as he clipped the hanger of the red pear-shaped ornament on a limb almost as high as he could reach.

"By golly, son, I do believe you're right," Frank said. "It does look a lot nicer there."

"The boy has a better eye for composition than you, dear," Gladys said with a chuckle, her dipper poised above the punch bowl. "More cider for my two favorite men?"

Frank shook his head. "I'm sloshing now, honey. And we're almost finished with the tree. When's Beverly due back?"

"Before eleven-thirty, or her date's in big trouble with a big, mean, tough Texas Ranger captain's wife."

"We'll save an ornament or two for her, then—maybe the angel to top off the tree." Frank picked up his son with an exaggerated grunt of effort. "Boy, you're getting to weigh as much as a yearling colt." He hoisted the youngster to let Frank Jr. put a silver bell ornament on a high limb. Then he lowered his son, patted him fondly on the rump, and said, "Okay, off to bed, like Billy. Santa won't come if there's young ones awake and about, you know."

Frank could tell from the excitement sparkling in the boy's eyes that his son wasn't going to get to sleep right away. The thought pleased him. Youngsters were allowed some fidgets on Christmas Eve. Even the youngest, Billy, past two and coming up on age three, probably would be up and down half a dozen times before dawn.

He settled into his favorite chair, lit a cigarette, and admired the tree as Gladys put Frank Jr. to bed. It was the most contentment he had had in months, maybe years. Vacation time at Christmas and a family to share the holiday with. A man couldn't ask for more.

Gladys came back into the room as Frank stubbed out his smoke. "Got them both down for the night, honey?"

"Not likely," Gladys said with a smile. She settled into Frank's lap, her arms about his neck. "But we just might be able to sneak in a little playtime before one or both pop up again."

She was still in his lap when a knock sounded on the door a bit after eleven. "Oh, good," she said. "Beverly's home early." She stood, straightened her skirt, strode to the door, flung it open, and yelped, "Boo!"—to the middle button of a tall young man's jacket.

After a moment's surprised silence the young man said, "I want Hamer."

Still smiling, Gladys called to her husband, "Someone to see you, dear."

Frank strode to the door and extended a hand. "I'm Frank Hamer."

The tall man ignored the offered handshake. "Could I see you outside, Hamer?" he muttered.

Frank stared at the man for a moment, but did not move from the open doorway.

The man's right hand whipped from behind his leg; light glinted from the metal of the gun in his hand. Before the weapon could fall into line, Frank swept his left hand from his side and hammered the would-be assassin alongside the head. The blow knocked the man head over heels from the porch and tumbled him down the steep front steps. The gun arched away and dropped into the hedge at the side of the house.

Gladys was at Frank's side before the man stopped rolling, his Colt .45 automatic in her hand. The would-be attacker scrambled to his feet and started running. Frank ignored the offered pistol, picked up a milk bottle from the porch and cocked his arm to hurl it after the fleeing gunman.

He never loosed the milk-bottle missile. The tall man raced around the corner and disappeared from view.

As Frank and Gladys stepped back inside, young Billy came tearing from his upstairs bedroom. "Is it Santa Claus? Is it Santa?" the boy yelped excitedly.

"No, honey, it isn't Santa," Gladys said. "It was just a man who *thought* he wanted to see your father. Go back to bed now, and give Santa a chance to come."

Gladys waited until the disappointed boy went back into his room, then said, "What now, Frank?"

Frank patted her arm. "Finish decorating and wrap some gifts. We wouldn't want Santa to find things half-done around here, would we?"

January 1925

Frank tossed the daily newspaper to the floor in disgust and reached for pen and paper.

"What's up, Captain?" Lee Shannon asked. "You look mad enough to whip a rooster and spot him five pecks."

Frank snorted. "The Fergusons are in. So I'm out."

"Resigning again?"

"I'm keeping my commission, just going on inactive status at least until after the next election," Frank said. "I'm not going to lend a hand while Ma and Pa Ferguson gut the Ranger force again. I've spent too much time, sweat, and blood putting it back where a man can be proud to call himself a Ranger."

Shannon sat across from Frank, sipped at his coffee, and shook his head. "I can't believe the voters of Texas. Ferguson gets impeached and can't hold office, so he puts his wife up for the job, she gets elected, and the old man's back in charge. Running things from behind his wife's skirt."

"He can damn well run things without me."

"I don't know, Frank," Shannon said. "I doubt it's going to be that easy for you to resign this time."

Frank put down his pen. "What are you talking about?"

"Public opinion." Shannon downed the last swallow of coffee and winced. "You've done a fine job here, Captain— except for making coffee. It still tastes like pine tar. Anyhow, I don't think honest Texans are going to let you ride off into the sunset this time. You've done such a good job they won't let you quit."

"Hogwash." Frank scribbled the last few lines of the letter of resignation and signed it. "I'm out, Lee. And if you don't want to work for some drugstore-cowboy political fanny kisser, you'll be right behind me."

Shannon refilled his coffee cup. "I would be, but I doubt you'll be gone long, Frank. The newspapers will raise hell, the voters will raise hell, and the Fergusons will listen this time."

"Don't count on it," Frank said glumly. "I'm going home for a few days, then hunt for a job. Maybe Harrison needs another agent down at customs."

"Where's your brother stationed now?"

"Del Rio." Frank picked up the box that held his few personal belongings and reached for his hat. "You know where the active case files are, Lee. I'll let you know where to get in touch with me when I land another job."

He strode from the Ranger state headquarters office into a biting north wind.

February 1925

Frank felt a lot less at home in the governor's office than he had the last time he'd been here and Pat Neff had sat in the chair behind the big desk.

Miriam A. "Ma" Ferguson, the new Texas governor, reminded Frank of a woman in need of an enema. Her close-cropped hair, wide-set eyes, prominent nose, and lips pulled into a thin line gave her the look of a mannish schoolmarm.

Frank had never cared for machine politics, especially where the Fergusons were involved. He wouldn't have been here now if Lee Shannon, Manny Gault, and most everybody else in the Ranger service—and even former governor Pat Neff—hadn't been on him like ticks on a brush-country cow to reconsider his resignation.

"Captain Hamer, I must admit I'm somewhat astounded at the outpouring of popular support you've garnered," Ma Ferguson said. "I know we've had our political differences in the past. I'm asking you to please set them aside for the good of Texas and the Rangers."

And the votes it would save for the Ferguson machine, Frank thought bitterly. He shook his head.

"I'm sorry, Governor, but I can't—"

She raised a hand. "Hear me out, Captain. You have my promise, my word—and that of my husband—that we will not compromise your position. We will force no hirings or firings upon you. You will be the boss where the Rangers are concerned."

Frank didn't believe a word of it. He couldn't bring himself to trust a Ferguson, be it Ma, Pa, or their house cat. At the same time he recognized a peace offering. He figured it to be an empty one, a stalling tactic. But she had made a point that pricked him. If he left the force, every good man carrying a Ranger badge wouldn't be far behind. The wholesale appointment of political lackeys and heinie-wipers would begin. And

that would doom the police agency Frank loved, as sure as a
.45 slug dropped a jackrabbit.

If he stayed in command, maybe he could slow down the
cancer that threatened to kill the Texas Rangers. He wasn't
naive enough to think he could stop it. But he could slow its
growth.

"Furthermore, Captain Hamer, you have my personal
pledge that the adjutant general's office will be instructed to
supply your men with everything they need to keep the peace.
Can we let bygones be bygones, in the best interest of Texas?
Will you rescind your resignation and remain in command?"

Frank made a decision he fully expected to regret.

"Yes. With those assurances, Governor, I'll take back my
resignation."

"Excellent, excellent," Ma Ferguson said, gushing. She
rose and offered him a hand. It was a large hand, and surprisingly strong. Probably got that way, Frank thought, from
squeezing all the graft money.

The next day, Frank strode back into his office, the un-
packed box of personal belongings under one arm.

Shannon lifted an eyebrow. "Talked you into it, did she?"

"Lee," Frank said, "I don't know if you've got a crystal
ball or a seer woman for a spinster aunt somewhere, but yes,
dammit, I'm back. I'm dumb, but I'm back. For now, anyway." He plopped the box onto his desk and glanced around.
Most of the headquarters staff and several field agents had
wandered in, all grinning like possums in persimmon trees.

"All right, gents," Frank said, "vacation's over. Get off
your butts and let's go catch some bad guys. Who's first on
the list?"

Llano
March 1927

Frank's fondness for chili kept him coming back to the small
café in Llano, where the cook never skimped on the grease.
It was passable chili, but could have used a touch more jalapeño to give it a Del Rio–style kick.

As he ate, Frank kept turning his latest problem over in his mind, hoping the constant stirring would bubble up an answer.

One of the biggest automobile-theft rings in the country was operating in central Texas, and his agents had been unable to pinpoint the ringleaders. Frank called in his field troops and took over the hunt alone.

A week's work brought him to Llano. A few more days of sniffing around and following leads from informants gave him the overall picture, including names of the gang leaders and their top thieves. But he wanted more than just the big dogs. An automobile was a major investment, and Frank was a firm believer in returning stolen property to its rightful owner. That was the thorn on this bush.

"More coffee, honey?"

Frank shook off the blonde waitress's offer of a refill, swallowed a mouthful of chili, and said, "No, thanks. I've had my fill for now."

"Haven't seen you around town before the last few days," the blonde said with a smile, "but you look familiar, somehow. Where you from?"

"Austin."

The woman's lips twitched; a flicker that seemed to Frank one of recognition glinted in her blue-green eyes. "Just passing through, or looking to settle here? We've got a nice town."

Frank's lawman instinct kicked in. The blonde was asking a lot of questions, and he didn't think she was just looking for a better tip. He had noticed the blonde and another waitress studying him between hopping tables. Something was going on.

"I'm just working here awhile," Frank said pleasantly. "I expect to be moving on soon, but it is a nice town."

"Care for some pie when you're done with the chili? We have peach and apple today."

"No, thanks. Maybe tomorrow. Keep the chili hot."

"We'll do that for you." She turned away to refill another customer's cup. The café was all but deserted. Sounds carried well in the small room, which was to Frank's liking. He always kept his eyes and ears open when working on a case.

A man never knew when a snippet of eavesdropping might turn up a key lead.

He returned his attention to the car-theft problem. The operation itself was sophisticated, yet simple. Car thieves from across Texas and even some adjoining states brought stolen vehicles into Llano County, where there was no shortage of buyers. Auto dealers and private citizens bought the cars knowing full well they could not get a clear title to the vehicles. Frank had enough information now to break up the ring, but it wasn't enough. He had to find a way to persuade the dealers it would be to their advantage to return the stolen cars and eat the financial loss.

He scraped the last bit of chili from the bowl, emptied his coffee cup, and reached into his pocket for a cigarette. The pack had managed to get itself tangled around a telegram informing Frank that a saddle-theft operation had been broken in San Antonio. He glanced at the telegram, fished out his cigarette, and tucked the pack and paper back into his pocket.

A few tables away, the waitresses stood watching him and chatting. Frank heard the blonde half whisper, "I'd give ten bucks to know what's in that telegram."

Frank pretended he didn't hear a word. He paid his bill and went to work. Two hours and half a dozen discreet inquiries later, he found his key to the operation, confirmed by the town gossip.

The blonde waitress was the girlfriend of a car dealer who was one of the theft ring's biggest operators. The man's name was near the top of Frank's list. And he had thought of a way to get the word out to the right people.

He strode to the telegraph office, ripped a blank message sheet from the pad, and wrote:

To Capt. Frank A. Hamer, Llano, Texas

Do not prosecute innocent purchasers who turn in cars. Arrest all others for complicity and hold in jail for criminal prosecution.

He signed the paper, "Aldrich, Adjutant-General."

An hour before the normal six o'clock supper rush, Frank

was back in the café, pleased to see that the blonde waitress hadn't left for the day. The fake telegram nested in a fold of his handkerchief.

Frank nodded a greeting to the waitress, took a seat at a table, ordered the special, and took his time over the meal. He finished his third cup of coffee and a slice of peach pie, put a dime tip on the table, and rose. He reached into his pocket for the handkerchief, blew his nose, and pretended not to notice as the "telegram" folded inside the cloth dropped to the floor.

As he paid his bill he saw the blonde hurry to the table, crouch, and scoop the phony telegram. She pounced on that like a duck on a june bug, he thought.

The next morning a knock sounded on Frank's door before he had a chance to go for coffee. A man stood in the hall.

"Yes?"

"Captain Hamer, I understand you're looking for some stolen cars out here," the man said.

"Yes, I am."

"Well, I think the car I bought several weeks ago may have been stolen. It's parked out front. I'd like to turn it over to you."

"Come on in," Frank said, "and I'll give you a receipt."

By midmorning, Frank had managed to grab a couple of cups of coffee in between accepting the keys to a steady flow of "this may have been stolen" cars. There were no parking places left along the street outside by noon. By nightfall, a vacant lot half a block away was almost full of recovered vehicles.

The waitress had certainly done a good job spreading the word, Frank thought as he signed a receipt for the fifty-second automobile of the day.

In addition to the buyers who brought in cars were several men on Hamer's suspect list, thieves and dealers who hoped to avoid prosecution by giving up their unsold vehicles. Frank gave no indication that they were under investigation; he gave them receipts and let them go, at least for now. He could hit them with warrants later.

By the time he made it back to his hotel room shortly before midnight, Frank had every pocket full of keys, almost

sixty cars to be returned to their rightful owners, and had to
send for another receipt book. Tracing the cars and notifying
the owners would take a few days, but there would be a lot
of folks out there happy to see their vehicles again.

Not bad for a day's work, he thought. "And bless the blond
girlfriends of the world," he murmured as he prepared for
bed.

CHAPTER SEVENTEEN

Borger, Texas
September 1927

"FRANK, I THOUGHT we'd cleaned this place up once al-
ready," Tom Hickman said as Frank nosed the unmarked
Ford into a parking space half a block from the Hutchinson
County Courthouse.

"Guess it didn't take," Frank said. "Like I told the governor, I've never seen a more corrupt town than Borger. What
they say is right—'Borger by day, Booger by night.' I think
it's even worse now than it was last spring."

Hickman surveyed the main street, crowded with oilfield
workers, speculators, gamblers, assorted thieves, drunks, and
shoulder hitters who made their livings beating up on anybody who got in the way of illicit profits. Pickups, oilfield
trucks, and automobiles jockeyed for space on the street. The
blare of car horns and shouted curses all but drowned the
music from bawdy houses and gambling dens. A dice game
went on in plain sight in an alley, the whoops and shouts of
crapshooters adding to the general commotion.

It seemed to Frank that every other building or tent they
had closed in the spring cleanup was back in business as a
speakeasy, gambling den, open bar, whorehouse—or all in
one, if the proprietor wanted more than one piece of the
boomtown pie. Once again, the oil strike had turned a little
one-horse Texas Panhandle town into a crime lord's dream

as forty thousand seekers of wealth and recreation flooded into Borger.

"Afraid you're right," Hickman said. "It's worse than Mexia. I thought we'd accomplished something here last time. Looks like I was wrong."

"We'll get it right this time, Tom." Frank shifted Old Lucky into a more comfortable position on his hip and tucked a spare automatic into its opposite-side holster. "At least we know who we're dealing with this time. Every mother's son we arrested in the spring seems to be back in town."

Hickman pulled his own .45 auto, racked the slide to chamber a cartridge, and said, "I don't know about you, Cap, but I'm getting just a tad tired of these oil-boom towns. Well, what's your pleasure? Get started now, or wait for the cavalry?"

Frank reached for the door handle. "The other boys are here—that's Jackson's car parked down the street. Might as well get to work."

"Same plan we talked over?"

"Yep. Start at the courthouse. That's where it all begins anyway, and we can get a lot of horse apples shoveled up before Dan Moody sends in the Guard troops tomorrow."

"At least we've got a governor we can work with now," Hickman said. "Ma Ferguson sure wasn't much help."

Frank grunted in disgust. "Never expected her to be. And she sure didn't disappoint me at that. Let's go."

The next day, an "extra" edition of the Borger paper hit the streets.

MARTIAL LAW, the headline screamed in the biggest type available.

Governor Dan Moody had signed the declaration. Texas National Guard troops under the command of General Jacob Wolters, veterans of the Mexia cleanup campaign, were en route to Borger from Fort Worth. In the body of the proclamation, the newspaper quoted Moody as citing "a conspiracy between the officers of the law and law violators," adding that "affidavits have been secured to the passing of money to peace officers for protection."

Within two hours of the Guard's arrival, the Hutchinson County Courthouse had been converted into a command post for Ranger and Guard operations, and a court of inquiry convened. By nightfall, nearly all Borger's city and county officials were suspended and most of them in jail.

It was a start, Frank thought, and this time we'll do the job right.

Frank stood on the courthouse steps and studied the dusty main street of Borger. The whoops and yells of drunken gamblers and carousing oilfield workers were all but gone, replaced by the sounds of shattering glass and ripping wood as Rangers and troopers destroyed confiscated liquor and gambling equipment and tore the roofs from speakeasies and gambling joints. The tent operators had disappeared almost overnight after the Rangers came to town.

Frank turned and went back inside as yet another car bearing the *Amarillo Globe* sign on a front door came into view. He had better things to do than pose for more photographs and dodge interviews. Newspapers and wire services trumpeted the cleanup of Borger on a daily basis, giving Frank the credit in headlines that thundered, LAWLESS TOWN FEELS IRON GRASP OF NERVY TEXAS RANGER, and the like.

The news reports didn't exactly endear Frank to the corrupt citizens who still remained at large for lack of proof enough to seek arrest and indictment. Beneath the signs of outward progress, tensions ran even deeper than they had back in the spring after the first cleanup of Borger.

He read through the stack of letters from one day's mail, separating the death threats and fan mail from routine correspondence and official reports. It was a slow day, he thought; there were just three letters telling Frank Hamer he had only hours or days to live. But that didn't count the messages and notes forwarded from Austin, including one postmarked in Chicago that added Governor Dan Moody's name to the hit list.

"Well, Cap," Tom Hickman said as he stepped into the office, "looks like you've made the big time now. Word around town is that bookies are laying odds you won't live another thirty days."

Frank lifted an eyebrow. "You place a bet either way, Tom?"

Hickman shook his head and half smiled. "Now, Cap, you know gambling's illegal. Besides, we've got other things to worry about right now. For instance, what are we going to do with the prisoners? The jail's packed to the rafters and there are more coming in by the hour."

Frank strode to the window and stood for a moment, thinking, then turned to Hickman. "We'll set out a trotline."

"Trotline?"

Frank nodded. "Get one of those heavy, long drill-rig chains. String it from that stout tree by the courthouse to the lamppost twenty yards down the street. We'll cuff the prisoners and chain and padlock them to the trot line."

"That'd work," Hickman said with a wry grin. "They may not like the accommodations much, but they won't be going anywhere."

"I'll get word out that any legitimate lawman who wants to run our trotline for wanted men is welcome to do so. Could be a big catfish or two out there that we don't know about."

October 1927

New Mexico State Police Sergeant Dan Lighthorse worked his way down the "trotline," peering into the faces of those chained there. Lighthorse stopped before a burly, bearded man.

"I'd like to have this one, too, Captain Hamer," the sergeant said. "He's wanted for robbery and murder in my state."

"You're welcome to him, Sergeant," Frank said. "The heaviest charge we can come up with against him is robbing drunks. You can put him away a lot longer than Texas can."

Frank watched as Lighthorse and his deputy loaded the three suspects they had picked from the line into the black car with the New Mexico state symbol on the door.

Tom Hickman, standing at Frank's side, said, "Well, there go a couple more. And good riddance. By my count that makes a couple dozen big fish hooked on our trotline for other lawmen."

"What's our arrest total up to now?" Frank asked.

"Hundred and seventy. Fifty-nine either charged or held for further investigation." Hickman sighed. "I don't know about you, Cap, but I'm fed up with Borger. Again. I'll be glad to turn this operation over to somebody else and get back to Austin."

Frank said, "Me, too. It's been a long time since I've spent a night with my family." He glanced around. "I guess it's safe to say we've gentled this bronc again. Maybe this time it took."

Austin
November 1927

"Hey, Pancho," Manny Gault called from his desk across the room at Ranger headquarters, "you've made the papers again."

Frank winced. "More publicity. Lord, you'd think they'd turn the faucet off after a spell."

Gault strode to Frank's desk and handed him the copy of the *Austin American*. "Appears you've cost some gamblers more money, Cap," he said.

Frank glanced at the paper, then went back and read the single paragraph more closely, a faint smile tugging at his lips. It read:

Time Up

Bets made at Borger that Ranger Captain Frank Hamer would be "bumped off" in thirty days after his drastic cleanup of vice and liquor conditions there, have come due. Captain Hamer was informed by friends that he would be dead in thirty days after he went to Borger. . . .

Frank dropped the paper in a desk drawer and grinned at Gault. "Hope none of our boys had bets on the bad guys," he said.

February 1928

Frank stared in disgust and growing anger at the sign tacked onto the telephone pole beside the narrow road.

The Texas Bankers Association had gone too damn far this time. Protecting their assets was one thing.

Setting up a wholesale murder machine for profit was another. It had to end. . . .

BOOK THREE

BANKERS AND BANDITS

CHAPTER EIGHTEEN

Odessa, Texas
March 1928

"WHAT THE HELL do you mean, you won't issue warrants?" Frank struggled to control his rage as he stared at the man seated behind the heavy mahogany desk.

The judge leaned back in the overstuffed chair and steepled his fingers. "Captain Hamer, you can't expect me to issue papers for you to go around arresting police officers for doing their duty."

Frank bit back a string of bitter curses; anger and disgust sat heavy in his belly. He glared in disbelief at the judge.

"Two innocent men were murdered here. Set up and shot down like stray dogs, just for easy money. And you aren't going to do one damned thing about it?"

The judge's face reddened. "Captain Hamer, you're treading a thin line here. If you were to use that language and tone of voice to me in open court instead of here in my chambers, I would find you in contempt."

"You wouldn't have to look very damn hard to find me in contempt of *this* court—Your Honor." The honorific came out with a sarcasm Frank seldom used. But then, he'd seldom been this mad before.

The judge leaned forward, a sudden wariness in his gaze. "Look, Captain, I'm fully aware of what you suspect. But the facts of this case are that two outlaws were preparing to rob our bank. They were caught in the act by duly commissioned peace officers and concerned citizens, and were shot dead."

"Innocent men were shot. Those two fellows were no more professional bank robbers than I am."

"That's your opinion, Captain, and nothing more. Bank robbery is the fastest-growing industry in Texas these days.

If a few more robbers are killed in the commission of such crimes, perhaps others would think twice before trying the same thing. This is an open-and-shut case, and you've given me no evidence to the contrary that would hold water before a grand jury.''

''No evidence?'' Frank snorted in disgust. ''I've given you a strong enough case to crack a murder ring, judge. And you choose to ignore it—''

''Hamer, that's enough!'' the judge interrupted. ''I'll hear no more of these wild accusations from you! To use one of your own favorite phrases, you're butting your head against a stump.''

Frank rose, seething inside. ''No, sir, I am not butting my head against a stump. I am butting my head against the Texas Bankers Association and their custom-made murder machine.''

''That's a serious accusation.''

''And I'm serious about putting a stop to it.'' Frank grabbed his hat. ''One thing you *can* take to your bank, judge, is that I intend to keep butting that stump until the stump falls over. As far as I'm concerned, murder is murder, and no man is above the law. Even bankers, crooked peace officers—and judges.''

Frank stalked from the office and slammed the door behind him. He paused on the street outside the courthouse, chastising himself for losing his composure with the judge. An angry lawman made mistakes. Frank Hamer didn't like mistakes.

The March wind, still tinged with winter's bite, stirred dust eddies along Odessa's main street as Frank strode toward his hotel room. A poster tacked to the side of a building fluttered in the gusty breeze. Anger flooded back into Frank as he ripped the flyer from the wall. It read:

REWARD

FIVE THOUSAND DOLLARS FOR DEAD BANK ROBBERS

NOT ONE CENT FOR LIVE ONES

Frank shredded the poster distributed by the Texas Bankers Association, let the scraps scatter on the wind, and idly wondered how much of the association's money went into the campaign funds and pockets of elected officials like the judge.

He was headed into a war.

And this one was going to be just as bad, and probably worse, than the bootlegger battles and border bandit brawls. At least with booze runners and rustlers, the game was simple. Catch them in the act and teach them the errors of their ways.

Dealing with the Texas Bankers Association was going to be a different matter. That much money and power carried the wallop of a howitzer shell in this state. Yet a simple little .22 slug in the right place could stop a howitzer. He just had to find the right place to put the slug.

Frank could identify with the bankers' problem, but not their solution. The judge had been right on one count: bank robbery was now Texas's fastest-growing business. Corrupt local lawmen and courts were less than enthusiastic about convicting or punishing bank holdup and burglary suspects. The activity had to be discouraged. But the bankers were going at it the wrong way.

The poster was the crux of the problem.

The first time Frank saw one, his hackles lifted. They hadn't gone down since. He had known at that first reading that it was only a matter of time until someone came up with the bright idea of luring people to a bank, shooting them dead, and pocketing the reward money. The dead didn't have to be bank robbers. Any cold body lying near a bank was worth a fortune.

His suspicions were compounded when the pattern became clear. Most of the "robbers" had been killed at night, by local peace officers. Frank knew professional outlaws. He'd spent most of his life crawling inside their heads, learning how they thought. No robber intent on a big score would hit a bank at night, spend hours breaking in and cutting through a vault, when he could get the same amount or more with a five-minute raid during regular banking hours. The scent of rotting halibut, Frank thought as he strode into the hotel lobby, was stronger now than ever.

In his room, he lit another cigarette, sorted several folders on the bed, pulled up a chair, and reviewed his files.

At three banks—in Stanton, Odessa, and Rankin—supposed bank bandits had been killed under circumstances Frank considered highly suspicious.

Those three "bank robberies" were the ones that smelled fishy and set him on the trail that brought him to this city on the dry plains of the West Texas oil country.

The more he dug into the Odessa job, the ranker the odor became. Two men had been shot to death at night. Neither had a criminal record other than an occasional arrest for drunkenness. They were, by no stretch of the imagination, professional bank robbers.

Of the tools recovered at the scene, the most incriminating was an acetylene torch, stolen earlier in the day from a local business. But nowhere on the men or at the scene were tips for the torch. Without the tips, the torch was worthless. It wouldn't cut one of Gladys's cakes. Tracks left at the place where the torch was stolen had been made by someone wearing high-heeled riding boots. Frank again studied the photographs of the dead men lying in the street. Both wore well-worn, low-heeled work shoes.

There was only one conclusion that could be drawn. The two men had been framed, lured to the bank on one pretense or another, and then shot down in cold blood for the reward money.

And there was a connection with the Rankin job, in which two men had been killed in back of the bank. Their car, parked a few feet from where they were gunned down, was loaded with torches and other tools designed for breaking and entering. Again, there were no tips for the torches, and the tools obviously had been planted after the fact. There was no trace of grease from the tools on the dead men's hands, none inside the car.

It was the same setup used in the Odessa killings. The Rankin shootings also had occurred at night.

Three men had split a $10,000 reward. One of the three also collected a share of the reward money from the Odessa job. It didn't take a genius to reconstruct the sequence of events. One man was the recruiter. It was his job to lure innocent people to the vicinity of the bank. Two others were the triggermen.

A few days after Odessa, three Mexican "bank robbers" were shot down by an officer and a citizen in front of the bank at Stanton, forty miles from Odessa.

The gunmen made a mistake at Stanton.

They had failed to kill one of the framed men.

Frank once again scanned the survivor's statement, signed and witnessed. There was no doubt in his mind the alleged robber had told the truth in the interview with Frank. No barely literate Mexican could have made up the story on his own. The Mexicans had been approached by a man who offered them work, told them to wait in front of the bank. Then they were gunned down.

The man who did the hiring shared in the Stanton reward money. The same name surfaced in the investigation into the Rankin job.

Of the three shootings, Frank now had solid evidence that linked the same two names to the murder-for-reward schemes at three banks. Signed statements, physical evidence. Bank records that showed hefty deposits in the accounts of two men a short time after the slayings. The paper trail was as solid as the physical and circumstantial evidence.

And he couldn't get one judge or peace officer to pay attention to that evidence. The murder machine was running smoothly, and he had reliable information it was about to strike again. Soon.

Frank gathered up the case files, stored them, and started packing. There was one way he could put a stop to it. . . .

Austin
March 12, 1928

Manny Gault strode up to Frank's desk at headquarters. "You've got a full house in the press room, Captain. Looks like every major daily paper in Texas and all the wire services are waiting. Made quite a stir when we put out word that the man who never said more than a dozen words to the papers had a big press conference scheduled."

Frank thumbed through the stack of stapled news releases on his desk. "It's the first time I've thought the press might be worth its weight where the law's concerned. I hope we've got enough statements to go around."

"We should have," Gault said with a wry grin, "we just about wore out every typist and typewriter available." The grin faded. "Pancho, are you sure you want to do this? The Texas Bankers Association's going to go nuts, and we're talking about a lot of money and power there."

Frank snorted. "Let 'em go nuts. They've stepped across the line, Manny, and it's time to let them know it." He tucked the stack of releases under his arm. "Let's go singe some bankers' tail feathers."

A babble of questions greeted Frank as he strode into the capitol press room and surveyed the crowd. Manny was right; it was standing room only.

Frank took his place in the front of the room and raised a hand until the babble died to an expectant murmur. "Gentlemen," he said, "I know that in the past, I haven't been exactly a fountain of words with the press. Now I'm asking for your help to stop one of the worst travesties of justice in Texas history. In a minute I'll be passing out copies of a rather lengthy statement to each of you. I would be grateful if you would see that it reaches print. If not in its entirety, please use it at least in part."

An Austin reporter stood. "Captain Hamer, you've never called a press conference before. That in itself is front-page news. I've heard from my own sources that this concerns the Texas Bankers Association. Is that accurate?"

Frank nodded. "That's right, Sam. We have a situation here where innocent people are being killed, shot down like wolves for bounty money." He raised his hand again to quell the sudden volley of questions. "I have a release here detailing the entire scheme. Each of you will receive a copy." He began passing out copies of the typewritten statement.

A wire-service reporter in the front row flipped through the pages, scanned the release quickly, then loosed a low whistle. "Captain, this is, shall we say, sensitive material. Are you charging the Bankers Association with complicity to murder?"

"Not direct complicity in a criminal conspiracy," Frank said. "What they've done may not be criminal in a technical sense, but what they've done is, in effect, to sanction a massive murder machine."

The Austin reporter raised a hand as Frank finished handing out the statements. "Captain, can you give us a brief summary of this release? I'll be needing to contact my editor, to let him know a major story is about to break." He glanced at his watch. "The editorial board meeting will be starting in twenty minutes to plan page one of the morning edition."

"Yes, sir, I can. As an illustration of what's going on here, there's a story I've heard from old Indian fighters. At one time the Apaches and Comanches had turned northern Mexico into a bloodbath, raiding and killing. The Mexican government put out a hundred-dollar reward for Indian scalps. A sizable number of Americans went into Mexico, hunting bounty scalps—"

"Excuse me, Captain, but are you driving at a point here?" the wire-service man interrupted.

"I am." Frank stared into the face of the reporter. "When Apaches and Comanches got scarce in Mexico, the hunters found out the government couldn't tell the difference between the scalp of an Indian and the scalp of a Mexican shepherd. So they killed innocent Mexicans, turned in the scalps, and collected the reward."

Frank paused for a breath and let the anticipation build. "And, gentlemen, that is what we have here now. The Texas Bankers Association's reward of five thousand dollars for a *dead* bank robber, but nothing for a live one, has led to that same situation. Innocent men and ignorant or half-drunk boys are being lured into ambush and killed for the reward money. What it boils down to is that the bankers of Texas are paying for Apaches and getting sheepherders."

"Captain," a Dallas reporter shouted over the sudden clamor, "aren't you in effect actually saying the Bankers Association is responsible for wholesale murder?"

"That," Frank said, his tone cold, "is exactly what I'm saying. This whole operation has the cold-bloodedness of a rattlesnake with a chill."

The frantic scratch of pencils against paper seemed loud in

the charged silence. Frank waved his original copy of the release. "In these pages I have outlined and detailed, as much as possible within bounds of legality and reason, the entire operation. I am asking you to print it in your newspapers."

"Captain Hamer," the Austin reporter said, "you're asking us to put the Bankers Association on trial in the press. Have you tried legal action?"

"I have, with no results." Frank consciously kept the bitterness from his tone. "I have gone before judges, district attorneys, any and all officials I have thought of who might be willing to bring individual cases before grand juries. None of them are willing to cooperate. I have asked the Texas Bankers Association to repeal the bounty system, yet they refuse to even admit that a problem exists and that innocent people are being murdered." He paused for a breath.

"My efforts in that regard are detailed in the release. It is my conclusion that only the pressure of public outrage is going to put an end to this practice. There is simply too much money and power at stake to trust the normal channels of justice."

Frank paused to stare into the faces of the assembled newsmen. "Gentlemen, even the lowest town drunk or itinerant drifter is entitled to the same protection under the law as the rich and powerful man. I ask you to consider that when you read this release in detail."

A Fort Worth newsman frowned. "The Bankers Association isn't going to like this one bit, Captain."

Frank nodded. "I know that. And I couldn't care less what they like. This has to stop. I know for a fact that other killings are planned—"

"Pardon the interruption, Captain," the Austin reporter broke in, "but I see here where you say you know the name of the man who shared in the Odessa and Rankin rewards and that this man is planning two more such framings in the future. Can you give us a name?"

"Not now, Sam. When I have arrest warrants or indictments, you'll have names. For the moment let's just say I have conclusive proof that will hold up in any honest court of law." Frank's gaze swept the crowd. "The most important thing is that publicity might prevent those and other murders for money. The sooner the public knows what's going on here, the more innocent lives will be saved." He reached for his hat. "That's all I have to say on the matter. Thank you, gentlemen." He started for the door.

"Captain," a voice from the back of the crowd called, "if we cooperate with you in this, does that mean you'll be available for interviews about your career in general and specific cases in the future?"

Frank snugged his hat down. "No, sir, it doesn't."

The newsman chuckled. "Just checking to make sure you haven't changed, Captain."

The next morning, headlines across the state and even in the national press blared Frank's exposé of the Texas "murder machine." Almost every Texas newspaper ran the complete article Frank had compiled, including the closing:

> "I challenge the Texas Bankers Association to appoint a committee for any number of their own members and let me put the facts before them that I have, and I will lay any wager that the committee will agree with me that no reward should have been paid either in the Odessa or in the Rankin job.
> "I extend this appeal to the peace officers, to the press, and to the people of Texas in the hope of stopping organized murder in this state."

Most of the stories quoted spokesmen from the Bankers Association and their lobbyists as "having no comment."

Manny Gault tossed the morning edition of the *Statesman* on Frank's desk. "Well, Cap," he said with a grin, "how's it feel to antagonize the biggest pile of money in the entire state of Texas?"

Frank sipped at his coffee and reached for a smoke. "When you go fishing what kind of fish do you like to catch, little ones or big ones?" He fired a match, lit his cigarette, and squinted through the smoke. "The bigger they are, the better I like to catch them."

The flood of irate calls from bankers Frank expected didn't materialize. The association wasn't talking to him—or to the newspapers.

It wasn't until two days later that Frank got the first direct threat, an anonymous caller who said the association would have his scalp and stop at nothing to get it.

"Friend," Frank said casually into the phone, "I've been threatened by experts. You amateurs don't worry me a whole hell of a lot," and hung up.

April 1

Frank strode from the Upton County Courthouse in Rankin with a fresh spryness in his step, two written confessions in his pocket, and a warm sense of satisfaction in his gut.

The break he needed in his battle with the bankers had come in a grand-jury indictment of the two men Frank had tracked down for murder for the pelt-money bank job. They offered no resistance to arrest. Then, faced with the evidence Frank had accumulated, they sang like mockingbirds, trying to save themselves from a death sentence.

It was no small victory, even if it didn't break the Bankers Association's hold. It meant that some men who otherwise would have been led to their deaths for blood money would live. It was the first chink in the association's armor.

Frank stopped at the telephone office on the dusty main street and gave the drowsy operator a number. He had promised the Austin reporter he'd have names when an indictment was handed down. He planned to keep that promise.

A few weeks later, with the press still nipping at their heels and under the steady weight of public opinion, the Bankers Association dropped the "dead bank robbers only" provision from their reward posters. The blood-money war had ended.

May 1930

"Honey," Gladys said, snuggled against Frank's shoulder as a mockingbird ran through a nighttime concerto outside the bedroom window, "aren't you about due for a vacation?"

"Soon, dear." Frank ran his fingers along Gladys's jaw, enjoying the faint scent of her freshly washed hair. "It would be nice to get away for a couple of weeks. We've got a standing invitation from Tom Mix. Maybe the kids would enjoy seeing Hollywood—"

The jangle of the phone broke the pleasant spell.

Gladys snuggled closer. "Let it ring, Frank."

"Now, honey, you know I can't do that." He twisted away, lifted the receiver, and listened for a couple of minutes. "Yes, sir, I'll get right on it. We can be there tomorrow if we drive straight through." He replaced the phone.

Gladys groaned aloud. "Now what?"

"That was Dan Moody. We've got trouble up in Sherman." Frank swung his feet over the bed and reached for his notebook of phone numbers. "A black man's been charged with raping a white woman. There's a lynch mob brewing. Judge Carter in Denton asked the governor for Ranger help. Pack a bag for me, will you, please, while I call the office and see who's available?"

Gladys didn't argue or grumble. It was one of the many reasons she was what Frank considered a perfect mate for a Texas Ranger captain; she didn't whine aloud at abrupt separations, though he knew it cut her inside just as it did him. She had plenty of practice at packing Frank's suitcase on short notice.

"Any idea when you'll be back, dear?"

"Can't say for sure, but I promise I won't dally around once it's over." Frank finished dressing, kissed Gladys, and reached for the bag. "Hug the kids for me, and apologize to them. I'd like to wake them and do it myself, but the boys and I have to get rolling if we're going to head off a lynching."

"I understand, and so will they. This must be big trouble if you're taking help instead of tackling it alone. Who's going with you?"

"Wheatley, McCoy, and Aldrich," Frank said as he reached for the door.

Gladys nodded. "They're good men." She lifted herself on

tiptoes and kissed him again. "Keep your hair on and your
powder dry, Captain Hamer."

Sherman, Texas
Friday, May 9, 1930

Frank stood at a front window overlooking the steps of the
Grayson County Courthouse, Old Lucky on his hip and a .45
auto pistol holstered on the off side, and studied the mob that
swarmed over the lawn and spilled into the street.

The sea of angry white faces reminded Frank of the Gulf
Coast shoreline in an approaching storm, an ebb and flow of
rage and hate with an undercurrent of violence about to break.

Many of the faces, he knew, belonged to Klansmen, adding
fuel to the race hatred; with the Klan, it didn't matter if a
black man was innocent or guilty. The charge of raping a
white woman was enough to trigger their blood lust. It didn't
matter a whit that the slender black man who cringed against
a far wall claimed the woman had seduced him.

Frank didn't know whose story to believe, and didn't really
care. Black or white, any accused man had the right to trial
by jury, not by lynch mob.

The woman claimed that the black had come to her farm
home in the rural community of Luella a few miles east,
shoved a shotgun in her face, tied her to the bed, and viciously
raped her. The black man's story was that he had gone to
collect some wages due him, was carrying the shotgun because he planned to do some hunting, the farm woman asked
him into the house, and all but dragged him into her bed.

Regardless of what happened, George Hughes already had
been convicted in the pages of the *Sherman Democrat* and in
the court of public opinion. All Frank could hope to do was
keep the black man alive until he could be moved to a safe
place to await trial.

It wasn't going to be easy.

The mob outside was an animal.

The resemblance of lawbreakers to four-legged predators
had always struck Frank; the comparison had seldom failed
him. Crooked politicians were like foxes, common thieves

like coyotes, professional outlaws and killers like mountain lions.

He was staring at a wild dog pack crazed by blood scent.

Frank turned from the window for a moment, surveying his defenses. They were thin at best.

Grayson County Sheriff Arthur Vaughan and Deputy W. B. Goode stood near the trembling, wide-eyed prisoner outside Judge R. M. Carter's courtroom. Rangers J. B. Wheatley, J. E. McCoy and J. W. Aldrich stood watch on the crowd gathered at the rear of the courthouse.

"Sheriff," Frank said to Vaughan, "we've got to get this man back to jail, where we could protect him."

"No, sah!" The prisoner's voice wavered in fear. "I ain't goin' through that bunch out there no more. They'd kill us all sure."

Grayson County Deputy Ollie Neatherly strode to Vaughan's side, out of breath, his shirt soaked with sweat. "We got a problem, Sheriff," he said. "Word's got around on the square that Hughes pled guilty. And there's a rumor the Rangers are under orders not to shoot anybody in the crowd if they charge the courthouse."

Frank mouthed a soft curse. "We're under no such orders. If that bunch tries to storm the courthouse, we'll let them know otherwise."

A shout rose over the surly rumbling from the crowd outside: "Get the nigger! Hang the black bastard!"

Frank pushed open the door, stepped outside, stared for a moment at the mob, then called, "All right, break it up! Go back to your homes and let the law handle this!"

"Law, hell," someone yelled from the crowd, "are you going to give us that nigger or not?"

"You're not getting him."

"Then, by God, we're coming up to get him!"

Frank glared steadily at the men in the front ranks of the mob. "All right, if you feel lucky, come on up. But if you start up those steps, there'll be a lot of funerals in Sherman tomorrow."

For several heartbeats a tense near silence broken only by subdued murmurs settled over the crowd. The men in front tried and failed to return Frank's steady stare. The mob wavered, then started to fall back. Frank breathed a silent sigh of relief. For the time being, at least, they had backed off. He turned and started back inside.

A voice bellowed from back in the crowd, "We don't need no damn outsiders comin' in here tellin' us what to do! Go back to Austin and let us handle our own!"

"Yeah! Leave Sherman's business to Sherman!" The yells spread, punctuated by curses and taunts directed at the Rangers. Frank paused for a moment, decided not to add wood to the fire, and went inside.

Seconds later a rock clanked from the wall beside the door. Glass shattered as a bottle slammed into a window. By the time Frank could draw three breaths, a hail of stones, bricks, and other debris peppered the building.

Frank yelled over the increasing din for McCoy. He jabbed a thumb toward the front door as the sergeant trotted up. "Keep an eye on that bunch out there a minute. I'm going to have a serious palaver with the judge."

He found Judge Carter still seated behind the bench, lips pinched and face pale. Carter's fingertips drummed against the polished wood.

"Judge, you've got to order a change of venue—*now*—or we're going to have one hell of a riot on our hands," Frank said.

"I—I don't know, Captain. We haven't heard all the testimony yet. The victim—"

"Judge," Frank interrupted, "a man's life is at stake here. Maybe several lives. You name a spot, anyplace, and we'll get Hughes out of here before this gets completely out of hand—"

"Cap, they're coming!" McCoy yelled.

CHAPTER NINETEEN

Sherman
Friday, May 9, 2:30 P.M.

FRANK SPRINTED TO McCOY's side and shouldered the door open. He drew his revolver as he and the sergeant stepped onto the veranda.

"Stop right there!" Frank yelled.

The crowd surged onto the lower steps. Frank lifted Old Lucky and fired twice, aiming low; two men went down, wounded in the legs. The crack of a pistol and a yelp of pain sounded from the rear of the courthouse.

The assault faltered as men in the front row of the charge pulled back from the threat of Ranger guns.

"We're not going to be able to hold them much longer, Cap," McCoy said, his brow creased in a frown. "We've got to get that man out of here."

A muscle twitched in Frank's jaw. "Hold on here for a minute, Sergeant. This time, by God, I'm going to get that judge's attention." He strode back into the building.

"Cap," Ranger Wheatley called from the back of the hall-way, "I heard somebody yell for a gas can! They're going to try to burn us out!"

"Get on the phone to the fire department," Frank said. "Tell them to get some men and equipment out here, now!" He spun to face Vaughan. "Sheriff, we've got to get Hughes out of here. Right now. We can't hold the courthouse against that mob. We can hold them off from the jail."

"But, Captain, how—"

"Shoot our way through if we have to," Frank snapped. He stomped into the district courtroom and strode up to Judge Carter. "Set a change of venue *now,* for God's sake! You don't even have to name a place! Dammit, man, that mob's going to burn the courthouse!"

The judge paled. "Okay. Change of venue ordered."

Frank hurried from the judge's office, offering a silent prayer that he could win the race against time. He was within three strides of the prisoner when a thud sounded from the county tax office; the odor of gasoline fumes hit his nostrils a split second before the *whoosh* as the gas exploded into flames.

Frank's heart skidded into his gut. "Oh, Christ," he muttered, "we've lost it—" A blast of heat washed through the courthouse. "It's no use, men!" he yelled over the roar and crackle of flames. "We've got to get out of here! Clear the courthouse! We can still make it through the back door!"

Frank blinked watery eyes, crouched to avoid the buildup of smoke, and scurried to the judge's chambers. The courtroom was empty.

He found Vaughan headed toward a fireman's ladder leaning against a second-floor window and grabbed the sheriff's shoulder. "Where's the prisoner?" Frank shouted over the surge of fire.

"In the vault!"

"What? My God, man, what's he doing there?"

"Judge said lock him in there. We gave him a bucket of water—judge said the vault wouldn't burn, he'd be all right."

Frank groaned aloud. "Dammit, he'll suffocate in there! What's the combination?"

"Don't know."

"Who does?"

"Nobody left in here who knows it." The sheriff glanced nervously toward the open window and the waiting ladder. "They've all left already."

"Call somebody, man—get them down here!"

Vaughan shook his head. "Can't—all the phone lines are dead. Must have been cut." The sheriff sprinted for the escape ladder before Frank could reply.

The last bit of faint hope drained from Frank's body. The black man was doomed. If he didn't suffocate first, he might well be cooked alive inside the heavy steel walls of the vault.

Over the crackle and hiss of fire, Frank heard the yells from outside: "Let her burn—let her burn!" "Burn that nigger! Then we'll get 'im!"

Smoke all but obscured Frank's vision as he and his three men, the last to leave except for the trapped prisoner, fought through a shower of fly ash and sparks to the back door. The mob in the rear of the building had moved back, away from the growing heat and embers that swirled on the wind. The crowd seemed strangely subdued now, more engrossed in watching the courthouse go up in towering flames and billowing smoke than enraged at the black man inside.

Frank glanced around and knew they had barely gotten out in time. The aged building and its contents, cured to tinder by time and drought, would be fully engulfed in a matter of minutes. Firemen stood by and watched, as helpless as Frank to stop the inferno. The packed streets blocked firefighting equipment; the few hoses the firemen managed to lay had been hacked through by pocketknives and hatchets wielded by the mob.

"What now, Captain?" McCoy gasped, wiping at his eyes.

"There's nothing more we can do here." Frank's words were tight with anger and frustration. "Get in the car—we've got to get to a phone and let the governor know what's happened."

"That won't help Hughes much, will it?" one of the Rangers asked as he slammed the car door.

Frank switched on the ignition and hit the starter. "Hughes is done for, but that's not all we've got to worry about." He threw the Ford in gear, leaned on the horn, and popped the clutch. Onlookers scrambled from the vehicle's path. "This bunch isn't going to be satisfied with one burned black man, if I know anything about lynch mobs," he said. "We've got to have help. I'm going to ask Dan Moody for the National Guard."

A half hour later Frank found a working phone almost twenty miles from Sherman in the Howe community. He rang up the operator and asked for long distance.

Dan Moody was on the line in less than a minute. Frank was in mid-sentence, briefing the governor on developments, when a voice broke in:

"I hope they lynch that nigger if he doesn't burn first."

"Get off this line, operator!" Frank shouted into the receiver. "This is official state business!"

"It'd serve him right, rapin' that poor white woman like that, givin' her all them nigger diseases—" Frank slammed down the phone.

He had to drive to McKinney before he could find a line relatively secure from eavesdroppers. Moody listened to Frank's report without interruption.

"All right, Frank," Moody said as Frank concluded, "I'll get the Guard on the way. We've got the Hundred-Twelfth Cavalry in Dallas. They can be there by nightfall."

Frank stood at the window of the Grayson County jail office, his gut churning in rage, frustration, helplessness, and disgust.

The crowded jail was now the command post for lawmen and Texas guardsmen. The problem was that peace officers and soldiers weren't in command. The howling mob in the streets outside, fueled by blood lust and a substantial amount of bootleg moonshine, was in charge.

Frank had counted on the early-evening arrival of the 112th Cavalry detachment to dampen the lynch-mob mentality of the five thousand or more who jammed the city streets. Instead of turning docile in the face of military uniforms and weapons, the mob had gone berserk; it was no longer a collection of individuals, but a single, raging animal.

The animal had gone on the attack before the soldiers could fully disembark from the InterUrban Railway cars from Dallas. Several guardsmen and a number of civilians had been wounded or injured in a skirmish at the rail station. Casualties on both sides mounted as the troops fought their way to the command post.

Not all the civilians on the streets were rioters. Women brought out their young children to watch the courthouse fire and enjoy the excitement. Teenagers, businessmen, workers, and other innocents mingled with the crowd and lingered on the streets well after the blaze died down.

A brawny man in bib overalls, unshaven, unsteady from moonshine, and carrying an ancient single-barrel shotgun, paused outside the window and stared at Frank through bloodshot eyes. The farmer made no move to raise the shotgun.

"You damn outsiders get the hell out!" the man bellowed, his deep voice booming over the tumult of the riot. "We can take care of this ourselfs! We know how to handle darkies! We'll have us a bait of nigger meat tonight!''

Frank didn't move or speak. He merely returned the man's stare. After a moment the farmer moved on.

"Captain Hamer," Colonel L. E. McGee, commanding the eight officers and forty-seven troopers of the 112th detachment, all but yelled into Frank's ear, "the only option left is a direct military assault. There's no other way we can disperse this mob. And in the absence of a formal declaration of martial law, I cannot order my troops to attack. You're ranking peace officer here."

Frank recognized the statement for what it was. Not a comment on the situation, but a request for suggestions. He shook his head. "An attack wouldn't solve anything, Colonel. Too many innocent bystanders would be killed. There's nothing we can do to help Hughes. He's a dead man anyway. The best we can hope for is that the mob won't burn the entire town."

"So what is your recommendation, Captain?"

Frank's shoulders slumped. "There isn't one damn thing we can do except wait and—" A yell from outside cut off his words.

"They're gonna dynamite the vault! We're gonna get that nigger now!"

Frank glanced at the clock. It read 11:30 P.M. He started for the door.

"Captain, you can't go out there," a Grayson County deputy called. "They'll tear you to pieces!"

Frank ignored the warning. He strode from the jail and joined the surge of humanity pressing toward the charred remains of the courthouse. Sergeant McCoy caught up with him a few yards from the jail. The two Rangers were within fifty yards of the courthouse rubble when an explosion hammered their ears.

As the smoke and debris from the dynamite blast cleared a couple of minutes later, two men clambered up the ladder placed against the ripped side of the tall steel vault.

"Here he is!" one of the climbers yelled. "We got the nigger now!"

A sudden hush fell over the crowd. Moments later the body

of George Hughes slid down the ladder and thudded into the ashes below. McCoy started forward; Frank grabbed him by the arm.

"We can't help him," Frank said.

May 10

Frank tried to blink away the sensation of grit under his eyelids and ignored the dull pain in the base of his skull. He rechecked his final report on the Sherman lynching and riot to be filed with the governor's office.

It wasn't pretty reading.

The mob continued its party long after George Hughes's body slid down the ladder. Frank couldn't say if the man died from suffocation, from the heat of the fire, or from the dynamite blast. There was no good way to die, but the fact that he was dead before the mob got hold of him was, in its own way, merciful.

Within minutes after the body hit the ground, knives winked in the glow of street lamps. To the cheers and shouts of the crowd, the mutilated body that had once been George Hughes charred atop a bonfire on the courthouse square.

The rioters hadn't finished with the black man even after the pyre flames died. They tied the grotesquely twisted corpse to an automobile bumper, dragged it through town to the Negro district, and finally hanged the remains from a tree for public display.

Even that didn't end it.

By sunrise, the heart of Sherman's black business district, the equivalent of two city blocks, lay in charred ruins, looted and burned by white rioters. Smaller, roving gangs broke off from the main mob to terrorize, rob, and burn out other black families. The roads leading out of Sherman filled with frightened ebony faces as entire families fled.

Today, a semblance of calm—to Frank, it seemed a smug contentment—lay over Sherman. Downtown streets were all but deserted except for National Guard patrols. Governor Moody declared martial law and sent more troops, a case of too little, too late, as far as Frank was concerned.

Frank and his Rangers identified several of the mob leaders, accumulated evidence against them, and turned the documents over to local authorities for possible indictment. Frank doubted the men would ever stand trial.

At least the phones were working again.

Frank dialed the operator and called home. Gladys answered on the second ring.

"Honey, I'm coming home," he said. "There's nothing more I can do here."

"Frank, are you all right?" Concern lay on Gladys's tone. "You sound—I don't know—just—not like yourself."

"I'm a little tired, that's all. And disgusted. I didn't get the job done. A man died here, in a way I wouldn't wish on anybody. Innocent people were hurt, burned out, run out of town." He sighed heavily. "I couldn't stop it, Gladys. I screwed up."

"Franklin Augustus Hamer, you quit talking like that," Gladys scolded softly. "You did your best, just like you always do. Some things are simply beyond one man's control. Now quit letting it eat at you and get yourself home. But stay overnight and get some rest first. I don't want to find out you've wrapped a car around a telephone pole on the way home."

Frank's jaw tightened. "I'll stop overnight a ways down the road. I don't intend to spend one more night in this gutless town. If I never see Sherman again, I'll die a happy man. . . ."

Austin
February 1933

The Fergusons were back in. So Frank was back out.

The day after the votes were counted and Ma Ferguson made her acceptance speech, Frank went on inactive status. It wasn't exactly resigning his Ranger commission, but it was better than fighting the Ferguson battles again.

He leaned back in his chair on the front porch, enjoyed the quirky Texas weather's unseasonably warm spell generally known as the "February thaw," and contemplated an almost impossible task.

A calico cat curled asleep in his lap. A tabby tomcat rubbed against his ankles. Porky Pig, the pet javelina Frank had found orphaned on a ranch and who had all but taken over the Hamer place, leaned against the side of Frank's chair. Frank tried to juggle the morning newspaper and drink coffee while alternately rubbing the scarred head of an aging blue tick hound lying beside his chair and scratching Porky's neck.

The javelina lifted his head for a chin scratch and grunted in contentment as the squawk of Gladys's pet parrot drifted through the doorway. The Hamer house had earned the nickname "Austin Zoo," pinned on it by Frank's and Gladys's friends.

Frank hadn't been so content in a long time. Or, he had to admit, so bored and itchy. It was a weird combination of feelings. Relaxed and tense, happy and feeling useless.

At any rate, the idleness couldn't last. He had a family to provide for and their limited savings were dwindling. Gladys was a wizard at handling money, but even magicians couldn't stretch a dollar as far as it needed to go.

And Frank had discovered he wasn't nearly as good a professional loafer as he thought he could be. He had been active all his life, which wasn't the best of practice for lounging around doing nothing. A man could only make so many trips to the post office, read so many newspapers, scratch so many hounds and javelinas, and pet so many cats.

Lately, the restlessness had become worse. Even if they'd had more money than the Catholic Church in the bank, he had to go back to work. Before Gladys physically kicked him out of the house or he went out of his mind without her help.

"Frank," Gladys called from the door. "There's a man from some oil company on the phone. Something about a job."

"Tell him we're not hiring," Frank said with a wink at Porky.

"Franklin Augustus Hamer, you quit teasing me and get your backside in here *right now* and talk to this man, or I'll send you to bed without supper for a week."

"Yes, ma'am, right away." Frank plucked the sleeping calico from his lap, put the frumped cat down, stepped over the hound, toed the javelina aside, gave Gladys a peck on the cheek as he walked past, and asked the parrot to hold it down while he was on the phone. The parrot ignored the order.

Five minutes later Frank hung up and smiled at Gladys. "Well, I'm back earning a paycheck," he said. "Better than five hundred a month as a special investigator for an oil company in Houston. Am I out of the doghouse now?"

Gladys's face reflected a storm of mixed emotions. "Do we have to move to Houston?"

"No. After a few days there I'll be able to make my headquarters right here and just go where I'm needed."

Gladys snuggled against his chest. "Then you're out of the doghouse—wait a minute! *How much* money did you say?"

Austin
February 1934

"Frank, dear, you've got company," Gladys said, peering out the front door as a tan Chevy coupe pulled into the driveway. "I think it's Lee Simmons. Wonder why he's come to visit?"

Frank rose from behind his desk and strode to the door. "I expect we'll find out soon enough. Make sure there's fresh coffee, will you, honey?"

Simmons, a lean, rangy six-footer, clean-shaven, his charcoal-gray suit rumpled from the drive, stepped from the Chevy. Frank met him at the bottom steps, hand extended.

"Lee, good to see you again," Frank said, his tone warm; he genuinely liked and admired the man whose slight build and too large shirt collar belied his rawhide toughness. Simmons's grip was as firm as Frank remembered, though it had been a while since the two had last met. "Come on in. Coffee's hot."

Simmons placed his narrow-brimmed silver belly hat and topcoat on the hall tree and gave Gladys a gentle hug. "You're looking as young and pretty as ever, Gladys," he said.

Gladys pulled back and studied Simmons's angular face. "When you get sugary and nice, Lee Simmons, I get the feeling this isn't a social call."

Simmons nodded. "Sorry, Gladys. It's business."

"Well, you men go on into Frank's office, if you can wade through the clutter. I'll fetch coffee and see if there's a slice of pie left in the icebox."

"Never mind the pie," Simmons said. "Just coffee's fine."

Frank led the way into a spare bedroom he had converted into a work area after the marriages of his daughters. The two men passed a few minutes in idle talk about old friends and shared experiences over almost three decades of law-enforcement work as Gladys brought coffee and excused herself.

"Something's on your mind, Lee," Frank said. "I can see it in your eyes, just like Gladys did. Might as well ride straight into the herd."

Simmons sighed. "I almost hate to bring it up, Frank, but I've hit the end of my rope. You're aware of the prison break at Eastham Farm a couple weeks back?"

Frank nodded. "I keep up with the news as best I can. Tracking down crude-oil thefts and keeping tabs on refinery security leaves me plenty of spare time. Sorry about your guard, Lee."

"They had no reason to kill him, Frank." Simmons's eyes narrowed. "The guards never resisted, not with forty-fives stuck in their faces. They just shot him down like a mad dog, killed him for the pure hell of it. It's a wonder the other guard wasn't killed, too."

"Who's on the case?"

"Everybody in the state who has a badge and a gun. Even amateur bounty hunters. So far, no luck. Dallas County deputies Ted Hinton and Bob Alcorn have been on the trail full-time for weeks now, but they've come up dry." Simmons sipped at his coffee and leaned back in his chair. "Frank, I want those people. I want them worse than I've ever wanted anybody. That's why I'm here. In my opinion, there's only one man in the state of Texas who could handle this job. I came to ask if you'll take the job of hunting down Clyde Barrow and Bonnie Parker."

Frank stubbed out his cigarette, his forehead creased in a frown. "How long do you think it would take to do the job?"

"That's something no man can guess. It might be six months, it might be longer. Probably, it will take you thirty days to get your feet on the ground before you start to work. No matter how long it takes, I'll back you to the limit.''

Simmons paused for a moment. "I know how it's been between you and the Fergusons, Frank. I've just come from the governor's office. I told them I need a special investigator, that you were the man I wanted on the case, and I have their assurance they won't interfere.''

Frank sighed. "I don't trust the Fergusons to keep their word, Lee, but I do trust you.''

"I'm asking you to accept an appointment as special investigator for the prison system, Frank. To work this one case. Run them down and put an end to it, one way or another.'' Simmons fell silent as Gladys entered, coffeepot in hand. He seemed reluctant to speak in her presence.

Frank took him off the hook. "Lee's asked me to lend a hand in the Barrow case, Gladys,'' he said.

"Bonnie and Clyde?'' Gladys's gaze flicked from Simmons to her husband and back. Her eyes narrowed. "Those cold-blooded killers and their gang have terrorized this country long enough. It's about time somebody put a stop to it.''

Frank said, "Go ahead, Lee. Gladys has the right to know what's been going on in here. Whatever I say will have to be okay with her.''

Simmons cleared his throat. "There is one problem. I know that you're finally making a decent salary for the first time in your life, Frank. If you take this job, it will be a major pay cut. I can't pay you but a hundred-eighty a month and expenses. It isn't much, and it would be a hardship for your family. . . .'' His voice trailed away.

Gladys put her free hand on her husband's shoulder. "Frank, you're the one man I know who can stop those mad dogs. If you want to do this as badly as I think you do, don't worry about the money. We'll manage.''

Frank patted her hand and smiled at her. "I didn't expect you to say anything else, Gladys.'' To Simmons, he said, "How many people will know I'm on the case—if I take it?''

"Almost no one outside this room and the governor's mansion. Hinton and Alcorn later on, when the time is right. We'll keep the operation under wraps, tell no one who doesn't need to know.''

"No newspapers?"

Simmons shook his head emphatically. "Absolutely not. We don't want the public—and especially Bonnie and Clyde—to know you're working the case. You'll have free rein, Frank. Develop your own sources in addition to a few contacts I have that can be trusted. Do whatever it takes to bring them down. How you do it doesn't matter."

"Well, Lee," Frank said, "if that's the way you feel about it, I'll take the job."

Simmons sighed in satisfaction. "I was hoping you'd say that, Frank. I brought along copies of the case files on Bonnie and Clyde and the hardcases they run with. I'll leave it with you while I take care of the paperwork to get your special investigator's badge. For practical purposes, you'll be on the highway patrol payroll. When you're ready to move, let me know." He rose. "The files are in the car."

"Stay for supper, Lee," Gladys said. "You've lost weight. You need some meat on your bones. I can always pour another cup of water in the stew."

Simmons half smiled, apparently relaxed for the first time since he'd walked in the door. "Thanks, Gladys, but I have to get things rolling. Another time, maybe."

After Simmons left, Frank sat at his desk, a stack of thick case files sharing space with his own clippings and notes on the Bonnie and Clyde rampage. An excitement surged in his veins that he hadn't felt in months.

Frank wasn't without reservations. He knew that despite Gladys's protest to the contrary, she'd have to squeeze some nickels awfully hard to keep the household running. And that he was now fifty years old. If things went wrong and he didn't make it, or got himself crippled, the family would be in bad trouble financially. Aside from that very real possibility, he didn't like working for the Fergusons. Even in a left-handed sort of way. But all that paled beside one cold reality.

Bonnie and Clyde had to be stopped.

Nothing else really mattered.

CHAPTER TWENTY

Dallas
February 10, 1934

FRANK SETTLED INTO the padded chair at his rented room in the small hotel off Industrial Boulevard, lit a cigarette, and flipped open the leather briefcase stuffed with files on Clyde Barrow and Bonnie Parker.

He had most of the files committed to memory, but didn't consider it a waste of time to go over them again. A man never knew when he might spot something he'd overlooked before.

Frank had never seen Clyde Barrow in person, but he was beginning to know Clyde inside and out—an explosive package in a small wrapping. Barrow stood just over five-foot-five and weighed 130 pounds, with brown eyes, fair complexion, clean-shaven, dark chestnut hair, the fourth child in a family of eight. Born at Teleco, Texas, in 1909, grew up in west Dallas.

After numerous brushes with the law on petty charges, he'd finally wound up at Eastham Prison Farm on April 21, 1930, to begin serving a fourteen-year sentence for auto theft. The admission exam showed Barrow had a heart-and-dagger tattoo and the initials EBW—for his alias, Elvin Williams—on the outer left forearm. His inside right forearm bore a USN and shield tattoo, ostensibly representing the U.S. Navy, though Barrow had never served in any uniform except that of an inmate. Yet another tattoo, on the outside of the arm, pictured a girl's face and the name Grace.

The big toe of Barrow's left foot was missing. Only days before his parole, in an effort to evade working in the state farm fields, he had hired a fellow inmate to chop off the toe with an ax. When he was paroled February 2, 1932, he left prison on crutches.

Less than three months later Clyde Barrow killed his first man, Hillsboro storekeeper J. N. Bucher.

It was then that Barrow discovered he liked killing.

From that Hillsboro shooting on April 23, 1932, until Eastham prison guard Major Crawson died in a hail of gunfire during the breakout on January 16, 1934, eight people went down under the Barrow gang's guns. Counting Crawson, six of them were law-enforcement officers.

If Clyde Barrow was a scary package, Bonnie Parker was even more so, Frank concluded. He had arrested a few women during Prohibition, but he'd never hunted a woman before. Especially one like her.

Bonnie stood four-foot-ten and weighed in at less than ninety pounds, perky, with an attractive if somewhat angular face, dark blonde hair tinged with auburn, a penchant for whiskey, and an outright love of the outlaw life and killing. Yet she took her pet white rabbit with her on her travels with Barrow, and had strong family ties. Even on the run, she and Barrow often risked capture for brief family reunions in the Dallas area.

The files generally checked out with what Frank had already learned in less than a day of quietly interviewing a handful of Dallas-area people who knew both Bonnie and Clyde.

Most of those he had talked to said they would never have suspected Bonnie Parker to take to a life of crime. Born in Rowena, Texas, in 1910, she had been an honor student, fancied herself a singer and poet, married at sixteen—some said fifteen—to a man named Roy Thornton. The couple soon split up, but when Thornton went to prison for robbery a short time later, Bonnie never filed for divorce.

"She just said it wouldn't have been the right and proper thing to do," one acquaintance of Bonnie's told Frank. The woman didn't know she was talking to a lawman who planned to run Bonnie Parker to earth. She thought they were just making idle conversation on a currently hot topic.

While waiting tables at the American Café in 1930, Bonnie met Clyde Barrow. They became lovers and, eventually, partners in crime. Bonnie was never far from Clyde's side except when he was behind bars. Even then she looked after "her man.'' She had once helped him break out of the McLennon County Jail in Waco, smuggling a gun to him. Clyde was supposed to have picked her up on his way out of the country, but for some reason, never did. She had to hitchhike back to Dallas. The episode didn't sit well with her, but she couldn't seem to stay angry with Clyde.

A few days later Clyde Barrow's days of freedom ended in Middleton, Ohio. He was sent back to Waco to await transfer to state prison.

Bonnie, Frank learned, had quite a taste for cars and speed. That fit right in with Barrow's talents as a car thief and as a driver. The man was good behind the wheel; with Bonnie at his side, Clyde thought nothing of driving a thousand miles or more without stopping except for gas or food.

Barrow knew every back road in a dozen states, and almost never used major highways. He was a master at eluding pursuit. Frank, no slouch behind the wheel himself, figured Barrow had missed his calling. He would have been a natural in the growing sport of auto racing.

Barrow fancied Ford V-8s, the fastest and most powerful vehicle currently available outside of specialized and expensive vehicles like the Cord. That bit of information wasn't lost on Frank. He had taken the trail behind the wheel of Gladys's personal Ford V-8 sedan; at least in that car, he was a match for Clyde—from a mechancial standpoint. Frank didn't delude himself that he could outdrive Barrow, but if it ever came down to an open road chase, at least he wouldn't be left in the dust in the first ten minutes.

When Barrow was in the Eastham prison, Bonnie wrote to him often, professing her love and expressing her loneliness. Her handwriting was neat, precise, her use of words almost poetic, and she was a superb speller.

Only a few of Bonnie's notes to her imprisoned lover had fallen into the hands of peace officers. Those few were enough to establish that the forced separation of prison only drove the two closer together. After his parole, they were almost constant companions. It was a complicated problem that sounded simple on the surface. Find one and you find them both.

And therein lay a problem that gnawed at Frank's gut.

He leaned back in his chair, stared out the hotel window, and sighed. He had never been forced to kill a woman, but this time he might have to. Bonnie and Clyde had vowed they would never be taken alive. The only chance for a bloodless capture was to catch them in a hideout somewhere, unsuspecting. Preferably asleep. He held out little hope that they would surrender peacefully. They had chosen a quick and bloody end in a shoot-out over death in the electric chair.

Catching them unaware wouldn't be easy. If Bonnie was like a bobcat, Clyde was a coyote—sly, wary, alert to the possibility of a trap at all times, even after twenty hours behind the wheel. The two had friends, real and imagined, across the country.

A sizable percentage of the public actually admired the cutthroat killers. To them, the story of Bonnie and Clyde was not one of mayhem and murder; it was a love story. The fact that it was a story written in blood did nothing to discredit the legend that grew around the fugitive couple.

In Depression-era America, there were few heroes. Hard times were fertile ground for the elevation of outlaws to legendary status. America *needed* a love story. Dillinger, Capone, Pretty Boy Floyd—all the major gangsters—were more admired than despised in general, but the big-name mobsters couldn't match the romantic saga of Bonnie and Clyde.

The legend gathered steam when the two lovers and others in Barrow's gang graduated from gas-station and grocery-store stickups to bank robbery.

Of all institutions, banks were the most universally despised in the nation. Banks and bankers evicted families, took over farms, closed small businesses. When robbers hit a bank, many poor folks cheered the outlaws. In much of the public eye, the bankers were only getting paid back for their ruthlessness and legal crimes against common folks.

There were stories that Bonnie and Clyde helped starving families or farmers on the verge of losing their land, handing out cash to those in need. That it was cash taken from others merely added to the Depression version of the Robin Hood legend. Frank hadn't been able to verify that the fugitives had, in fact, helped out many poor folks. Their creed seemed a variation on the Robin Hood theme: take from anyone with money and keep it yourself.

Frank shook away his musings, lit another cigarette, and returned to the cold truth. He had murderers to track. There was no place for legends and love stories in the life of a lawman.

Only reality.

He spent several minutes studying newspaper photographs and original snapshots of the fugitives. Bonnie and Clyde obviously enjoyed seeing their pictures in the papers. Most of the photos, taken with Bonnie's Kodak by Bonnie, Clyde, or other members of the gang, were posed along the same lines. Bonnie playfully holding a shotgun on Clyde. The two leaning against a car, guns in their hands. Individual photos, all displaying weapons; one showed Bonnie smoking a cigar, but something didn't look right about that picture. Frank suspected it had been retouched by a newspaper artist. Clyde occasionally carried cigars, but mostly fancied Bull Durham roll-your-owns. Bonnie smoked Camels.

He noted the license-plate numbers visible on cars in the photos, then put the pictures aside and flipped through the case reports, reconstructing the sequence of events that brought him onto the case.

A short time after Barrow's parole, Bonnie and Clyde befriended a small-time bootlegger and thief—slightly built, pale, blond Raymond Hamilton. The Barrow gang was in business.

The gang had also included Buck Barrow, Clyde's brother, and Buck's wife, Blanche, until a bloody shoot-out in Missouri in July 1933. Buck died of a police gunshot wound as a result of that raid. Blanche was captured. Bonnie and Clyde, both wounded, escaped and disappeared into a hideout somewhere to recuperate. When their wounds healed, the robberies and killings began again.

The cumulative string of slayings now covered three states. Frank ran down the list of dates and victims once again:

Deputy Sheriff E. C. Moore,
Atoka, Oklahoma,
August 5, 1932.

Butcher Howard Hall,
Sherman, Texas,
October 11, 1932.

Lumber salesman Doyle Johnson,
Temple, Texas,
December 5, 1932.

Deputy Sheriff Malcolm Davis,
Dallas, Texas,
January 6, 1933.

Constable J. W. Harryman
and Detective Harry McGinnis,
Joplin, Missouri,
April 13, 1933.

City Marshal Henry D. Humphrey,
Alma, Arkansas,
June 23, 1933.

And the latest,

Major Crowson,
Eastham, Texas,
January 16, 1934, when Bonnie and Clyde broke Ray
Hamilton out of prison.

The list of crimes attributed to the Barrow gang included an impressive number of robberies that hadn't resulted in murder. There was even a notation of a rape. That didn't seem to fit Clyde's character, but it could have been committed by someone else in the gang.

Frank reviewed again the details Lee Simmons had provided on the background of the prison break. Floyd Hamilton, Ray's brother, had asked Clyde Barrow to help spring Ray and fellow Eastham convict Joe Palmer. On the night of January 15, Clyde and Bonnie drove to Eastham with an ex-con accomplice, Floyd Mullin, who had inside information from one of his contacts about the route by which the prisoners were to be escorted to the fields for the next day's work. Mullin hid a pair of .45 automatic pistols behind a log under a small culvert near the wood yard where the prisoners were to labor.

The following morning, guards Major Crowson and Clem Bosman, escorting the work detail, didn't notice Palmer slip behind the log. The next thing they knew, Palmer had a .45 aimed at their heads. Hamilton grabbed the other .45 from behind the log. Bonnie and Clyde were in a waiting automobile a few yards away. Who fired the first shot wasn't established, but that one trigger pull set off a barrage of slugs from weapons in the hands of Bonnie, Clyde, Hamilton, and Palmer.

That Bosman escaped alive was little less than a miracle.

When the shooting stopped, prisoners Hamilton, Methvin, Palmer, Henry Bybee, and J. B. French piled into Barrow's Ford. The escape had gone according to plan.

Bybee and French had joined the breakout on impulse. Shortly after the break, the two were let out of the car to go their own ways. The others made a clean escape.

Frank stubbed out his cigarette and stood. It was time to start the real legwork. Work he would do alone before he hooked up with the Dallas deputies.

New Boston, Texas
February 16, 1934

"Thanks, Dink," Frank said into the public phone in the cluttered country store alongside the narrow two-lane blacktop outside the small northeast Texas town. "And don't worry. You know nobody'll ever hear about this from me."

He dropped the old-style wall phone earpiece back onto its hook, ordered a cup of coffee and a ham sandwich from the matronly woman behind the greasy lunch counter, and reviewed his information.

It was solid. Reliable sources, even gossip that turned out to be more fact than fiction, the well-used maps he studied almost constantly led to the same conclusion.

Clyde Barrow and Bonnie Parker invariably traveled a circle from Dallas to Joplin, Missouri, to Louisiana, and back to Dallas. Sometimes their route varied, even far afield into

Indiana or Iowa or west to New Mexico. But like most animals, they eventually returned to their favorite hunting circles.

And as hunted animals invariably did, they returned to a safe den when the heat was on. That den couldn't be too far from this town near the Louisiana line. Find the den and eventually you find the animals.

He had known for days the hideout had to be in Louisiana. Bonnie and Clyde were hot in Texas and Missouri; they had robbed and killed there. They had killed no one in Louisiana. It was a notable omission.

Despite the strong family ties that took them back to Dallas for clandestine visits with relatives, Texas authorities hadn't been able to catch up with them.

Catching them was not Frank's major objective at the moment. It was learning their movements, their habits. He was beginning to get a handle on how Clyde Barrow's mind worked. He nodded his thanks to the woman behind the four-stool counter as she topped off his cup.

"Sandwich will be ready in a minute, mister," she said. "New around here, or just passing through?"

"Traveling," Frank said with an encouraging smile. The woman was obviously looking for conversation. A man never knew where idle chat might lead. "Heading into Texarkana."

The woman frowned. "Lived there most of my life. Got too busy, too crowded, too many darkies. Seemed like somebody was always killin' or robbin' somebody. The mister and me left there five years ago, and we sure don't miss it none."

Frank nodded in sympathy. "I know what you mean. Worry some myself, spending so much time on the road away from home. Lots of people out and about would kill a body for a dollar bill or a car these days."

He sipped at his coffee as the woman assembled the sandwich and plopped it on the counter before him. He took a bite and smiled. "Mighty fine sandwich, ma'am. Where in the world did you find fresh lettuce?"

"Got it off a truck out of Mexico a few days back. Feller who's got a truck farm down there stops by here ever' trip north. Keep it fresh in an icebox out back. Tomatoes, too."

Frank chased the bite of sandwich with a swallow of coffee and nodded. "Nothing tastes quite as good as fresh lettuce, especially if it's out of season. Bet you sell a lot of it.''

"Sell or swap. Funny thing," the woman said, "just the other day, this young couple stopped in for gas and a bite to eat. The girl was so tickled to see fresh lettuce they bought a whole head to take with 'em. Said it was to feed a pet rabbit.''

"Lucky rabbit," Frank said casually between bites, even as his heart rate picked up. "This couple—was she a little bit of a thing? Not even five foot tall, sort of red-haired?''

The woman winced. "Yessir, and I tell you, I never seen such a bad dye job on any girl's hair. Didn't even come close to matchin' that red dress she was wearin'. Seemed like a nice, polite young girl, though. 'Cept for one thing. She was drinkin'. Smelt it on her. I tell you, I sure don't hold much with no young girl drinkin' whiskey. Ain't ladylike.''

Frank finished the sandwich, pulled a photograph from his shirt pocket, and handed it to the woman. "Was that her, by any chance?''

The matron squinted at the picture for a moment, then nodded. "That's her. The skinny young feller in the pitcher was with her, too. You know 'em?''

"Yes, ma'am, sort of. I've never seen her, but I've seen quite a few pictures and know some folks that know her. That's Bonnie Parker. The man is Clyde Barrow.''

The woman gasped and dropped the photo as if it were a hot plate. "Bonnie Parker? Clyde Barrow?" Her face paled. "My God! We could have been robbed or—or kilt—''

Frank tucked the picture back in his jacket pocket. "Oh, I don't know about that. I hear they're past robbing stores and filling stations. Moved up to banks, I understand. How long ago did they stop here?''

The woman's brow wrinkled. "Six, seven days ago, best I recall.''

"Did you notice if anyone else was with them?''

"They was two men. Boys, really. One of 'em had pimples real bad. Seems like I've run across that boy someplace before. He looked mighty familiar.''

"I'll bet it was Henry Methvin. I hear he's been running with Bonnie and Clyde." Frank raised an eyebrow. "That name mean anything?''

"There's Methvins over in Bienville Parish in Louisiana. Out by Gibsland. Farmers. The ma and pa used to come to revival meetin's at our church back when we lived in Texarkana." She shook her head. "Lord, I still ain't got over the shock. Bonnie and Clyde. They could of kilt us, sure."

Frank shook his head. "If they had money and didn't figure you would call the law on them, you were probably not in much danger."

"Oh, they had money. Bought near five dollars' worth of gas and groceries, more cash than we see here in a whole week most times."

"Did they mention where they might be headed?" Frank asked.

"Well, the girl got kinda upset when she found out we didn't have no whiskey for sale, but the man told her don't worry about it, they'd get some on down the road." She looked at Frank with renewed interest. "You're sure askin' a lot of questions about them two."

Frank forced a smile. "The whole country's curious about them, ma'am. Bonnie and Clyde are bigger than Dillinger and Floyd and the other gangsters. I suppose it's because they're homegrown outlaws. *Our* outlaws, so to speak." He stood. "I'd better be getting on down the road. How much do I owe you?"

"Fifteen cents. You stop by and see us again, mister," she said as she handed him his change.

"I'll do that for sure, ma'am. I surely will. Thanks for the conversation, too. Man gets to needing talk, traveling by himself."

"My pleasure. Now, you watch yourself." She waggled a finger at Frank. "You see that Bonnie and Clyde, you steer clear of 'em. Some folks think them two's heroes or somethin', but I don't hold with killin', even bankers and lawmen. It's agin the Good Book's teachin's."

Frank smiled. "Yes, ma'am, I'll do that. And it surely is."

Northwest of Texarkana
February 20, 1934

Frank unbuttoned his coat despite the bitter north wind that spilled over the rocky outcrops of pine-forested hills.

There was no mistaking the rock bluff up ahead. It was the same one in the background of a photograph of Clyde Barrow, clad in suit and tie, his white hat in his hand.

Frank had found the hideout.

He pulled Old Lucky from his holster, stepped from the road into the cover of pines and brush on the hillside, and followed the tire tracks to within thirty feet of the shallow cave carved by wind and weather into the side of the distinctive rock bluff. He stood, sniffing the breeze, listening intently, for a half hour.

There was no sound except for the wind in the evergreens and the occasional call of a bird or rustle of animals in the tall grass, no smell of wood smoke. Still, he kept the revolver in hand as he approached the cave entrance.

The place was deserted, but not empty.

Around the cold ashes of a long-dead fire were two dozen or more cigarette butts. More than half were Camels. Bonnie's brand. The others were the remnants of roll-your-owns.

An empty quart whiskey bottle lay on its side along one wall. Bonnie's brand, bought at a little store near Logansport. Clyde seldom drank. When Bonnie boozed, she did it with a passion. She usually put away so much liquor that she couldn't keep her legs under her. He had numerous reports that Clyde had to carry her to the car on several occasions.

They had been here. The signs said the camp was at least five days old.

Frank holstered his handgun, squatted beside the ashes, and studied the scooped-out hollow in the hillside. A bit of refuse caught his attention. It was a wilted lettuce leaf. Food for Bonnie's white rabbit.

He left the cavern as undisturbed as possible, brushing out his own tracks as he withdrew. He ignored the biting wind at his back as he strode the quarter mile to his Ford. He fired the engine, waited for the heater to warm, and studied his next move.

He had the trail. It was a cold trail, but it was a trail. His informant, a small-time heroin dealer who harbored a personal grudge against Clyde Barrow, had told it straight. The man also had said a lot of folks, including some lawmen, in the area weren't to be trusted. Barrow's network of spies and informants was as extensive as Frank's.

Methvin, Frank concluded, was the weak link in the chain. It was a link that could be used.

He shifted the Ford into reverse, backed down the narrow, rutted road until he could turn around, and drove into Texarkana. He stopped at a gas station and made a call while the attendant filled his tank.

"Zeke, Pancho," he said into the phone. "You were right about the hideout. Now I need another favor. Get word to Methvin's dad that the law is onto the cave, and that unless the camp's moved the feds will be on them within a week. Do that for me and it'll save some grief, okay?"

He listened for a moment, nodded, and wondered why people did that; the man on the other end couldn't see the nod. "Much obliged, Zeke. Maybe I can return the favor." He hung up and strode out to the Ford just as the attendant closed the hood.

"Oil's okay," the pump jockey said. "The spare was a few pounds low. I aired her up for you. That'll be two-eighteen." Frank handed him three one-dollar bills and followed the attendant inside to collect his change. "Heard the news on the radio?"

"Not today," Frank said.

"The Barrow gang broke into the National Guard Armory over in Texas, place called Ranger, last night. Loaded up a mess of BARs—Browning Automatic Rifles—a mess of forty-five pistols, and a bunch of ammunition." The attendant counted out Frank's change. "Sure would hate to be any lawman tangles with that bunch now. I was a BAR man in the army. Those things are bad news. Thirty-caliber, full automatic. Make a bunch of big holes in a man real quick. Shoot clean through an engine block."

"So I've heard," Frank said. "Any word on which way they went?"

The attendant shrugged. "Nah. The cops are running around like chickens with their heads cut off, rounding up anybody related to Clyde or Bonnie. They won't find 'em, though. Nobody can catch Clyde."

Frank said, "You're probably right. Thanks for airing up

that spare. I'd hate to get caught in the middle of nowhere with a flat and nothing to do about it.''

He eased back behind the wheel, fired the engine, and headed for Texas.

Wichita River
February 21, 1934

Frank knelt in the small clearing in the cottonwood grove along a bend in the Wichita and studied the campsite.

Again, he was a couple of days late. Bonnie and Clyde had been here. Stubs of Camels and hand-rolled cigarettes lay beside the ashes of the campfire, along with the remnants of nibbled lettuce leaves. A depression in the sandy soil bore the distinct imprint of blankets and indentations where two small, slender people had lain. Tire tracks a few yards away matched those issued as standard equipment on new Ford V-8s.

In the wide-ranging search after the Ranger armory burglary, other officers in the hunt had missed this particular site. The only footprints around were those of a woman with a tiny foot and an assortment of men's-shoe imprints.

A slip of paper fluttering at the edge of a wild plum thicket nearby caught Frank's attention. He plucked the paper from the bush and held it to catch the dim rays of lowering sun. It was a sales slip for a woman's dress, belt buckle, and ascot bought in a Dallas store. Frank tucked the slip in his pocket. It was another bit of insight into the wanted pair's tastes and habits.

He was getting even deeper into Clyde Barrow's mind and habits. As the Ford rumbled to life Frank felt sure he could anticipate their next move.

Chances were they were in Dallas right now. . . .

CHAPTER TWENTY-ONE

Dallas
February 27, 1934

"YES, SIR," THE slender, gray-haired salesclerk in the downtown clothing store said, "those are my initials on the sales ticket. Is there a problem with the merchandise?"

Frank shook his head. "No, ma'am, not to my knowledge. I was just hoping you might remember making the sale, and could let me know what the items were."

The clerk's brows lifted. "May I ask why you wish to know, sir?"

"I'm trying to locate the young woman who bought this clothing, ma'am."

"I see. Are you a relative?"

"More of a family acquaintance. I've been asked to help locate her." Not a word of that was an outright lie. It just wasn't the complete and entire truth.

"Is she a runaway, or in some kind of trouble?"

"Yes, ma'am, you might say that. The family's quite concerned about her." That wasn't a lie, either. The Parkers *were* worried about their wayward daughter. With good reason.

The clerk sighed and shook her head. "Poor dear. Of course I'll do what I can to help." She studied the list for a moment. "These are fairly common stock items. The dress was a medium weight, fine cotton, ankle length, high neckline, full sleeve. I remember we had trouble finding it in such a small size—she was such a tiny thing—in the color she wanted. Red."

Frank scribbled a few lines on the back of an envelope.

"She wanted to accessorize it," the clerk said. "I outfitted her with a red-and-white-striped ascot, gray stockings, a plain but fashionable two-inch silver belt buckle, and a perky little hat, a sort of tam-o'-shanter or beret style. A quite attractive outfit, except that the dress color clashed a bit with the tint in her hair. Of course, I didn't try to impose my personal taste on her." The clerk smiled. "Antagonizing customers isn't my job."

"I noticed she paid for the purchases in cash," Frank said.

"Yes. Actually, the young man with her paid."

"Did you notice anything else about her or her companion?"

"There was one thing. When she came in, I noticed quite a few white hairs on her dress—a blue one, with a Victorian neckline. I believe it was rabbit fur." The clerk shook her head in disapproval. "Young women shouldn't waste hard-earned money on rabbit coats. Unless they're top-quality manufacture, they shed hair as badly as the rabbit itself."

Frank retrieved the sales slip and touched his hat brim with fingertips. "Thank you very much. You've been a big help."

"My pleasure." She clucked her tongue in pity and concern. "There are so many terrible things that can happen to an attractive woman these days. I certainly hope you find her."

"So do I, ma'am. So do I."

An hour later Frank was back in his West Dallas motel room, on the phone to Ed Portly in Joplin, Missouri. Portly was a good officer and a man who could be trusted. Frank gave him a description of the items Bonnie had bought in Dallas.

"There's a good chance they may be headed into your area, Ed," Frank concluded. "Since they broke into the armory in Ranger they've got more firepower than any officer. Remind your people what they'll be walking into if the Barrow gang shows up."

Frank hung up and scanned the mail he had picked up at the post office downtown. The envelopes were addressed to Mr. Frank Hamer, General Delivery, Dallas, Texas. He read the letter from Gladys first, and sighed against the tightness in his chest. All was fine at home. Except that he wasn't there.

The letter postmarked February 15 in Huntsville, Texas, from Lee Simmons, acknowledged receipt of Frank's latest report on the investigation. Simmons wrote that a car believed to be Barrow's had been repaired at a shop in Rhome, northwest of Fort Worth, and that the fugitives were believed to have been spotted in Vernon. There, the trail seemed to end.

Frank folded the letter, a bit disappointed. It contained nothing he hadn't already found out. Frank had learned that a rural road outside Rhome was a favored gathering spot for the fugitives to meet with their families.

He also had information that didn't appear in Simmons's letter, and possibly wasn't yet known even to the Dallas deputies hunting Bonnie and Clyde.

In Vernon, Ray Hamilton stole an automobile—he was even more accomplished a car thief than Clyde—drove to Wichita Falls, and picked up a convict's wife, a woman named Mary O'Dare. The two had rejoined the Barrow gang in Wichita Falls.

It was, Frank mused, a rather interesting development. There were now two women in the fugitive band. Women and money often led to strife among outlaws, especially when they were thrown together and on the run.

The question now was, which way had the Barrows headed from the Wichita River camp? Logic said they would follow the wide circle, cross into Oklahoma, and eventually return to their home range in northwest Louisiana. Like wild horses, they ranged far and wide, but always returned to familiar pastures.

Logic didn't always apply to Clyde Barrow. The man was less predictable than most outlaws. Frank couldn't shake the feeling that the Barrow gang was somewhere nearby. If he had learned anything over the years, he had learned to trust his hunches.

He almost picked up the phone to call Lee Simmons, but abandoned the idea. Since the affair in Sherman, he trusted long-distance operators even less than he had before. He had taken a chance calling Ed Portly. If he called Simmons and a nosy operator who had connections with the wrong crowd overheard Frank Hamer talking with the state director of prisons about Bonnie and Clyde, the fact that he was on the case would no longer be a secret in Dallas. Or anywhere else, if the newspapers found out.

Frank stubbed out his cigarette and glanced at his watch. It was mid-afternoon, and he hadn't eaten since before daybreak. He walked the block to the nearest restaurant.

With the noon rush ended and a couple of hours to go before suppertime, the small café was almost deserted. He ordered a bowl of chili and cup of coffee.

"Guess you heard the news," the cook in the grease-stained apron said as he clanked the coffee mug down before Frank.

"What news would that be?"

"The Barrow gang hit the Lancaster bank today." The florid-faced man chuckled aloud. "Serves them damn bankers right, somebody taking money from *them* for a change."

Frank casually sipped at the coffee. "Anybody hurt?"

"Nah. Just walked in, stuck up the place, and hit the road."

"The law catch 'em?"

"Ain't no laws gonna catch Bonnie and Clyde." A note of pride tinged the cook's words. "Not with Clyde drivin', they ain't. They drove a stole car to the bank, switched to another one over in Hutchins. Got clean away with over forty-four hundred dollars, the radio says."

"That's a lot of money."

The cook chuckled again. "Sure would like to of seen that banker's face when Clyde and Ray stuck them big pistols up their noses." He spooned chili into a bowl and put it before Frank.

Frank reached for a cracker. "Ray? That would be that Ray Hamilton fellow?"

"The same and only." The cook paused to top off Frank's coffee cup. "Bonnie was waitin' outside, keepin' the car runnin'. Clyde and Ray done the job, then Clyde popped behind the wheel and took off. That Barrow bunch's been makin' the local laws look downright silly. Outsmart 'em and out-drive 'em all the time, that Clyde. He's a caution, sure enough. How's the chili?"

Frank tasted the dish and suppressed a wince. It was bland to the point of being tasteless, about three peppers short and a cup too much fat, but he nodded his approval anyway. The cook wanted to talk. He might clam up if Frank told him the truth about his cooking.

"Hear which way they went?" Frank scooped up another spoon.

"Nope. The laws got every highway blocked off, but Clyde, he don't drive the main roads. Even if he did, there ain't no roadblock he can't run. Done it a couple times already."

"So I hear."

"You know, Clyde come in here once a spell back," the cook said. "Right after he got paroled, it was. Set right over there on that end stool and had the businessman's special—fried steak, red beans, and mashed 'taters." He chuckled again. "Guess he's a businessman, sure nuff. Business of stickin' up banks. More chili?"

Frank pushed the empty bowl away. "No, thanks. That'll hold me for a while." He reached for a cigarette. "I'll just finish this cup and be on my way. Got to get back to work."

"What kinda work you do?"

"Varmint trapper."

"How's business?"

Frank shrugged and lit his smoke. "There's always plenty of varmints around."

The cook drifted away as other customers trickled in.

Frank sipped at his coffee and pondered his course of action. There was no future in trying to join the immediate chase. The Barrow gang would be long gone by now. The best he could do was try to outthink them, anticipate where they might be headed.

His best guess at the moment was Oklahoma. From there, they could head in most any direction. They had pulled a bank job in Lucerne, Indiana, stolen a car in Illinois, and shot their way out of a police trap in Platte City, Iowa, between May 8 and July 20 of last year.

The pattern varied somewhat—Clyde was too smart to follow the same circle when on the run—but the trail more often than not led through Oklahoma northward, then turned back to hideouts in Arkansas, and invariably returned to their base camps in northwest Louisiana. From the base camp it was a short drive, at least in Clyde Barrow terms, to the Hamilton, Parker, and Barrow clans in and around Dallas.

Frank didn't expect to catch up with them. Law-enforcement officers in a dozen states had lost hot trails. Federal Bureau of Investigation agents who joined the hunt after bank robberies and kidnappings hadn't had any luck, either. One man wasn't likely to run Bonnie and Clyde to earth.

But one patient man could lay the groundwork. And he now had a good idea how Clyde's mind worked.

The key was patience. The patience of the Indian.

Only this Indian would be traveling by Ford V-8 instead of horseback, and facing a lot of miles. It looked to Frank like he was going to be living in his car for a spell.

Poteau, Oklahoma
March 2, 1934

Frank settled into a rickety chair with a frayed cane bottom at the table of a hardscrabble farm on the northern outskirts of the small Oklahoma community and studied the slope-shouldered man seated at the rough pine table across from him. The man looked beaten, aged a decade or two beyond his forty-odd years, a lifeless expression in the pale blue-gray eyes.

"Mr. Barker, I appreciate your agreeing to visit with me for a few minutes," Frank said. "I know it's getting on toward planting time."

"No need goin' to the trouble," Barker said, despondent. "Ain't gonna make a crop this year, neither. If it ain't too dry, it's too wet. Price of cotton's gone down the outhouse pit anyway. I'm gonna lose this place, sure as skunks stink. Should have went to California with all them other folks." He pulled a sack of Bull Durham from his pocket and felt the cloth. The sack was empty.

Frank shook a cigarette from his pack and handed it to the farmer. Barker pounced on the smoke as if it were a dollar bill. Frank felt a deeper sympathy for the beaten man. He had been broke himself a few times, back in his early years of cowboying and sharecropping. But he had never been truly hungry or totally on the edge of despair like this man.

Frank said, "I understand you were in the bank when it was robbed."

"Yessir, I was." Barker took a deep drag on the cigarette and sighed. "Like I told them G-men and the local laws, I was tryin' to manage a loan for seed. Can't plant no crops without seed. Anyhow, me and Silas, the bank owner, was just about to make a deal when them robbers come in and messed up the whole thing.''

''You told the officers the robbers were Clyde Barrow and Ray Hamilton?''

''Told 'im I *thought* it *might* have been Barrow, but I wasn't gonna swear to it on the Bible. I seen pictures of Barrow in an Oklahoma City paper at the feed store. Spent my last quarter there on chicken scratch. Couldn't be sure, though. I never told the sheriff nothin' one way or t'other about Hamilton. Didn't pay real close attention except that whoever them two was, they was holdin' mighty big pistols.''

''Any pistol's big when it's pointed in your direction,'' Frank said sympathetically. ''Did you see a woman with them? In a car outside, maybe?''

Barker shook his head. ''I was facin' the wall, just like I was told. Heard 'em take off, though. Car was a Pontiac. They got a special motor sound.'' He puffed at the cigarette until the shrinking butt threatened to burn his fingers. ''Heard the Barrow bunch hit the bank over in Durant, too.''

''It's possible,'' Frank said. ''Some folks identified them. But people have identified Bonnie and Clyde in places they couldn't possibly have been.'' He pulled the cigarette pack from his pocket and slid it across the table. ''Keep it. I've got more out in the car.''

''Much obliged.'' The farmer's fingers stroked the nearly full pack as if it were made of solid silver. ''Wish they was somethin' else I could tell you, but I reckon that's it.''

Frank stood and offered a hand. ''You've been a big help, Mr. Barker. Thanks again for your time, and good luck to you.''

The farmer's grip was callused and firm. ''You, too, mister. I heard them Barrows was the ones hit the First National over in Galena a week or so back. That a fact?''

Frank shook his head. ''I have my doubts about that, Mr. Barker. The woman in that holdup was wearing men's clothes. I don't think Bonnie Parker would ever do that. She's a touch on the vain side. Likes to look and feel feminine all the time.''

"Come to think on it, all the pictures I ever seen of her she was wearin' a dress." The farmer scraped a palm over his gray-stubbled chin. "By the way, what outfit did you say you was with? You ain't FBI. Them G-men ain't the friendliest folks I ever met. Talked to me like I was some darkie field hand, them in their high-dollar suits and shiny shoes."

"Sometimes federal agents can seem a bit abrupt, Mr. Barker. It's their training, I guess." Frank reached into his pocket and produced his badge and identification card. "I'm with the Texas prison system. Special investigator." The farmer squinted at the badge and card. Frank sensed the man couldn't read. He flipped the wallet closed. "What's the best highway to Joplin?"

Terre Haute, Indiana
March 14, 1934

"Yes, sir," the apron-clad woman seated across the lace-covered table from Frank said, peering at the photographs he had spread, "those people were here, for almost a week. And I would not be completely truthful if I did not say to you that I was truly relieved to see them leave."

"When was that, ma'am?"

"A week ago tomorrow." She sniffed in disdain. "They made a terrible mess of my rent house. Holes in the wall, broken dishes, cigarette burns on the furniture—just a horrible amount of damage. And all the shouting and cursing and arguing and noise at all hours of the day and night—why, it was enough to make one's blood boil."

Frank nodded sympathetically, though he had heard the story before. The Barrow gang wasn't especially noted for its tidiness, either in rural camps or rented homes.

"And that girl," the woman in the apron said with a haughty sniff. "Simply disgusting. She was—*drinking*. And smoking cigarettes constantly. It just isn't—isn't *seemly* for a young woman to be so intoxicated, day or night, that she couldn't even walk. Perhaps I'm old-fashioned, but I do not approve of women smoking. I find it abhorrent. If they had not paid in advance and I not needed the money desperately, I would have evicted them.''

"It's a good thing you didn't try, ma'am,'' Frank said. "You might have been hurt. Those people were the Barrow gang.''

The woman's face went as white as the apron she wore; a hand went to her mouth. "Oh, my Lord! Are you sure?''

"Yes, ma'am. You've identified the photographs, and your descriptions match them, even down to the white rabbit.''

"Oh, my Lord!'' she said again. "Those—those murderers? In my rent house?''

"I'm afraid so. Did you by any chance hear any of them say where they might be headed?''

A bit of color returned to the woman's face. Her brow wrinkled in thought. "In all the shouting and noise, it is hard to say. But I do recall one of them, a man, screaming something about going home, and that the man he was shouting at could go somewhere else. Well, he said it a bit more crudely, in language I could not bring myself to repeat. I *am* a Christian, you know.'' Her cheeks colored. "I could paraphrase a bit, I suppose, and say that he told the other man he could go to the hot place.''

Frank pondered the information for a moment. If the man doing the shouting was Clyde Barrow, by "home,'' he could have meant either Dallas or Louisiana. "What happened after the argument? The one where the 'hot place' was mentioned?''

She sighed. "Shortly thereafter—not more than perhaps an hour—they left. Strangely enough, they drove away in two automobiles, even though they had arrived in only one. I don't know where they obtained the second vehicle. It was a Plymouth coupe, quite similar to the one owned by my late husband, may he rest in peace. I had to sell it. I never learned to drive. Does that have special significance?''

Frank nodded. "Yes, ma'am, it does. Apparently, the gang has reached a parting of the ways. It happens rather often among criminals, and it's usually a dispute over money.'' He didn't add *or women;* the poor Christian lady across the table had already had enough shocks for one day.

Frank nodded at the photographs. "Could you show me the one who left in the Plymouth?"

She tapped a finger on Ray Hamilton's photo. "This one. There was a young woman with him. She would have been pretty, except for that dreadful overuse of makeup, like some"—she flushed again—"cheap—I'm sorry, I can't think of a more acceptable word—hussy. I don't see her photograph here."

"Her name is Mary O'Dare," Frank said. "I haven't managed to find a decent picture of her yet. Did the others leave together, in the other car?"

"Yes, sir. I think it was a Pontiac, or something like that. It had this strange hood ornament—an Indian head. And there was a dent in the left front fender, like they'd hit something." She tapped a fingertip on each photo as she spoke. "The man in this picture—the one you said was Clyde Barrow—was driving. The girl, Bonnie, sat beside him. This boy with the terrible complexion was in the backseat, along with this other young man who seemed quite pale and unhappy."

"The pale one was Joe Palmer, a prison escapee," Frank said. "He has a bad stomach and becomes ill when he rides in a car. The one with the skin condition is Henry Methvin." Frank gathered the photographs and tucked them in his suit pocket. "Do you mind if I take a look around in the house they rented?"

"Of course you may. It's right next door. The white one with green trim. But I'm afraid you won't find much. I cleaned the place up except for the damage. It took me two days."

Near Shreveport, Louisiana
March 23, 1934

Frank sagged against the driver's seat of his car and sighed. It had been a long road.

He had ridden many a long trail in the early days, after rustlers or patrolling the border, but for some reason travel by car took more of a toll on Frank's strength than riding horseback.

His shoulders felt too heavy to move. The dull, aching itch in his legs and stiff back muscles were a nagging reminder of the almost constant driving and sleeping in the backseat. The rear seat of the Ford sedan wasn't designed for the comfort of a man his size.

He had temporarily stored Old Lucky under the driver's seat. It was difficult to position the oversized revolver so that it didn't dig into his hip or ribs when he drove for extended periods. The .45 Colt semiautomatic pistol was more compact and comfortable on his belt, and it carried more cartridges in its clip than the revolver's six rounds. Frank knew if he happened to tangle with the Barrow bunch alone, he would need all the firepower he could get.

He traveled with his .35 Remington rifle—a more powerful replacement for the .25 that had served him so well—within easy reach on the passenger's side, just in case. He didn't delude himself. If he met up with the Barrow bunch alone, he would have almost no chance in a shoot-out. They had the advantage in numbers and firepower.

What added most to Frank's physical discomfort at the moment was his own odor. He wafted a scent reminiscent of wet billy goat to his nostrils. The inside of the Ford reeked with sweat and unwashed-man smell, the odor of scores of cigarettes, and the ripening remnants of a ham-and-cheese sandwich he had forgotten to toss out the window. He wondered idly if he would ever be able to get the car cleaned up enough that Gladys would be willing to ride in it.

Frank could cope with tired muscles, stiff joints, and the occasional flare-up of aches from the bullets and buckshot he still carried in his body. At the moment it seemed he could feel every one of his twenty-three bullet scars. He didn't cope as well with feeling grubby.

He hadn't had a bath in four days or a shave in two. The stubble rasped at the skin where his jaw and chin met. His neck itched beneath the jawline and at his shirt collar. Tonight, he promised himself, he would check into a hotel, soak for an hour in the tub, and get a good night's sleep in a real bed.

Yet, he conceded, the trip had been anything but wasted. He had missed Bonnie and Clyde at every stop—sometimes by days, sometimes by hours—but now he had crawled completely inside Clyde Barrow's mind. He knew the man's habits, his hunting range, what he looked for in picking a remote campsite or hideout. He knew the brand of sardines and type of sandwiches they preferred, the brand of whiskey Bonnie drank, the clothes they wore, the weapons they favored, the numbers of extra, stolen license plates that Clyde carried in the car and often changed.

And now he knew for certain that the gang had split up after the argument in Terre Haute. Four days ago Ray Hamilton, his brother Floyd, and another man had robbed the bank at Grand Prairie, Texas, of about fifteen hundred dollars.

Bonnie and Clyde would never see a dime of that money unless they took it by force from Ray, Frank knew. The old saying about honor among thieves didn't hold water when money was involved. Or when an outlaw had a chance to save himself from the electric chair by turning on an accomplice.

More importantly, Frank was now convinced that Henry Methvin was the key to bringing in Bonnie and Clyde.

Methvin wasn't a true career criminal. He was more of a small-time thief, a hanger-on, content to go along for the ride. Frank had not uncovered a single instance to date of Methvin's actually participating in a bank robbery or holdup. Methvin could be used. Frank was still trying to figure out how.

He started the Ford and glanced at the odometer. He had driven more than three thousand miles in the last eight days, interviewing people from Texas to Missouri to Indiana and back, learning as many side roads in northeast Louisiana as he could, developing contacts, finding out which lawmen could and couldn't be trusted.

He glanced around, saw no approaching traffic, and pulled onto the narrow blacktop leading to Shreveport. He could have the car serviced tomorrow. He and the Ford both needed a rest.

Bienville Parish
March 28, 1934

Frank Hamer didn't believe in cursing, but this time he indulged himself.

He stood at the door of the abandoned shack at the base of a pine-covered ridge and stared at the trademarks of Bonnie and Clyde's camp. It was the litter he had seen many times, even down to the nibbled lettuce leaves and the empty quart whiskey bottle.

He had missed them again, by no more than a few hours. Days of work down the drain, through one of those accidents that plagued a peace officer on the trail.

He couldn't blame the force of local and federal officers for reacting to the rumor that the Barrow gang was in Ruston, just down the road, and launching a major sweep through the town the day before.

Clyde and Bonnie heard the news, probably even before the raid got to the final-plan stage. They quit the country again. It would be weeks before they came back.

The raiding party hadn't known that Frank had found and staked out Clyde Barrow's hideout. The officers didn't know because he hadn't told them. Maybe, he thought, that had been a mistake. But it had been a gamble worth taking. If his approach had worked, it could have saved lives.

His plan to take the fugitives without any shooting—just slip in while they were asleep, crack them alongside the head, and cuff them—was gone, probably for good. But if he had called in the FBI and a force of local officers, more lawmen would have been killed for certain.

The shack was not a trap for the fugitives as much as it was a fortress. A good shot armed with a powerful weapon like the BAR positioned on the bluff above, and another firing from inside, could have dropped half a dozen men before the attacking force even realized what was happening.

Frank knelt and plucked an object from alongside the depression where they had made their bed. It was a button from Clyde's coat. The dark blue one, an expensive imported Italian-made suit he had bought in Benton, Arkansas. Frank dropped the button into his pocket and strode toward his car, concealed beyond the bend in the winding dirt road.

Who tipped off Bonnie and Clyde that the Ruston raid was about to happen was a matter of mild curiosity, but not all that important in the overall scheme. It could have been any one of their many friends in the area, or Methvin's kin. They could even have heard of it on the radio. Newsmen made it all but impossible for a large group of police officers to move anywhere in secrecy, and Bonnie and Clyde always carried a radio.

Frank paused every few strides to examine the tangled brush and fallen timber along the twisted logging trail, even though he knew most every foot of it by heart after three previous scouting trips. What he was looking for was nearby. He could feel it.

Wanted criminals needed information as desperately as the men who hunted them. Especially Bonnie, Clyde, and Methvin, given their strong family ties. That meant a message-drop point, a fugitive's mailbox, where communications could be exchanged. Find the mailbox and, sooner or later, you find the criminals.

Frank knew it was somewhere in Bienville Parish. He also knew it was not in a town. Being seen in the same place too often by too many people was too much a risk for people on the run. The mail drop had to be in a rural area. It would be near a paved all-weather highway, or at least a graveled side road, where it could be checked for messages when rains turned the rural dirt paths into ribbons of mud, impassable even to good drivers like Barrow.

It had to be where there was some, but not too much, traffic. A spot where passing motorists would think little of a car stopped at the side of the road. It had to be where the road was wide enough and the shoulders firm enough for an automobile to pull from the traffic lanes onto the side of the highway.

Frank had driven every such road in the parish at one time or another since he had taken the trail. He thought it likely that he had passed within a few feet of it at least once, perhaps several times. Clyde's mailbox could be anywhere in the heavy pine forest, dense underbrush, marshes, and bogs of the parish.

He slid behind the wheel of the Ford and climbed back into Clyde Barrow's mind. Clyde had been spooked here. Easter Sunday was coming up. Bonnie had a thing for family visits, even brief ones—and especially on holidays.

Frank hit the starter. Bonnie and Clyde were in Dallas.

He had to go back there and start the hunt all over again.

CHAPTER TWENTY-TWO

Grapevine, Texas
April 3, 1934

FRANK EASED THE Ford to a stop before the farm home near the hill that overlooked an isolated stretch of road a few miles northwest of Dallas, and glanced at the graying sky.

The rains would come soon, he thought, and wash the blood from the soil of the nearby field.

He tapped on the door frame and waited patiently. The muted sound of a radio and voices from beyond the door told him someone was at home.

After a couple of minutes the door cracked a bit. A lean man whose weathered face spoke of many days in the fields peered through the screen door.

"Mr. William Schieffer?" Frank asked.

The man nodded, his gaze flicking warily from Frank to the Ford and back. "I'm him."

"I'm a special investigator for the Texas prison system. I'm told you were a witness to the shooting deaths of the two highway patrolmen here last Sunday."

"I saw it. I've already talked to the law about it."

Frank nodded. "I realize that, sir, but I was hoping you wouldn't mind telling me about it again. I've read the newspapers and police reports, but I prefer to get my information firsthand when possible. Newspapers sometimes are not entirely accurate. For that matter, neither are police reports."

The farmer glanced over his shoulder and stepped outside.

"Hope you don't mind talking out here," Schieffer said. "I got a houseful of kinfolk. I'd as soon the young ones didn't hear about it again."

"That's fine with me, sir. Now, would you tell me the whole story, in your own words, from the beginning?"

Schieffer dug a pipe and tobacco pouch from the pockets of his overalls and leaned against a porch support. "How much you already know?"

"For certain, only that Highway Patrol troopers E. B. Wheeler and H. D. Murphy were shot to death just off the road that runs by the field across the way. And that you'd identified Clyde Barrow and Bonnie Parker as the people who shot them."

The farmer seemed to relax a bit as he struck a match and lit his pipe. "Well, yessir, that was what happened, sure enough. I was standing right about there"—he pointed toward the gate of a hog wire fence that enclosed a garden—"when I noticed this car pull up in the field. Didn't think much of it, on account of young people come up here quite a bit. It's a popular spot for sparking among young folks."

Frank nodded. It was also, he knew, one of the Barrow gang's favorite meeting spots for family visits. Or gathering forces to plan a bank job. "Had you seen that particular car up here before?"

Schieffer shook out his match and tossed it into the yard. "Couldn't say. It was a Ford, four-door sedan, black. Lots of them around these days. I didn't pay much attention to it at the time, just noticed it set there for quite a while."

"Like whoever was in the car was waiting for someone?"

"It sort of looked that way." Schieffer puffed at the pipe and blinked as the smoke drifted into his eyes. "I didn't really pay it much mind until I heard the shots when they killed those trooper boys."

Frank lit a cigarette. "Did you see the patrolmen before the shooting started?"

"Yes, I—well, sort of. I heard the motorcycles drive past. Glanced up because when I was younger, I wanted one of those things." Schieffer paused to flip the spittle from the stem of his pipe. "Anyhow, the two police slowed down, but rode on past the first time. After a spell, I heard them come back along the road, then slow down again. Wasn't until I heard the shooting that I realized they'd stopped by that car. Don't suppose they knew who was in it, or they'd have brought some help along.''

"No, sir,'' Frank agreed, "they probably didn't realize what they were walking into. What happened then?''

Schieffer worked the pipe for a few seconds. "Well, it wasn't but a few seconds until I heard the shots. First I heard a shotgun, then four of five rifle shots. Real fast, like a machine gun.''

That would be one of the Browning Automatic Rifles Barrow carried, Frank thought. So far, almost everything the man said jibed with the newspaper accounts and police reports.

"There were pistol shots, too. They don't sound like shotguns or rifles, you know. I can tell the difference. Used to hunt a lot, before it got so crowded around here.'' Schieffer paused for a moment. "Anyway, there was two men standing beside the car. One of them was Clyde Barrow. The other was that Ray Hamilton fellow.''

The farmer was mistaken there, Frank knew. The second shooter had to be Henry Methvin. Ray Hamilton hadn't run with the Barrow gang since the split in Terre Haute. From a distance, the mistake was understandable. Ray and Methvin were about the same size. So now, Frank thought, Methvin had finally dropped a hammer on a man. It was Methvin's first kill that he knew of.

"That's when I saw it, what really spooked me,'' Schieffer said. "Bonnie Parker. She got out of the backseat. Had a shotgun in her hands. She walked up to this one trooper laying there and looked down at him. Then she sort of stepped back, raised that smoothbore, and shot him again. Twice. I'd swear I saw his body bounce when those shot charges hit. You know the worst part?''

"What was that?''

"She laughed.'' The farmer's jaw clamped onto the pipe stem. "I swear she laughed. A high-pitched laugh, kind of a cackle, like that was the funniest thing she'd ever seen.'' He sighed. "Well, sir, then all three of them jumped back in that car and went tearing off.''

Frank nodded. "Are you sure the woman was Bonnie Parker?"

Schieffer nodded. "Picked her out of a bunch of police pictures later that day. Well, the next thing I knew, the place was crawling with lawmen. I told them what I'd seen, and they asked me down to the courthouse to tell it again and look at the pictures. That's about all I can tell you."

Frank nodded his thanks. "You've been a big help, Mr. Schieffer. I appreciate it." He turned to walk to his car.

"Mister?" Schieffer called.

Frank turned. "Yes?"

"You think Bonnie and Clyde might come back here? To kill me, I mean, since I saw the whole thing?"

"I doubt that, Mr. Schieffer. I expect they're long gone from Texas by now." He tried to reassure the farmer with a smile. "But just to be on the safe side, make sure you know who's at the door before you open it. And call the sheriff if you see a car—any car—acting suspicious."

The farmer swallowed, his Adam's apple bobbing emphatically. "Sure hope you catch that Barrow bunch. I'd rest a lot easier, knowing they were dead or locked up."

Frank touched his fingers to his hat brim. "So would a lot of folks, Mr. Schieffer. We'll get them."

He slid behind the wheel, started the Ford, and waved as he turned onto the road toward Dallas.

Some things in Schieffer's story didn't quite fit, Frank thought as he drove. According to the official reports he had read, Schieffer had picked out photographs of Billie Mace, Bonnie's sister, and Floyd Hamilton, Ray's brother, instead of Bonnie Parker and Clyde Barrow.

Frank had already quietly checked out Billie and Floyd. Billie had been at her home in Oak Cliff all of Easter Sunday. Floyd Hamilton was nowhere in the Dallas area. They both had solid alibis, with witnesses to back them up. It hadn't made any difference to the Dallas lawmen. They had already arrested Billie Mace, along with a lot of others who had ties to the Barrow and Parker families, in a general sweep of the Dallas area.

The botched identifications worried Frank. They could be a problem if the case ever came to trial. Yet he didn't doubt other elements of Schieffer's account. Most everything else checked. Investigating officers had picked up shotshell hulls and spent cartridge casings for both a BAR and a handgun at the site of the killings.

The Barrow bunch always traveled with an arsenal. Bonnie preferred a shotgun. Clyde was a BAR man first, then a pistol shooter. He wasn't sure about Methvin, but Henry likely had fired the first shotgun blast if Bonnie was in the backseat. Clyde wouldn't have had time to drop a shotgun and grab a rifle.

The car was a different vehicle from the one Frank had been tracking. Clyde apparently had ditched or hidden the Pontiac somewhere. Frank would lay odds the Ford parked in the field had been stolen.

He hadn't been able to verify all the details or compare notes with the two Dallas deputies assigned full-time to the Bonnie and Clyde case. Ted Hinton and Bob Alcorn had left Dallas on the chase a short time after the shootings. They would be somewhere in Oklahoma by now.

Frank felt a twinge of sympathy for Hinton. The Dallas County deputy had a three-month-old baby. Hinton, his wife, and the infant were out for an Easter Sunday ride when Hinton heard of the shootings. They were on the site within a half hour. Now Hinton was somewhere to the north. It might be days or even weeks before he saw his wife and child again—if he didn't catch up with Bonnie and Clyde and get himself killed.

The thought pained. Frank hadn't seen his own family since February 10. And no matter how hard a man worked, he couldn't keep his mind totally occupied with the chase for twenty-four hours a day. On the day the two troopers were shot down, Frank should have been emerging from Easter church services with Gladys and the family, maybe on the way to a picnic in the countryside.

Austin seemed farther away than China at the moment.

Frank shook aside his brief trip into loneliness. He had work to do—contact Lee Simmons, fill him in on the latest developments, then check out of his hotel and take to the road again.

Frank had a hunch it wouldn't be too long until the Barrows were heard from again. And somebody else might die.

Fort Scott, Kansas
April 8, 1934

Frank Hamer knew he was looking at a lucky man.

Miami, Oklahoma, Police Chief Percy Boyd, seated on the padded bench beside Frank, knew it, too.

Boyd's partner, Cal Campbell, hadn't been so fortunate. The sixty-three-year-old constable had taken a bullet through the heart in a muddy, rutted road only a few miles from the far northeastern Oklahoma community of Commerce, a few miles north of Miami.

The bandage around Boyd's head still showed a spot of pink from the slug that creased his scalp.

Bonnie and Clyde's death count now stood at an even dozen, nine of them police officers. That they had kidnapped, and then released, Boyd, wasn't particularly unusual. The outlaws seemed to enjoy making a game of kidnapping people. To abduct and terrorize a lawman was the height of humor in their book.

Frank already had the bare bones of the story, most of it from an interview with truck driver Charles Dodson, who had come upon a Pontiac mired in the mud near Miami. Dodson pulled the vehicle from the ditch and back onto the more passable road, and was about to leave when Boyd and Campbell, tipped by a passerby that a car with a bullet hole in the windshield was stuck in a ditch, drove onto the scene.

Dodson told Frank—as he had Hinton and Alcorn, who had interviewed him a day earlier—that the occupants of the car opened fire almost immediately when the officers stopped. The first bursts from a pair of "machine guns"—the BARs—killed Campbell and injured Boyd. The wounded chief of police was disarmed, forced into the Barrow car, and driven away. The Pontiac crossed Stepp's Ford Bridge over the Neosho River, headed west and north.

The Pontiac made only three miles before it became stuck again. Clyde and Methvin forced a farmer at gunpoint to pull the car free. The farmer hadn't seen Boyd. Law officers feared the chief had been executed and tossed from the Barrow car somewhere along the muddy back roads.

Instead, Bonnie and Clyde had kept the chief prisoner for a day and a half before releasing him at a farmhouse near Fort Scott.

"That's pretty much the way it happened," Boyd said as Frank reviewed his information on the shooting and abduction. "I expected them to kill me anytime, but for some reason they seemed to take a liking to me. Bonnie, in particular. We had quite a talk."

Boyd paused, for a moment, thinking. "You know, Frank, if what Bonnie and Clyde told me is true, those two highway patrolmen were killed just because Bonnie wanted to give her mother a white rabbit for Easter. Bonnie and Clyde were waiting for family when the troopers rode up."

Frank handed a cigarette to Boyd and lit one for himself. "They could be telling the truth. Stranger things have happened."

The two fell silent for a moment, smoking, each with his thoughts. Frank retraced the last couple of days in his mind. Like Hinton and Alcorn, he'd been several hours or even days behind Bonnie and Clyde. They had been spotted in Durant, Oklahoma; in Texarkana, Arkansas; dodged a roadblock northwest of Texarkana; and killed Cal Campbell in Oklahoma before heading into Kansas.

It had been a long, muddy, and so far futile trip.

"Funny thing," Boyd said, breaking the momentary silence, "Bonnie asked me to do her a favor. She said she didn't want her public—that's what she called it, 'her public'—to think of her as a girl who smoked cigars, like the newspapers say, because nice girls didn't smoke cigars. She was pretty mad about it. I told her I'd set the record straight when they turned me loose."

"I thought there was something strange about those pictures of her holding a cigar," Frank said. "And it makes sense that she'd want it known. Except for her habit of killing people, she takes pride in being female."

Boyd stubbed out his cigarette. "I didn't know until they stopped in Fort Scott and bought a newspaper, a few hours before they turned me loose, that Cal was dead. He was a good man."

The police chief fell silent for a moment, then said, "Frank, those two have to be stopped. They won't be taken alive, and that car they're driving is a rolling arsenal. I counted two sawed-off shotguns, half a dozen pistols, and three BARs. There was ammunition and loaded clips all over the place. Anybody who tries to stop them is going to get killed."

"There is a way, Chief," Frank said. "But it isn't likely to happen while they're on the run. All we can hope is that nobody else gets killed before then."

Fort Smith, Arkansas
April 10, 1934

Frank tossed his suitcase on the bed of the hotel a block down the street from the courtroom where Isaac Parker, known as the "Hanging Judge," had once dispatched outlaws and killers to the gallows, and immediately reached for the telephone.

He got through to Texas Highway Patrol Chief L. G. Phares within a couple of minutes.

"Chief, Frank Hamer," he said. "I've got license plate and motor numbers of the Pontiac Clyde and Bonnie drove when they killed Cal Campbell. And other plate numbers they're known to carry in the car with them."

He flipped though the pages of his pocket notebook, read off the string of numbers, and waited as Phares read them back. "That's the list," Frank said. "It may not be much help. They'll probably be in another car and maybe with even different plates by now, but at least it's something."

"Anything new on their movements?" Phares asked.

"Not really. The trail petered out not far from Fort Scott. Every highway in four states is either patrolled or road-blocked, but I doubt it'll do any good. Clyde will be driving the back roads, and he knows every logging trail and cow path."

"Any ideas?"

"Just a hunch, but I'd say they're either headed back to the Dallas area or to their hideouts around northwest Louisiana. If I were a betting man, I'd put my money on Louisiana."

"Okay," Phares said. "Frank, Lee Simmons and I have decided to send somebody along to lend you a hand. You can have any man you want."

Frank didn't hesitate. "Is Manny Gault available?"

"He is. He left the Ranger force, but he's still on the Highway Patrol payroll."

"Then he's the man I want. I've worked with him before. Each of us knows what the other's thinking and what he's about to do most of the time. I'd sure like to have Manny alongside when or if the shooting starts."

"You've got him. Where and when do you want to meet?"

"Make it Dallas," Frank said. "Give me a couple days to nose around Louisiana and check out some sources. Say, on the fourteenth?"

"I'll get the word to Manny just as soon as we hang up. Frank, I know you and Manny would get the job done, but it's time we hooked up with the Dallas people on this case. Hinton and Alcorn have been working exclusively on the Barrow hunt for weeks now. With what they know and you know, we'd have a better chance to run Bonnie and Clyde down."

Frank frowned, but didn't object. "Could be we could use some extra firepower at that, Chief," he said. "I haven't spent much time with them, but the deputies seem like good men. They deserve to be in on the windup."

"Have you talked with Hinton and Alcorn much?"

"We've compared a few notes here and there, but mostly we've gone our separate ways. I got the impression the Dallas County sheriff wasn't real enthusiastic about my moving onto his turf and working his case."

Phares chuckled. "Smoot Schmid doesn't want to admit his boys can't handle it on their own. He would have bowed his back like a mad cat if he hadn't owed Lee Simmons a favor. Let him sputter and do what you have to do."

"Okay, I'll play," Frank said in resignation. "The deputies haven't had much luck, but neither have I."

"Frank, it might be a good idea to let Hinton and Alcorn think they're in charge."

Frank sighed inwardly. "All right, Chief. I'll see if Manny
and I can't point them in the right direction without them
knowing it. Tell Manny to bring along a BAR or two and a
couple of shotguns. It'd be nice if we had nearly as much
firepower as Bonnie and Clyde."

Southern Missouri
May 14, 1934

Frank glanced at Manny Gault as brake lights winked on the
car up ahead.

"Looks like Hinton and Alcorn are pulling in for a gas
stop," Frank said. "I could use a break myself."

Gault flexed narrow shoulders that belied the strength in
his wiry body. "Me, too. I feel like I've been rode hard and
put up wet, as we used to say in the old days."

Frank cast a quick wink at his longtime friend and frequent
partner in the bandit-chasing business. "You look like it, too,
Manny. Reckon you're getting too old for this game?"

Gault grinned back. "I'm not that old, Pancho. Study on
it some, you'll realize you're not the sprightliest rooster in
the barnyard yourself anymore." He sniffed and wrinkled his
nose. "Getting a bit ripe, too. Riding with you makes a man's
eyes water."

"Ah, that's leftover baloney sandwich you're smelling.
Wouldn't be so bad if you didn't have them covered up with
onions all the time."

"Just give thanks I don't have a craving for turnips and
cabbage," Gault said. "Riding in a closed car with a man
who eats that combination and breaks wind isn't exactly like
walking through a rose garden. And the onions aren't as bad
as those sardines you live on. Smells like a stack of fish guts
in here. Least you can do is throw out the tins once you've
eaten the sardines."

"Would," Frank said agreeably, "but I can't find it in the
rest of this mess. Gladys is going to have my hide nailed to
the barn door when she sees what we've done to her car."

"Serve you right." Gault shifted his weight and sighed.

"You know, I don't remember a saddle being as hard on the butt as these car seats are."

Frank eased the mud-spattered Ford to a halt outside the rural store. "May be some truth to that, Manny, but at least a Ford doesn't buck a man off on a frosty morning. Toss a blanket over that arsenal in the backseat. I'd hate to have to explain to Simmons and Phares that some young punk stole half a dozen guns from two of their best ex-Rangers."

"Might be a problem, at that." Gault reached over the seat and covered the two Browning Automatic Rifles, pair of shotguns, Frank's .35 Remington with its special thirty-round clip, and an assortment of revolvers and semiautomatic handguns. "Reckon we've got enough guns here, Pancho?"

"I sure hope so, Manny. I'd hate to come up one short." Frank climbed out, locked the car doors, and stretched as the two Dallas deputies stepped stiffly from the car ahead, a Ford sedan the same make and model as Frank's.

The decision to take the trail in two cars served a dual purpose. If one broke down, they still had transportation; in case of multiple flats, they had multiple spares; and it wasn't nearly as crowded. Four men in one car loaded down with half an army company's weapons and ammunition wouldn't have room to sweat, let alone bring a firearm into play if need be.

"Reckon those two fellows know what they're doing?" Gault said with a nod toward the Dallas County deputies.

"So far I'd say so—except for stopping at this same little country store three times in less than two weeks. For all we know, the man who owns this place might be Clyde's favorite uncle. Hinton says the man can be trusted, and he lets Ted use his phone."

Gault grunted an agreement. "I'd worry about that some, myself. Could be the telephone operator's Methvin's favorite aunt, keeping Clyde posted on where we are and what we're doing."

The comment brought back the bitter taste of Frank's experience with the telephone operator in the Sherman disaster. That was a long time back, but it still rankled. "It's a chance we have to take, Manny. At least now we're headed in the right direction. When we catch up with Bonnie and Clyde, it'll be in Barrow's hideout country. I'd bet a year's pay on it.''

Gault tugged his narrow-brimmed felt hat down against the glare of afternoon sunlight. ''I know better than to bet against you, Cap.'' He paused for a moment, then said, ''You know, we don't exactly look like Tom Mix's version of a posse of lawmen.''

Frank had to agree with Gault on that point. Hollywood posses were clean-shaven, white shirts pressed, silver conchas on their saddles, polished boots, six-guns tied down on the thighs of new Levi's, riding tall in the saddle. Not four tired men with stubbled faces and wrinkled shirts, who reeked of sweat, baloney and onions, and empty sardine tins.

''Nature calls,'' Gault said. He strode on bowed legs toward the sagging door marked GENTS at the side of the country store.

Frank reached for a cigarette, noted it was the last in the pack, and mused on Manny's evaluation of the posse. Manny had it pretty well pegged. As Hinton had said yesterday, they ran a fair chance of being arrested by some local lawman for being bums and suspicious persons—scruffy, rumpled, unwashed, smelly. And tired.

Hinton's swarthy, round face showed lines of fatigue, and the slump of his shoulders marked him as a man who had seen little rest over the past couple of weeks.

Frank knew the feeling. He also knew it was going to get worse before it got better.

Deputy Bob Alcorn, despite the rumpled clothes and whisker stubble on his heavy jaw and prominent chin, managed to look surprisingly fresh for a man who had made every mile Hinton had logged in the pursuit of Bonnie and Clyde. If he was as exhausted as he should have been, it didn't show.

Manny Gault looked worn down and used up, too. But then, Manny always looked like that. The craggy face, lined and weathered, and graying hair earned by years of chasing outlaws, made the slightly built former Ranger appear older than he really was. The expression in his eyes and set of his jaw hadn't aged over the years, though. Anybody who brushed Manny Gault aside as an ineffective old man had just made a serious mistake. Gault was tough as a badger and just as stubborn. Frank couldn't think of another man he'd rather have at his side with trouble up ahead. As it surely was. Frank sensed it was only a matter of time now.

That the Dallas deputies had narrowly missed catching Bonnie and Clyde three or four times in the past didn't diminish Frank's respect for the officers. He doubted any other lawmen would have fared better. And they had common sense. Back in Durant, Oklahoma, they had met Bonnie and Clyde, driving in the other direction down a busy main street. Alcorn nixed any attempt to turn around and start the chase. Durant was crowded that day. Innocent people could have been run over or shot if the posse had jumped Bonnie and Clyde.

It was the right decision. Frank would have done the same thing.

The deputies' other failures had been either just plain bad luck—a fact of life for lawmen—or, in the earlier stages of the hunt, an underestimation of the game they hunted.

The Barrow bunch had shot their way past Hinton twice, the last time blasting their way through a roadblock manned by more than a dozen officers. Hinton's other attempts had come up short for a number of reasons, not the least of which was Clyde's uncanny driving ability.

Frank finished his cigarette and strode to the country store. He paused at the door to discard the crumpled empty pack as Hinton stepped outside.

"Anything new, Ted?" Frank asked.

Hinton snorted in disgust. "A white rabbit showed up at Bonnie's mother's place just a few days ago. They were in Dallas while we were running all over three states chasing shadows."

Frank wasn't particularly surprised at the news. He had been halfway expecting it; when Bonnie Parker made up her mind to do something, it usually got done. Even delivering a pet rabbit to her mother. "Anybody see Bonnie and Clyde?"

Hinton shook his head. "The sheriff figures they didn't want to take the risk themselves, so they had a friend deliver it. He and the Rangers are rounding up everybody they can think of who might have a line on Bonnie and Clyde. It looks like there's only three of them riding together now. We've had several sightings of Bonnie, Clyde, and Methvin, but not Joe Palmer. That cuts the odds down more.''

Frank nodded his agreement. The Barrow gang was thinning out. Raymond Hamilton was back in custody, pulled over near Sherman a short time after he'd robbed a bank in Lewisville on April 25. Mary O'Dare, Ray's sweetie, had been picked up April 23 at an apartment in Amarillo. That left three of the original gang still on the road. The three most dangerous ones.

Hinton sighed. ''Guess we'll be heading back to Dallas now. Again.''

Frank scratched at the stubble on his jaw. ''I think it'd just be a waste of gas, Ted. They'll be long gone from Dallas, They're likely headed for their old hangouts in Louisiana.''

''You're probably right. Anyhow, Sheriff Schmid left it up to us. No specific orders except to stay after them until we get them. Might as well get the tank topped off on your car, Frank. We've still got a long list of tips to check out.''

Hinton clucked his tongue. ''I'll swear, it seems everybody in the country has seen Bonnie and Clyde in the last week except us. We've been into, over, under, around and through every swamp and hill in Louisiana, Arkansas, and Oklahoma. Missed them by a day here, two days here, three there. We've had Bonnie and Clyde sightings reported every day in half a dozen states, all at the same time. The best we can claim so far is that at least we're keeping the pressure on them, keeping them on the run.''

Frank said, ''They'll make a mistake. They all do. Call your family?''

A slight smile touched Hinton's lips. ''Yes. Everything's fine at home. The baby's growing like a weed.'' The smile faded. ''I'll be glad when this is over. I could count on one hand the number of times I've seen my son since he was born.''

Frank clapped Hinton reassuringly on the shoulder. ''I know how you feel, Ted. I haven't been home myself since February. I've got a feeling we're close to the end of this. Meantime, we'd better stock up on baloney and sardines.''

CHAPTER TWENTY-THREE

◆────

Ringgold Highway
Bienville Parish
May 19, 1934

FRANK BLINKED AGAINST the scratchy feel inside his eyelids and pressed the accelerator as the Ford started the climb up the hill nine miles south of Gibsland. Reflections of the auto's headlights winked back from the underbrush beneath heavy pines and bits of gravel laid over the asphalt road base.

The powerful V-8 engine responded to the touch of his foot, kicking the speedometer reading back up to forty on the uphill grade. Frank had driven the road twice before, once in a heavy rain, again in wispy fog; tonight, under clear skies, it was as if he were actually seeing it for the first time.

He glanced at Manny Gault, who dozed in the passenger's seat after being behind the wheel of the Ford for four of the last six hours. Even in sleep, Manny's craggy face looked drawn and angular in the faint greenish-white glow from the dashboard lights. Frank would let Manny sleep; within two or three hours, they would be in Shreveport and in a real bed for the first time in days.

The gleam of small, close-set eyes in the car's headlamps at the side of the road atop the hill broke Frank's train of thought. He eased off the accelerator, slowed, and watched as the skunk ambled across the road from south to north— Frank abruptly jammed on the brakes.

The slight jolt brought Gault upright. "What is it, Cap?"

The hairs on Frank's forearm tingled. "I think we've found it, Manny."

"Found what?"

"Clyde's mailbox." He eased the car to the side of the road and twisted the wheel to point the headlamps at an angle toward the west side of the road. The lights illuminated the stump of what had once been a sizable tree a few feet from the edge of the dense forest. "I should have noticed this before."

"Noticed what?"

"A perfect spot for a mail drop," Frank said. "Clyde's mailbox. From the crest of this hill, Bonnie could keep watch in both directions for any traffic, keep the motor running while Clyde checked for messages. The road's all-weather, wide enough for a car to pull partly off the road if need be. That stump's a distinct landmark. And we're less than ten miles from Irvin Methvin's farm."

Frank heard the breath catch in Gault's throat. "By God, Pancho, you just might be right for once in your misspent life." Gault reached for the door handle. "Let's take a look."

The search didn't take long. A weathered board lay near the edge of the woods behind the stump. Frank and Gault, flashlights in hand, squatted beside the board for a moment.

"No sign anybody's used it in the last day or two," Gault said, "but it looks like it's been moved since the last rain."

Frank cautiously lifted an edge of the board and peered beneath it. A couple of white grubs squirmed in the moist earth. Frank's heartbeat picked up as his flashlight beam touched a bit of paper, little more than the size of a match head, impaled on a splinter at the back edge of the board.

"It's been used, all right. By God, Manny, I think we've got the hole card in this game now." Frank eased the board back into place with care. The two hunters crabbed backward, brushing out their tracks, until they reached the edge of the graveled asphalt.

"What now, Cap?" Gault asked.

"We'll go on into Shreveport, catch up with Hinton and Alcorn. Then I'm going to give Henderson Jordan a call and let him in on the plan. He's one sheriff I know can be trusted to keep his mouth shut."

"We've got a plan?"

"I've had it in mind all along." Frank slid back behind the wheel of the Ford and waited for Gault to climb into the passenger's seat. "We know Clyde's got a hideout around here somewhere. It won't be far from his mailbox. Sheriff Jordan and I both know Henry Methvin's old man is Clyde's postmaster. If we stake out this place, set a trap, we can take them.''

''Could be a long wait,'' Gault said casually.

''Could be.'' Frank released the parking brake, shifted into low, and pointed the car toward Gibsland and the connecting highway to Shreveport.

''When do we let Hinton and Alcorn know what we've found?'' Gault asked as the Ford picked up speed.

''Not right away. I've got to talk to Henderson Jordan first,'' Frank said. ''We may just have one shot at Bonnie and Clyde, Manny. No disrespect to the Dallas deputies, but I want Henderson in charge of this operation. It's his bailiwick, anyway, which technically puts him in charge. He'll go along with the plan. I'll ask him to put it to Hinton and Alcorn as his idea. They'd be more likely to agree to it, coming from Henderson.''

Gault nodded, his face grim in the pale dash light. ''Good idea, Pancho. Those Dallas boys are fair-to-good trackers and decent lawmen, but I've had a feeling all along they'd as soon not have us tagging after them. I don't think they want to share the credit with a couple of old beat-up ex-Rangers.''

''They can have the credit,'' Frank said. ''All I want is to get Clyde Barrow off the road—one way or another—and go home.''

The two men rode in silence for several miles before Gault said, ''Pancho, I've never popped a cap on a woman before, should it come to that.''

''Neither have I, Manny, but I'm afraid that's the only way we'll take them. I don't like the idea of shooting a woman myself. When the time comes, just remember how Bonnie Parker stood over a dying trooper and put two loads of buckshot into him. And laughed.''

Shreveport

Frank tossed his hat onto the bed in the Inn Hotel and reached for the telephone.

It rang several times before a groggy voice answered.

"Henderson? Frank Hamer. Sorry to be calling you near midnight, but I need your help. . . ."

He talked for nearly fifteen minutes, pausing only to answer an occasional question or ask one himself, then offered his thanks and hung up.

"Henderson's bought in, Manny," Frank said, turning to Gault, who had already stretched out on the bed. "He promised he won't pay any attention to any other lawman, federal, state, or local, until we've given this a shot. And he'll keep it quiet. He'll bring his best deputy with him when we make the move. Bryan Oakley may look like a bookkeeper, but he's a good lawman and a top hand with a rifle. And we can trust him."

"Sure wouldn't hurt to have an extra gun around, at that," Gault said. "Now, if you're finished yammering on that blasted phone, hush up. I'm tired as a mule that's just pulled a plow for a quarter section."

May 20, 1934

"Man, I'd forgotten what it was like to have a *real* meal under my belt," Manny said as he pushed back his plate at the diner next door to the Inn Hotel.

"And no onions," Frank said reverently, "a blessing for which I am duly thankful."

Gault snorted in mock disgust. "Give you a night's sleep, Pancho, and you start gigging a man right off. Think I'll put in for a new partner."

Frank leaned back in his chair, his belly full of honest food instead of baloney sandwiches and sardines for the first time in days. He didn't remember ham and eggs ever tasting quite so good. He studied the men around the table as the waitress refilled his coffee cup.

They all looked a sight fresher this morning, he thought, and smelled a darn sight better. A good sleep, a bath, shave, a change to clean clothes, and a full belly did wonders for a man's spirits.

"Well, Ted," Frank said as Hinton swabbed up the last bit

of over-easy egg with a biscuit, "what's the schedule for today?"

Hinton popped the biscuit in his mouth and chased it with a swig of coffee. "It's Sunday. I think we've earned most of the day off. I plan to rest up, write a few letters home, maybe call my wife. Along toward evening, we'll go back to work." He glanced around, made sure the waitress and other customers were out of earshot, then lowered his voice. "This evening we'll call on Police Chief Bryant and let him know we're in town again. That sound okay with you two?"

Frank nodded. "Fine by me. I noticed a little church down the street a ways. Thought I'd catch morning services if I had a chance. It's been a spell since I've been to church."

"You may miss out on a good card game," Alcorn said. "I'd hoped to take a few pennies from you boys today."

"Later, maybe," Frank said, "but I think I'll pay a call on the Big Dealer Upstairs first."

"Man ought to confess his sins, sure enough," Gault said, "but Pancho, you haven't got a whole week, and I figure you owe the Man at least that much time, just to catch up to ten years ago or so."

Frank waved to the waitress. "Miss," he said, "would you please stick a biscuit in this old coot's mouth? It's the only way I can figure to get him to shush up."

Shreveport Police Chief Bryant leaned back in the oversized armchair behind his desk and peered at the two deputies seated across from him, then glanced at Frank Hamer and Manny Gault, who leaned against the wall beside the weapons rack.

"Men, I sure appreciate your letting me know you're in town. And your information's accurate. Bonnie and Clyde not only are in the area, we darn near caught them just last night."

Frank's heart sank. If the Barrow bunch had been spooked by the local police, they would have quit the country. They could be in Iowa by now. Or New Mexico.

"What happened?" Hinton asked.

"Well, about midnight, two of my patrolmen drove past the Majestic Café—it stays open all night—just cruising along slow, checking things out. Normal routine. They didn't know Bonnie and Clyde were parked outside. We didn't have a description of the car or anything.''

Frank allowed himself a mental curse. Bonnie and Clyde had been within rifle shot of the Inn Hotel at about the time he and Manny Gault checked in.

"Bonnie and Clyde were in the car with the motor running," the chief continued. "When they saw that police car ease past, they thought they'd been spotted. Threw gravel all over the place when Clyde hit the gas. My men chased them a good ways, but never did catch up. That Clyde's some kind of driver."

Frank groaned inwardly. A chance encounter with a police car had blown all those weeks of work.

"But the funny thing was"—the chief paused to light a cigarette—"there was a young fellow inside the café at the time. He'd ordered a stack of sandwiches and soft drinks to go, and was waiting on the order when Clyde gunned the car. When he saw that, he jumped off the stool and ran out without even waiting for his sandwiches, or paying for them."

Hinton glanced at Alcorn. "Henry Methvin," he said.

Frank's hopes soared. If Methvin had been left behind, Bonnie and Clyde wouldn't quit the country. Methvin was sort of a younger brother to both of them, and Barrow wasn't one to abandon a friend if there was any other choice. It had been different when Ray Hamilton split with Barrow. Hamilton hadn't been a friend.

"Well," Bryant said, "I'm not sure it was him, but the thought had entered my mind. The waitress said she'd never seen him before, but she'd sure know him if he came in again."

Frank glanced at Gault, saw the knowing expression in Manny's eyes, caught the slight head nod. Hinton abruptly stood and offered a hand to Bryant. "Thanks for the information, Chief. We'll check it out."

The next morning, the four officers had just finished breakfast at the Majestic when the woman who had waited on the man left behind came in at Hinton's request, relayed through the café manager. She was a bit rumpled from lack of sleep;

she worked the night shift, but had agreed to come down early to talk to the lawmen.

"Ma'am, I sure appreciate your interrupting your rest to come in," Hinton said. "We're looking for the young man who ran out on you Saturday after he'd ordered sandwiches. It's a rather important police matter." He pushed his plate away and spread several photographs on the table. "Do you see anyone here who looks like that man?"

The waitress didn't hesitate. She tapped a finger on Henry Methvin's photo. "That's him. Same eyes, same pimply face. There's no mistake about that."

Frank finally relaxed. The trap was not only still in operation, but it was now baited. With Henry Methvin.

Hinton thanked the woman for her time and help, paid the check, and led the way outside. The four lawmen waited for a couple of early strollers to pass and they could speak in confidence.

"Well, men, the trail just got hotter," Hinton said. "With Methvin afoot and out of touch, I'm betting Bonnie and Clyde will circle back to Old Man Methvin's place, looking for Henry. We could stake it out and take them there." He glanced at Frank and Gault. "You fellows know the Black Lake area where Methvin's folks live?"

Frank nodded. "I know it some." He didn't say that he'd cased the Methvin place several times and already abandoned plans to catch the Barrow gang there. "Hardscrabble farm carved out of deep forest, where the swamp rises to a series of rocky ridges. Not many ways in and out."

Hinton fell silent for a moment. "Bob and I know it pretty well, too. We've prowled around over there quite a bit, we know Old Man Methvin's habits, and there's no mistaking that old Model-A truck he drives. We'd be taking some chances. Around here, you never know who Clyde's friends are. And if somebody happened to make us for the law closing in on them, they'd run six states before they slowed down. Still, it might be worth the risk—"

"Ted," Gault interrupted, "there's one man who knows that country like it was his own pumpkin patch. Henderson Jordan. If anybody knows a way to dig them out of that Black Lake area, it'd be Sheriff Jordan."

Frank cut a quick glance of thanks at Gault. His partner had jumped it at just the right time. Hinton thought on it for a moment, then nodded.

"It would be common courtesy to let Jordan know we're back in his area of jurisdiction, anyway," Hinton said. "We'll make a run to Arcadia this afternoon and call on him."

Minden, Louisiana

Frank downshifted, tapped the brakes, and prepared to steer the Ford off the Highway 80 blacktop onto the path used as a detour around a bridge being rebuilt.

Hinton and Alcorn, better than a hundred yards ahead, were almost past the construction. Hinton's car had to pull over to the side of the detour to make way for a tan Ford to pass, headed west.

Frank brought the car to a near stop, barely rolling, as the tan Ford neared. The young man behind the wheel of the car said something to the woman beside him as they passed. Frank's heart skipped a beat. The woman could barely see over the dash. Both wore dark glasses, but there was no mistaking them.

"Cap," Gault said, jerking upright in the passenger's seat, "either I had some bad mushrooms for lunch or we just met Bonnie and Clyde."

"Nothing wrong with your lunch, Manny. That was them."

"Reckon Hinton and Alcorn spotted them?"

"They'd have to be asleep or blind not to," Frank said. "They were just about an arm's length away when the two cars met. I didn't see Hinton's brake lights come on. Good thing Hinton decided not to chase them. It could have blown the whole plan. We'd never catch Barrow, not in his home country. All we'd do is spook them."

Gault twisted his head to stare out the back window at the tan Ford, now fading into the distance at a moderate speed. "Think they made us?"

"No. They've never seen us before. They didn't run and didn't shoot, so they didn't recognize us. Or Hinton." Frank realized he had been squeezing the steering wheel and forced himself to ease his grip. "Notice anything else, Manny?"

"Yeah. There was nobody else in the car with Bonnie and Clyde, at least that I could see. I'd guess they haven't picked Methvin up yet."

Frank exhaled the smoke through the open window. "I doubt Methvin has had time to get a message to Clyde's post office, Manny. We've still got our ace in the hole."

Gault settled back into the seat. "Let's just hope," he said, "that Clyde Barrow's not holding the joker."

Arcadia, Louisiana
May 22, 1934

Bienville Parish Sheriff Hamilton Jordan dropped the phone back into its cradle and swiveled his chair to face the group of patiently waiting men.

Space was at a premium in the small office in the quiet town of three thousand. Manny Gault shared an unpadded bench with Bob Alcorn. Parish Deputy Prentice M. Oakley, commonly known as Bryan, had the single chair across from Jordan. Frank and Ted Hinton stood, leaning against the wall. A haze of cigarette and pipe smoke laid an overcast against the low ceiling, a man-made cloud that eddied on currents drifting in through windows opened against the muggy heat.

Hamilton Jordan, Frank mused, could have been the movie-star cowboy Tom Mix had wanted Frank to be. Jordan's high cheekbones, cleft chin, strong jawline, expressive eyes, and mouth that seemed forever on the verge of a laugh would have played well to the camera. So would his trim six-foot, athletic frame; the sheriff moved with the fluid grace of a boxer.

Jordan was anything but a movie star. He was a top lawman who knew when to be tough, when to ease up on the reins, and he had a network of friends and informants throughout Louisiana.

"Well, men," Jordan said, "looks like it's time to mount up. The word is that Bonnie and Clyde will be checking their mailbox in the next day or two for a message from Methvin. This is the break we've been waiting for." He rose and reached for his gray rancher's-style hat. "By the way, if you Texas boys have never spent a spring night in northwest Louisiana, you're going to be making friends with some of Ma Nature's least friendly critters. We've got bigger and meaner bugs here than you've ever had the misfortune to meet. Watch out for snakes, too. Everybody set?"

Hinton nodded. "All set. Sheriff, are you sure you can trust your source on this one?"

Jordan shrugged. "This particular informant's never steered me wrong before. You all know the plan. Let's move."

Ringgold Highway
Bienville Parish
Monday, May 23, 1934, 2:30 A.M.

Frank settled in behind the tangle of pine branches and other tree limbs the lawmen had built into hunting-style blinds over the last hour along the east side of the road. He ignored the constant hum and buzz of mosquitoes and gnats about his ears.

Jordan warned them to watch for snakes, but that wasn't their main source of torment. It was the mosquitoes, deerflies, and other biting insects that were obviously delighted to find unexpected fresh human meat out here in the middle of nowhere. And the chiggers and ticks. Frank suspected that in a few hours, he'd have tiny red spots under his belt, the waist of his shorts, the tops of his socks. It could be a long night.

Frank ran through the setup in his mind once more. He could find no flaw. Their cars were several yards off the main road in the middle of a stand of moss-covered trees, out of sight. There was no danger that a point of light reflecting from headlamp beams would give them away to anyone approaching on the highway.

The men were spaced about ten feet apart. Frank, his .35 Remington with its thirty-round clip inserted and a cartridge chambered, and two .45 auto pistols at his belt, had the southern post in the line of lawmen.

Manny Gault was at Frank's right, Hamilton Jordan next,

then P. M. Oakley and Bob Alcorn, with Ted Hinton on the north end of the line.

They didn't lack for firepower. Hinton carried a Browning Automatic Rifle with twenty rounds of steel-jacketed ammunition, a shotgun at his side, and packed a pair of sidearms. The others also had powerful rifles and shotguns, with handguns for backup and close-in work. At least they had Bonnie and Clyde matched or even outgunned in the weapons department. If there was a consolation to the prospect of going into a gunfight, it was the idea that at least a man had an even chance. Even better was the assurance he had a slight advantage. That assurance wouldn't stop a bullet, but it helped.

Frank had been through fifty-one gunfights in his three decades of law enforcement. He hoped to make the fifty-second his last.

Waiting was the hardest part.

Frank had known many a brave man who wouldn't hesitate to plunge straight into a gunfight to panic or make a fatal mistake under the pressure of boredom overlaid by the constant strain of pushing hearing, sight, and smell to the limits for hour upon hour. None of the men in this group showed any sign of strain. They were professionals. That was reassuring. This was no job for amateurs.

The stump that marked Clyde's post-office drop across the road was barely visible in the faint starlight. Frank could only hope that his and Jordan's information was correct, that Bonnie and Clyde would stop at the mailbox shortly after sunrise.

A mistake would mean disaster. Given this group of lawmen, he didn't think it would happen, but in the dark there was always a faint chance that a car driven by an innocent couple might decide to stop at the wrong place and wrong time. If shooting started, the target had to be a dark tan Ford Deluxe sedan stolen in Kansas and, if Clyde hadn't switched the plates in the last few hours, bearing Arkansas tag number 15-368.

Drainage ditches lay along each edge of the road, leaving no room for a car to turn around without having to stop, turn, and back up at least once. Barrow's mail drop was a trap when it was covered by half a dozen men with big guns.

Frank heard the cough of engine and whine of downshifted gears before the word came down the line.

"That's Old Man Methvin's truck," Manny whispered. "Jordan's going to stop him."

Frank nodded to himself. Irvin Methvin wasn't likely to be driving this road at this time of day unless something was afoot. Like delivering a message from his son to Bonnie and Clyde.

The battered Model-A truck shuddered and clanked to a stop. Irvin Methvin's eyes went wide at the sight of six men armed with heavy weapons fanned out in the road.

Henderson Jordan opened the truck's door.

"What brings you out this time of the morning, Irvin?" Jordan asked. "Looking for your boy, or Bonnie and Clyde?"

"I ain't talkin' to you or any other laws, Sheriff. I'm just out a-drivin'." Methvin's voice quavered slightly. He had trouble holding Henderson's gaze. The farmer obviously had something to hide, Frank saw at a glance.

Jordan reached for the door handle. "Well, Mr. Methvin, I'm going to have to ask you to step out of that truck. We're going to be using it for a while, and we're going to have to discourage you from leaving. So you won't mind if we take you off the road a ways, out of sight. You'll be safe—and I expect you to just sit quiet for a time." Jordan turned to his deputy. "Take him back to the cars. Cuff his arms around a tree, but leave it so he can either stand or sit. And leave him some water."

"You can't do that, Sheriff!" Methvin squawked. "I got rights! The FBI's going to hear about this!"

"Right now, Mr. Methvin, there's something more at stake here than your rights. And there's no FBI here, so just do as I say. Play along with us, and we'll see if we can convince a judge you helped out, maybe make it easier for your boy. Okay?"

Oakley led Methvin into the darkness of the forest. Alcorn slid behind the wheel and turned the battered Model A around so that it faced into oncoming traffic. The officers jacked up the right front wheel and removed the tire.

"Bait for Clyde," Jordan said to Frank. "He'll know at a glance that's Old Man Methvin's truck. He'll at least slow down, maybe even stop to offer help."

9:10 A.M.

Frank dropped his cigarette, ground the half-smoked butt beneath a heel, and glanced over his shoulder at the sun.

Daylight had come slow to the Bienville Parish forest, the buzz of night insects reluctantly giving way to the calls of birds greeting the new day and the hum of mosquitoes that worked the day shift.

It had been a long night for Frank. He suspected the others in the group—with the exception of Manny Gault, an old hand at the waiting game—had suffered more than he had. The stubble on his cheeks itched as much as the bug bites. Bienville Parish mosquitoes were able to tap a man's blood even through the layers of a suit coat and shirt. Frank would happily trade a week's pay for a cup of hot coffee at the moment.

Throughout the night, the only sounds had been those of the forest, the infrequent passing vehicle, and the barely audible fussing and cussing of Old Man Methvin cuffed to a tree back in the woods.

What galled Frank most, though, was the message that had come down the line just a few moments ago. If Bonnie and Clyde didn't show in another twenty minutes, they'd call in the dogs and quit the hunt—

The hairs on Frank's forearms prickled.

The sound was faint but unmistakable, the distinct hum of a powerful engine moving at high speed. The engine of a Ford V-8. Frank made it three miles away, to the north.

Frank flicked off the safety of the .35 Remington. The hum of the engine grew nearer, more distinct, by the moment. His breathing settled into a steady rhythm, his heartbeat only slightly elevated.

The pitch of the approaching car's engine changed as the vehicle began to climb the hill. Seconds later Frank heard Hinton's voice, the words tinged with excitement:

"Here they come! It's them!"

The car topped the rise, slowing rapidly. Behind the wheel of the Ford sedan with the Arkansas license plate, clearly visible in the climbing sun, was a small dark-haired man and an even smaller woman. Frank caught the flash of red as sunlight fell on her dress. Bonnie and Clyde.

The Ford slowed still more, then came to a stop beside the stump a few feet away. Frank couldn't see Clyde's face. Both Barrow and Bonnie Parker were looking away from Frank, toward the stump.

"Halt!" Alcorn yelled.

The man and woman started at the sharp command. Frank stepped from the blind into the road; he saw Bonnie's shoulder dip, her hand come up clutching a sawed off shotgun. The bore of the shotgun swung toward Frank.

He fired, saw the woman's body jerk, heard a high-pitched scream. He shifted the muzzle toward Clyde Barrow, pulled the trigger, and saw windshield glass shatter before Barrow's face. Then the crack of his Remington was all but drowned in the thunder of five other weapons all firing as rapidly as actions would work. Paint chips and glass flew from the Ford as slugs tore into the vehicle; the bodies of the occupants jerked and twitched as lead and steel-jacketed rounds ripped their flesh.

The barrage of gunfire seemed constant in Frank's ears as he fired round after round through the windshield of the Ford; the *brrrp* of Hinton's BAR stopped, its magazine emptied in less than two seconds. The thump of shotguns and handguns came into play as the lawmen dropped empty rifles. The Ford lurched into motion as Clyde's foot slid off the clutch; the vehicle started rolling forward, buckshot and bullets still tearing into the metal.

Frank moved aside as the Ford lurched forward erratically, traveled ten yards past him, veered left, and finally jolted to a halt in the roadside ditch.

The gunshots stopped.

Frank shifted the Remington to one hand, drew his .45 auto pistol, and started toward the car, Manny Gault a couple of strides behind him.

"Be careful, Cap." Gault's warning sounded hollow and

distant through the ringing in Frank's ears. "They might not be dead."

The dust kicked up by the Ford settled, the powder smoke from the weapons drifted away on the wind. Frank sidled up to the car and peered through a bullet-riddled window.

Blood spattered the inside of the Ford; scarlet streamed down the woman's slack face from her open mouth and the dark hole between her nose and upper lip. A sawed-off shotgun lay at her feet.

Clyde Barrow slumped against the driver's-side door, the back of his head a tangled mass of blood, brain matter, and hair. Frank thrust his pistol beneath his belt, propped his Remington rifle against the side of the car, and yanked opened the driver's door. Barrow tumbled out, his Browning shotgun and Frank's rifle falling atop the bullet-torn body. The slight lurch of the automobile as Frank yanked the door open sent Bonnie Parker's body forward. Her head now rested between her knees.

Frank pulled his pocket watch and checked the time. It was 9:17 A.M., May 23, 1934. The end of Frank's 102 straight days on the trail of Clyde Barrow and Bonnie Parker. That end had come in about twelve seconds of gunfire.

Frank pocketed the watch and looked inside the bullet-torn Ford again. A half-eaten sandwich lay beside Bonnie, soaked in the blood that stained her red dress. In the backseat, among an arsenal of rifles, shotguns, handguns, and hundreds of rounds of ammunition, rested Clyde's saxophone. The musical instrument seemed out of place, almost unreal, in such a setting, Frank thought.

He turned to the silent, grim-faced officers gathered around the car. His gaze settled on Manny Gault.

"It's over, Manny," Frank said. "We can go home."

Epilogue

On May 25, 1934, Frank Hamer attended the funeral of Clyde Barrow in Dallas; the next day, Bonnie Parker was buried in West Dallas Fishtrap Cemetery.

A short time later Frank testified for the defense in the murder trials of Billie Parker Mace, Bonnie's sister, and Floyd Hamilton, Ray Hamilton's brother, charged with the shooting deaths of the two highway-patrol officers near Grapevine. Largely because of Hamer's testimony that Bonnie and Clyde had committed the murders, both Billie and Floyd were acquitted of the charges.

Frank helped obtain a pardon for Henry Methvin for crimes committed in Texas, having made such a promise to Henry's father. Methvin was later tried for crimes committed in Oklahoma and sentenced to death. The death sentence eventually was commuted to life in prison, and Methvin was finally pardoned by the governor of Oklahoma. Hamer and Methvin exchanged letters from time to time.

The other major player in the Bonnie and Clyde escapade, Raymond Hamilton, was sentenced to ninety-nine years for bank robbery, escaped from prison, was recaptured in Fort Worth, and died in the electric chair May 10, 1935.

Perhaps Frank Hamer's greatest contribution to Texas in the Bonnie and Clyde case was not the removal of two killers from society, but the rescue of the Texas Rangers from oblivion. The Texas legislature had planned to abolish the Ranger force, but the outpouring of public adoration and support of Hamer—as a Ranger—was so strong that the lawmakers were forced to abandon their plan. It was the second time that Frank had, in effect, "saved" the Rangers.

Hamer never exploited his role in the Bonnie and Clyde case for personal gain; in fact, he turned down numerous lucrative offers from book publishers and movie producers for his story.

He continued to work in law enforcement and eventually founded a security-guard service with former Houston police chief Roy T. Rogers, an association that lasted thirteen years.

The most painful day of Frank Hamer's life came in May 1945, when he received word that his younger son, Billy, had been killed in action in the storming of Iwo Jima. Billy, a marine, was buried with full military honors in 1946. Hamer's eldest son, Frank Jr., served as a marine pilot in World War II, and eventually served in various law-enforcement positions.

Gladys's two daughters married, one to a rancher, the other to a prominent architect.

Frank Hamer's many wounds continued to bother him throughout his later years, especially in the humid Houston climate. In late 1949, at age sixty-five, he sold his partnership in the security firm and returned to Austin. In 1953, he suffered heatstroke, and on Sunday, July 10, 1955, the man who survived fifty-two gunfights and twenty-three bullet wounds died peacefully in his sleep. Pallbearers at his funeral included former friends and associates W. W. Sterling, Lee Simmons, Tom Hickman, and other officers with whom he had worked over his long career in law enforcement.

Texas Ranger Chaplain P. B. Hill, in the eulogy at Frank Hamer's funeral, called him "one of the greatest men I ever knew . . . a man who feared Almighty God but never feared the face of any man. . . . He was the personification of those qualities that make a great officer, the qualities that made Texas Rangers famous."

Gladys Hamer continued to live at their home on Hillside Drive in Austin until her death.